# DELTA SQUAD - BLACK

### DELTA SQUAD BOOK 6

### JESSE WILSON

Copyright © 2024 by Jesse Wilson

Layout design and Copyright © 2024 by Next Chapter

Published 2024 by Next Chapter

Cover art by Jaylord Bonnit

Large Print Edition

This book is a work of fiction. Apart from known historical figures, names, characters, places, and incidents are the product of the author's imagination. Other than actual events, locales, or persons, again the events are fictitious.

All rights reserved. No part of this book may be reproduced or transmitted in any form or by any means, electronic or mechanical, including photocopying, recording, or by any information storage and retrieval system, without the author's permission.

# 1

The footsteps were the first sound he heard that didn't originate from inside his own head. His senses were still sharp, but the darkness and time had made him question everything. All the things he'd seen before coming here, the dark was a blessing he had trouble accepting. It was better than the reality he'd come from.

Still, the footsteps only got louder, and on instinct, he tensed up. There was no reason to escape. The insanity was out there. The devil, all the cosmic things. The end of the world was out there, and it was safe in here in the dark.

Then his cell door opened. He could feel the pressure and temperature change on his torn skin. It wasn't time for the torturing bastards to come back. There were still at least thirty minutes unless they changed their schedule.

"I heard you were having a bit of a bad couple of years?" a voice asked. Cody didn't know who it was. He tried to place it, but there was nothing. "They took your eyes. I guess you would have reacted to the light when I turned it on," the man said, doing his best to ignore the blood-coated walls and horrendous odor of rotting flesh in the room. The man chained here in the center of the room looked more like a corpse than a man.

Cody felt a callused hand reach under his neck and lift his head up for a second. Cody tried to speak, but without a tongue, nothing came out but blood. The man recoiled before the blood could hit his skin, and Cody's head fell back down.

"They have beaten you worse than I thought. Well, just listen for a few minutes. Not like you have much else to do," the man said, his voice still alien to Cody.

"Incredible, really. Did you know you were meant to be the last ones? That's right. You and your idiot friends were supposed to go to war with 188 and die," the man said, and Cody's pain faded. He would have looked at the man had he still had his eyes and the strength to do it. He changed his breathing enough, however.

"That got your attention, good." The man read Cody as if he were a book. The change in breathing told him everything he needed to know. "You won. You managed to do the unthinkable. Imagine our surprise when you pulled that trick. It was as impressive as it was inconvenient," he said.

Cody wasn't sure what this was all about, but he knew whoever this was, wasn't his friend. He wasn't sure if he had any friends left still alive. He didn't understand why he was still alive. Maybe just to suffer. It was almost time for the torturers to come back. He could feel his healing kick in. The soft tissues always healed the fastest.

"Not only did you win. You just wouldn't stop. You took down every threat, new and from the past. Beyond the imagination even, and somehow, you just didn't fall. You gave everything you had —" Finally, the beaten one spoke.

"And it wasn't enough." Cody's words were racked with pain and almost weren't words at all.

The next thing he felt was a punch across the face that knocked him to the side, but the chains holding his wrists moved him back into the center. The pain faded in a few seconds.

"What, are you going to cry now? You helped save the Omniverse from the worst threat it has ever known and saved untold amounts of lives and your world as well, and you are crying over a few lost lives who knew the price from the beginning. Who died in service to their country, their beliefs, and you are broken up about it? Do you think they would be this broken up? Do you think they shut down when the whole team was supposedly vaporized?" Cody thought about this. The man was right, but he was getting mixed signals.

"Of course not. There's no damn crying," the man said, and Cody grit his teeth. "Delta Squad don't know how to cry, we never figured it out," Cody said, his words better now, vision starting to return. His eyes burned as if sand were filling the sockets, and he closed them tight. "What do you want?"

"Death is a part of the business, kid. You've been in this dark hole for six months, and the world is a miserable place now that the Syndicate has power over everything. Your team needs you."

Cody shook his head. "Is this a new torture? I know everyone is dead. We've lost. I've lost everyone," he replied. "That sounds a lot like crying to me, stop it," the man said, and Cody couldn't help it. He was sure everyone had died, but when did he start thinking that? Nothing made sense.

"What are you talking about? Who died? The world still needs you. The Syndicate is waging war on the whole world. No one can stop them. Millions are going to die for their utopia. Don't you understand? The Syndicate is the enemy. It always has been," the man said. Cody opened his eyes. They burned and itched, but even that was fading away.

He could see the man for the first time. He was

an older white man, with gray hair and an equally gray mustache. He didn't look impressive, but at the same time, there was something off about him, too. He had on a faded blue uniform, no name tag, and held his broom in his left hand.

"I know you, don't I? You're the janitor at Blackfire. What in the hell are you doing here?" Cody asked and knew at once he was losing his mind. This wasn't possible. The man did not fade away as he stared. Again, nothing made sense. He felt as if a crucial piece of information was missing somewhere.

"Yeah. I'm real. With this job, they don't pay attention to me. I called in a favor from some friends of mine. Time is running out. Want out of this hole or not?" he asked, getting to the point. Cody didn't want to stay here anymore. Still, this could have been some elaborate trick. Something to make him talk, make him hope again just for the bastards to crush him again at the last moment. He would not put it past his captors. Still, there was a chance this was real.

"Fine, let's get out of here," he replied and pulled against his chains. Something was draining his energy. He had felt this way since he had been shackled here. "I don't imagine you brought a key or something?" Cody asked.

The man smirked and lifted his broom. It seemed like a normal one, wooden handle and all, but with one quick swing, the handle sliced through the chains. The links fell to the ground. "Stand up, Commander. Like I said, the real battle is about to begin," he said. Cody took a deep breath and stood up. His muscles screamed as he forced his body to rise.

"How come every battle that is coming up is the real one? Were the others just practice?" Cody asked. The man just shrugged. "Hell if I know. It's just a saying. Before you do anything, you need a shower. Do you smell you? My god, man, it's enough to choke a maggot," he said. "I'm aware," Cody replied.

The two of them moved towards the steel door. The man looked out both ways. "Come on, let's go," he said, and they walked out. Cody did his best to ignore the pain while the rest of his wounds attempted to heal.

## 2

"What do you think of this life? It's everything you deserve. It's more than everything you deserve. It's paradise, and it's ours," she said to Blake as the two of them sat on the porch. Blake still had no idea how he ended up here. One minute he was in a chaotic nightmare, the next, wherever here was. A white mansion next to the beach. Everything was perfect. The weather, the drink, the chair he was in. Perfection. Six months of perfection, it was starting to get old.

For all he knew, she whipped this scenario up in just a couple of seconds. It might not even have been Earth at all. He pushed all that stuff out of his mind.

"It's great, still I can't help but feel that I was stolen away from everyone when I could be trying to make things right again," he replied with a smile. She glared, it was a little scary, and Blake knew how close to oblivion he was.

Her eyes softened along with the rest of her.

"Oh, you know I like it when you complain about worldly situations, but your blue toy soldier leader sealed off the world from dear old Dad. You know what? He can't get in. I can't get out. You're stuck with me, at least for now," she said and looked back at the ocean. Blake shook his head and laughed.

"How long is it going to be before they find us? What about the Chronovore? Emily isn't herself lately. I'm pretty sure she's near indestructible. Something the guys and I specialize in dealing with. I wonder how they are doing. As amazing as you are, I do miss the fight. I think I always will. I might have an addiction," he said, half not thinking about what was coming out of his mouth.

"You miss the fight? Well, you can always fight with me."

Blake's eyes shifted in her direction just in time to see her fist come at his head. He got out of the way, making sure not to spill his drink in the process.

"No, I don't want to fight you, really. I'm totally not missing the fight that much, I promise," he tried to tell her, but it was pointless now. She swung with her right fist, it was slow. He dodged the attack, stood up, and grabbed her by the neck, for all the good it did. Her flesh was iron in his grip. He wasn't sure if he could move it at all, even if he wanted to. There was never any reason to hold back.

"Aww, look at you. Getting all aggressive, I like it!"

Nero snapped her fingers, and a shockwave sent Blake flying from the porch, over the shore, and ten feet into the ocean. He hit the surface of the water and thought for sure he felt something inside snap, but there was never any pain in this place. Sometimes he was sure that this was the afterlife.

Blake flipped over to his back and opened his eyes. She was standing over him, studying him. "You know this is entirely unfair," he said, and she laughed. "Sorry, I got carried away, but don't worry, I'm sure it'll happen again," she replied. Blake tried to smile.

"Well, you really are dying here, aren't you? Dad was right about people all along. You can give them everything you think they want, and they'll wither and die without the challenge. Humanity was created with violence in blood. Go home. I'll wait for you to complete whatever it is you feel you need to do," she said.

"It's not about the challenge. It's knowing people are out there dying, suffering, and I can stop it. I can try. It's about doing the right thing if you can do the right thing," Blake replied.

"Then go be my hero and go do the right thing," Nero said.

She knelt, put her hand on his chest. "Thank you." It was the last thing he was able to say before everything went white.

His vision returned just as fast. It was night. He was alone in a dark alley. The thing that let him know the last six months were real was the fading scent of the sea.

The place was quiet. Blake stood up and was dressed in a black uniform. He knew it at once as a Syndicate patrol guard uniform. "This your idea of a joke?" he asked while getting his bearings. He picked a direction and walked out of the alley.

He made his way to the main street and looked up and down the road. There was nobody out on the streets, and the flag of the Syndicate hung where the American flag should have been. For a minute, he thought he was sent to some alternate dimension. Then a more horrifying thought arrived.

This was his world, and something worse happened than he even considered. Nothing he could do here. He picked a direction and started to walk. It was a few minutes before the sound of an engine could be heard.

Blake stopped and turned around to face it. He was ready to kill everyone as the big black armored vehicle pulled to a stop. "You there, what are you doing?" the man on the main top gun asked. Blake blinked.

"I got separated from my unit. We met up with some resistance and were not prepared for it. In the retreat, I got lost in this city. It's been a bad day and I'm a transfer. Don't know this place yet. Mind if I hitch a ride back to HQ?" Blake asked with a shrug.

The man looked him over. "The ROD is heavy in these parts. I'm surprised you're not dead. Get on, we'll take you back," the man said, and Blake smiled. "Thanks!" He made his way to the side, grabbed on to a handle, and pulled himself up. It took everything Blake did his best to not laugh when the guy told him about the heavy rod.

The second he was secure, the man up top pounded on the roof, and they started to drive, destination unknown.

# 3

"Winning, there isn't anything like it," Emily said and looked around the battlefield. The resistance and the Syndicate soldiers, frozen in time in mid combat. Both sides behind rubble and broken streetcars. Bullets trapped in time. Explosions frozen in place. "How long do you intend to chase me?" Emily asked.

"No, there isn't, but look at you now. The last great enemy of the world. They want me to kill you. Of all people, they pick me to kill you," he said, "and chase you, as long as it takes to fix whatever this is." When he said that she almost smiled.

"They? The mighty 188 reduced to an errand boy, an assassin. How did you get so weak?" Emily asked. Her green eyes burned bright. Her skin cracked as she moved.

Jake shrugged. "I was replaced as a threat when you showed up. What am I to a beast that can eat time?" he asked, and she stopped.

"Yeah, you of all people they ask to hunt me down and kill me. How's that going?" she asked him as her green eyes flared with power. Jake stopped. "They asked me because we used to have a connection. I don't know where Emily starts and the monster begins. Maybe there is no difference now," Jake replied.

Emily smiled. "You can examine me, nice and thorough, all the inches. Maybe then you can find the dividing line," she said, and Jake rolled his eyes. Not to say he wasn't tempted to look.

"Chronovore, let her go. This world is at peace, or it will be soon. Everyone is going to get what they want."

Emily scoffed at the idea.

"Let her go, she wanted this. I wanted this too. Look at us. For the first time, we really get to make a difference, and no one is going to stop us, this world is mine," she said.

"What are you going to do? I mean, endgame, what is it?" Jake asked, and she looked at the ground.

"To do what I was born to do. End time, stop all the noise. Take a look around, we are on a battlefield. Idiots versus morons. This is all pointless, worst of all a waste of delicious time."

Jake had heard enough. He didn't care what her endgame was. He lunged forward as she lifted her arms to do something. He took her wrists in his hands and with some effort forced them back down to her sides.

She didn't seem to be fighting back all that much.

"Oh, you still care? How did that happen, we tried to obliterate you with a tactical nuke, remember?"

She got close. Jake didn't recoil. He wasn't sure if the whole nuclear weapon thing happened or not. It was kind of a footnote in history compared to all the insanity that happened since then.

"I really didn't care. It didn't kill me. Mark did that, but now everything has changed. You don't need to do this. They created you, it is a matter of time before they find a way to kill you. Please, I am trying to save you." Jake tried getting her to showing any amount of humanity, but not the kind he was expecting.

Emily put her head against his and did nothing for a time. "You don't understand. Your time is up. Everyone's time is over. I'll miss you most of all, I suppose," she said, closed her eyes before pulling back out of his grip.

Jake didn't have time to do anything before she punched him, knocking him to the ground. It was only a second until the battle began to rage around him again, nobody seemed to notice the missing time. Jake looked around for her, but there was no sign. She was gone.

"Damn it, Emily, why won't you listen to me," Jake said to no one as the battle erupted around him and all the noise that came with it. He was getting sick of the sounds of war after all this time. He took a deep breath but didn't stand up. "Oh, yeah. Resistance. I almost forgot you were still here." He was surprised that Emily didn't kill him, maybe she couldn't yet. It didn't matter right now.

"The Syndicate are on the retreat, don't let up, kill them all." Jake heard someone yell this from the other side, over the gunfire and chaos of war. He shifted his head a little. The Syndicate forces must have been taken by surprise. Several of their number were dead. Jake shifted his eyes to the right, more corpses. No one had noticed he was here. He supposed a time skip would have that effect. "Well, a loss to these idiots just wouldn't look good."

Jake's eyes began to burn with the golden light, at once everyone on the rebel side noticed the corpse on the ground come back to life.

He levitated up back to his feet to face the enemy. "Oh god, oh god no." Someone yelled. The gunfire concentrated on him. The bullets smashed against his flesh and crumbled to the street.

His hands lit up with gold fire. "Listen up rebel

scumbags. America is finished. You can surrender and be brought to justice for your crimes against the Syndicate, or you can die here. You have five seconds to stop shooting me," he yelled, amplifying his voice over the weapons.

He counted to five in his head, the rebels made their choice. Not one of them gave up the fight. "Make it easy, fine with me," he said.

Jake lifted his arms and golden light shot from his hands. He stretched his arms out in a sweeping motion and watched as the resistance turned to ash and their weapons melted where they stood.

In just a few seconds it was over. The resistance and the cover they used as a defense were wiped out, replaced with flames. Jake powered down, then turned to face the Syndicate.

"You idiots got taken by surprise. If it happens again, it won't matter if you win the fight. I'll kill you all, or what's left of you," he said. The soldiers in black didn't know how to react at the sudden appearance of 188.

"Yes, sir, it won't happen again, sir." Jake assumed it was the leader. He didn't know anyone in this unit. He'd never seen them before and didn't plan too ever again. Faceless grunts, nobodies in the big picture.

"Good, get these fallen men back to base so they can have a good cremation and get back out there to end this fight," Jake ordered them, then shot off into the air. Emily had left, he had to find her or none of this would mean anything at all.

## 4

"So, this is the infamous Flesh Tearer. Well, he doesn't look so tough now, does he?"

There was a crowd of people gathered around the rim, looking down into the special cell made for Josh. He was chained like a dog in the center, a long, thick chain fastened to an equally thick bar running across the opening. He could walk around the cell, but only so far. Josh could hear them talk. This place was made so their voices echoed down into the pit.

The Syndicate loyalists were granted special privileges to see the monster. The worst part was the propaganda that played every ten minutes over the loudspeakers.

"Come see the butcher of America. Josh, code

name Flesh Tearer, last name unknown. This monster murdered an untold number of innocents over the past several years. He is a psychopathic monster that has no soul. A brave group of men subdued the beast, doing the impossible and capturing him at no small loss to their own group. Now this wild animal is on display in prison, here for all to see as a reminder of the past. No one can stand against the Syndicate, witness the living proof," the monotone announcer's voice said.

It was maddening. The same thing over and over for months. One weird explosion and otherworldly things, then he woke up here. One meal of disgusting gray soup a day, one shower, but their shower was just them nearly flooding the tank up to his neck for a few minutes. Hate was all he felt. The shackles around his neck keeping him here burned. He wasn't sure if that was a mental thing or real. It didn't matter.

He didn't wonder where everyone was. They had to be dead. They would have come for him by now, he was on his own.

"I bet I could take him. Look at him. He can barely stand." A woman's voice echoed into the pit. Josh stopped.

He looked up at the three people above and glared at them. "Oh, Bonnie, I think he heard you," one of the men said. "Teach him a lesson," the other said, and Josh watched as the skinny man hit the red button.

A powerful electric shock tore into his neck through the collar and dropped him to his knees. The current wouldn't stop until they stopped. He wouldn't scream. The pain was bad, but nothing he couldn't handle.

"Take it, bitch. I'd kill you if they'd let me," she yelled at him. Josh closed his eyes then after what felt like forever, the current stopped. By the time he looked up again the three were already gone. It'd only be a matter of time before more people came to look.

He hated everyone, everything, but he had to control himself. Josh took a deep breath and sat in the middle of the cell. The pain was already gone.

There was a red line on the floor of the cell close to the edge, a solid circle. He picked up his empty food bowl and threw it past the circle. A minigun activated and turned the bowl into a million pieces in a second, then a tiny disk robot shot out from the slot in the floor to vacuum up all the pieces before disappearing back into the wall.

The weapon high up on the wall made him miss his old weapon. He wondered where it was right now, then he figured it was in a million pieces or melted down.

That thought was enough to make him almost

feel depressed, but he couldn't give in to despair. Not yet.

He started his breathing exercises again to control his rage. This was a time to think.

# 5

Dustin sat against a wall in a black cell. There was one light far above, and he couldn't mess with it. It was dim. One plate of food a day. He thought so anyway. In the black cell, he kept himself sane with memories of the past. He had been in here for far too long.

He supposed they kept him alive because killing him was not as easy as it looked. Maybe somebody in the ranks of power wanted to keep him alive for some reason, torture he imagined. Revenge maybe. Dustin smiled in the dark. He knew that if it was him on the other side doing the capturing, he would have killed the prisoner, not kept them locked away in a hole. Why take the chance?

He hated the dark. Somebody knew what they

were doing when they put him in here. Delta Squad member or not, you hated what you hate, and nothing would ever change that. All he had left now was the quiet, the one meal a day, memories to keep him company. The memories were starting to warp. Did they really fight against the Devil. Did all that cosmic stuff really happen? It felt like a dream now. The more he tried to remember, the more uncomfortable it became.

Dustin's mind began to wander in the dark. Sometimes memories didn't seem quite right. Other times he was sure that when the giant monster rose from the sea, they were able to change the Viper into a giant robot to fight it off. Or did that ever happen? It made him smile. It was an entertaining idea. Then he thought of the clowns and how they feasted on the bones of his friends. Shapes in the dark, something horrible lurking just beyond the dim light. He shook his head. More thoughts rushed in.

Memories of rainbow bears in the magic forest, when did that happen, did it happen? Dustin hated the dark so much. He pulled his knees up to his chest and sat next to the wall.

"Just make it to the next meal. Just make it to the next meal. Just make it to the next meal." It was the mantra. The only thing keeping him attached to this reality.

Then the light started to flicker.

Wyatt was pinned to a wall in a dead white room, hovering between being awake and suffering at any given time. Whoever oversaw keeping him decided that he needed to suffer. They had used his own throwing knives, stabbed through the palms of his hands. A blood stained metal beam around his waist kept him in place, and two more blades were through his feet.

He knew full well whoever did it had a twisted sense of humor, a mockery of Christ, or something. It didn't matter.

He hated this wall, the room, the sameness of it all was worse than the pain, it was driving him mad and perhaps half blind because of how bright it was.

Once a day some water would turn on from the ceiling. Sometimes it was hot. Sometimes it was ice cold. Its main purpose was to wash the blood out of the room, his body, and down the drain in the middle of the room. He could only imagine what nightmares it was being used for, but there wasn't much else to think about here in this cell. Not much other than the past and how it all went wrong after saving the world, or half-saving it anyway.

Every few hours, the blades in his limbs would twist in a full circle to increase the blood flow and the pain. Wyatt winced as they did so again. There was no way he was going to let them win.

Before he knew it, the ordeal was over, and the countdown to the next time started. All he could do was wait and cling to hope.

Hope was going to drive him insane faster than anything else in this nightmare that didn't have an end.

# 6

"Do you think these bodies can handle the project?" Mark asked while he looked down through the glass.

"Who knows, really, no one knows. Now that the cosmic players are out of the picture. We don't have to worry about any uninvited guests. Everything is working out just the way we planned. The time eater's days are numbered. Does that sound funny? It sounded funny to me, I guess," Solaris replied, smiling to himself.

"Yeah, funny. Whatever. Let's not waste time. It's been six months and no activity from the squad. It makes me nervous when they just do nothing for so long," he replied, looking at the two ladies in the tanks below.

"Mark, listen. They are captured. Not getting

out. Ever. We won, you know?" Solaris asked, and Mark spun around, grabbed the doctor by his white lab coat, and slammed him against the wall in one move.

Solaris had the wind knocked out of him.

"No. You listen. They are the most elite force in the world. You forget there is a whole ass load of those bastards out there. More than just five. They have a habit of showing up when they are least expected," Mark said, and Solaris turned his head, not comfortable with how close the man was right now.

"Mark, please. It's a new age of science. The Squad is a relic of the past, just like you, but you happen to be on the right side. We control everything. My project will make the Squad look like rookies on their first day," Solaris said and smiled.

"I promise. Like I said, they have four of them locked up tight, and the last hasn't been seen since. None of the others are doing anything either. The Resistance of Delta is a joke. We've already won. This project is just the icing on the cake we've worked so hard for. Now, get off me, General. You wouldn't want to cause drama, would you?" Solaris asked. Mark backed off, setting him back on the floor. "All of the BOBO soldiers have been distractions in the past, all attempts to control them have failed. What is going to make this any better?" Mark asked.

"Finally, a question worth answering. One I

need to keep secret. Like I said, General, you need to trust me, and like you said, the remains of the Delta Squad could strike at any time. If I told you all the secrets and you get captured, then you'd know all the secrets, and believe me, I bet they could make you talk, then they'd know everything too," Solaris replied. The two men glared at one another.

"You're lucky we still need you, at least for now," Mark replied as he took one last look down at the science lab and walked out of the room.

Solaris smoothed out his lab coat and cracked his neck as he walked back to the observation window. He knew it was just a matter of time before his creation would be perfect, but Mark had a point. His time was running out. Keeping secrets could keep him safe for only so long.

# 7

The house was blue and small, on the outskirts of a town none of them knew. "Six damn months of running, we could fight back, why are we watching him instead?" Tyler asked, staring at Joey.

"Do you understand anything? We used to be friends. Why do you insist on treating me like a monster? I'm not Silence anymore," Joey said.

"Well, Joey. You used to be Grandmaster Silence. You killed friends, countless people, you've done horrible things. We're not friends anymore. You're an idiot, but we've decided to keep you alive. We don't know why. Stop screaming because you'll give us away," Brianna replied, keeping her voice down.

Angel looked out a window but didn't see anything. Since the Syndicate's takeover, it made the enemy easier to spot. "I think we're good," he said, and Brianna didn't feel relieved. "Of course, we're good, no one's looking for us. They think they've won. We're fine," Joey said and rolled his eyes.

"Yeah, sure. Three superpowered beings and a has been cosmic dumbass serial killer. I'm sure no one is looking for us, that's the logical conclusion to make, idiot," Tyler replied, leaning back in his chair.

"It has been half a year. Maybe the idiot has a point," Angel replied, doing his best to relax.

"What we should do is get a good night's sleep, armor up and go kill as many of the invaders as we can. Maybe we die, but so what? Everything's lost at this point anyway. We could ditch this guy and go on our own," Angel said.

"You'd just ditch me?" Joey asked. "Yep," Tyler replied.

"Yeah, we could, but this guy was a host for Silence and didn't die. Who knows what those Syndicate bastards could find in him? If even a spark of that power still exists, they will find it and the nightmare will start over. Hell, if he dies and that thing is still in him, it might just find a different host. We don't know," Brianna replied and looked at Joey.

"Don't think I am protecting you because I like you. In fact, I should just kill you now and get it over with and take our chances with Silence finding a different host," she said and glared at Joey with a hateful look in her eyes.

"You can't kill me, you can't kill anyone," Joey said and regretted saying this as soon as he finished.

"Oh, can't kill anyone? Joey, have you not been paying attention? The world has changed, we have changed. You're liable to kill everyone, you almost did. You're a monster, Joey. We have to keep you in check so something like that never happens again."

Brianna screamed at him. Joey looked away. The words hurt. Silence did those things. Not him, but he couldn't make them understand any of that. Every time he tried to explain it, the words never got out of his mouth because he couldn't justify them in his head.

There was no excuse. He took the power of the monster when it was offered. "All of you had power. Everyone around me had power. I was a nobody. Someone offered power and I took it. Anyone would have done the same. No one would have known how it was going to turn out. I get it, you hate me but that was the past," Joey said all at once.

"You could have said no. Does it look like anyone's life got better because we got power? Does it look like everything's a paradise now?" Tyler asked.

Joey looked at the floor. "No," he replied.

"Six hours until daylight. Looks all quiet. I suggest we take showers, find whatever food is left in this place if any, then get some sleep. I'll take first watch," Angel said and crossed his arms.

"I'm not going to kill you all in your sleep," Joey replied. "I don't trust you," Angel replied, and Joey rolled his eyes. "I'd just try to run away first."

"That's why we watch you. You run and anyone finds you, who knows what could happen. No one wants that, and if you really felt the least bit bad about what you did, you wouldn't want that either," Brianna said.

Joey didn't have anything to say to that. "I'm taking a shower first, you find food," she said to Tyler, stood up and walked out of the room, and he did the same.

"Dish wars, then?" Joey asked. Angel sighed, reached into the dark bag beside him and pulled out two decks in plastic cases and tossed him one. "Practically have all the cards in these decks memorized. It kind of takes the fun out of the game," Angel replied.

"It almost does," Joey replied. The two of them began to set up their decks.

# 8

It was raining in the city. He had spent six months on the run while the Syndicate turned every form of resistance in their path to dust.

The Delta Squad had been defeated, the Guardian Angels, too. Lots to think about but not a lot of time to do it. Today he was a nobody, walking in Cleveland, in the middle of the night in a rainstorm passing under the black flags of the Syndicate that seemed to be attached to every building. The rain had a sinister effect on them. Almost made them seem alive.

He supposed they didn't want anyone to forget who owned the country, and maybe the world by now.

Bryan was at a loss of what to do now. He could

fight, he knew that he could do damage to the Syndicate's forces, but one man, even one such as him, would fall eventually and do no good. Too many thoughts.

Then lights lit the rain up from behind. "Damn it," he said under his breath. Usually, the patrols didn't bother coming out in the rain. This must be someone looking to impress someone else, just his luck.

"You there. You're out after curfew. Turn around, show us your hands and your papers," Bryan did as they asked but kept his head down the entire time. "Hands first or papers, it's hard to do both at the same time," he replied.

"Don't be a smart ass, papers, identification. Why are you out here?" the man asked. Bryan couldn't see him due to the spotlight shining in his face. He hated spotlights.

"I am a leader of the Guardians, Zodiac Corps to be specific," he said in a calm voice, over the rain. This statement got a bit of a laugh out of the soldiers in the vehicle. Bryan was unsure why that happened.

"Great, another crazy out wandering the streets," the one in charge said. Bryan looked up, he couldn't see any of them through the lights, but the light didn't hurt his eyes.

"Alright leader, come with us and you won't be

hurt. It's wet anyway and surely one such as yourself should be in a dry place, right?"

"No, I think I'll pass. Thanks anyway," he replied with a shrug.

"We will not say it again, come with us or we will open fire."

The gun on the top of the thing aimed towards him, it was a small movement.

"If you really think you should waste the bullets, that's up to you. Me, on the other hand, well, you know I'd rather save the ammo. You might need it later for something more important."

Bryan heard someone snap their fingers.

The gun on top opened with a burst of fire and at once, he was knocked off his feet and onto the pavement. Bryan gritted his teeth as he hit the street. The bullets burned his flesh where they made impact, these were big bullets. He didn't fall.

"That hurt. Do you think you could, you know, not shoot me?" Bryan stood up. The pain was intense, it had been a while, but he was determined to not let scum like this see him react.

The lights still blinded him, but he felt the energy from them change to panic. "Holy—" Bryan held up his right hand.

"No, son. Not exactly what you'd call holy," he said with a cough. "Now, what am I to do with you now that you shot me?" he asked. He was sure the rain covered his question and everything else he said anyway.

"What the hell are you doing, shoot him again, you must have missed," Bryan heard the same voice yell out, thick with panic.

The machine gun began to shoot. He ran to the left towards the middle of the street just a little faster than the gunner could follow. These people couldn't be allowed to live, they'd seen his face, seen him take machine gun bullets and not die. No, they'd tell someone for sure and that just couldn't happen. He slid through the water and turned toward his attacker at the same time.

In his right hand a green bolt of lightning appeared and formed into a weapon. Not just any weapon, Soul Sabre, Theron's weapon, a gift from another time. The blade burned with a brilliant blast of bright green energy, crackled through the rain.

"What in the hell? Kill it," the man behind the light screamed. Bryan's blade let loose a brilliant bright green ray.

The energy cut through the vehicle and the same energy exploded from the black windows. The spotlight died, the tires exploded.

The men were nothing more than a pile of ashes being washed away in the rain, now. The armored truck would never run again as the melted parts steamed in the rain. The Soul Sabre disappeared as he finished inspecting his work, pleased with it. So much for keeping a low profile. Someone was going to call this in.

"Sorry guys. I just don't have time to chat. I have a team to put back together. I have work to do," he said and walked away, fading in the rain.

# 9

Tony was stuck working the reconstruction. "Hey, Tony, I need the hammer. I got a stubborn nail," Randy said. It shook him out of his thoughts. "Sure, buddy," he said, picked up the thing, and gave it a light toss in the man's direction.

The humid Florida night was brutal, but the reconstruction unit never took any time off. Day and night, twenty four hours, nonstop work.

The Olympians made a mess of Tampa when they showed up, and now it almost resembled a city again. The same was happening all over the new Syndicate States.

Slave labor. Tony picked up another plank of wood when a pair of guards walked by. "Worker, this is the worst wall I've ever seen. Look at how you pounded in those nails, the wood's chipped to hell, and these joints won't hold together, one hurricane and this is all coming down. Take it apart and do it right, then report to the lash camp so you learn your lesson," the man said, then the pair walked away laughing.

Tony heard the words, but they didn't seem mean spirited. He was sure the guard didn't care. Tony had no intention of going to get whipped. The wall was fine, and he knew it. They needed to lift it up, put it on the truck so the next unit could do what they wanted with it.

"Yeah, no," Tony said and turned back to Randy, who'd watched the whole thing. "Are you really not going to the lash?" he asked.

"Why would I? They have thousands in each unit. You think they keep track of us all? Not a chance. Those idiots will forget me by the time they have to yell at someone else," Tony replied.

Randy looked nervous. "If you say so. I won't remind them. This heat, am I right?" he asked. Tony wiped the sweat off his brow and nodded.

"Say, while I was getting nails from the truck, I heard the guards talking about the resistance. Apparently, they took back Anchorage. I guess the Syndicate doesn't fight well up in the north," he said, and Tony nodded again.

He also didn't believe any of that stuff. He knew the Syndicate liked to play games with people's minds. False hope gave people the will to live and wait for rescue instead of fighting back. It was just a ploy. On the other hand, there was no reason to tell Randy or anyone anything different. Losing hope, even if it was false, was dangerous.

"Come on, help me finish this wall, and then we can get back to the barracks. This heat is going to kill me before the Syndicate does," Tony said, and Randy nodded.

The two of them started to lift the wall when, from just down the path, there was a scream, a woman. Tony closed his eyes. "Fourth time this week," Randy said. "I still can't believe we lost to these red-eyed bastards," he finished, they slid the wall onto the truck.

The guards had no reason to treat the slaves like people. They could use them however they saw fit. The men were treated better because they could do more work. "Give me the hammer," Tony said. Randy got chills. Tony's voice had changed. It was dark and cold now.

Randy handed him the hammer. Tony took it and started to walk in the direction of the screams. "Man, what are you doing besides getting yourself killed?" Randy asked. Tony narrowed his eyes. "This has got to stop," he said and moved past Randy.

The trip didn't take long. Tony moved less like a construction worker now and more like a shadow as he avoided the work lights. Randy followed him but couldn't quite match his movements.

Tony turned a corner and saw the same two guards from before that had just found a woman, alone, and cornered her. She was on the ground, bleeding from the mouth. Tony knew what was coming next. "What's the matter? Don't like being alive anymore? Don't like doing what you're told? Still got that old freedom stuff in your brain?" the guard on the left asked.

"I'm gonna screw you so hard that you won't even remember your own name, bitch, let alone anything else," the one on the right added. They both laughed at her whimpering.

Tony heard enough. He gripped the hammer so tight his knuckles turned white. Then, from the shadows, he started at a dead run. At the same time, he flipped the hammer around to the claw end and swung. The claw sunk into the back of the left guard's neck. Tony pulled the hammer to the side and tore all the flesh out with it, making the blood spray.

The other guard was in shock. Tony lunged, knocking the man to his back, pushing his rifle aside with ease.

Tony began to bash the guard's face over and over with the tool without hesitation. After six strikes, the man's head was a bloody mess with bits of skull and brain in all directions. Once Tony was sure the man wouldn't be getting up again, he stood up.

Looking at the woman, he nodded. "Get away from here. Go to the barracks and say nothing about this to anyone. If they ask about your face, just say you tripped. Go," he said. Before she could say anything, he turned and walked away.

"Dude, what the hell was that? No, really, what the hell?" Randy asked. Tony looked at the bloody hammer.

"Just putting right what has been wrong. It's the little things," he replied. He looked behind him and saw that the hammer had been leaving a trail of blood from the scene. "We need to clean this up before the shift ends, cover the blood trail," Tony said with that same cold voice.

"Right, sure," Randy said and started to kick dirt over the blood. Tony looked at his blood covered hand and knew he must be covered in the stuff.

There wasn't time to regret or worry about his choices now. The sun was going to come up soon, and more guards were on the way, the shift change, too.

"Always something," he said, sighed, and looked for a way to clean himself up.

# 10

The Angels and the Zodiac Corps sat in the dark dimension together. "How long has it been now? Four, six, ten million years? I can't take it. I can't. I can't do it. The walls are closing in. Why are the walls closing in? There aren't even any walls here! Why is this so hard? Why is this happening? Where is all the cheese?" Gemini screamed into the dark and started to roll around in the dust.

"I will literally pay you to kill him," Dani said, holding her head. "It's only been six months, I think. Maybe. Calm down, will you?" Tiffany asked him, but it was no use. Cole flew off into the dark.

Alex looked up at the members of the Zodiac on the other side. "Why the hell did I ever listen to you in the first place?" he asked.

Samantha just shrugged. "Hindsight is always perfect," she said.

"Sam has a point here. We trusted the wrong people. Who would have guessed the meeting was a trap?" Matt added.

"I did, I totally did. I said it was a trap the whole time and we shouldn't go meet the Syndicate in any capacity because it was a bad idea. Once again, for the millionth time, I told you so," Melissa said, and Dani rolled her eyes.

"Yes, we get it. We so get it," Brittany replied. "Ladies, please, we've done this conversation a hundred times. Can we please not do it again?" Alex asked, and the two of them stopped.

"One room, one mistake. Mark talked a good game, didn't he?" Matt asked and started to laugh. "We were gonna work together to rebuild the world and then before you know it. Poof, one dimension beam later, and we're all here. Trapped. Forever," he said and tossed a rock into the distance. If it landed, it never made a sound.

"So, anyone have a deck of cards? Because I forgot mine back on the ship," Matt said.

Alex looked at Samantha in the dim light and smiled.

"No cards, but I am sure I can find something to do, you know. I'm pretty resourceful when I need to be."

She caught his stare and smiled back. "I like to

break things, you know. All kinds of things. Doesn't matter if it's small," she replied with a cold stare in her eyes. Alex got the message, and everyone else did too.

"I want my goddamned cheeseburger, and I know you have it. You can't keep it from me forever," Cole screamed out of the dark and put his blade through a six foot tall rock. "No cheeseburger. What am I going to do? How can I even stand this anymore? Why do I even exist?" he yelled, then fell to his knees as if he were a machine that ran out of power.

This caught the attention of everyone else.

"Is he always this way?" Hale asked.

"Yeah, sometimes he's actually weird. You need to watch out on those days. This isn't too bad," Ariana replied. The other Zodiac members nodded in agreement, as if they had seen things.

"You know, I just had a scary thought. Bob and the others were banned from Earth realm, right? Well, we're not on Earth anymore," Matt said, and the words made all of them widen their eyes at the truth of the message.

There was a rumble in the distance, like thunder. No sign of changing weather or anything else that might be the cause. Just a sound in the distance.

"Yeah, thanks. You just screwed with fantasy time. Now I have to be serious," Ariana said, staring at the Guardian Angels. She sighed.

"You know, we were both tricked. When we make it back home, why don't we just team up to kill every member of the Squad and their Syndicate? I mean, we both hate them and have nothing to lose. Now that your friend here brought up that disturbing fact, I think we should start coming up with a plan," Alex said.

"Oh, now you want to come up with a plan. Six months and now you want to work together because something has a chance of showing up?" Tiffany asked, and energy began to crackle between her fingers.

"I'm going to ask you another question here in a minute," she finished.

"Stop it, please. We don't even know if it's been six months or not. This is progress, and the man makes a point. We are stronger together, yeah?" Dani asked, and Sam looked at Tiffany.

"Not now, Tiff. The Guardians have a point. We should work together, at least to get out of this nightmare," Samantha said.

"Fine."

"It's okay. Once we get back home, we can have a spa day, I promise," Ariana said and looked at the Angels. "You can come, too. Ladies only," she said.

Alex and Matt looked at one another. "Trust me, that's not one conversation you'd want to be a part of anyway," Alex said.

"We'll hit up the cheeseburger joint and keep

the crazy guy happy," Matt said. "Fine, if you say so," he replied.

Both groups stood up and began to stretch out. No one had any ideas of what to do yet, however.

"I have an idea we can try. We should try and make it back to Hell. At least there we will be on our own turf and can get back home," Hale said.

"Hell, you want to go to Hell? Why would you--" Tiffany cut herself off. She knew this is where the Angel Corps were trained. This was home to them.

"Yeah, we could go there, but we don't know how to get there from here. This place is called a prison for a reason," Dani replied.

"Yeah, what a shame, we can't find our way into Hell. That's just too bad," Samantha said sarcastically, but nobody laughed. "Well, someone go get the rock whisperer, and let's get looking for a way out. Nothing but time, right?" Alex asked and looked around. Everything here looked the same. He didn't like it. Nobody liked it.

"Cole, we're leaving," Sam yelled at him.

"Can I keep my rock?" Cole asked, and Sam sighed. "Yes, you can keep your rock. Let's go," she replied. Cole walked out of the dark with a vague person shaped rock in his right hand. "It's Ben. See? Ben says hi," Cole said.

The Zodiac members missed Ben. "Not funny," Matt said. Cole frowned. "Oh, I just thought…"

Sam smiled. "It's okay. We all miss him. Let's go.

Maybe he's in Hell somewhere, and we can bring him back ourselves," she said with a forced smile.

"Yeah, oh, I can't wait to go to Hell. Let's find a way there quick," he said and flew off into the black sky.

"You heard him. Let's go to Hell," Alex said, then picked a direction. It didn't matter in this place, he supposed. Then he and the group started to walk into the unknown.

## 11

"What do you mean, real battle? How much battle can be left? I don't think anyone has any fight left in them after all of this," Cody asked as the two of them walked down the hall.

"Yeah, you'd think that, but you're not an idiot, you know there is always something more, something else. Or are you really that stupid, Commander?" the man asked him.

"Guy, stop calling me that. I'm not a commander anymore. I'm not even a member of a team anymore. I quit. I appreciate this, but once I am out these doors, I'm gone. Understand me?"

The man stopped.

"Don't you get it? Once you're chosen for this job, you keep it until the day you die. You have a hard time dying. We've all watched you. We've been impressed so far, but this sounds a whole lot like crying," he said.

He never turned around, never looked at him. When he was finished, he just kept on walking forward.

Cody shook his head, all he could see was all the times he failed and how it all led to him being trapped in a torture cell. He didn't feel like he deserved to walk among the living right now, but he still drew breath, still alive. It was hard to get the doubt out of his mind when all he wanted to do was disappear.

"Who are you anyway? You break me out of that hole, and, how? It makes no sense. The only one who might be good enough to get through the defenses is—" Cody blinked and it all became clear.

"You got it. Now, let's keep going before I decide to leave you here. We need to get your armor back," the man said and kept a steady pace down the hall.

Cody couldn't help but notice the doors beside him, bars in the small windows leading into black cells.

"There are people behind these walls. People like me. Special enemies," Cody said, realizing this, slowly coming out of his depression long enough to see it.

"Yes, but don't be fooled. Not everyone is worth breaking out. They'll kill you and everyone else if given the chance. They stay here," the man replied and did not slow down, but it didn't matter. The alarms in the place started to blare.

"Damn it. This'll end bloody. I hope you're going to snap out of that stupid emotional state soon. I'll need your help," the man said and came to a stop.

"Don't have a choice or any weapons," Cody replied, barely being heard over the sounds of the alarms. Cody wasn't sure what direction the guards would come from. If he was unlucky, it would be both sides. He didn't feel lucky. The footsteps were coming in from the left, a whole group of people were running in their direction.

"You go first, leader. Show me some of that spark," the man said, and the armed guards came around the corner and began to fire. The man had pulled a door he was closest to open for cover against the bullets.

"What the hell are you doing?" Cody asked as the guards started shooting, the bullets deflecting off the metal door.

The rescuer didn't know what to expect, but as he heard the thump of a body hit the ground, he could only sigh. Taking a quick look around the corner of the metal door, he could see the body of the commander on the floor, bleeding. "You'll be fine, walk it off, champ," he said and waited behind the door.

"Well, great. Mister high and mighty Commander decides to display his super bullet sponge skills. Shoot him again to be sure, then cuff him," one of the guards said and watched Cody twitch a couple of times as a pool of blood formed under him. The pain was intense. He'd almost forgotten what it felt like to be gunned down. Still, he lived, here in his own blood. No bullet ended his life when it could have.

Fate, maybe. Of course, it could be the guards had bad aim. His pain was already beginning to fade. A slew of nightmares clouded his mind. What if this was just another cosmic trick? What if all of this was an illusion? An old stranger does the impossible to save him—that didn't make any sense, but the pain sure felt real enough. Cody's mind raced, but a stronger force pushed all of it out.

The will to live. His eyes opened slowly. He could see them moving in his direction.

Cody didn't move a muscle. He waited until the guards were closer. The four of them weren't careful. His bleeding had stopped, but they didn't notice. "Come on. Someone cuff this son of a bitch so we can put him back. Then get a mop and we can pretend like this didn't even happen," one of them said through the helmet.

One of the guards kneeled to grab Cody's wrist. He did, and Cody reached up with the other arm, grabbed the rifle, and pulled it down.

"What the hell," the man yelled as his weapon was stolen, shocked at the speed the blood covered man had.

The feeling didn't last long as the weapon spun around and fired. The back of the guard's head exploded with the helmet, blood splattering onto the other three. The other three reeled back, weapons drawn, confused at what happened.

Cody rose, covered in his own blood, the blood of the guard with the black weapon in hand. He flipped the switch to single-shot mode and shot each of them without hesitating in the neck, watching them fall to the floor.

"I hate wasting ammo," he said to the dead and turned to look at his rescuer, turned the weapon on him.

"I'm not sure if this is a dream or who you are. I know I won't shoot you in the back, but I don't know if the same is true for you. You go first and lead the way. Any tricks, anything I don't like and, well, you know."

He picked up one of the bloody guns from the guards and tossed it to the janitor, who caught it. "Of course, wouldn't have it any other way," he replied and at gunpoint, took the lead once more, and the two of them began to make their way out.

"I knew you had it in you, champ," the old man said. "Yeah, thanks for all the help. Keep moving. How did you even get here anyway," Cody replied.

## 12

"So, they lost the battle. Damn it, what good is a resistance if they don't listen to orders? It would be so easy if they just did what they were told," Heath was angry. For the past six months, Nick, Roger, and himself had been transmitting the orders to anyone who could hear them.

Roger put his head in his hands. "They aren't soldiers. This isn't a *Terminator* situation. You can tell them what to do all day, but they're just people against an overwhelming force. Plus, we have some success. If we didn't, no one would be left to listen," Roger said.

"Plus, the orders are basically the same as video game missions. Take out site X. Destroy this, disrupt that, kill this one," Nick said and adjusted a dial. "Not exactly the greatest battle plans in the world, are they?" Nick asked.

Heath just took a deep breath.

"Six goddamned months with you two in this junk abandoned base, and I'm about to lose my mind," he replied.

Nick and Roger just looked at one another and shrugged. "This old place isn't so bad. I mean, it has hot water and ten years of food, crappy food but still. It could be worse," Nick said.

"Yeah, everything still works, not like the island right? We wouldn't want to be there now anyway. I'd say we're lucky to be out of sight and still useful," Roger added.

Heath rolled his eyes. "Just shut up. I'm aware," he replied.

"Take a look at the Syndicate's map. I hacked into a couple of old satellites and look. The western half of America is fighting like hell. The country is split down the middle. The easterners have all but given up, it seems. Half a country is better than none," Nick said.

Heath shook his head.

"The world. Look at the world. Every major city has their flag. They own all three of the most powerful weapons in the world, all the strongest people," Heath said.

"Why won't the other delta members fight?" Nick asked. Heath just shook his head. "They are fighting. Look at that map again and tell me how it is the country is cut in half but it's not enough. There are only so many, and the Syndicate armies are, well, limitless," Heath replied, falling back into a chair, tired, more than just tired, drained.

"Listen. Let me take over for a couple of days. Abdul is out there kicking ass, and others too. The war will still be here when you get back, I promise," Roger said, and Heath nodded. "I know. I know it's just, yeah, you're right. Good luck," he said and stood up.

"If you lose the damn war while I'm gone, the Syndicate will be the last thing you have to worry about," he said, rubbed his eyes, and left the room.

"How the hell did we get here, man?" Nick asked. Roger turned his eyes back to the map. "Bad luck," Roger replied.

"It feels more than just bad luck. Man, I miss the good old days when we had all the fun weapons to fight wars with. I want to get out there and do something," Roger said.

"We're doing enough here. We can see everything. We can get people out of danger and make the Syndicate suffer where it counts. Shut up and let's get the next mission ready and hope there are people still willing to fight," Nick said.

"Yeah, I don't want to get shot by Heath for losing the war," he replied.

"Shot? No. Heath would take his time, inch by

inch. When 188 first appeared, he had to get information out of some of the red eyes. Those boys looked more like steaks before they died. I've seen some stuff, but I never want to see that again," Nick said.

Roger nodded. "Thanks for the tip," he said and hoped that wasn't what the future had in store for him.

"Oh my god, look," Roger said and pushed a few buttons.

# 13

Brian woke up in the ditch where Emily left him. The last thing he remembered was fighting with Emily, and after that, nothing. When he woke up, he had the worst headache he could remember but was otherwise unharmed. The chaos of the battle surrounded him.

He had no idea how long he had been in this ditch, but some time must have passed by. Rust was forming on the broken steel already, but only faint traces.

"Can't stay here," he said and pulled himself back to the road, speaking to make sure his voice still worked, and started to walk away from the old battleground.

For hours he walked in a line. The sun above

him hardly seemed to move, but the air was cool. There was a slight breeze too. It felt like winter was on the way, or fall maybe. He was lost in his thoughts when he looked up. There was a small town in the distance, complete with a giant blue water tower, the tallest structure in town.

Brian felt good about this and quickened his pace toward the place. At the very least, he could get news of the state of the world.

It wasn't long before he got to the first houses outside of town. No one was out. The place appeared lived in, but still dead. His first idea was that a plague came through. It didn't matter, however, he had to keep moving.

Brian moved until he came to the school. There he looked at it, empty as every other place. There was something off about it—the flagpole. At the top, there was no American flag. Instead, it was a black flag with a red cross in the middle.

"Damn it," he said. It was all he needed to see to know things went bad somewhere along the line.

As he approached the pole to take the offending flag down, the first signs of life came, almost as if they had appeared out of nowhere.

"You there, away from the flag, and prepare to present papers." The voice came from behind, and Brian turned around to see a group of black clad soldiers there. They didn't have their weapons pointed at him yet, but he knew it wouldn't take much for this to change.

"My name is Brian. I am, well, I am lost. Tell me where I am?" he asked them while raising his hands. It was an honest question. He had no idea when or where he was.

"Region Six," the man replied. "Now, your papers." The man never flinched, and Brian could see the grip get tighter.

"What is Region Six?" With this, the soldiers raised their weapons, took aim. Brian wasn't threatened by the gesture.

"I am going to tell you one more time. Present your papers," the leader said, furious at having to repeat himself.

"Well, no. See. I don't have any on me you'd take and—" The men opened fire. It took a few seconds to realize that the bullets were just bouncing off. "What the hell are you?" one of the soldiers screamed while shooting.

"I told you. My name is Brian." He said this and jumped, closing the distance in the process. When Brian hit the ground, he did it with enough force to knock the soldiers back. He grabbed the legs of the closest soldier and spun, using him as a weapon. This was more than enough to shatter the bodies of the others, sending bone and blood in every direction. The man he used as a weapon was dead.

He tossed the body to the side and it hit the brick wall of the school. The remains slid to the ground. "Morons picked the wrong side."

It was then he heard the faint beeping from one of the bodies. He rolled his eyes because it could only mean one thing. Trouble. Brian thought about running, but then the thought passed. It was clear there was a war on. Where there as was war, there was always resistance.

It didn't matter if he was the last fighter in the country or not. He had time to make up for and a job to do.

Then the ground began to shake. The vibrations caused the flagpole to shake, the windows of the school too.

There was a tank rolling down Main Street. It seemed a little extreme. He looked up into the sky and saw a glint in the sky. A drone had seen everything he'd done, too. Now it made sense.

Brian turned towards the tank and cracked his neck. "Hit me with your best shot." The tank didn't look like one he recognized. It looked from the future. Or at least how he imagined one from the future would look.

It fired.

Brian saw the shell coming. In his mind, he saw himself punching the shell in slow motion and watched as the explosion surrounded him in an awe inspiring thing for all to see and to give the enemies something to be afraid of.

The second he thought of this plan, he was knocked off his feet by the explosion and thrown back into the air into the ground several feet away. Leaving a crater where he landed.

Brian coughed, then groaned.

"Alright. I admit it. That was a pretty good shot as shots go. My turn." He looked down at his clothes. He would need new ones. These were toast.

Brian decided to stop being stupid and pulled himself up, took off running. He leapt high into the air. Brian landed in front of the cannon.

Not wanting to get blasted in the face, Brian walked forward with his arm under the long cannon. He walked up the front of the tank and ripped off the turret in the process. The metal made a horrid wrenching sound, then he tossed the hunk of steel to the side.

Inside there were two men who were terrified. "You shot me with a tank."

"It's really not nice to shoot people with tanks. It's not the polite thing to do." Brian was going to crush these two, but he noticed a crowd starting to form.

People brave enough to come out of their homes. They were all scared, dirty, and looked as if they had been starving. Brian got a better idea. He reached down, grabbed, and tossed them on the ground beside the ruined tank. Then he jumped down beside them.

"Alright everyone, these guys are yours. You can kill them if you want." No one said anything. He wondered if there were more soldiers in town. There was no indication there were, not nearby at least.

"By Cyranthis' mercy. We owe you everything," a man in black said. It caught Brian off guard for a second. "Are there any more around town?" Brian asked.

"No, sir. One tank, a small unit. There were more when they took the town but in exchange for obedience, they pulled out, left the small guard unit behind," the priest replied. Brian nodded.

"Our god has answered our prayers," someone cried out from the crowd, and like someone lit up an applause sign, the rest of the people let loose with a cacophony of praise and affection. Brian wasn't used to this. These people worshiped Cyranthis, and that religion was crazier than a bag of cats. However, crazy was the only game in town right now.

"What is your name, savior?" the priest asked.
"Brian," he replied.
"Come with us, Brian. You have delivered us from the Syndicate's grasp. We need to celebrate a great victory," the priest said.

"Sure. I could use some new clothes as mine were destroyed by, well, you all saw."

"Yes. Clothes, a feast, all the things. Welcome to our town. Cyranthis be praised!" The priest said as the crowd cheered then, and all of them began to walk towards the houses. For now, at least, everything was looking up for him.

## 14

Josh was in his cage and the visitor chime kicked in again. Josh cringed at the sound of it and knew what came next. However, when he looked up to see the face of his next tormentor, there was someone in a black cloak standing there.

"Cosplayer," he said. It looked like Grandmaster Silence from here, but he knew that was impossible. There was always the chance he was going insane, too. The figure stood there. The moon made the scene all that more dramatic.

The person cocked his head and then tossed something down into the pit. Josh saw the metal glint through the air, and then it landed on the floor with barely a sound. It was a thin piece of steel wire. He looked up, and the figure was gone.

He knew that he was in deep Syndicate territory,

and the security here had to be intense. There was no way that a freak with a cloak would just be able to walk through the front door. No, someone planned this.

Or it was a trick. Josh stared at the wire and wondered if he took it, if the miniguns watching him wouldn't open fire and remove one of his arms for fun. The thing that represented freedom represented everything else too.

"Screw it," he said and shuffled over to the wire and picked it up. Nothing happened. Josh rarely ever got nervous, but tonight he was.

He reached around and found the electronic lock that held his collar in place. Josh couldn't help but smile. It was good enough to hold prisoners, but anyone who knew what they were doing could break them if they had something to do it with.

Today, Josh did, thanks to a mysterious benefactor. He took a breath and slid the metal wire in the crack and twisted it. He could feel the thing loosen. He pulled the thing off his neck, and some skin came with it. The chain was attached to the top. With the walls protected by miniguns, escape must have been deemed impossible.

Nothing. Had there been no one watching him this whole time? Was it all automated? Someone had been giving him his food, but for all he knew it was a robot, too. Didn't matter, he flexed his hands, grabbed hold of the chain and pulled it to make sure it wouldn't break. Once he was sure it wouldn't, he started to climb. One hand over the other. His muscles burned, and he wanted to quit.

Each time he moved up, the night air got cooler, fresher. He could smell freedom with each handhold closer to the top.

Josh groaned and grabbed the middle of the bar that had held his chain, wrapped his legs around it, and started to shimmy to the edge where the cloaked one stood. He crawled over the edge and got over the edge.

Josh investigated his former cage for the first time, and all he could feel was hate. He walked to the button the visitors were able to press and torment him at will. Big and red, 'Tame the Beast' in big black letters over it. Rage hit like a wave, and he smashed the button in with his fist. It felt good to hit something.

The red button shattered like glass. He extended his hand and watched the shards fall off his skin. He looked around and saw that his cage was just for him. It was like a silo in the middle of a city. The person who helped him was gone, but the black cloak was on the ground. He picked it up and put it on. The thing fit.

He looked off into the distance and knew that this situation wouldn't last long. He had to get out and wondered if he could just walk through the front doors. Maybe no one would notice. He slipped the hood up over his head and put his hands in his pockets.

Inside the left pocket was a piece of paper. Josh pulled it out and read it. Three simple words.

'To The Museum.' Josh had no idea what that meant. If this was a plan, he didn't want to mess it up by doing his own thing. At least not for now.

Towards the exit hall, he turned and walked towards the door. If a cloaked man entered, hopefully, one would be able to leave. With any luck, the elevator ride down wasn't a trap. Josh was paranoid now but doing his best to not show it.

Josh walked outside. "Hey," a voice said, and he stopped. "What'd you think of the freak?" he asked. Josh turned his head just enough to see the guard at the door and imagined tearing him to pieces.

"I wouldn't want to meet him in a dark alley," Josh replied, the first thing that came to mind, his first human interaction in months. He was rusty.

"You said it, have a good night," the man replied with a smile. Josh realized this was just a worker paying the bills. He almost felt sorry for this one, if only he hadn't called him a freak.

"You too," Josh replied and glanced at the monitor above the man's head. It showed Josh was still in the center of the cage, secure as ever. He had questions.

"Oh. I'm new. I heard the museum is a good place to visit. Any idea where it is?" Josh asked, and the guard shrugged. "Just a few blocks from here. You should have seen it while on the observation deck."

Josh remembered seeing something that looked important from there. "Thanks," he replied, then walked out the door.

# 15

Those blades, they were beginning to turn again. The pattern was repeating itself as it had countless times before. Wyatt had no choice but to sit there and take it as the blades carved their pounds of flesh from him. Sounds from the white void.

Gunfire.

The sounds of battle were not something you could forget when you have been involved in something like this for so long. This just confirmed it for him. He had lost his mind.

He gazed down as he watched his blood flow towards the drain when the door on the opposite side of the room had something sliced through it. It was a blade, not his. He could tell his from anywhere, but this one seemed close.

"What is this?" he half said. Maybe it was just his mind. He wasn't sure anymore.

He trained his eyes on it, trying to look for any sign this was not happening, but it all seemed real. Still, he knew just how convincing illusions could be. The blade pulled back. There was a kick, there were sparks, and the door fell to pieces.

He looked at his rescuer but had no idea who it was. He was dressed in a suit of armor. It was primitive, Wyatt knew that much. It was more than enough to overpower most people.

"Hey there, can't talk long. Major reinforcements are coming," the man said as he walked. Wyatt was confused. "Who are you?" It was the first time he had heard anyone's voice in quite a while.

"No time for that." He pulled all the blades out and tossed them on the floor with a soft clanking sound. Wyatt's arms didn't fall. The blood was so thick and crusted, it glued him to the wall. Same with his ankles. There was a thin strap of metal holding him to the wall as well. "God damn," the man said. Wyatt could tell he was doing everything in his power to not throw up at the sight. Despite getting rinsed off, it wasn't enough.

The man grabbed Wyatt's blood crusted shirt and pulled him off the rack with a hideous slurping sound as fast as he could. He fell to the floor, landing on his hands and knees.

Everything hurt.

"Listen, we gotta get out of here. It was hard enough getting through. Hurry up and get right so we can go." He heard the words, but the pain was immense. Nothing was working the way it was supposed to.

"Do I have to carry you out? I will. Don't make me do it."

Wyatt wasn't feeling any better. "No time to waste, let's go."

Wyatt took the hand offered to him and managed to get to his feet. His savior still needed one free arm and managed to give Wyatt all the support he should have needed. His feet, they refused to work.

"Damn, I can't--" Wyatt was cut off by the other. "Shut up and breathe more. You'll get better. They said you might be worse off than the others." Wyatt heard the words. Others, they were still alive. It didn't seem possible.

This was the first time Wyatt had seen what lay beyond this door since he woke up. "Others, they are still alive?" Wyatt was sure that the others should have been killed. There was no reason to keep them alive for any reason. It made no sense.

"Yes. Others. Now shut up and heal." They got through the door, and he looked both ways. To the left was filled with bodies and bloody floors. The right was clear.

"You do good work," Wyatt said and tried to laugh.

"Thanks, come on, we need to keep moving," he replied.

Wyatt was able to make his left hand into a fist, and it didn't hurt so much. "I'll be fine soon. Starting to feel better already." He looked down and put his feet flat on the floor. It was painful, but he could do it at least. "Nice work, maybe in a few hours you can learn how to tie your shoes. Let's go, princess, but we don't have all day, let's go."

"Take the suit off, and I'll show you how to use it. Could have got in here without being seen, I bet. You're clumsy and stupid, nothing like the ninja you're pretending to be. I'll take being a princess over that any day," Wyatt replied. The man in the armor looked at him.

"Shut up," he replied. Wyatt just smiled. Wyatt also knew deep down he would have approached this rescue mission the same way. Kill them all. There was no way he was going to say that out loud, however.

The two of them began to make their way down the hall. The alarms were blaring, but no one was coming. "How many of them did you kill?" Wyatt asked. "If we are lucky, all of them. Now, please shut up and go." Impatient and harsh, this guy reminded Wyatt a lot of himself, always in a hurry.

"Right," Wyatt said and was walking on his

own now. The pain had faded, and he was feeling like his old self. He looked at the sword. A closer look told him that it was rarely used. Whoever sent this guy to his aid must have had a sense of humor.

"Oh, I was told to let you have this," the man said and tossed him the sword. Wyatt caught it. The thing felt good in his hand.

"You're on your own once we get out. Get to the tower," the man said. Wyatt didn't know anything but supposed that everything would be simple once he saw the bigger picture.

## 16

Dustin was lost in his own thoughts in the black room. It was years. It had to be at this point because what was time anymore? One tiny dim light to see outlines of things, a sink, toilet. No bed. He got to sleep on the cold stone floor.

For twenty hours a day the light was off. He was sure he should have run out of air long ago, but there must have been a vent somewhere. He never heard a fan.

Nothing mattered anymore. He was sure this was hell, he wasn't alive, just didn't remember how he was killed. God knew he deserved it for all the people that he'd killed over the years. No, he needed this punishment. Deserved it and earned it even.

Yeah, this was forever. He felt like he was alive. He knew there was no way he could be. Not anymore. A horrible trick. He crawled into his corner, the one where he slept, and began to fall asleep again to have the most vivid dreams of the past.

Just before the dream took him, the wall across from him began to explode into a shower of sparks.

This woke him up with a start, and he crouched away from the sparks as the source of them began to move down the wall. This must have been it. Hell must have been tired of letting him off easy, and now it was going to flood into his tiny little room and eat him.

Yes, he was afraid of the sparks that appeared there and watched them travel inch by inch until they hit the bottom. They stopped, and the red glow on the seam began to fade away. Then the impacts began. Something was trying to get in, and it was working. Each time the unknown force slammed against the other side, the door slid in that much further until it caved in with a crash as it hit the floor with the loudest sound he'd heard in, he didn't know.

Dustin closed his eyes tight and waited for the worst, but there was no demonic thing on the other side. No fire, no anything. Just a hand reaching out and the light shining into the cage. "Take my hand. You're free," a voice said.

An angel to pull him out of Hell? It couldn't be,

could it? He didn't know who it was. He didn't trust it either.

This was home. This was where he was safe from the evils out there.

A wave of cold, fresh air flooded the room. It felt different. It felt alive for the first time in forever. Dustin gathered his courage and reached out to the hand, took it, and it pulled him out. He was blinded, and as he tried to stand up all the way, his back cracked along with most of his bones as he moved more than he had in months.

This action caused him great pain. The light, the cold, everything was painful out here, and for a short time, he thought it was just a different kind of hell, one he never imagined. He couldn't see anything, but someone grabbed him.

"Listen to me. Don't open your eyes, just walk. That's all you need to do. Just walk." Dustin agreed with not opening his eyes. They burned as if someone had thrown glass into them. The light was horrible.

The other led him in. He didn't know what direction they were going, everything was chaos now. He could hear people running. It seemed like they were getting closer. "Come on, it won't be long now," the voice said, and just a few minutes later he heard a door opening and the air got even colder.

"Open your eyes now." Dustin heard this and didn't want to do it. It was all pain if he did. But the voice had done nothing to hurt him yet, so he had to trust it.

He slowly opened his eyes to darkness. The sky was black, filled with stars. They were in a city, but the dull streetlights did nothing to cause pain.

Dustin was still confused. He didn't want to look at himself.

"Not so bad out here, is it?" Dustin didn't respond as he looked around. "Listen, go to the alleyway just over there," the man pointed. "Go down there and look for a brown sack. In it, you'll find fresh clothes and a weapon. After that, make your way to the big tower there. I'll meet you there. Hurry." It was a guy, but Dustin never got to see who it was. When he turned around, whoever it was, they were already running away.

He walked down to the alleyway and turned down it. There was, just as the guy had said, fresh clothes, and a weapon, a gun. He looked at his hands. His fingernails were long and gnarled. He put his hand to his face and felt a beard there.

Dustin knew he couldn't work a weapon with these hands. The fingernails alone made it difficult. So, he took a breath and smashed his hands against the brick wall until the brittle nails snapped into pieces. It hurt. The pain was welcome, however. It meant he was alive.

Dustin spent the next few seconds doing his best

to tear off the broken nails until he was satisfied with the results.

It was a simple pistol. Felt good in his hand, the cold steel, the weight and smell of the oil and gunpowder.

Now to change clothes and find a tower.

# 17

Paxton was in his room in his, well, someone's apartment. He sat in their chair and watched their television. CNN was going around the clock reporting on the success of the new overlords and, in true fashion, highlighting all the great changes to come while ignoring all the bodies.

They called themselves SNN now, Syndicate News Network. Paxton smiled. When you said the old or new way, it just sounded like Sin.

He opened another can of someone else's beer and took a drink. Bitter, but it did the job.

The coma left him with a headache. Syndicate hospital rooms sucked. Paxton discharged himself when no one was watching. There wasn't much to that story, and he didn't like to think about it.

Paxton thought a lot about the past sitting here

doing nothing. Without armor, he was a nobody, and that was fine.

Another sip out of the can. Too many ideas with nothing to do. He hated it and kind of wished there was a fight he could join. The idea of fighting without his armor was terrifying. So, what if he was a coward? They lived when so many other heroes died, blasted to pieces with strange weapons and powers.

Even the Delta idiots rarely fought without armor either. There was no reason to judge him. He had the powers of a god and still, after all that, he lost everything time and time again. Fear and anger were turning out to be a terrible mix.

Paxton drank the last of the bitter liquid and tossed the can at the former owner of the apartment. The dead man caught it with his chest, then it rolled to the floor with the other cans.

"New York City, grand jewel of the Syndicate. We'll investigate how much has improved since the liberation of the city, tonight at ten," someone on the television said.

Paxton could only laugh. He wondered how many idiots believed this. Of course, the world had been at war in one form or another for years now. Maybe the Syndicate finally meant peace. People were giving up their rights for security in droves.

He stood up from the chair and walked to the

window. Peace was just the quiet time between wars, and he'd had enough of it.

The night was quiet, just like the last and the one before that. Of course, he knew things from the past that might have been useful. Secrets that might upset the fragile balance of power.

He traced his finger on imaginary lines on the pane of glass in the shape of a skull. It reminded him of happier times when he was more of an artist.

"No one asked you," he said to the dead man, but didn't bother looking at him. He was starting to smell bad. If he had to wait much longer, he'd have to find a new apartment. At least it would be something to do for a little while.

## 18

"Well, this is fun. We've been up here forever. Do we actually have a plan, or are we just going to keep on watching?" Skye asked with an annoyed sigh.

"This was the plan until it wasn't," Chris replied.

"Yeah, putting all our power together into one form and giving it to a psychopath—what could have possibly gone wrong? Here we are. Stuck on the moon," Stephanie said and threw a red rubber ball against the wall over and over, catching it each time.

"Will you stop doing that? I don't know what's worse, you or that stupid ball," Chris said with a glare.

Stephanie caught it. "I'm worse," she replied.

"Oh, come on, I was kidding. I know you're not that bad," Chris replied, and she smiled a little.

"Thanks."

"Hey, we voted on that psycho. After all the insanity, who knew it was going to end the way it did?" Amanda asked.

"Too bad none of us knew any psychics," Chris said with a slight laugh.

"The Typhon armor was removed. How did they even manage that? I guess it doesn't matter, but we should get that back. We still didn't get what we started out to do. I'm anxious to have another crack at those rust bucket armors," Matt said and looked out a window, to see the white surface of the moon, and the deep nothing of space.

"It's not so bad up here. The Syndicate is taking over everything and have left us alone. Even if we go back, we'll either work with them or just fight until we die. If they don't bother us, we shouldn't bother them. It's only fair," Skye replied.

She had a point. The others had their taste of fighting and all the insanity on Earth.

"Well, we did have a good run. Olympians, it was fun for a while even, fun until it wasn't," Chris replied. He remembered fighting Gemini and others. All that power and still outclassed. They were supposed to be rulers of the world.

Now they were isolated on the moon. Yesterday's news.

Then the one sliding door into the common room opened.

"We'll get it all back. First, look at these new upgrades I've been working on," Megan said.

"Upgrades?" Skye asked, and the confusion they all felt had a voice.

"The armors are gone, Typhon's on Earth. What could be left to upgrade?" Stephanie asked, and Megan nodded.

"I know, I get it, but if you thought we left all our best tricks on Earth, well, you don't know me well at all. You should know me well enough by now, right?" she asked as the others stood up.

"Come on, follow me. I have such sights to show you," she replied and walked back through the doors.

The others looked at one another, nervous now, but then they walked through the doors after her, curious at what she and the future were about to put into their lives. "As she always been so weird?" Chris asked. "I think so," Skye replied.

# 19

Dr. Solaris was sitting in his office, sipping on his favorite drink, enjoying the victory. The Syndicate had it made, and there was nothing to do but wait.

It was late, and he had settled into a comfortable routine. Drink at the office, daydream about future projects while low classic rock played. Now, however, Mark entered his thoughts, and the rest of the Syndicate.

Mark was right. Once he was done and disposable, they would eventually kill him off. He had to keep an eye on him and all the rest of the nutjob generals he had to work for.

Solaris had the urge to throw his glass against the wall in frustration. How could they think the way they did?

It was too late to run now. Too late to stop working on the project, too. His fate felt sealed.

In a way, however, everyone's fate was sealed with the Chronovore still out there tearing up everything in sight. A world ending threat everyone ignored. Solaris couldn't help but laugh because maybe nothing mattered in the end anyway. She'd end all of time, destroy history.

As insane as that sounded in his head, it was the truth now. Maybe death was better. There was no telling what the time eater would do to him. At least with the Syndicate, it would be more traditional.

He took a sip of his bright red liquid, halfway learning how to accept his fate at the hands of his employers when the alarms began to sound on the desk console. Special ones. Them. He closed his eyes and set his glass down.

"I told those idiots to spread them out," Solaris said and sat up, turning the alarms off.

He didn't know if anyone else was aware of what was going on or not. He didn't care either, not anymore.

"Damn it."

It was all he could say.

"Well, better do my duty, I guess. Don't need to give them a reason," he said.

He pushed a button on his desk.

"I don't know what happened, send the special

security to the museum. All hell's about to break loose, and we should attempt to stop it."

He released the button and leaned back into his chair. He needed a good distraction. Letting the info out into the world about how to the Delta Squad out of their cages might be enough to save his life, or at least make them forget long enough so he could disappear. It was possible the team did nothing after getting out too. That'd ruin his plans.

"I wonder who picked up the info, I'll have to thank them if I meet them," Solaris said, turned his music up, and refilled his glass with bright red liquid.

"A toast to the dead, whomever that may turn out to be," he said while he lifted his glass, then he started drinking again.

## 20

Blake was at the headquarters, and to his relief, no one even looked twice at him. Apparently, picking up strays was common.

The minute he got there, the first thing he wanted to do was find a computer, something with access so he could try to find out information, where he was, anything important. However, the place was so thick with Syndicate soldiers that it proved to be impossible, so he did what the rest of the soldiers did.

He sat in the commons and waited for a chance to do something. He hated every second of it but tried not to look too obvious.

The night dragged on, and the various conversations blended into one another. Blake was already wishing he was back with Delacroix more by the second when something cut through the crowd that seemed to attract everyone's attention, too.

"A CD One situation is unfolding, possible targets heading toward the museum." The message was short and to the point. The others seemed uneasy at the words, as if someone transmitted them by mistake. Blake got an idea.

"Hey guys, let's go check this out," he said to the guys who had picked him up. The men stared at him as if he had lost his mind.

"Are you crazy? We're just street guards. Nothing like that applies to us. We just pick up transmissions like that sometimes." Blake shook his head at these words.

"Oh, my mistake. I thought you wanted to move up in the world. It's alright if you want to remain bottom feeders forever. We'll just keep to ourselves and do nothing."

Blake had no idea where this museum was, and if he was going to check this place out, he'd need a guide.

"Who the hell do you think you are talking to us like that?" The man said with a fair amount of justified anger. Blake turned around, and his eyes had changed. Now he had the eyes of a killer that burned through these soldiers.

"Alright, you got me. Name is Tyler. I am part of the Chemical Dragon division, working undercover to find worthy members for the unit. No one has been worthy or willing to take a goddamned risk, so I am resorting to blowing my cover to find a few good men. Are you them, or do I keep walking?"

The mood around the table changed at once.

The others had a dead stare on their faces.

"Chemical Dragon? They're the Syndicate elite. Hell yes, we can go to that museum," the captain said, and the others seemed to be just as excited now. A chance to get out of grunt work was worth the risk. Blake smiled.

With no orders to do so, the men piled back onto their armored vehicle and pulled out of the camp. Blake made sure to take his place on the side once again.

"Let's move, top speed. If we miss this, you are out of chances," Blake said.

Someone in the background was ordering them to stop. Blake heard this, looked back, and smiled at them just before they turned a corner.

Blake also had no idea what he was getting into. It could have been anything, but anything was better than sitting in that place for another minute doing nothing at all.

So what if he had to lie to get things moving? He couldn't believe he was living in a world where the Chemical Dragon unit was considered to be elite.

## 21

Josh wandered down the street. He looked at everything and had no idea what city he was in anymore. Nothing looked the same or as it should. He didn't look the way he should. He had a long beard, and his eyes were sunken in and bloodshot. He looked like a ghost or some evil wizard in this cloak.

Standing out here, he was sure he stood out. He wondered why that guard let him go in the first place looking like this. Maybe he didn't get paid enough to die.

Shops were dark as if a plague had come through. In a way, one did. The Syndicate's flag was on the corner in front of him on a pole flapping in the wind.

Josh narrowed his eyes at the black thing in the streetlight in the distance.

The streets were worse than dead. They were empty, and he could almost feel all the memories that it used to have and feel them echoing around him. Like walking through a school after hours, or a theater after it closed.

A creepy feeling washed through everything.

He knew there were people here. He saw them every day, they saw him. It must have been a curfew. That was the only thing that made sense.

Voices in the distance shattered his thoughts. He looked over and saw firelight coming from an alleyway. People were there. Josh decided to investigate and walked across the street to see what was going on.

In just a few seconds, he could hear what they were talking about. For now, he just decided to listen from around the corner.

"Dude, man, that freak in the cage, man, what's his deal?" One of them asked with a laugh. "Flesh Tearer? You don't know?" The other laughed, and two more laughed with him. Four of them were there, one was a girl. Josh could smell the perfume. She wore too much.

"That maniac is a monster. The Syndicate said out of all the Delta Squad, he was the worst one. Killed thousands of people with his armor, and nobody knows how many without," she said in a hushed tone, faking seriousness.

"I went to see him a couple of months ago, creepy. I mean, stare death in the face like that, and it changes you," another said, his tone of voice feeling honest to Josh.

Another scoffed at the idea.

"Really, thousands? I don't believe that. He couldn't. Hell, I could take that sorry sack of s---." The kid felt a hand come down on his shoulder from the black behind him.

The others had looks of terror on their faces and backed off.

"Yes, I am sure you could take him on. All by yourself," Josh said.

He bolted to the others. Josh let him go. From their perspective, he was standing there, his eyes reflected the light of the flames and hid half of him in a shadow that danced around him, never revealing his full face.

The teenager got a burst of courage once he was with his friends.

"Damn right I could take you. I'll be a hero. I'm not sure how you got out, but I'm putting you back."

Josh just smiled, but stopped once this punk reached into his pocket and pulled out a red packet, opened it up, and swallowed it in a hurry. Then he smiled.

"Crimson Eye." Josh said. Someone was still making it in this nightmare.

"Yeah, this stuff makes me invincible. Cost me a fortune too. I was gonna share it with them, but the universe had other plans," he said. Already his voice started to get more manic. His voice started to become deeper as well.

The other three were confused at the drug use. They had no idea what was going on.

"Yes, and now I will become a legend. I will kill the monster even the Syndicate fears," he screamed for no reason, then lunged at his enemy.

"Yeah, good luck with that, your brain is already melted." Josh stepped aside and watched as this kid hit the wall, bouncing off.

"Oh, see, that's a wall. I'm over here," he said and shook his head. Josh hated seeing anyone take this stuff. It was a disease. There was no cure. He watched the junkie turn around. Already he looked less human than before.

That much crimson was a one way ticket to hell.

"You've killed yourself," Josh said and saw the rage of the BOBO soldier inside now. The teen screamed. It was a roar, then started to run.

The charge was uncontrolled and fast.

Josh grabbed the kid the second he was close enough, used the momentum he had, and with one easy spin, the infected was picked up and thrown face first into the barrel of fire.

The screaming was something horrible, but Josh held him in the fire. It wasn't easy, but soon the kicking stopped. His fingernails burned away along with the skin on his hands. The pain was intense.

Josh pulled away and watched his hands as they repaired themselves, then turned his attention to the rest.

"He took the drug. Once you take that much, your life is over."

The smoke and the smell were terrible. The others were doing all they could to not throw up, but when he said what he did, something occurred to them.

"Mister, sir, guy, um, that 'drug' as you call it was handed out in our school in small doses. It's, well, it's encouraged to take it to help prevent colds. Most don't," she said with a weak voice. Josh grunted in disgust.

"Tell everyone to not take it. It'll kill you, and if it doesn't, you might end up killing people you care about. Trust me." They didn't know what to say or do with this information.

"Well, get the hell out of here," Josh yelled at them, and the other three took off running. The smell of burning flesh was bound to attract attention from others. Standing here wasn't an option anymore.

Josh pulled his cloak close and continued his journey.

## 22

Dustin was paranoid. Every sound in the distance made him pause to make sure no one was close to him.

He was holding the gun close to his chest, but he saw no one.

This place was strange. There was the scent of burning flesh in the air. He couldn't tell where it was coming from or if it was even real. Dustin ignored it. None of his business.

He kept walking down the street when he heard a noise. Somebody was running in his direction. Many people had stopped walking.

"They found me, this is it."

He pointed his weapon in the direction of the noise and waited. The wait was not a long one as three figures burst out of the dark. He didn't ask any questions and opened fire. The three figures jumped back into the dark.

"I see you over there. You can't hide from me. I'll kill you all. I'll do it. You'll be dead. I'll kill all of you." They might get him, but there was no way Dustin was going down without a fight. He held his gun into the dark, waiting for the first sign of movement.

"Stop shooting at us! We can't shoot back." A woman's voice came out of the dark.

Dustin narrowed his eyes. "Yeah, and how can I be sure you're not really demons coming back to take me into the pit?" he asked.

"Dude, we're not demons, I promise," she replied.

He lowered the gun. "Come out, I won't kill you," he said and waited, even though he was nervous.

The three of them came into the light, and they were all terrified. Dustin looked at her, up and down. She looked human enough. The other two guys he wasn't too sure about. "How did you know where I was?" Dustin asked, still ready to shoot at the first sign of trouble.

"Find you? We're just trying to get off the street. You happened to be in the way." Dustin knew she was just acting calm. He also knew all of their eyes were on that gun.

"Home, you live here? Where am I?" Dustin asked.

"You're in, well it used to be called Atlanta, but now it's just city number six. The Syndicate likes to number everything for order."

Dustin knew this name, both of them, but it was as if his brain had been turned off in places. "Syndicate, why didn't I know this?" he asked, trying to remember the difference between reality and stuff he made up in his head.

"You three. Get out of here. I'm sorry for shooting at you," Dustin said and continued, "you woman, do you know where I can get a drink in this town?"

She frowned. Dustin narrowed his eyes.

"Sorry, but all that was banned by the Syndicate. All the bars and stuff were shut down. The whole country is dry except for the runners, but there can't be many of them left alive," she said, and something inside of Dustin snapped.

"Right. Go home, and thanks. Sorry for the whole, you know, gun thing," he said, and the three of them took off running once again.

"Dry," Dustin said, trying to get his head around the idea. He heard the others talking as they ran off.

"Didn't that crazy homeless guy look like one of those squad people we saw in school? I thought they were all dead." It was the last thing he heard as they disappeared into the dark.

"Not dead yet," he said, then kept walking.

## 23

Wyatt heard gunshots echo through the night. "Oh, they are starting the party without me? I don't think so."

He started to run in that direction only because it came from the direction of the tower he was supposed to go to. For all he knew this was someone he knew, maybe. No, no need for hope just yet. He controlled his thought process and focused on each step so he didn't trip and stab himself with the sword.

Six months impaled on a wall did him no favors, either. His legs burned with each step. His lungs threatened to explode. All Wyatt wanted to do was stop, but he pushed through all of that. Eventually, things would go back to normal. It was a matter of time.

This would take some getting used to again. Every step he took he felt like he was going to fall over, but this was no time to hesitate. He turned a corner and slid to a stop in such a hurry, he nearly fell forward.

There, at the far corner, there was a patrol car. Three guards were having a smoke break, talking about something he couldn't quite make out. It didn't matter what they were talking about. It was choice time. These were the ones responsible for the state of the city, world, he didn't know how far the Syndicate's grip went.

He thought about going back where he came from, around the corner, and finding another way. Or, kill them all. Wyatt tightened his grip on the blade.

Wyatt ran forward. When he was halfway there his footsteps attracted the attention of the guards.

"What the hell?" one of them asked.

"Stop," another yelled as they drew their weapons. Wyatt grit his teeth but did not stop. "Shoot the bastard."

The guards began to shoot. Wyatt knew what they were going to do, the same thing every idiot with a gun did. They shot at him. Wyatt shifted to the left and the bullets sailed into the night. Without missing a step, he threw the sword. The thing shot through the air and stabbed the left guard in the neck.

He fell to the ground. "What the hell?" the one in the middle said, covered in the blood of the victim.

Wyatt had already closed the distance between them in the time it took them to talk. Grabbing the hands of the center guard, he pushed the weapon under the face mask of the other and pulled the trigger. The man was dead before he hit the ground, face obliterated, turned to blood. At the same time, the blade was pulled out of the neck.

Wyatt swung it again. The sword wasn't as sharp as his own and only made it to the spine of the guard, who was tossed to the ground. With a tug, the blade was removed.

"Still got it," he said. Then looked at himself. He was covered in his own blood. He imagined that looking like a psychopath wouldn't be an ideal way to show up to wherever he was going. Even if there was no time limit given, he couldn't help but feel the pressure.

"Need a change of clothes."

Wyatt stripped the cleanest pieces of uniform he could off the bodies and changed into them. These guys were all bigger than him but not by much, Tightening the belt fixed the problem. There was still some blood on pieces of the uniform, but it was nowhere near as bad as it used to be. Feeling better already, he wiped off the sword and wished he had a place to put it.

It was now he heard the quick footsteps of somebody running up from behind him. He was sure nobody was left alive to call for backup. He turned around, ready for a fight, not ready for this. Three kids were running towards him as fast as they could.

The two guys were screaming something, trying to tell him something, but he couldn't understand either of them. They didn't have any weapons, but they were scared out of their minds.

Wyatt waited until they were close enough. He revealed his blade and with one quick motion brought it up to their necks. They slid into the sharp side of the blade, trying to come to a stop. Wyatt retracted with them without losing contact on their skin until they stopped.

"Don't move." Wyatt sized them up, face hidden by the helmet.

"Friends of yours, miss?"

"Sir, please forgive them. We know it's after the curfew, but we have important information," Wyatt sighed.

"Of course you do. Tell me your story. Not you two dwips, the girl."

They almost started babbling at once. He applied a bit of pressure to their necks with the blade to make his point and they shut up.

"Well, we were out, and you'll never believe it, but The Flesh Tearer escaped. He killed Bill after he took the vitamins you guys gave us a couple of months ago. He threw him in the fire and burned him to death," she said in a hurry.

He lowered the blade.

"If this is true, the three of you are in terrible danger. This monster, this is his game. He kills one of you, then he lets you go to hunt you down one at a time, for fun. Look at the guards, it all makes sense now. He's close. You better run."

Their eyes went wide with terror. They noticed the dead men on the ground for the first time. It was dark. They were scared and not so close to see that they had no uniform.

Wyatt didn't feel too bad saying this because knowing Josh, this is actually something he might do for fun. But was he there? Was this story real or just something to get them out of trouble? The look on their faces was almost impossible to fake.

"Listen. Go home. Tell no one what you saw. Those vitamins, don't take them, trust me," Wyatt said to them in a low voice.

The three of them looked to the rooftops, to everywhere, looking for a sign of this monster that had to be chasing them. "Go, now. I'll hold the monster off. He can't be far away. Run." The three of them took off.

For the first time, he felt hope. The others might be here. They didn't all get killed. Why not?

"I have so many questions." With that, he took

JESSE WILSON

off running towards the destination someone picked for him.

## 24

Cody made it outside with the others. "We go our own ways from here," the man said. Cody turned around and couldn't believe what he saw. "God damned office building," Cody said and almost laughed. It was so obvious it hurt.

"Your target is over there down the road. Tall building, lights on. One of the prides of the Syndicate. Think you can make it?" he asked. Cody turned back to see the building. "It's not far, I can make it."

"Good luck, Commander," the man replied as he walked away. Cody started walking in that direction. The streets were dead. The faint smell of burning flesh hung in the air, too. It was something you never forgot.

No time for that now. He took a deep breath of the outside air. Then he ran. Faster than he remembered running before. It felt so good to just move, to be free at last.

He came around a corner and had to stop. There was a group of people already there. A black truck, people in black uniforms. He didn't know any of them. However, Blake was standing there.

Cody couldn't move. This didn't make sense. Did he betray all of them? Was this some kind of plan? He shot back around the corner.

"The hell is going on." This was no time to lose it. There was one thing to do from here. Cody took a deep breath and decided to get his answers.

"Hi guys," Cody said with a wave.

Blake turned to look at once. It was him, just wandering up to a group of Syndicate soldiers out in the open.

Blake couldn't believe what he was seeing. Did he develop a death wish in the six months he was gone? This didn't make sense. Also, the commander's face looked like he hadn't looked in a mirror in the same amount of time. A wild beard covered most of his face.

"Who the hell is this?" the captain of the guard unit said. The others were quick to follow. Blake just played stupid for now, praying he didn't just blow his cover.

"Hi, Blake. How's it going? Long time no see,

you little prick. Why do you come to me in my dreams now? Do you think this is some kind of joke? All I have to do is wake up and all this goes away." He laughed, and the gun hung at his side. He still had his hand around the grip, however.

The rest of the guys turned to look at him then. "Who's Blake, who's this guy?" the captain asked.

Blake shrugged, then put his arm around the neck of the man beside him and broke his neck in an instant. He reached for his and his victim's side arms and pulled them both out at the same time, beginning to shoot the others in the head in rapid succession.

The action was over in seconds, and Blake was surrounded by dead men and blood.

"Dude, that was amazing. You killed all of them and didn't even blink. I like the dream you. Very effective," Cody said with a laugh.

Blake didn't know what happened to him. "Cody, I don't know what's wrong with you, but you're awake. This is real, not a dream," Blake said.

"Sure it is, buddy. Watch this trick. I am going to summon all the rest of our dead team too. They all died, you know. I'm the last one left. We don't even know what happened to you. You just disappeared. Here we go."

Cody turned, spread his arms out, and sure enough, just like he said, the others began to emerge from the darkness in their own directions.

Blake was impressed. Maybe Cody was right, and this was all a dream. A simulation. Maybe Delacroix was just playing a mind game with him this whole time. Everything felt real enough, smelled real too.

"See, Blake, all dead. This isn't real. Don't you think I haven't imagined this a million times over?" He turned the gun on Blake.

"I could shoot you, and you'd be just fine. Watch." He pointed the gun at Blake's head in an instant, and just before he could pull the trigger, Blake got out of the way. "You know what, if this is a dream then this won't hurt." Blake put his fist into Cody's jaw, an uppercut that knocked him off his feet and onto his back.

This did hurt, and Cody expressed the pain weakly.

"Ow, why'd you do that? We're friends, I thought. Jerk," he said as he started to get up.

"Dreams don't hurt, dwip. This is real," Blake said, just in time to see Wyatt start attacking Josh and Dustin in a fit of rage.

"Oh, what the hell?"

Blake made his way over to the other three.

"Hi, nice to see you again. Stop killing one another," Blake said. Wyatt lunged at Josh, who got out of the way and punched Wyatt in the stomach. Neither one wanted to back off.

"You let me rot in that hell," Wyatt yelled.

"You never looked for me, not even once," Josh yelled back as Wyatt stabbed Josh in the shoulder with the blade. Josh pulled the sword out and ignored the pain. "Toothpick, you always seem to have one," Josh pushed the blade aside and punched him in the face.

"Why is everyone fighting?" Dustin asked, trying to decide who to shoot first.

Blake rolled his eyes.

"So good to be back," Blake said and took aim.

"Time for a quick therapy session, Delta style." He proceeded to shoot all three of them in the leg, ending the fight. They dropped to the ground.

"Now, let's talk about this like sane people," Blake said and looked up.

"Yes, like sane people. Let's see how you do," Strom said, and Blake glared at him. "Shut up, ghost. I'm busy."

The others were on the ground looking at him. "Alright, guys, it's been a while. Why don't you tell me what the hell happened?" Blake asked.

"This is the most intense dream of all time," Cody said and started laughing about it. Blake turned around and shot him in the leg too. "Shut it, Commander. Not a dream."

"Oh god, why do my dreams hurt so much now?" Cody said as he hit the ground.

He looked back to the others and sighed as even now Wyatt was still glaring at the other two. "Just a bunch of idiots," Blake said and shook his head in disappointment. They were just shadows of their former selves, but time was running out. An elite unit was heading their way, and time was running out.

## 25

"Does anyone know how to get to hell?" Tiffany asked. They had been walking for hours in this wasteland, and everything felt the same besides the swirling sky and the occasional sound of thunder in the distance that they were trying to get away from.

"No. Nobody knows the way to hell besides dying on Earth and a few portals that lead there from Earth. Guess what. Nobody wants to die, and we are not on Earth, so our chances of getting there aren't great. Our best chance is to find Bob or Theron and--" Gemini cut Alex off in an instant.

"Bob is bad, you know. I don't think we should go looking for the omnicide monster that wants to kill everything. This seems like a bad idea to me. Even the rock says it's a bad idea too."

"The rock has a point," Dani said, not believing she was agreeing with the crazy one.

"Yeah, well, I don't have the power to break through that barrier the idiot commander put up. None of us do because it's powered by the Nexus itself. I don't see any other options, so if anyone has a good idea, feel free to speak up at any time," Alex said.

"You know, you have all that supposed power, and we have sparks of Theron. Maybe we could use our energy, combine it, and make a dent or a hole to where we need to go?" Samantha asked like it was the most obvious thing in the world to do.

"Yeah, that'd work, but you know what? Power in a dead world would attract anything that might still be alive right to us, like, you know, the whole moth and fire thing," Hale replied.

"Well, we have to try something. I refuse to die here," Samantha replied with a twinge of fear.

"Don't worry. We can't die here, at least by starving, and none of us get older, so, yeah. Chill out, lady, we will be just fine," Dani replied, trying to keep calm.

"Fine, hey, wait, didn't Fort DIAB have a portal to this pile?" Matt asked.

"Yeah, they did, but who knows what it looks like on this side? If there is even a portal, it could just be an energy field entrance that just appears out of nowhere," Tiffany replied.

"I'll find it," Gemini said and took off into the sky.

"Well, at least he's being helpful," Alex said as they all watched him take off.

"Think he'll ever come back?" Brittany asked.

"Doubt it. He'll find a rock to talk to and forget what he was doing," Ariana replied with a sigh. It felt as if the situation was getting worse as they walked in this dead world.

## 26

"Why the hell are you attacking one another?" Blake asked, trying to make sense of all of this.

"He never came back. He abandoned us. Dustin gave up, Cody sold us all out to the enemy. Everyone but me gave up," Wyatt replied, doing his best to contain himself.

Dustin was doing his best to get away.

"I did what? Did you not see that explosion? I was in the middle of all of that. If it wasn't for Typhon's armor, I'd be a greasy spot on the rocks right now. I was finished. That's why I didn't come back, but right now, I'm going to make you eat your own sword," Josh replied.

He couldn't believe that Wyatt had that in his

head. "When I woke up, I was in a cage," Josh replied.

"You're all demons. Get away from me. You're trying to take me to the bad place again," Dustin said in a panic. Blake rolled his eyes and shot him in the other leg. "Shut up," he replied and turned his attention back to the others. "Still DIAB. At least some things don't change much." Blake said.

"You didn't even see Theron bring the others back to life. Erin and Dana were brought back to life, but we couldn't fight back. Everyone just gave up, too weak to fight. I couldn't save anyone. Didn't stop me from trying." Wyatt said, and these words made Cody take notice.

"Wait, what did you say?" Cody asked.

"Yes, seriously. Theron brought them back to life before he and the others left as a final gift of thanks to us. Minutes later, the Syndicate swarmed us and took everyone. The Zodiac and those stupid Guardian Angels did nothing. I don't know what happened to them." Wyatt replied.

Blake's eyes widened, and Cody was up on his feet.

"What do you mean? They are alive? Everyone is? This dream is better than I thought because I remember, I watched them be killed by, that one guy, Typhon. Being alive is only possible in a dream world," Cody said, still sure this was all in his head.

Wyatt pulled himself to his feet and charged past Blake as soon as Cody said this, grabbing him by the neck.

"This is reality. Everyone was taken. I don't know where they are. We can find them, and we can save them. Wake up, or I'll just keep beating you until you realize what is real and what isn't."

Wyatt's sword went for the commander's neck. Cody escaped with a step back, ducked the wild swing with ease, lifted his gun, and held it against Wyatt's side.

"You can't beat me in real life. You have no chance here in my dreams either. I control everything!" Cody said to Wyatt. Neither one flinched, inches from death.

Then a new sound broke through the silence. An engine. Someone was coming.

"Oh really? Well, tell that to them. I think they missed the memo." Wyatt said and took a step back. A strange, large armored truck pulled around the corner and stopped, headlights blazing.

"This must be the Chemical Dragon Unit," Blake said.

"The what?" Dustin asked.

"You heard me the first time," Blake replied.

"Are we going to smash them, or what's the plan here?" Josh asked. "Don't know. I have a feeling we weren't supposed to waste time yelling," Cody said.

"Yeah, starting to think that, too," Blake replied.

"I say we just run," Dustin said.

"Shut up, Diab," Cody replied as the doors of the car opened and the lights shut off. Then five figures got out.

Five figures dressed in familiar looking armor.

## 27

"You know, I think they stole our armor," Josh said.

"Yep. You can tell that's ours. The commander's armor is nanotech and, well, I'd know mine anywhere. It's not Wyatt's blade or our weapons. The armor is ours, but the weapons are aftermarket models. They can still tear through us like butter, I'd imagine," Dustin said with a few quick glances at the ones who had arrived.

"But they could be demons, too," Dustin added.

"Not demons," Wyatt replied, "demons have more hair."

"Well. Look who it is. The heroes of yesterday, all beat up and worn out. We were called out for this?" the one in the dark blue nano armor said and started to walk forward. Cody was beginning to think this wasn't a dream anymore.

There was no way he would have let someone else wear his stuff, but he was happy to see it still existed, at least.

"I thought these dwips were dead," Rory said as he stepped ahead.

"I guess someone lied," Winnie replied.

"Does it matter? We can make this quick. Anyone could have done it," Yoshi replied.

"Our past selves are here to test our worthiness in a dream battle. How typical and predictable. Am I really this boring?" Cody asked.

"Yeah," Wyatt replied.

"We can take these losers. They want to fight on the wrong side, then they'll pay for it," Josh added.

"Oh sure, we can take them. Just get past the super armor, the weapons, and it's easy sailing from there," Blake said.

"I have an idea," Dustin said, way too loud.

"Well, that's right, let the armored freaks know about it too. Good plan, DIAB," Josh replied.

"Yeah, we run the hell away," Dustin said and started running towards the building.

"That was the best idea he's ever had. You better run," Vera said, but put away her sniper rifle. There was no need for it here.

Blake aimed both pistols at their leader and emptied the rest of the ammo into the armor. The bullets bounced off. "Well, okay, running seems like a good plan." He took off running with Wyatt and Cody.

Not Josh. He stood his ground.

"Armor or not, I'll take you down," he said and was all ready to attack them when Blake came back for him.

"We need you alive. Obviously, they think we're defenseless. Let's go," Blake said. Josh took another look at his old weapon.

"You better run," Winnie said behind that blue armor. With one last glare, Josh turned and ran inside.

"Commander, why did we let them live?" Jin asked.

"We owe them a chance. There was a time they could have wiped us off the map, but they didn't. Now we are even. Let's go," Winnie replied.

"Besides, it'll be fun. When was the last time we got to have any?" Vera asked.

"Been a while, this could be the last time, too," Rory replied. After their prey disappeared through the doors, the hunt was on.

## 28

"So, running inside. Good plan, good start anyway. Did you have anything else to this plan?" Wyatt asked.

Dustin started pressing the elevator button, but there was no response.

"Seriously, the elevator? When was the last time we ever had any luck with that? You should be thankful it doesn't work," Blake said and Dustin stepped back, threw his hands up in frustration.

"Trapped, just like old times," Wyatt said.

"Hated old times," Josh replied.

Cody turned around. Behind him was a sign with five armored figures on it in shadow: "Delta Squad Historical Exhibit, come see the weapons that nearly destroyed the world on the top floor, today." In big red letters.

"Well, would you look at that?" Cody asked and the others turned to look.

"That has to be why those weird people pointed us in this direction. If they have our armors, what is up there?" Blake asked.

"Almost as if it was planned by someone," Dustin said.

"Who cares, let's get up there. Maybe it still works," Wyatt replied. No one had to say any more about it. They took off running to the main stairs at the back of the place without knowing how far up they had to go.

After three flights of stairs, Dustin was picked up from behind and pushed into a wall. Nobody saw who did it.

"Stealth," Dustin said as he rolled over, revealing his bleeding face. After this, it was silent.

"They're just screwing with us," Blake said, looking around in the dark for anything obvious. He didn't see anything.

"Come on out. Anyone can be invisible and take down an enemy. You want to be a real Delta member, you come out to play with us face to face," Blake said. He didn't think it'd work and thought of all the times he did the same thing in the past.

Josh was hit in the face, slammed into a wall hard enough to crack the surface. His jaw broke, everyone heard it. He stumbled, but refused to fall. Instead, he pushed himself off the wall in the direction of where his attacker was, hoping they didn't move.

He connected with the invisible enemy. Both of them went over the rail.

Wyatt and Blake both reacted at the same time and managed to grab Josh before he went over the edge. They watched as Vera hit and dented the floor below, then turned visible. The two pulled him up with ease.

"Yeah. Like we were going to let you kill yourself again," Wyatt said.

"I didn't kill myself the first time," Josh said, his jaw still cracking into place as he spoke. Blake looked at his jaw.

"Is it just me or do we heal faster than we did before?" Blake asked.

"Yeah, I think we do," Josh replied, "but I don't think now's the time to worry about it. Let's keep moving," Josh said.

Dustin felt his own face. In all the action, he didn't even notice when the pain faded away. All the wounds were gone.

"I can get used to this," he said as the others started to run up the stairs again. They understood why they weren't dead yet, they had to make the most of it while they could.

## 29

The minute they got to the top floor, they could see broken glass everywhere. By the window, they saw the shadows of the enemies.

"What, you thought we would just walk up the stairs when we could just, you know, fly up the side of the building and wait for you? Yeah, that wouldn't make any sense now, would it?" Winnie asked, stepping inside in the broken glass.

"Well, you know. It was worth a shot," Cody said and shook his head. "Well, I guess we lost. I am just gonna wake up now. This dream isn't fun anymore," he said and closed his eyes.

Yoshi took the initiative. His armor sped towards Cody, its black hand wrapped around Cody's throat, and picked him up.

"If you don't mind, I'll be the one to kill the

commander today," he said, acting without anyone telling him to.

Cody opened his eyes as the iron grip tightened. He put his free hand around the arm of the one trying to kill him. Maybe it wasn't a dream after all. "Kill me? Right." Cody still had his weapon and put it to the side of Yoshi's head.

"I may be a little rusty, but the last time I checked, this kind of armor doesn't do too well against weapons like this." He said it with a smile, but the grip was intense, and he didn't know how long he could last against it. He could already feel the air running out, but he had to stay calm.

Yoshi looked at the gun and knew that any sudden movement would be a gamble. He dropped the commander.

"See, that's what I thought because--" Too much talking was distracting him, and with his other hand, Yoshi grabbed the weapon and crushed it.

"Well, alright. You had a point. Had," Yoshi said.

"Let's get 'em, gotta die sometime anyway," Josh said. The four of them threw caution to the wind and ran at their enemy.

Winnie was confused. Rory's armor started to glow blood red, and he slammed his left foot into the floor.

It seconds before they were sent flying back

across the room, slamming into the wall, and sliding to the ground.

"I almost feel bad for everyone who ever had to go through that," Wyatt said and coughed up some blood.

"Not the time to start feeling bad, can't feel much at all right now," Josh replied with a groan of pain. He couldn't move.

The others didn't feel like saying much. "Guys, take a look. Over there," Dustin said and pointed. His left arm cracked as he straightened it, bones popping back into place.

"Our suits. We were supposed to get them, I assume, undetected," Wyatt replied, still gasping for breath.

"Last mission and we screw it up. That sounds about right," Josh replied, and Dustin was the first one to make it back to his feet.

"Those suits. Since you're about ten seconds from death anyway, I guess you should know that we found them on the Viper. Never could figure them out. DNA-locked or some nonsense. They look great on display like that, right?" Vera said.

Winnie glared at her.

"Did you have to tell them any of that?" Winnie asked as she pulled out the plasma cannon to finish the job. Vera just shrugged.

"No, just kill them and it won't make a difference anyway," she replied, and the rest of them laughed about it.

This was all the time Dustin needed, and he started running to the armor.

Yoshi beat him to it, took hold of the empty suit, and threw it so hard that it sailed out the open window behind them.

"No chance," Yoshi said with a sneer in his voice.

Dustin never stopped running. Instead, he changed direction and jumped out the window. "Son of a—" his voice trailed off into the night.

All of them watched in disbelief.

"Well, what can I say. He's always wanted to die on his own terms, good on him," Wyatt said with a weak smile.

# 30

Winnie was tired of the games and prepared to pull the trigger. None of the remaining four flinched in the face of death. Winnie couldn't believe this is what it had come down to, but the Syndicate had won. It was a new age, and these people would never accept the new world order.

This was needed. The old world had to die.

A strange noise was coming from the dark. Winnie thought it was in her head at first, but then turned to look in that direction. The others did too.

"No. It's not possible, is it?" she asked.

Wyatt and Cody glanced at one another. They started to stand up, making as little noise as they could while the others were distracted.

Josh and Blake followed their lead.

The noise sounded familiar, a high-pitched

whining sound. Rory walked over to the edge of the window and looked over the side to see if he could see anything in the dark, but there was nothing there. Not even with the thermal vision.

"Nothing out there. It could just be a patrol drone on the fritz," Rory said, looking around.

"Sounds like that, just kill them so we can get out of here," Yoshi replied.

"Yeah, take care of business," Jin replied, "or I will," he finished.

Convinced it was nothing, Rory turned around to move back to the team. "Winnie, the others—" Rory had time to say when something came up from behind, grabbed him by the back of the neck, and ripped him out of the window. All anyone saw was an orange blur.

"Not possible," Winnie said as she stood there in disbelief.

"While you weren't looking like an idiot, they all went for their armor," he said and pointed. They all looked just in time to watch the last three of these things come to life.

What was once an easy extermination mission now turned into a terrifying experience. Fear slammed into all of them, and there was silence. Cody was sitting with his back to the wall.

"I didn't see my armor on display. Looks like this one's all yours," he said.

"Now it all makes sense," Josh said and flexed

his fingers. It all felt the same, but it was clear there was more than a simple upgrade to these things. There was a lot he didn't understand right now, but he felt better already.

"Agreed. Let's take out the old armors first," Wyatt said, and the three of them took their first steps forward.

The other side began to move back as they got closer. Winnie shook her head and pointed the plasma cannon at Cody. "Stop right there or I'll--" she watched as a blade sliced through the cannon in one strike, sending electric blue streams of plasma energy in every direction.

"Or you'll what?" Wyatt said as he stood there, in front of her and the others. "Impossible, I didn't even see you move. How?"

Wyatt responded, swinging the blade again. Winnie tried to catch it in her hands, missed, and watched as the blade slammed into her chest, burying itself in the armor.

"Holy sword movement! I wasn't even trying." One was amazed, the other was horrified. "Oh, I've wanted to do this for a long time," Wyatt said.

Jin lifted his minigun up and tried to open fire on all of them. The gun was already spinning when Josh grabbed the barrel of the weapon and stopped it cold. "You planned on killing me with this gun? I don't think so. This weapon has history. Its owner wouldn't appreciate you using it like this," Josh said. His altered voice made Jin want to run.

Looking at the skinned armor didn't help either.

"Please, sir, I was just following orders. You were a threat, so we had to kill you. You know how it is to follow orders, right?" He was pleading with him now.

"Of course I do, but I also know what it means to break them too. A lesson you never learned." He pulled the weapon away, and it was attached to his armor as well. The second it came loose, there was a shower of sparks to follow it.

"No, please. Don't do this."

"Funny how arrogance always turns to fear in seconds." He dropped the weapon to the ground and had a choice to make. Would he use his new weapon or his hands? Jin put everything he had into a left hook. Josh was distracted by deciding how to kill this one when he was hit in the face.

Josh never saw it coming, and the attack was as strong as he could manage. The old armor was still powerful. It knocked him into the far wall, but he was able to keep his balance.

"Damn, it's too bad you're trying to kill me. I think I might like you, but you have to die. I think I'll take my time, too," he said and started walking back towards Jin.

# 31

Blake stared at the Hell Razor armor. "You and me, are you ready?" It was a plain question. There was no response.

Blake couldn't help but imagine Wyatt in this armor. All the things it's been through, all of their armors being used by anyone else was wrong. He would rather see them destroyed than anyone else use them.

Technically they didn't belong to the Delta Squad, but now, in the current situation, he figured it was okay to claim them.

The very thought of somebody else using them at all was enough to make him cringe. Too many memories, nobody else was worthy to wear these suits.

Yoshi attacked Blake with two throwing knives

while he just stood there waiting for an answer to the question.

Blake caught the blades in the air as if he were picking a flower from a garden. He twisted the ends of those blades a slight degree. It was simple enough and there was no hesitation to throw them back as soon as he caught them. Yoshi, on the other hand, was not able to catch the blades in the same way, and they sunk into his chest.

"No!"

It was all he had time to say before they discharged their electric power into him. Blake was hoping they didn't change how electricity worked on the suits.

Yoshi panicked as the suit took the charge and was forced into a hypercharge state. "DNA match not detected," the computer said in his helmet.

"No, God, abort this. Stop it now," he screamed, trying everything he could to make it shut off, but nothing was working.

The self defense protocol activated. Blake stepped back and watched the armor and the person inside of it burn itself out with a massive electric current.

"You don't mess with the team and our stuff and get away with it," he said as he watched the figure fall to the floor and the smoke rise. "You won't be getting up again," Blake said as he walked over and picked up the blade. He swung it down, and with one swipe, he severed the head from the body.

"Heal from that one."

He stepped back, expecting more blood, but it was burned shut from the inside.

While he didn't trust the armor's effectiveness and didn't know if they could heal from this, it just didn't pay to take chances. Syndicate cancer needed to be cut out, and this was a small step in accomplishing that goal.

## 32

He didn't know why he ran and jumped out the window to go after the armor. The only reason he could think of was maybe he had a death wish after all. It was all a blur. He touched the armor and it opened around him.

Dustin hit the ground at full speed, but the green shockwave canceled out the impact. It was as routine as it had ever been. Without any hesitation, he shot into the sky as fast as he could go. He sounded like a missile. At least that's what he imagined. Inside the armor, it was just quiet.

Timing was everything. He shot past the window and reached out. The second he could do it. He grabbed Josh's imitation and took him.

Dustin tossed the man onto the roof, then he landed behind him. All these months in the dark, powerless, now faced by someone who worked for the people responsible, he had a new feeling. Rage.

"Alright, reject, you're going to die for even thinking about wearing the armor of my friend. I'm going to cook you alive," Dustin said as he landed in front of Rory while he stood up. Dustin wasn't sure why he spent all that time talking. It was a stupid thing to do, now the freak was able to stand up. He got ready for a fight.

Rory pulled the minigun out and started shooting. Dustin strafed to the left as the bullets tore up the roof. "You're too slow. Do you always shoot where your target is? Who taught you how to fight?" Dustin was disappointed.

Just as he said that, Rory used his zipline and hit Dustin in the chest, pulling him forward off his feet, into the roof.

"Syndicate's finest simulations. I must have killed you a thousand times," Rory said as Dustin slid to a stop. He had to admit to himself, using the zipline was good thinking. Dustin almost smiled because it wasn't quite good enough.

He shot up into the air, and the hooks at the end of the line snapped off just as a barrage of bullets hit a second later.

"Let me show you why they call me Flame Genesis."

His arm mounted miniguns unleashed a white flame from both wrists down onto the roof. The fire was expelled with so much pressure that it exploded in all directions. Dustin never even felt the heat of the flames despite being this close.

Rory's armor started on fire, and he tried to escape to the air.

"No, you wanted to be in the fire, you get to play in it with me." Dustin turned the white flames towards the sky.

Rory was engulfed by the wave of flames, blinded by the fire, and he fell back down to the roof. Dustin walked to his victim. The flames covered his body as he did but never stuck to him.

"You made a big mistake not just killing us." It was all he could say or wanted to.

With one last look at his enemy, he lifted his right foot and put it down on the head as hard as he could, and he and his enemy went through the roof, sending a firestorm down on everyone on the floors below them.

## 33

Wyatt was taking on the replacement commander and the sniper all on his own. He was fast in his new armor, but the two of them still had an edge. "The old guy is quick, but look at him go," Vera said and tried to shoot. Wyatt kept moving. He knew the armor he had on had been updated, but he didn't want to take any chances.

"Don't let the bastard slow down," Winnie said, still pissed this guy wrecked the plasma cannon. There wasn't much she could do right now about anything. Wyatt was just toying with Vera right now. Winnie was just waiting for him to attack.

It was annoying to fight like this because they would take turns in the attack against him and he couldn't get close. Well, he could have if he wanted to, but he had a plan, an idea in his mind that was going to make a point.

Always looking for the best win he could, his plan was to line them both up and take them out at the same time. He was waiting for the perfect chance to do it. Just a few more twists and turns and it would all be perfect.

Then his plans were ruined when Dustin came crashing through the roof. Rory's burning body landed on Winnie as he fell through with torrents of flame coming with him.

Everyone stopped what they were doing to do their best to avoid the fire as it rained from above.

"Dustin, what the hell were you thinking?" Wyatt screamed, backing away from the flames. Dustin stepped off the bodies, ignoring him.

"Well, look who it is. Other Blake." Dustin and Vera looked at one another.

"Yeah, and you're dead because--" Dustin lifted up his arm and from the top of his wrist fired a blazing red beam into and through Blake's old armor. The figure inside said no more, fell to her knees, and was dead in one shot.

"Shut up."

"Holy hell, Dustin, do something about the fire," Cody said, backed up into a corner, shielding his face.

Dustin turned, lifted his arms, and started to spray water out of his weapons. "Better living through nanochemistry, gotta love it," he said as he put the flames out, drenching Cody in the process.

"Yeah, I'm lovin' it," Cody replied, thankful the heat was retreating, kind of wished he wasn't being drenched. More important, he needed his armor back.

## 34

Jin had been afraid before. He'd seen the monsters of the past. Worse, he'd seen the state of the victims Josh and the others had left behind. Now that killer was coming for him and had all the reasons in the world to kill him.

Jin backed off. He considered fighting, but to what end? Might get lucky, get in a good hit or two, but no. No chances here. He did the only thing he could think of.

"Let me live. I'm sorry, orders and all that. Let me live and you'll never see me again," he said, and Josh stopped in his tracks.

He hated it when people begged. There was no reason to show mercy. The fight would be over soon. He could feel it.

"Lose the armor," Josh said. Jin hesitated, but the slightest movement forward caused him to jump. Then the armor opened.

Jin stepped out. A fine soldier for any armor, sure, but mutated from the BOBO strain. He'd never fit in anywhere again.

Seeing the enemy like this just made him tired of killing idiots.

"I'm gonna make you a deal. I'm going to throw you out the window. If you live, you live. If you die, well, I gave you a chance," making up his mind on the spot.

His eyes got big. "No, wait. I changed my mind. Just make it quick. Please," he said, backing off.

Josh grabbed him by the neck, picked him up with one arm, and tossed him out the window with ease, through the glass and into the night, with any luck out of his life forever. It was about now Dustin crashed through the ceiling.

Josh turned around to look at what he saw. Dustin looked like so many pictures of the devil standing in a ring of hellfire. Almost scary from a distance like this.

Josh walked over to the others. "So, you get your new stuff and you can't wait to blow something up. Glad to see you're still the same." Dustin turned to look at him. "They had it coming," he replied.

"What are we going to do about Captain Delusional over there?" Blake asked. The flames around them were growing.

"I have an idea. Where is his armor?" Josh said, looking around for it but couldn't see it. "Is this it?" Wyatt had wandered off towards the display and found a strange-looking vial of dark blue liquid in a glass container.

"This could be it. Hand it to me," Josh said. Wyatt did. "It looks like the same thing she's wearing," Dustin said. "Analysis says it's nanites. I mean, it could just eat him alive too," he finished.

Josh looked at the liquid and nodded, making up his mind again.

"Commander, you're going for a ride," Josh said with a happy tone of voice. Cody looked up at him as all he saw was a hand coming down for him. "Wait, what are you doing, this isn't what I want, this isn't the dream."

Josh said nothing. The others had no idea what he was going to do. Josh smashed the vial of blue liquid into Cody's back and threw him out the open window in one fluid motion. Cody's scream disappeared into the dark.

Josh felt like he might be getting addicted to throwing people out of high buildings. It was entertaining, at least.

"What the hell?" Blake asked, shocked like the others.

"Oh, big idea that was, good job. You might be

insane, you know that?" Wyatt asked. "On the other hand, that was funny," he finished. Josh nodded.

"I thought it was fun, at least," Josh replied.

"Commander or not, we need to leave. This place is about to be leveled. It's time for everyone to get the biggest wake-up call of all time," Dustin said, and with this, his whole armor began to glow all around him.

"So much for the element of surprise," Wyatt replied.

"Ah, damn it, why do you have to--" Blake said, trailed off, and decided not to waste any more time. There was no changing his mind, and he didn't like this place anyway.

Dustin remained behind, and the other three took off through the shattered window.

They all looked but didn't see Cody anywhere. They didn't have time to look for him. They landed on the roof of the nearest skyscraper behind them and turned to watch.

For a second, nothing happened.

"Matchstick short out or something?" Josh asked. Wyatt just shrugged. Then the entire top of the building exploded with light. With it came a heatwave they could feel through their armor. The windows shattered on all the buildings around. With the light, it looked as if someone threw several tons of glitter into the air.

The explosion ripped through the building floor by floor, moving down until it hit the bottom. Leaving the whole thing, a towering inferno remained.

"God damn," Wyatt said.

## 35

"Well, I guess he likes his new armor," Wyatt said as he watched the tower burn.

"More importantly, anyone see Cody? Or do you suppose he's toast?" Blake asked. He looked around, saw nothing, and when he didn't see anything, it was a bad sign.

"Nope. No sign," Josh replied as the skyscraper began to collapse. He was more interested in that than looking for Cody.

Considering his brother had lived through worse, he wasn't too worried about it. Not yet, anyway.

Blake and Wyatt were watching the blaze continue when something shot past them both. The two of them looked to their left. "Where'd Josh go?"

Wyatt asked. Blake just shrugged. "For being sight oriented, you sure do miss a lot," Wyatt replied. "Getting old, I guess," he replied.

"Throw me out a window, you rat bastard." Josh was hit so hard and fast that he wasn't aware of what happened at first, but the words told him everything he needed to know.

Then Josh hit the side of a building. The concrete shattered on impact, and he felt himself be pushed inside.

"Nice to see you too," Josh managed to say when Cody put his right fist into the side of Josh's helmet, sending him through the concrete and the steel, deeper into the crater. "Threw me out a window. Not cool, bro," he repeated himself.

Cody was going to deal out more punishment as Josh sailed off into the dark, but his visor came to life. Erin appeared. This was a prerecorded message.

"Great, an info dump. Just what this story needed," Cody said, crossing his arms.

"Hello, Cody. Sorry to be typical, but if you're seeing this, something bad has happened. I don't know why you needed this armor, but your old suits have been destroyed or stolen. With any luck, the traitors couldn't tell the difference between these new armors and the ones they were our best creations for the time. You've seen the Horseman and the Olympians. These armors were created with experimental materials and never meant to be used," she said.

"Should have shot them into the sun," Cody replied under his breath.

Erin paused as if she knew he'd say something. Once he was done, she started to talk again.

"I always figured that someday it would come down to who had the bigger guns, so I made sure that it would be the Delta Squad," Erin said.

"This is the ultimate armor class. I am sure if I had time I could improve on this model, but time is short. The others were given a similar message. This armor is several times better than your old suits. It should put you above both the Horsemen and the Olympians."

"Sure," Cody replied. The didn't look all that confident.

"With the help of the Guardians, we were able to install the true weapons as well. Pray you never have to use them," she said with a nod.

Cody wasn't so good with the concept of praying anymore.

"This is all I can do for you. After this message is over, it will grant access to the full power of the suit. I wish you luck. Hopefully, we'll see one another again, but if not, thanks for all the memories. Oh, take care of the armor. They can self-repair, but there aren't many repair bays left if things get real. Good luck," Erin's voice died out, the image faded, and the second it did, the armor's full power was accessed just as she said.

With it, a part of his old self felt as if it returned as well.

"If only this were a dream," he said and turned back to the burning building. "I think we could have done without that," he said to himself.

Three of them landed on the ground just in front of the massive blaze. "What the hell happened to you?" Blake asked.

"Cody was unhappy I threw him out a window. We had words. I think he'll be okay."

Blake shrugged. "Glad to see we still solve all our problems with violence," he replied.

"Violence is always the answer," Josh replied as an explosion ripped through the front door. Dustin walked out with the blaze, his armor smoking, but otherwise undamaged.

"Hey guys, where's Cody?" Dustin asked, brushing some ash off his shoulder.

"I'm here," Cody said as he landed beside Wyatt. "Oh, good of you to finally join us," Wyatt replied and looked at the fire.

"We should go," Cody finished.

"Yeah, but any ideas on who got us out?" Wyatt asked, ignoring him. Cody looked around. "Yep, this is the perfect time for this conversation. Here under a burning building in an occupied city. Just perfect," he said, frustrated.

Since they were determined to make this happen, there was no reason to fight it.

"All I know is that the janitor from the island got me out," Cody said and shook his head. "Still can't remember his name or why he was there. Nothing made much sense," Cody said.

"Janitor? Dude, you must have been delusional. I think you just got out on your own and were seeing things," Dustin replied.

"Who knows at this point," he replied.

"Yeah, somebody wanted us out, but is this help or more of the Syndicate's games?" Blake wondered out loud. "Games? Letting us all out would be a pretty damn dangerous game, don't you think?" Wyatt was quick to shoot the idea down.

"Who knows what they, whomever they are, have planned or anything at all about."

All I know is that we are out, and we have work to do," he said and looked over as first responders and soldiers were closing in on the disaster. Something small flew overhead in the dark.

"Guys, I'm picking up a radio signal that's repeating something over and over. It's a target list of some kind. Heath is giving out the orders too. I'll link you up," Dustin said, and he tuned in to the same signal for the others.

"Well, looks like we know where to start. Let's

take this list out," Wyatt said. They all turned to look at Cody. "What do you say, one last time?" Wyatt asked.

For a few seconds, there was no response. He looked down.

"Yeah. Just don't die on me, alright? Let's do this our way. The only way we know how, but let's keep the whole last time part out of it, we're three last times into all of this," Cody said, then noticed they had an audience. Soldiers had arrived, first responders, too.

"So much for the element of surprise," he said under his breath.

They were all soldiers, but not a single one of them was shooting. Josh walked towards the line and extended his mini guns that were attached to his arms. He didn't understand how it worked yet, but he thought it was nice to no longer have to hold his weapons. They were more of a part of him.

"Does anyone want a piece of this? I have plenty of bullets for everyone here." There were firefighters and others here, more slaves of the Syndicate. There was no way to engage with the soldiers and not kill them too.

He had to try this first.

To his surprise, the soldiers backed off and lowered their weapons too.

"I wasn't in the mood to kill defenseless people anyway," Josh said and returned to the others.

"Why'd you have to scare them like that? You getting soft in your old age?" Dustin asked.

"Shut up, let's get out of here. The sooner we leave, the better."

"Oh, now you want to leave," Cody replied.

With that, they all took off into the night sky, leaving the inferno behind.

## 36

Blue had been ignored. Maybe even forgotten. The ice and the cold he moved through didn't bother him. Night into day, back into night again as he moved south without a word. With no one to kill and nothing to do but walk, it gave him time to think about most of his life.

All of the important bits anyway.

It was so long ago, what was the name of the town? Goldwater, Gold something. It didn't matter.

Hot, dusty town in the middle of a desert, where no town should have been.

Blue sat in the local saloon, drinking whatever excuse for whiskey they had in the town, lost in thoughts of robbing a bank when the swinging door opened and she walked in.

Woman, not native to this part of the world. She

was something else, dressed in bright colors, long black hair, and deep brown eyes. Skin the color of a deep brown rock that might have been in the sun too long.

It was the first thing he thought of when he saw her.

"Hey, you," Blue said as he stood up to meet her. "What's your name?" he asked, and she didn't pay him any attention.

Blue was the forgiving type. There could have been all kinds of reasons she didn't pay attention. He'd try again.

"Lady, hey, what's your name?" he asked again and grabbed her wrist. She pulled back in shock, her eyes glinting in the sunlight for a second.

"Kezia," she said and pulled away.

The name enchanted him from the second he heard it. "Blue, maybe you should leave the woman alone," the man behind the bar said. Blue tore his eyes away from the lady and looked at the bartender.

"Three days I've been in this rathole of a town, and I hadn't killed anyone. Maybe that changes today?" he asked, resting his hand on his gun.

"Sorry, I just thought—" the man trailed off, eyes on that weapon.

"Please, I'm just here for the radium salt, please," she said, and Blue let her go. "Radium salt.

New medicine, never trusted science that much," he said.

"Anyway, how about you and me go up to my room later tonight? We can talk about, uh, science, always liked biology," he said, and she rolled her eyes.

"My father would never allow it. I must return," she said and turned. She reached into a pocket on her dress. Blue wondered if the dress was homemade. He'd never seen one with pockets before. She pulled out a shiny gold coin and it hit the bar. Blue was familiar with currency, yet the markings on this coin didn't look like any he'd seen before.

Now he had another reason to try again. The barkeep took the gold coin and slid a gray box to her. "You be careful with this now, too much is dangerous," he said.

Kezia smiled. "Yes, thank you," she said and turned to leave. Blue hadn't moved. "You wouldn't happen to have another one of those coins, would you? I'm something of an expert and I haven't seen one like yours before."

Kezia looked down. "No, please, let me go," she said and tried to get around him. Blue knew the other patrons of the bar might be afraid, but together wouldn't hesitate to stand up to him.

He stepped aside and she walked out.

"Barkeep, where's she from? Not around here, I figure."

JESSE WILSON

The man behind the bar stepped back. "Gypsy. Roma tribe. Not sure what they're doing here, but they don't bother anyone, and no one bothers them. They'll be moving on for cooler weather in a week, maybe two. All I know is the gold is good and that's all I need to know," he replied.

"Gold and women, my only weaknesses," he said.

"Don't go fooling around, Blue. Stick to banks," the man replied.

"Oh, you know me, Ed, nicest guy in the world. I wouldn't try to rob some poor defenseless desert people of their gold. Not me," he said, drank the rest of his whiskey in one shot. It burned its way down while he put the glass on the bar.

Blue had plans for tonight.

What did he do the rest of that day? Blue didn't remember. He tried to, but it was just a blur. Too much time had passed to remember. However, the night. How could he forget the night?

No moon in the sky, a billion stars in the sky. The camp below, wagons, horses, all the things a roaming settlement might have.

A raging fire in the middle. "Hell of a party, eh boys?" Blue asked. "You sure about this? You don't even know if they got more gold. This feels bad," Joe said.

"You always got a bad feeling about everything," Mike replied. "Jeremy's right. I can smell the gold from here. A whole damn pirate's chest of it, I bet. We gonna be rich for weeks. Not to mention these people just steal everything anyway. We're just taking it back," Mike added.

"You got to trust Mike, he's never wrong," Blue said, and Joe took a deep breath.

"Guns blazing, just like that small town in South Dakota?" Joe asked. Blue just smiled. "You got it, brother. Let's go get paid," he said.

The three men made their way through the weeds towards the blaze in the distance. If anyone had seen them coming, no alarm was raised.

Blue remembered the air being cool that night as they moved into the camp.

No one noticed them. Everyone seemed to be in some kind of trance. Kezia was twirling around the fire, her dress looked like it was liquid as she danced, not the same one as before. This was colorful, deep red and gold, some blue in there too. The others were playing strange music none of them had ever heard.

The strange rhythm and all the wild dancing made Blue forget why he was here. The trance was strong. Something in the smoke made him relax for a minute. Then, out of nowhere, a gunshot into the air brought everything to an end.

When the music died, Blue came back to his senses and drew his weapon too. All eyes were on them now.

"Alright, Gypsies. We're here for the gold. Hand it over nice and quiet, then you can get back to your, whatever this is," Blue said, weapon pointed at them. Outnumbered, yes, but it was rare that groups wanted to lose people. Guns made people much more agreeable.

"Gold? You must be mistaken," someone replied. He looked like a chief or leader—something—but everyone appeared to be in some kind of costume tonight. Blue didn't care who was what.

"I saw the lady pay with it today. I know you have more. Where is it? I'm usually not this kind, but it's late, and I want to get back to town to spend my gold while there's still some night left," Blue replied. The other two watched the crowd to make sure there weren't any heroes among them.

"The gold. You want the gold. White man never has enough, do they?" an old man asked, and Blue had heard this song and dance before.

"White, black, red, yellow. It doesn't matter. All men can never have enough. I have the guns, so I'll take the gold," Blue replied.

The old man looked into the fire. "Fine. Life is more important than gold." He pointed at two younger men. "Go get it," he said.

They hesitated but then ran off into the dark.

"You get your gold and you leave," the leader said.

"That's the plan, chief," Blue replied.

It was tense while they all waited. Even their guns were starting to get heavy. Then, just as Mike predicted, the men brought back a chest, one on each side.

The box looked ancient, had strange markings on it none of them had ever seen. "What the hell did I say? A goddamned pirate chest," Mike said as he and Joe ran up to it. The men opened the lid.

Not just gold. Gems, too. Diamonds, rubies sparkling in the firelight.

"Goddamn," Joe said, picking up a ruby he couldn't close his fist around.

"Take it and go, monster," Kazia said, and something in Blue snapped. Being rejected and disrespected three times in the same day wouldn't be allowed to slide.

"Bitch, you want a monster, you got one," Blue said. He remembered saying that and what happened next.

He drew his other weapon, aimed at her, then pulled the trigger. He watched her fall in slow motion. It was one of the most replayed memories in his mind. She fell like she danced, a slow spin, then landed on her back.

That last breath left, and she gazed toward the starlit sky.

"Blue, what the hell? We have what we came for," Joe asked. Mike just howled into the night as if he were a beast.

The crowd didn't scatter, scream, or do anything you'd expect a crowd to do. The chief rose, leaning on his long walking stick, fury in his eyes—only the kind an old man could make.

"Kazia." It was the only word he could say, staring at her. Nothing he could do.

"Blue, let's get back to the horses," Mike said, his excitement turning to fear. Before Blue could say anything, the man stood up.

That walking stick came into the firelight for the first time, covered in snakes, or something that looked like snakes. He lifted it and put the end back into the ground. A sickly and bright green mist erupted from the ground.

It moved as if it were alive. Joe and Mike disappeared from his vision, and those screams they made were inhuman.

Blue would never see them again.

"Sendrax Tarum." The man said it three times. His voice echoed like thunder in his brain. He didn't know what it meant. The last time was too much. Blue fell to the earth. His brain tormented with inhuman nightmares, things that shouldn't exist but did. Things that tore him to pieces only to put him together again in chaotic ways.

Ten thousand years, forever. The nightmares took him places—alien cities deep under the sea. Vast gulfs of space filled with fleshy nightmares full of teeth.

Then, he woke up. Eyes opened to a familiar sight. Grass, blue sky. Sunlight.

No sign of the people, the gold, his friends. He was in an empty field. He did the only thing he could do: pushed himself out of the dirt and stumbled back into town. Even the horses had disappeared.

He would never see any of those people again.

Blue walked down this road, remembering his life to this point. Animals fled from him. When he got to town, every horse went wild when he got close. Nothing made sense, and he had to leave.

Wandering between the towns, life became cold.

People hated him more than usual. Blue became an outsider, wandering through history. Every town the same, every person became the same. No matter how he acted, no matter what he did or how, all they could see was a monster. Even if they had never laid eyes on him before, he was an outsider now.

Even time seemed to reject him. While it moved ahead, he felt like he was stuck. Each new town brought small changes in how people talked, how people dressed. Tiny things, new things. Blue remained the same. Unable to change.

The next ten years turned into a blur, and the only thing that changed in him was his rage. People hated him, so he would hate them right back.

Blue grit his teeth in anger as he moved towards

his destination down this lonely road. He saw a white sign on the side, old peeling paint on the surface, with words in pale blue: 'Jesus loves you' inside of a deep red cross. Some church sign, outdated now.

All it did was remind him of the day he learned the truth.

He walked into a church after the sun went down. Some grand cathedral, he couldn't remember where now. The priest turned and grabbed his cross as if some great evil had invaded the house of God. "You can't be here," the man said, his voice echoing with authority.

An authority Blue ignored as he moved forward.

"I need an answer. Give me what I want and I'll go away," Blue replied and moved up to the man who was doing his best not to tremble in Blue's presence.

"Sendrax Tarum. What do those words mean?" he asked, picking the man up with his left arm as if he weighed nothing.

The priest closed his eyes in terror. "I don't know," he replied.

"Start talking, or I'll nail you to that cross up there. You'll be closer to your boss that way," he said.

The priest turned his head. "I'd tell you if I knew. I swear it, please," he begged for his life. Blue was frustrated and prepared to do what he said when a door opened.

"Put him down. He doesn't know anything. I do," the man said. He didn't look like a priest. Looked more like a professor than anything. Blue dropped the priest.

"Follow me," the man said and turned back towards the door, disappearing through it. Blue followed.

"Sendrax Tarum is a Roma curse. We've been following you for a decade. You've only been getting worse. What the hell did you do, who'd you kill?" the man asked.

"What do you mean, curse? I killed a woman, crime of passion," Blue said it as if it were any other thing. The man looked at him and crossed his arms.

"And you never tried to make amends? Never looked for the one who did it?" the man asked, and Blue shrugged.

"Looked a little, lost interest, didn't know I was cursed. Thought it was just bad luck. How do I get rid of it?" Blue asked, getting to the point.

"It's a curse. You don't get rid of it. Only the one who laid it can break it. You got to make up for what you did," he said.

"I don't feel bad about what I did. She had it coming. Rejected me twice, no, three times in the same day," Blue said, and the professor couldn't believe what he was hearing.

"Jeremy, listen. This curse is called empty soul. It's burning you away. If you die without lifting this curse, you will become something we call a scourge. A literal monster that does nothing but destroy everyone that crosses your path. You don't want to be that. Find the one who did this. Make up for it and move on with your life. Start over," the man said.

Blue thought about it.

"Fine. I'm tired of being the outsider. Where are they and I'll go," Blue said. The man smiled.

"Near the Old Snake Trail, Colorado. Know it?" he asked, and Blue shrugged.

"Been through once or twice. Nasty bear problem, Colorado. I can get there in a few days," Blue replied.

"Get a move on. They are heading west, but you should catch them in time," the man said.

Blue felt something for the first time in a long time. He asked the stranger his name. The stranger gave it. Time had erased that memory.

Blue was on the road, he was going to undo the curse. The journey was going fine until he came to Montgomery.

A boom town caught up in the silver mining business. Bustling and chaotic. Blue remembered the name because he knew a Monty once, killed him because he took offense to Blue sleeping with his wife. Friends were supposed to share, weren't they? Monty had to die.

It had been a while. He just wanted something to eat.

From the second he sat at the bar, he felt eyes on him. Nothing new.

Blue got his food. It wasn't special, but it was the last thing he'd ever taste. Eggs, bacon, some burned toast, and bitter coffee. The taste felt so distant now, but if he tried, he could go back to that.

"Jeremy Blue, come out with your hands up or we will shoot you," a voice came from outside. The law. In his rush to get to the trail, he had been less cautious about showing his face.

Blue remembered finishing his meal. All the eyes in the place were on him. He didn't say anything.

"Alright," he said and stood up and walked outside to face the law. He didn't bother putting his hands up.

"Blue, you're wanted for robbery, murder, and a whole lot of other things I don't have time for right now. Come quietly so we can hang you before the weekend," the man said.

Blue just smiled. "I'm afraid I can't do that. See, I'm cursed, and if you kill me before I can lift it, it's gonna be bad for everyone. Just let me go," Blue replied.

"Nonsense. Save some paperwork before the

weekend," the sheriff said. Blue drew his weapons and shot two of the officers in the chest, the rest opened fire. Blue felt like he was being hit with several hammers before dropping to the ground in his own blood.

Blue didn't know what happened next. He woke up. It was night. Just on the edge of town. He was covered in blood, surrounded by it.

He turned to face the town. The place was destroyed, burning, littered with people dead on the streets. Not one soul was seen alive from what he could tell, and all he could feel was his rage building again. The jagged edges of the buildings felt like they were just begging to be torn up even more.

When Jeremy looked down at himself, it was in a body he didn't recognize. Pure muscle, and the ground felt like it was far away. His arms were strong, and all he wanted to do was rip and tear until everything was leveled.

Then, it wasn't long after that the Syndicate and their Delta Squad came into his life, and the rest, as they say, was history.

Things he didn't care to remember.

It didn't make any sense, but this is where Brian was. He could feel his blood calling out to him. What was stolen so long ago.

It was near dawn when Blue arrived. He didn't

see this place as it was. He only imagined what he was going to do to it.

## 37

The leader of the Syndicate had a great-looking office, simple inspirational pictures on the wall, even a nice digital clock that counted the seconds, and an even better door. It was solid oak and shiny brown. It matched well with the rest of the gray room.

Then, the door slammed open. It hit the wall so hard that the prized digital clock hit the floor, shattering against the dark carpet.

Mark made his way through the opening.

"I know this had to be planned. You let them out, why?"

The man behind the desk looked at his clock. "Do you not know how to knock? Look at what you did, you broke it. I've had that clock for years. I remember the day I got it. Now, shattered on the ground," he replied.

Mark looked at the clock. "I'll buy you a new one, sorry," he replied.

The man smirked.

"Anyway, calm down. The Syndicate won, sure, but there are worse things out there. This victory was handed to us. It was so easy after all this time. You couldn't beat them. Nobody could. It was pathetic. Chronovore is still out there, and we need an exterminator. Jake isn't going to talk her down, we both know it. The Delta Squad seems to accomplish the impossible. I say we give them a chance," he replied.

"Yeah, we have the upper hand, but for how long? Like you said, impossible is what they tend to be good at. They'll never stop, and they have access to things that shouldn't even exist. As soon as they take care of Emily, we're next. What if they get the Viper back? Then it's over," Mark said.

"You make a good point, as always. However, the squad is not the only threat. We just needed to get them all within killing distance, close, you know. I have a plan. You need to trust me." The man smiled, not a hint of worry on his face. "It's time to gather the Generals."

Mark narrowed his eyes but thought better of making a bigger deal. Trust the plan.

"Alright. I'll make the call, but I still think this is a big mistake." Mark believed he had too much faith in this Dragon project.

"They are going to hit where the resistance has been trying to get, you know that, right?" Mark asked.

"Yes. The plan won't be perfect, but what is? We can take a few hits before we win. Trust the plan, trust me, too," he replied.

Mark walked out of the room, closing the door behind him, making sure not to slam it. Then he wondered who else was a threat, but it hit him all at once that the Typhon armor was still on base, wasn't it?

He had been kept out of most of the information lately. Too busy with other things, biding his time to the point that anything might be going on. It was still on base, right? With everything that had been going on in the past six months, he'd been too busy to check.

The way to the holding chamber for the Typhon armor was short, but he was walking pretty fast. Of course, when he got to the door, there was no guard posted. He walked to the hand scanner and pressed his hand against it. It scanned, and the screen turned green, the steel door opened with a hiss. When Mark got inside, it was empty and dark.

It had been emptied for quite some time,

judging by the dusty ledges. "What the hell is going on?" he asked, then wondered why he was kept out of the loop on things like this. He left the dark room, not sure what to do next.

## 38

The Leviathan sat vacant in the frozen north at a secret Syndicate base. A blizzard raged around the giant ship.

"I hate this place," Bella said as she flipped a switch. The lights turned on in one of the many weapons control rooms on the thing.

"I hate that we're basically janitors. Keeping the thing clean until they decide to use it again," Keith replied and pulled the mop out of the water. Despite not being used, the dust built up fast anyway, and orders were to maintain.

He started to mop the floor, and she started to clean off a console. "What would happen if I pushed this button that said Ion Cannon on it?" she asked and laughed.

"The rest of the crew would get a heck of a

wakeup call, and you might shave off the top of a mountain somewhere. Also, good chance you'd get executed," Keith replied.

Bella pushed the button anyway. Keith jumped and waited for the result, but nothing happened.

"First time on weapons deck, no power to the main system anyway. Push all the buttons you want," she said with a laugh.

"God damn, I thought we were about to end up in the Headless Valley," he said, heart still racing.

"Not today," she said.

The two of them laughed it off and then got back to work. A few minutes later, the alarms did go off.

"What? The power's off. Nothing should have fired," she said, looking around.

"Wrong alarm. Intruder alert. Someone boarded the ship," he said and dropped the mop. "No drills today, it's real," he said and ran for the exit, she was close behind.

The two of them suited up, grabbed their weapons, and made it to the deck of the ship. There was the ice, the wind, and piles of snow, but no evidence of intruders.

"Is this some kind of prank?" Bella asked. Keith looked around, squinting through the snow.

"No, look. There's light over there. We're just on the wrong side. Come on," he replied.

The two of them started to run in that direction.

JESSE WILSON

The basic suits of armor made traction easy as they moved through the ice and snow. Once they made it past the center of the ship, they slid to a halt.

"What?" Keith asked.

"From the files, it's the Olympians. We are screwed. What are they doing here?" she asked, unsure if they should just run and hide or fight.

The two of them watched as Hades' black chains tore through the chest of three people with ease and tossed them over the side as if they were some sort of tendril. Then they watched as Zeus hit another group with so much energy they just turned to ash.

"I'm out of here," Keith said and turned to run. Bella nodded and did the same thing. It was hopeless.

Poseidon was right behind them as they turned and picked them both up by their necks, one in each hand.

"What are we to do with you?"

"Let us go?" Bella asked, tossing her weapon to the deck. Keith did the same. Poseidon nodded.

"Sure, why not? It'll make a good story to tell your kids someday," he said and tossed them both off the side of the deck without a second thought.

Maybe they lived, maybe not. He didn't care. They didn't matter in his story. Once they disappeared into the howling blizzard, he made his way over to the others.

"You think this will be enough?" Amanda

asked. She was still getting used to her armor again and all of its upgrades.

"Of course it will. The Syndicate did all the groundwork for us. All we have to do is move in and take over. It'll be easy," Megan replied.

"Now that the housekeeping is done, what do we do now?" Skye asked.

"Hera, we take this ship for a ride," Megan replied.

"Alright, I suppose we'll just have to make a good first impression," Skye replied.

"Do whatever makes you happy," Stephanie said as she walked to the main hatch. "Don't suppose we can open this without breaking it?"

"Just break it, it'll repair itself. Nano metal, remember?" Chris replied.

"Oh, sure," she replied, grabbed the locking wheel, and tore the thick metal door off its hinges.

"Wise Athena, always trying to overcomplicate things when the direct approach is the best way to do it," Amanda replied.

"Well, sorry, it's not like they make spare parts," she replied.

"Just move it already," Matt said. Megan took the lead and walked through the door.

"Do you even know where the bridge is?" Chris asked. "Of course I do. I can read the signs on the wall. Let's keep moving," she replied.

The six of them made their way to the bridge, to a terrified looking crew. Megan lifted her hands.

"I am Zeus of the Olympians. If you value your lives, you'll bring this ship to life. If you wish to die, please stand up. I don't want to wreck any of the consoles," she said, electricity crackling from her fingers.

No one stood up, and they got to work.

"Good choice," she replied.

"Oh, before we go, I have something to do," Skye said and left the bridge as the work continued.

The monstrous ship roared to life once more after a long silence. The base on the ice below the ship was in a panic as the Leviathan lifted into the blizzard. As it did, a figure flew off the deck of the ship. The personnel of the base below never noticed.

Hera's hands lit up with the prism beams, and she fired the deadly rainbows down into the base.

The explosion was terrible. The ice shattered. Everything that was standing there was engulfed with flame.

What the explosion could not destroy, the water claimed. The ice opened beneath them. The living and the dead were sucked down into the icy water in minutes. No signs of life were detected by her suit.

Hera gazed upon her work, where once stood a

base was now just a black lake that would freeze, leaving no trace of what was before. Satisfied with her work, she returned to the Leviathan as it disappeared into the storm.

# 39

Bryan needed a place to do his work, but the Syndicate scum was everywhere. He watched as the blood sizzled from his blade and kicked the severed head away from him.

"Don't you morons ever take a few hours off?" he asked no one, knowing that now that this had happened, more would be showing up. He had no choice but to move.

At least it had stopped raining.

Tonight was a good night. Most of the city lights were out, and he could see the stars. The stars were chilling. They were either wrong or right, depending on your point of view. The stars were great tellers of the future for those who could read them. They were all screaming the same thing: Disaster was on the horizon, but at the same time, their patterns were supposed to create a cosmic lock.

Few people knew this, and even fewer understood the meaning behind it. The idea that the stars held something out was a myth even to the Guardians. Bryan was never one to disregard the concept of a myth.

Everything came from somewhere, and this had to be no different. Then it hit him—a wave of inspiration.

"The stars, of course, Bryan, you're an idiot," he said to himself and looked up. The answer was getting high. He figured he'd never mention this to anyone and proceeded with his plan.

There was a building close by, and it was high enough. He ran right towards the front doors and got inside, only to meet a group of soldiers there using it to take a break.

"Are you kidding me right now?" he asked with his sword still in hand. The guards didn't even take the time to ask questions, pulling their weapons and starting to shoot.

He didn't have time to play this game again and ran to the left as fast as he could, outpacing their aim. At the same time, his sword lit up with green fire. He swung it in their direction and watched as the group was torn apart at their waists, falling to pieces in a few seconds.

"You shouldn't have stood there." Bryan took

his eyes off the dead and found what he was looking for.

Stairs.

Ten minutes later, he stood on the top of the building. It was high off the ground and away from the prying eyes of anyone who might want to get in the way.

Bryan stood there with the blade in his hands. He had no idea how he was going to manage this, but he would do his best. The blade was of cosmic origins, so it should be able to get the job done.

"Ok, sword. Let's do this." Bryan lifted it into the air, concentrated, and swung into the air at nothing, only to watch the end of the blade slam into the rooftop. He narrowed his eyes—there had to be a way to accomplish this.

He took a deep breath and swung again. Nothing happened. He just made another dent in the roof. "A little help, come on," he said.

"You know, if you want to open the path, you need a better reason than, 'bro, do what I need you to do,'" a voice said from behind. At once, he turned around, blade pointed at the source.

"Theron, how?" Bryan asked.

"Relax, not really here. I gave you my weapon. We have a connection. What are you trying to do, Leo?" Theron asked.

"Trying to get the team back together," Bryan replied.

"Zodiac. Of course. You're missing a few members too. It's too bad you ended up fighting on the side of chaos for so long," Theron replied. Bryan nodded. "Nothing we can do about that now. Can you help me?" he asked, trying his best to remain respectful.

Theron smiled. "How could I say no?" He reached out. A small green spark leapt from his fingers to the edge of the blade. Now the thing glowed with an alien light.

"Good luck," Theron said. When Bryan took his eyes off the blade to reply, he was already gone.

"Thanks." He took a breath and concentrated on what he wanted to happen. "When you get a cosmic assist, best not waste it."

He held the blade above his head and swung it down. The thing caught on something in the air, sunk in, and began to cut down through, as if cutting through slime. The harder he pushed down, the more resistance it gave. Dimensional walls were things not easily broken.

All he could do now was hope he was cutting into the right place. He pictured it in his mind but had no idea if it was enough to do the job.

# 40

Quentin was stuck. He had been here for six months, but it wasn't so bad. He had company, at least.

They needed someone to keep the robot cat company. Sparky and he were both relics from a bygone age now, but that didn't stop the living machine from trying to kill him to pass the time. Sometimes he'd win, sometimes he got pieces taken out of his arms and bled for a while.

Both of them could heal. There never was a winner.

Around the fifth month, Sparky stopped attacking. It was the little things that mattered the most in this nightmare.

Now the two of them were almost friends. There were bad days, but not many. Quentin and Sparky were stuck in a house in the middle of nowhere. There was no way to tell where this place was. Sparky spent most of his time outside, sleeping in the grass near the electric fence.

Every time it tried to fly out, sensor-activated machine guns knocked it down. It was a machine, but when it was full of holes, it would always seem to bleed before repairing itself. It made Quentin feel bad every time. Quentin was sure he could have escaped, but to what? The world was not friendly to him anymore. For now, he had everything he needed. Out there was nothing but the unknown. Living here was nice enough.

Six months of monotony, besides one thing.

Someone unseen would leave behind the strangest books at the front door. Whoever did it was stealthy enough to avoid the machine guns and the electronic cat.

They would vary from simple picture books that looked like they were made for kids to horrifying things—books with symbols and stories of things that seemed impossible.

The doorbell rang again, just as it had each and every time. He sighed, got up, moved to the door, and opened it. Just like all the other times, there was a package on the step.

"Thanks," he said to no one and picked it up. Old brown paper tied with even older string. Or at least someone wanted it to appear that way.

Just another thing that didn't make sense.

He moved back into the living room, glancing out the window. Sparky was just laying out there in the sun like it always did. Nothing new. He sat back down in his chair and put the package on the table.

"Let's see what kind of nightmare you brought me today," he said and undid the string. While they were all strange, this one was by far the strangest just by looking at it.

The cover felt like leather, but it was different. Quentin opened the thing.

"Per Ostium Sub Mari," he said. Somehow, it didn't seem like the right thing to say, but there it was.

It was the first book he got that wasn't in modern languages. The others had titles like *Unspeakable Cults* and *Massa di Requiem par Shuggay*.

This one was different.

The ink was black, but it was almost as if the letters were just black holes in the paper instead of ink. Written by hand, but what kind, he couldn't tell. The writing was perfect.

It felt older than the others. As he looked over the letters on the first page, he felt relaxed. As he gazed into those pitch-black letters, they started to make sense. Nothing changed, but he felt as if he had been reading this language his whole life.

He read on.

Turning the pages, the words told a story of

power that was beyond the walls of the universe. Power for anyone who had the courage to reach out and grab it. It spoke of ancient lands that had sunk beneath the sea and a door that waited.

More pages, more words. Words of how to get there, where to go. The second part of the book made him feel more relaxed, yet horrified at the message. Not a message he was unfamiliar with. The idea that humanity had been nothing more than a mistake was appealing.

It meant all the things he did or would ever do would be meaningless. There was comfort in that. Life didn't mean anything, no one's did.

Reading this made him think of all the worst things he'd ever done, and he could undo all of it. All he had to do was go to the door under the sea. Undone, all of it. How nice would that be? Stranger thoughts filled his mind, too.

"I know what I have to do now," he said, coming to the end of the book, and closed it. "I know what I have to do, where to go," he said with a wide grin.

"I can bring all of this to an end," he said to the book, as if it were alive. He walked to the door and stepped outside, book under his arm.

The electric fence loomed high in front of him, but new knowledge was gained. Now there was a reason to leave. He looked at the dual machine guns there on the gate. Stupid machines made by equally stupid people.

Quentin picked up a rock and tossed it between the two at the gate. The turrets turned in on one another as the thing flew past. In the same second, he jumped on top of Sparky and leapt to the top of the fence behind the left turret. He wrapped his hands around it and pulled it up and off. It was harder than he expected. There were more sparks, too.

Sparky followed and tore the other one to pieces with his claws. "Nice work," he said. The metal cat just jumped to the other side.

The minute Quentin hit the ground on the other side, he realized that he was starving for something more than the pink paste that came out of a tube in the kitchen.

His first mission was to go get something real to eat.

"Food, new clothes, and then we go to the ocean. I am going to undo all of this mess," he said. The cat said nothing as they walked away from their former cage.

With this old, grimy book at his side, all things would be revealed. He was going to save the world.

## 41

"The world has a hidden past, you know? One that is barely touched on in the stories of writers, people unlucky enough to glimpse things in their dreams. You've heard of it. Maybe you haven't. I don't know really, but I do know it is not far from the truth," Adam said, shaking his head, flipping through a book.

"Oh my god, how the hell did we get stuck with you? Shut up," Lindsey said. "I swear if you tell this story again, I'm going to tear your teeth out," she said, staring out the window at a snow-covered landscape.

"I'm with her," Haley said.

"I don't have much else to say. You two seem rather aggressive toward a person who can make your intestines come to life and chew their way out with a couple of words. Maybe you should just let an old man ramble. I mean, it's really not so bad, is it?" he asked and took another sip of his coffee.

"No, I suppose it's not so bad after all," Lindsey replied. Adam smiled. "Besides, you might need to know some of this. Could be a quiz."

"A quiz on stuff no one cares about but weirdos. Can't wait, should be fun," Haley replied, staring at her sword leaning in the corner, thinking about better times.

Adam smiled. "It'll be fun." Then his smile disappeared.

"The first things, you saw them both. They aren't alone. They have a whole family out there in constant combat. But Bob and Theron were clever. They created the nexus. They used the stars of every universe that is as a kind of lock against the dark outside. Cool story, right?" he asked.

"Every night I go out, and I look up into the sky, and each time the stars are just a tiny bit shifted out of place. All the chaos, all the insanity. The cosmic seals are coming apart, and no one is bothering to fix them. It can only mean trouble," he said.

"That's great, why aren't you out there fixing it?" Lindsey asked.

"I am pretty great, sure, but the amount of energy to fix it would take a huge gathering of us. With the Syndicate watching and some of the Guardians working for them, it'd be impossible to do it. It's almost as if the Syndicate wants everything to break down. I know that sounds insane, but that's what it feels like," he replied.

"Why are we hiding out here? We should join with the resistance. Do something," Haley replied.

"The Syndicate has to be tapping into things nobody should even know about. How do you fight something like that?" Adam asked and stood up. It was late. His coffee had barely been touched. "I need to rest now," he said and stood up.

He'd always claimed to be some powerful something or another, but to the women, he just looked like an old man. Acted like it too.

"You two get first watch, whatever. Just don't—you know what to do," he said and wandered out of the kitchen.

Despite all the banter between the three of them, it was hard not to feel bad for the guy. Adam acted as if everything was coming to an end, but he also acted a little like a crazy person on a street corner, too.

"He's been afraid ever since we left. I think he's losing his mind. Who can blame him? The Syndicate and everyone who's anyone is hunting us. We had to hide out here in the frozen north," Lindsey said. "Not the happiest of places," she finished.

As if on cue, the overcast sky started to snow. It looked nice.

"At least we're not hungry or freezing. We've

had worse places to hang out," Lindsey replied. Haley nodded.

"I don't know. This story he tells, it feels real. Do you think there is any truth to it? I mean, at all?" Haley asked. She had a hard time not believing this story. "I mean, think about it. We've literally been to other dimensions. Seen some things," Haley said. Lindsey shook her head.

"Okay, other dimensions or places exist. But you heard him yourself. Even his own people think it's just a story. Something to keep the others busy. I don't think we need to worry about a maybe when the Syndicate is breathing down our necks," she replied.

"Yeah, it's all just a story. The real enemy is the Syndicate. We should really get back into the fight, and soon," Haley replied.

"Yeah, but later. Right now, one of us should get some sleep. These Canadian nights are long," Lindsey said.

"You go. I'll be fine as long as I have the coffee and the television," Haley replied. "Nothing like some SNN to keep you company. See you in a few hours," she replied and walked off.

Haley turned on the Syndicate News Network to see how much the Syndicate was winning today.

"Five dangerous criminals have escaped today, hours ago. The only details we have are—" The newswoman looked into the camera, her eyes wide.

"The Syndicate has everything under control. Everything's fine," then the screen flipped to a technical difficulties screen.

"Son of a bitch, they're not dead," she smiled. It was the first time she smiled in months. Also, she wanted to tell the others, but it was late. They needed their rest, and she was too excited to sleep.

# 42

Brianna, Tyler, and Angel were walking down a road. The house they were staying at started to feel a bit too comfortable. Complacency in a world like this just got you caught or killed.

"Guys, can we get something to eat? Really. I'm pretty hungry, and it's been twelve hours since we ate last." Joey liked to complain, but it wasn't needless.

They were all hungry, cold, and miserable.

"Joey, shut up. You do realize we are running because of you. You do realize most of this is because of you. Why, why in the hell did you have to take the powers of Silence?" Brianna asked him as they walked. Nothing Joey did made sense, and the frustration was rising.

"How many times do I have to say it? Everyone around me was special. You got those cool armors, the Delta Squad, everyone we were involved with was special, everyone but me. I just wanted to fit in. I took the powers and had no idea it would consume me like that," Joey laughed a little. "Hindsight and all that," he added.

"Yeah, I get that. You didn't need any power. We were friends. We didn't ask for this," Angel said. All he wanted to do was punch Joey in the face.

It was true. Joey did everything. The other four had it forced on them. Joey didn't feel too hungry anymore. He didn't even know why they kept him around. Those thoughts were thrown out of his mind as soon as a house came into view.

"We'll see if there's anything to eat there," Tyler said and pointed at the house.

"Sounds good," Brianna replied.

Joey heard something else, however. He looked up and saw a glint of light in the cloudy sky. "I just saw a drone. We're about to have company. I can't see how walking down a road in the middle of the day could have ended well," Joey said as the others looked up just in time to see the drone disappear into the clouds.

"Oh, yeah. Drones," Tyler said.

"We need to get out of here," Angel said.

"Thank you, Captain Obvious, wasn't aware,"

Brianna replied. They had no idea what direction to run. Despite the drone, there was nothing else around.

"Maybe it was just a recon drone, and we're okay. By the time they get here, we'll be long gone," Angel said.

"Maybe, but let's get to the house all the same. I don't like being out here in the open like this," she replied. With that, the four of them started to run toward the house when, from both side streets, big, black armored vehicles roared around the corner and blocked them. Two came up the road behind them as well.

"Well," Joey said, "I'm saved from you idiots. Finally, I get to eat." He put his hands up. He started walking forward. "I surrender, I'm not with them," he started to say when the gunner on top of the left vehicle shot the ground in front of him.

"Stay where you are, lay on the ground. You are all enemies of the Syndicate. Get on the ground and put your hands behind your back," a voice rang out.

"Arrested. I mean, that's really not my style," Brianna said under her breath, clenching her fist. "If you do not comply, we will open fire. Get on the ground now," the voice said again. Joey had no issue with following orders. He just laid down, thankful to get away from these maniacs.

"We have to fight," Tyler said.

"No, just give up. It's better that way," Joey said as he put his hands on his head.

"Joey, these people are not your friends anymore. They are going to put us in labs. You think you're being saved, but come on, man, think about it. We've all had power, there is no way we're just going to be left in a cell," she replied.

"Last warning. On the ground or we shoot." Joey winced. The woman had a point after all. Surrendering just kept him in the dirt.

"Fine," Joey said and pushed himself off the road. "I guess it's time," he finished.

"Joey, what are you doing?" Brianna asked.

"I've put up with your antics enough, but you have a point. The Syndicate aren't going to do us any favors. You three can help or watch. It's up to you, but this won't take long," he replied. Joey sounded different, more confident than he did five minutes ago when he was sure his ordeal was over.

Joey closed his eyes, took a deep breath. When he opened his eyes, they were no longer human. Instead, they burned with silver flames. Brianna and the others took a step back.

"What?" Angel asked, but Joey just kept walking toward the new enemy, then broke into a run.

His left fist rose up, and he lunged forward,

closing the distance in a hurry. The impact came with such force that the front end of the armored vehicle caved in. At the same time, it flipped end over end, then landed into the house they were heading towards.

Before anyone could react, Joey dashed to the other vehicle and ripped the door off. Joey reached inside and tossed a man in black armor out, throwing him back into a streetlight. The body of the man was torn in half at the waist.

The three watching cringed at the sight, then started running to the right. "We'll ask questions later, let's go," Angel said.

The sight of the sudden violence shocked the men in the cars behind them. When they ran, no one started shooting.

The other armored carrier rocked violently, then blood began to seep out of the door. The gunner on top was pulled down screaming, and blood shot up like a geyser. The three observers turned around just in time to see it.

"What is happening right now?" Brianna trailed off as the front of the vehicle tore open. Joey flew the distance between the cars and used both of his fists to crush them both at the same time. They looked as if they had crashed full speed into trees.

The steel was mangled, the bodies inside crushed. Broken limbs hung out the shattered windows. Joey flipped both the hulks of twisted metal, and they landed upside down with a hideous crash.

He was covered with blood now. His eyes still solid silver as he turned to look at the other three.

"I guess I should explain," he said with a shrug, trying to flick the blood off his hands, uselessly.

## 43

Heath was gazing at the big screen. The despair was coming in waves now. Every time another section turned red, he knew what it meant. Another 'unit' had hit the retreat signal.

"Damn it, stand up. Fight. Do something, you morons," he screamed at the map in frustration. Nothing changed, however.

He put his face in the palms of his hands. It was over. All of it. The war, the resistance. Everything was coming to an end right in front of him. There was only one thing left to do.

Get drunk and wait for the death squads, fight until they died.

Heath walked to his excuse of a desk and sat in the folding chair. The only thing he had managed to take from Blackfire Island.

An ornate black bottle, engraved with writing he couldn't understand. No one could understand it in the modern age, at least.

"A gift from the Guardians," Heath said, looking at his reflection in the black glass. The bottle was still cold. It was always cold. "Booze from Atlantis," he said, remembering how one was given to Dustin to convince him to come back.

Only three bottles were had. The third one was still somewhere on the island. Heath moved his fingers on the outside of the bottle, feeling all the ridges. Wondering who carved them, how they were made.

It was now he missed the old days the most. He was just about ready to open it and call the others in the office. His hand gripped the top, then, just as he began to twist, something happened on the screen.

A section turned green. "Huh?"

Then the door opened behind him. He put the bottle back in the drawer before anyone saw it.

"Heath," Nick rushed beside him, but there was no response at first.

"Hey, snap out of it, you need to see this," Nick said, and Heath looked up at the screen as Nick flipped the channel.

"I saw the green section, but what is all this? Turn it up."

Roger came into the room a second later. "Oh

my God." Too excited. Heath wanted to punch them both but decided to wait until he saw what the big deal was.

Nick turned it up, a little too loud, but Heath wasn't complaining—yet, at least.

"If you're just joining us, earlier tonight, the terrorist group known as the Delta Squad has escaped and attacked. There are at least forty casualties that we know of. The following images are not suitable for children. They are graphic."

The newscaster said, then a smaller screen in the corner filled the screen and started playing. The camera panned over to see soldiers dead on the ground, blurred out but obvious.

Then the camera panned over to a scene of devastation. The whole building had collapsed into a burning, jagged mess as far as the eye could see.

"Can you tell us what happened?" a voice behind the camera said, turning towards an injured man on the ground.

"I can tell you. Those bastards blew everything up, and when we tried to put the fire out, they started shooting. I was lucky, I tripped and fell when the shooting started. All I could do was hope they left," the man said, holding his bleeding head.

"They want to kill us all," he said as the camera switched back to the anchor.

"This is all the information we have here at SNN. We repeat: The Delta Squad is at large. If you see anything, call this number at once. Anytime, anywhere. These criminals need to be caught before they strike again, and a manhunt is underway," she said with a blank stare. Heath could have sworn he saw hope in her eyes. Maybe just a little. Maybe he was losing his mind.

"Holy hell, shut this trash off, get them on the radio. What are you waiting for, you should have led with that. I should just—bah, get them on the line." Heath had so many emotions going at once, he was just doing his best to keep his head.

For the first time in a long time, he smiled.

"Admit it, you're happy," Roger said.

"Yes, but I still might shoot you, so don't push it. Get them on the radio," he replied as he put his hand on his sidearm.

"Fine, I get it, we'll do our best," Roger replied, then got to work, knowing Heath would have actually shot him if he didn't.

## 44

The Delta Squad was flying through the air faster than they ever had. After six months in hell, none of them had much to say. Right now, they were just enjoying the ride and the freedom that came with it.

"Guys, what did they do to you?" Dustin asked. There was no response for a bit.

"Do we really need to talk about it?" Wyatt replied.

"Yes, we should," Dustin replied, but he could tell they weren't interested in talking.

"Listen. They kept me in a dark place. Nothing to do. One dim light. I lost my mind. I figured you were all dead. Cody, why didn't they just kill us?" he asked.

"I don't know. I was in a cage for six months or

something. It was bad, and I don't think I want to think about it anymore. Let's just move on," Cody replied. The more he thought about his ordeal, the more upset about it he became.

"I'm with him," Josh said. Blake didn't want to tell anyone what happened to him.

"Yeah, let's move forward," Blake added.

Cody was about to tell them what was going to happen next when all of their radios crackled to life at once.

"Cody, is it you? It has to be?"

The words made all five of them stop in their flight.

"Yeah, it's us. The Syndicate didn't kill us for whatever reason. Thanks for the rescue. Six months, have you been running a bit slow lately?" Cody asked.

There was silence on the other end for a bit.

"I am glad to see you are free, but I don't know how you got out. It had nothing to do with me. I was sure you were dead after we saw you get hauled off," Heath said. "You should know Theron did some kind of magic and brought people back to life. Back to life just in time for the Syndicate to swoop in and catch everyone, it was insane," Heath replied.

"We don't know where anyone is. Hell, we only knew where Josh was, but the security around there was insane, we couldn't do anything," Heath said. Cody ignored that last part.

"Don't take this personally, but I don't think we're going to take orders from you. We need to do this our way. If you want to keep up, all you need to do is pay attention to the news, we'll start with your to-do list," Cody replied, then shut off the radio.

"What are we going to do?" Josh asked.

"We're going to piss the Syndicate off," Cody replied.

"Great, how?" Wyatt asked.

"Heath gave everyone a good starting point. There is a supply train heading out to California. Let's wreck it," Blake said.

"Looks like we have a train to catch. It's about three miles west of here," Dustin said, "at least according to the map," he finished.

"A train, Cody. Really?" Wyatt asked. He was annoyed at the situation—they all were.

"Yeah, is it going to be too difficult for you? Too much work?" Cody asked.

"Come on, guys, it'll be fun. It's a train. How hard could it be? Ten minutes tops, no problem," Dustin said, trying to break it up.

"Fine, ten minutes, but don't tell someone you're not following orders, then start doing everything they want done," Wyatt replied.

## 45

They sailed through the sky with purpose now, toward the west, toward a train.

Dustin pointed down at the train, the only train heading west. "I think that's it," he said.

"You're an idiot," Blake replied. Josh just laughed.

"I might be an idiot, but take a closer look. That damn thing is armed to the teeth with weapons. No one is getting close to it," Dustin replied.

"We could take out the rails ahead of it," Wyatt said.

"Yeah, we could, but we have no idea what's on that thing. The disaster could kill too many. We need a new plan," Cody said and was about to say what was on his mind.

"No, I'll take care of this. We don't have the

time. Stay out of my way," Josh said, his voice filled with rage.

"What's he gonna do all by himself?" Blake asked, but nobody wanted to guess at what he had planned. "He needs to hit something. When he needs help, we'll be here," Cody replied, and the four of them watched as he chased after the speeding train alone.

In the dark, the thing looked black, but as he got closer, it was silver. Just as many guns, and there were gunners on top too.

Josh made no sound as he flew through the dark. The men on the train scanned the dark, looking for any signs of trouble. Josh had to admire how dedicated they were to their jobs. Too bad they were on the wrong side.

His old armor only had one minigun, effective but limiting. This suit had one attached to each arm. With a thought, they extended. Josh took a second to admire the work they put into it, and his weapons began to spin for a couple of seconds.

As silent as his armor and weapons spinning were, the gunfire was not. The roar of the miniguns even overcame the sound of the train.

The gunners were first. By the time they reacted to the sound, Josh had already turned half of them into red mist trails as the train moved forward. The ones who managed to shoot back could only aim for the flash of the miniguns.

Josh watched the flesh of the enemy get shredded. He missed this more than he realized.

"Now for the front of the train." Josh started to fly to meet it.

As he came into range, the guns of the silver train focused on him. It was an automatic response to anything—it had to be.

Josh rolled as the cannons began to fire. They missed, everything beside the train began to explode as shells hit the ground.

"Might take longer than ten minutes," he said, then wondered why he was talking to himself so much. He couldn't be nervous, could he?

He flew farther than the weapons could aim and thought he was safe for a minute to make a new plan when a strange looking weapon rose from the top of the train's roof. Josh had never seen a weapon like this and decided it was good to stay out of its direct line of fire.

Just as he started to weave to the left, the automated targeting system kicked in and fired a bright blue beam at him. There was no way to avoid it because as soon as he saw it, it blasted him into the ground. His armor was smoking, but this felt more like some kind of force beam to push him back.

"Stay back. This train is mine." He didn't have to look to know that they would try to provide backup after this. He took to the air again, as fast as he could go this time, low to the ground, and moved ahead of the train.

There was no way he could attack the train from the sides or above without getting blasted again. Innocent people? There were no innocents left. You either joined the Syndicate or you fought them. Anyone who fought them wouldn't be near here.

There was only one move left, but he wasn't sure if he could pull it off or just become a greasy spot on the tracks.

Life was overrated anyhow.

He flew into the nose of the train and kept pace as it moved ahead, retracted his weapons.

Then he made contact with the front.

His claws dug into the steel with ease. He put all of his strength, the armor had, and lifted the front end of the train off the rails, and didn't stop.

He lifted it into the air and brought it down onto the second car of the train. He then put that same power into pushing the silver train to the right and tipping both cars over. The second he accomplished this, he flew away.

The rest of the train followed the pattern, falling off the track.

Twenty eight sections of the train derailed, slamming into one another with excessive force. Some of them exploded, others were crushed. Josh hovered just above the new disaster he made.

He waited for people to start crawling out of the

wreck. He was going to kill anyone he saw. Also, he was still mad that they hit him with that blue thing. He gave it all back to them. Just what they deserved. Maybe, maybe not. He didn't know much about what people deserved, nor did he care about that. If they were shooting at him, it was only responsible to shoot back. If they hit him, they deserved to die. Life was simple.

The others made their way to him. "Did you just suplex a train?" Wyatt asked. He was in shock—they all were.

"Yes," Josh replied in a calm voice that only made them nervous.

"Nice work. Now let's find a Syndicate headquarters outpost and see what we can see," Cody said and looked around at the mess Josh had made of the place. He almost felt sorry for the people inside, almost. He wasn't going to say anything about any of the earlier concerns.

"I know right where to start looking," Blake said, and continued. "I'll lead the way."

"Lead on," Cody replied. Blake nodded and took off toward the East. The others followed, leaving the disaster behind.

If nothing else, it sent a hell of a message.

## 46

"Well, has anyone seen Cole since he left?" Tiffany asked.

"I bet he's on a hot date with another rock," Dani replied. "I wouldn't be surprised, but we really should keep track of him," Samantha replied.

"Yeah, he's insane. We should leave him here. It's safer for all of us," Brittany replied.

"Guys, he's crazy but loyal and good in a fight. We need to keep him around," Ariana replied. "Fine," Alex said, "but let's keep looking for a way out first. We can wait for him. He always seems to find us in this nightmare," he finished.

"Come on, keep walking," Brittany said. "If we keep talking, something horrible is going to hear us," she finished.

"Yeah, something terrible," Matt replied,

looking around into the dark, but besides the dull green glow at the edge of the horizon, saw nothing. "This whole place is something horrible," he said and rubbed his hands together.

It wasn't cold, but something was chilling him to the bone out here. He didn't want to say anything about it, afraid the feeling might spread.

Cole, meanwhile, had sailed through the dark looking for anything. He didn't know what or why. To him, this place was a place of unlimited adventure. You never knew what rock had a story to tell. Or what you were going to find next.

Then, he saw a rock shaped like a man. "You," he said and landed beside it. "Hello," he said to the rock.

"Hello," the rock replied. Cole smiled. "What are you doing way out here, man?" the rock asked him, and Cole crossed his arms.

"Me and my new friends are trying to get back home. We think if we can find a way into Hell, that we can find a shortcut back to Earth and then, well then, it's totally payback time, but first, a feast of cheeseburgers. That has to come first," Cole replied to his new rock friend.

"Really, they want to go to Hell? Tell me, where are your friends now?" the rock man asked him and materialized a block of cheese in his hands and handed it to Cole. Gemini's eyes lit up.

"For me? Oh, you're like the best guy ever," he said and took the cheese.

"I know, I'm pretty awesome. So, about those friends. I'd find them myself, but everything looks the same around here, you know? I'd like your help. I bet I can show them a way out," the rock man replied.

Cole thought about it, then took a bite of cheese. It tasted exactly how he imagined it. "Usually, rocks just like to stay where they are. We have a nice conversation sometimes and then I go. No one has ever wanted to come with before. Why do you want to meet them?"

The rock man crossed his arms. "I already said. I know this place like the back of my hand. I can help find a way home," he replied, and Cole smiled.

"Yeah, I trust you. Come with me! I'll show you where they are. What could go wrong?" Cole asked. "You need to keep up. Let's go," Cole said, finished his cheese, and flew into the dark. The rock man followed him.

Cole was fast, but the rock kept up with him.

It was a few minutes before the people came into view.

"Guys, I found someone who can help," Cole said as he landed in front of them with his new friend.

They all looked at the same time and stopped in

their tracks. That same look of fear spread through their eyes.

"Hello, you," Bob said to them with a smile.

"I did good! I am awesome," Cole said, oblivious to the danger. "You know, we are doing fine," Samantha replied with as much confidence as she could summon. It wasn't easy.

This was no time to be disrespectful.

"Oh, look, Theron's toy soldiers all boxed up. The Guardian Angels are right alongside them, a collector's dream. How special. Now, I assume here isn't where you want to be. Now, what can we do to change this little problem?" he asked.

"See, I told you he could help," Cole said and crossed his arms. "The rock knows his way around this place," he finished.

"Cole, that's not a rock," Dani replied. Cole tilted his head. "What, no it's a rock person," he replied and took a closer look. Then, whatever illusion was there wore off. "You son of a bitch," Cole said, and punched Bob in the face as hard as he could with his right fist.

The shockwave caused everyone to brace themselves. Cole was still standing there, and Bob had stumbled back just one step.

His blue eyes now burning. "Did you just punch me?" Bob asked, voice still calm. "Yes, I'll do it again. You pretended to be a rock. Why would you trick me like that? Not cool," Cole replied. Bob stood up and calmed down.

"Okay, I admit it, but I was a convincing rock, right?" Bob asked. Cole crossed his arms. "Yeah, you were a good rock," he replied.

The others weren't sure what was happening right now. They also wondered why they weren't dust yet.

## 47

"Bob, we're not dead, so you must want to help us. We know what you do. Everyone knows. You make some kind of deal, and then you come for payment at the worst time," Samantha said. She figured if that punch didn't kill them, he had to have a reason. It was best to get to the point.

"Young lady, this is true. All things come with a price, don't they?"

Nobody saw him move, but he was right behind her, hands on her shoulders. They were ice cold to the point of burning. She pulled away from him and turned around. Everyone else kept their distance.

Now was not the time to complain.

"I see your point, but it doesn't make sense.

You're you. Why would you want anything?" she asked. Bob nodded.

"You all feel this way? You all feel entitled to free stuff? Typical humans. All this power, and you think you still deserve more than what you're worth? Everything needs to make sense, everything needs a reason?" His eyes flashed bright blue.

The monster had a good point—sometimes life didn't make sense, and everything had consequences, a price.

Alex stepped forward. "What's the price? What would you want from us?" Bob looked at him.

"Well, that's easy. You'll just need to kill the Delta Squad. The saviors, the ones who convinced you to fight against me and the rest, just for this to happen anyway. I'm sure this wouldn't even be much of an ask. You hate them, right? As a bonus, I'll bring back the rest of the Zodiac team for added firepower. You know, for old times' sake." Bob said with a sinister smile. Even in the dim light, his teeth seemed to glow with an eerie white light.

The group looked at one another. There had to be more to this deal.

"You can break through the barrier to get us home?" Dani asked him.

"I can't get through to that Earth for a little while, but you can. The Logos barrier was made for us cosmic types. You see, you're way too flawed to be captured by this net. It's complicated and unimportant for the issue at hand," Bob replied.

"So, ladies, gents, what do you say? Interested?" he asked and waited for their answer.

"There has to be more to it besides just killing the squad. I mean, sure it's not a big deal, but come on. That's it? This is Bob here, you know. Mister Abyss, supreme supervillain—we can't trust him," Tiffany said.

"Maybe not the words I would have used standing right in front of him," Ariana replied. Bob crossed his arms. "Don't trust me? I've never gone back on my word, woman. Watch yourself," Bob said, standing behind Tiffany now, uncomfortably close.

She felt her body temperature drop. "Sorry," she said, swallowing her pride. It wasn't easy. She wanted to hit him, but at the same time didn't want to die—or worse.

"That's a good girl," he replied and walked away.

"We kill them or we stay here, forever. Even if we get into Hell, it's still Hell, not like a walk in the park, not like an easy path. Not to mention, if Lucifer is back there, it's going to be even worse than it was when we were there. I say we take the deal and worry about it later," Alex said. Really, it was between here, Hell, and going home and killing some people they didn't like anyway. The choice was obvious. If Bob was here, it was clear there was no other way out for them.

"Fine, damn it all, we'll take the deal," Samantha said. The others looked at her. It was clear that there was no other choice, but speaking for them—well, there might be some fallout for that move later. Sam was sure she wouldn't hear the end of it for a while once they got back home.

"We get our friends back, at least," Sam said, trying to find the bright side to all of this.

Bob was about ready to open the path home when a bright green light started to burn through the air beside them. For a second, Bob thought Theron was doing something, but that wasn't possible. He was barred from the world just like him.

This was something else—it was Theron's blade opening the portal. Bob knew something else was going on.

"Well, there is your way home. You better go," Bob said with a slight shrug. "Remember your part of the deal. I'll expect results. Remember, the barrier will weaken eventually, and not even death can save you from me. I'll find you anywhere if you fail," he said with the same calm, trusting voice that he always had.

It was a threat, but it sure didn't sound like one. Bob disappeared before anyone could reply.

At first, they couldn't see the other side as the

bright green light burned through the dark, but it was soon apparent that Bryan was on the other side. The hole was big enough to walk through.

"Bryan, what are you doing here?" Ariana asked over the strange electrical noises coming from the tear.

"Wow, it's so electric and weird," Cole said, trying to grab the random sparks before they disappeared, as if they were fireflies.

"Shut up and get through. Not sure how long I can hold it open," he replied, visibly struggling with the effort it took to keep it open. No one needed to be told twice. They ran through the portal as fast as they could. Alex and Sam were the last two through.

"We're good," Alex said, and Bryan pulled the sword back. They watched as the rift sealed up as if nothing was ever there in just a few seconds.

"We made a deal with Bob. He said he would bring back the fallen Zodiac members to help kill the Delta Squad," Sam said.

Bryan made the blade disappear in a second and took a breath.

"You did what? I can't believe you made a deal with that one. You're an ex-Guardian—you of all people should know better," he said, shaking his head. All of his happiness to see his old friends just disappeared in a heartbeat.

"Why, what's the big deal? We kill the tin cans,

get our payback, and our friends back from the first time we met. I don't see a downside here, Leo," Matt said.

Bryan ran his hands through his hair.

"There are things you don't know. The Delta Squad can't die. I mean, no, they can, but their power is connected to the altar on Blackfire. The altar is how the Logos barrier was formed—it keeps them alive and this planet safe at the same time. Those idiots tapped into the energy, and now each team is healed and tough to kill," he said.

"It's just five of them," Samantha replied.

"No. When Bob makes a deal, he screws you over. If he said kill the Delta Squad, my guess is he meant all of them that remain. You'd be hunting them down for years—you might never find some of them. They like to disappear. Also, if you kill them all, that means the barrier will weaken as a whole. Each member of the squad is like a battery," Bryan said.

"So, oh my god, they're literally saving the whole world all the time and don't even know it?" Alex replied.

"How did you find out?" Tiffany asked.

"Aura sight. If you look at these people with it, you'll practically go blind. It's the same color as the Nexus, same energy," he replied.

"Oh, you can do that?" Ariana asked. "Yes, that's not important right now. What is, is that you made a deal to kill all of them and help make the barrier weaker, forever," Bryan replied.

The Zodiac didn't know what to think. "So, we can still kill them, right?" Cole asked. "No, not unless you want all of reality to get flipped on its head or just erased," he said, then blinked. "No more cheese if you do," Bryan shifted his position on the fly.

"No more cheese. We must not kill them. We can't let them die. We must save the cheese," Cole replied, and Ariana sighed. "Always the smallest things that inspire the strongest people," she said under her breath.

"I want my ship back," Alex said. Bryan shrugged. "I haven't seen the Predator since the big cosmic dust up six months ago," Bryan replied.

"We were in that hellhole for six damn months —it felt so much longer," Brittany replied. The other Angels looked just as pissed as she did.

"The others haven't been alive since the 1800s, and Jason was vaporized by Bob, I think. I don't know if it's going to make a difference in what we have to do. If Bob did bring the others back to life, he never said where they'd be. He never said he'd make them easy to find or bring them to us," Bryan said.

"You raise a good point," Sam said. "They could literally be anywhere on the planet right now and confused in a whole new world," she finished.

Bryan took a deep breath. "Well. I don't know about the Angels here, but I'm getting the band back together. You lot can work with us if you want, or not. We're on the same side—no Zodiac member will attack you while this situation of ours exists. The Syndicate has to be beaten. We need to find a way to break our deal with the Abyss," Bryan said.

Alex looked at the others. "It'd be stupid to fight you—no point. We're allies for now. We really should find my ship—it might be useful," Alex replied.

"Well, now we have a plan. Let's get the hell out of here," Bryan replied.

Sam looked up to the sky. "Does anyone else feel that?" she asked. The other Zodiac members became aware of it too.

"Bob wasn't lying. The others are back. I can feel them," Bryan replied.

"Nope, I don't feel anything," Alex said.

"No, we always know where one another is. Not like, exact location, but general direction. We need to find a place to meet," Ariana replied.

"Great. This should be fun," Dani replied.

"Oh, my friends are all back—this is going to be awesome," Cole said and took to the sky.

Bryan shook his head. "I guess we find a place where no one's looking. Zodiac members, pick an

Angel to take with us. We gotta fly," Bryan said and took off.

"I call dibs on Samantha," Alex said and smiled. She just rolled her eyes. "Do anything I don't like, and I'll drop you," she replied.

He just smiled.

# 48

Lance and Nate were thrown into a special prison made just for them. It was the best thing that ever happened to them.

"Get me another beer, would you," Nate demanded. The female guard standing at attention next to his recliner, with nothing on, walked away without a word.

"We should have just done this. Trying to take over the world is stupid," Lance said. "You said it, man. This is the life," Nate replied.

A few minutes later, the guard with the vacant look on her face walked back with an ice-cold bottle. Nate took it. "Thank you," he said, and the lid of the bottle just popped off on its own, zipped into the trash, and he took a sip.

She stood back at attention, as if she were a statue.

"It's amazing what the power of illusion can do over a couple of months," Lance replied. "Telekinesis doesn't hurt either," Nate replied and flipped the channel. It was the SNN network.

"Oh my god, the news, change it," Lance groaned.

"Look at the train," Nate said and turned it up.

"The criminals known as the Delta Squad have destroyed a train filled with food and medicine heading out to the war ravaged Western Territories. This senseless act of terrorism is just the first of what is expected to be the start of a whole string of devastation, according to experts," she said as the camera attached to a drone hovered over the burning train and the whole wreck.

Lance pushed the mute button.

"The Delta Squad, alive?" Nate asked. "Why didn't they just kill those idiots?" Lance asked the obvious question.

"No idea. Do they know we're still alive? I don't want to give all this up," Nate replied, looking at the guard. He didn't even know her name. "Life's kind of fun here," he said and looked back toward the television.

"I hope not. I mean, if we don't go after them, they shouldn't come after us. They have bigger problems, and I'll bet they're pissed as hell, too," Lance replied.

Nate nodded. "Yeah. Common sense says that. Common sense is a trash fire. Chances are good that the universe will lead them right here for some stupid reason, and then everything is gonna go straight to hell," Nate said.

"I hate it when you're right," Lance replied.

Then the alarm light came on above the television, as if the universe was listening to their conversation.

Nate turned the channel with his mind to switch to the surveillance setting. "Not the squad, they wouldn't pull up to the front gate."

"Windows are tinted, can't tell who it is," Lance replied. "We'll let Alyssa handle it," Lance finished.

"I like her. I hope she doesn't get killed. Training replacements is tiresome," Nate said. The two of them watched the screen as the situation unfolded.

---

Paxton pulled up to the gate. It was weird. Every prison had two guards, and they were always armed. He rolled down his window and looked up. There was a woman there dressed in the uniform, but she was disheveled. Her eyes were glazed over. It didn't even look as if she noticed him at all.

"No visitors," she replied, like a machine. Paxton recognized the look anywhere.

"Damn it, Lance, I know you can hear me in there. Let me in," Paxton replied. The guard didn't react.

After a few seconds, like a machine, she reached over and pushed the button. The gate slid open without a sound. "Thank you, both of you," Paxton said, then pushed the car through the gate. The prison was a ghost town. That wasn't surprising anymore.

He walked to the front door and made his way inside. An empty hall in front of him. No one at the desk to sign in with.

All the security doors were wide open. "Figures," he said and walked down the hall.

There was only one hall leading inside. At the end, there was a large room that was in desperate need of some circulation. Paxton had smelled some stuff in his time, but this had to rank in the top five of terrible things—a college dorm with no off season.

"Christ, turn on the fan," Paxton said as he walked inside.

Lance and Nate shrugged. "Must be a nose blind thing, it happens when you never leave a place," Lance replied.

Paxton noticed the naked guard standing beside Nate. "I see prison's been good to you."

"It has its perks," Nate replied.

"Paxton, long time no see, buddy. What brings you by our place?" Lance asked, he was in a good mood.

"The Squad has escaped. I was wondering if you wanted to get involved. They don't seem to be in the best of moods, and anyone against them will be a target," Paxton said.

"Yeah, we know. I saw what they did to the train after they blew up the building," Nate replied. "I thought they were supposed to be the good guys or something. They murdered all the firefighters at the scene. They didn't do anything," Lance said, and Paxton looked to the side.

"No, well, see. The actual story is the Syndicate sent a silencer to the scene and had them all killed so the public would buy the terrorist story. The Squad let them live," Paxton said.

Lance and Nate stared at him.

"Did you kill all those people, and how do you even know?" Nate asked.

"Would you even care if I did and when was the last time the killed a large group of people with clean headshots?"

"Not really. I didn't know any of them, and never. They're the messiest people on the planet," Nate replied.

"So, what is it you want?" Lance asked. "Well, I built new armor, but I can't get to it. I've been rendered inactive by the Syndicate. I want to make a difference, you know? All I need is your help to get the armor. After that, you can go your own way," he said.

They looked at one another. "What's the goal? For or against the Syndicate?" Nate asked. "Against, of course. I do want a rematch with that Squad. I think my new armor is up to the task. I copied the new Hell Razor armor and added my own special touches to it. It's finished, but I just need to get it."

"Sure, why not. It's boring here anyway. The Syndicate put us here knowing full well we'd take the place over. Why would we want to leave? Well, I guess they didn't count on some action," Lance said.

"Yes, but you two need to take a shower and get some fresh clothes. My car's out front. I'll wait for you outside," Paxton replied.

"Sure, whatever," Nate said, and the three of them separated.

Twenty minutes later, they walked out of the place wearing guard uniforms. They looked like actual soldiers again, and smelled like people, too. Paxton waited for them to get in. Lance in the front, Nate in the back.

"What are you going to do with the fembots?" Paxton asked. "Don't worry, without us around, they'll snap out of their trances in a couple hours wondering what happened. It'll be fine, let's go," Lance replied.

"Alright, sounds good to me," he replied, turned the car around, and drove away from the prison.

Fifteen minutes into the drive, Nate and Lance got a taste of reality. The symbol of the Syndicate was on every flagpole. Posters were plastered on walls.

"You think they overdid it with the propaganda thing?" Nate asked.

"Yeah, you know how super evil organizations get when they win. They just spray their material over everything," Paxton replied.

"A hundred ways you could have said that, and you picked the grossest one possible?" Lance asked.

"Yep."

Nate looked at all the flags, posters, and other things as they drove down the road. With a thought, all the material tore and fell to the ground.

"It's a start," Paxton said.

"Weird, this is what we were fighting for back in the day. Feels weird to be against it now," Lance said. "Last time, we were included. This time, we were prisoners. It doesn't feel that weird to me," Nate replied.

"Good point," Lance said.

# 49

It was early in the morning when there was a knock on the door. Brian and the people of the town were still relaxed from the impressive victory. No one heard it at first inside the community center. Then, it happened again, this time the whole side of the wall vibrated.

Everyone went quiet.

"What's that?" a child said. Brian didn't see who it was.

"It could be the Army. I heard on the radio they were fighting near here. I'll go look," a brave teenager said. He looked like he could have been captain of the football team once upon a time. Before anyone could stop him, he ran to the door. Brian had a terrible feeling about this and stood up.

"Hello there. Is there a Brian here?"

The voice came through the door, and Brian's blood froze. He knew this voice, and it meant everyone here was going to die.

"I'm here. Leave these people be. Your issue is with me," Brian said. He'd hardly had a chance to relax, and this happened. It seemed it was destiny, or maybe it was the cruel design of a plot he couldn't escape.

Either way, it was obvious to him that resting was out of the question.

"Ah, noble Brian, I'll be waiting out here, don't make me wait long, boy."

With that, the shadow retreated from the door. The teenager turned around. "That sure as hell ain't the Army," he said.

Brian took charge and stood up.

"You people, thanks for everything. You need to get the hell out now. I'll hold him off as long as I can. Just leave," Brian said.

"Wait, what's going on?" the mayor asked.

"Death's come to visit, that's the long and short of it. Get your people out the back. Take nothing, waste no time, hide, don't hide here," he replied. Brian moved toward the door and walked outside.

Blue was there in the street, standing like a statue with the sunlight behind him.

"So, someone let you out of the ice hole, congratulations. You could have gone anywhere on earth, and you walked five thousand miles right to my door," Brian said and stepped onto the street.

"I would walk five thousand more if it meant I got to kill you," Blue replied and stretched his fingers.

"Really, you need to get new hobbies. This is getting old," Brian said and wanted to laugh, but he knew that this excuse for a human would never change.

"Come at me if you're not scared," Blue said and rested his hands on his guns at his side. They'd be useless in this fight, but that's not why he did it.

"Scared? Are you alright, Blue? Usually, you'd have this whole town leveled trying to get to me. You would have killed the kid at the door in a second. All that time in the ice must have cooled you off," Brian replied.

Blue just shrugged.

This was nerve wracking, strange, and alien. A passive Blue? Brian decided if he was going to do this, he'd do it right. The minute he started his advance, Blue pulled out a strange-looking switch from his pocket, opened the cover, and pressed the button.

"Someone left their explosives laying around. Wouldn't want to waste them, you know how it is, right?" Blue said.

A second after he said it, the building he just came from went up in flames as the force of the explosion knocked him forward. Brian looked back in horror.

"You just killed all those people." Brian wasn't sure, but he hoped they got out.

"Not me, you did. You came here and killed them all because you should always know I'll follow you until you're dead. I just wanted you to have some real fire. Now come at me like you mean it. We won't be doing this again," Blue replied.

Brian had all the motivation he needed to do everything he could to make that come true.

Brian grabbed a burning chunk of cement and threw it at Blue as hard as he could. Blue caught it and only had time to look up for a second to see a fist coming at his head. Brian had closed the distance with one jump and connected with power enough to stagger the monster back three steps on impact.

While the right fist did its work, the left fist slammed into Blue's stomach and sent him into the air, and to the ground on his back. Despite all this power hitting Blue was still like hitting solid steel.

"Well. I see you have some fight in you, good." Blue stood up.

Brian was not afraid of this monster, but he knew full well there was little he could do to stop him. The one who managed to do it and seemed to cause any lasting damage was Josh, but he wasn't here.

Brian stood against something no one has ever defeated in a fair fight. He had no idea what he was going to do besides be murdered.

Brian hoped he'd think of something before Blue turned his face into slime.

Brian lunged forward again, but this time Blue stood his ground. He grabbed Brian's wrists, spun around, and slammed him into the street, and through it, sending up a cloud of dust and blood. "Oh, did I hurt you? I'm sorry. I meant to kill you. I'll keep trying until I get it right," Blue said, holding those broken wrists.

Brian grit his teeth and rammed his head into Blue's chest, causing him to let go. Then he grabbed Blue's guns and pulled them back as his broken bones healed.

"Heh, you plan to shoot me with them? They won't do any good. You better give them back before—" Brian crushed them in his hands as if they were tin foil, then threw them to the sides.

"See, now we can have a fair fight," Brian said and knew what he did. If there was anything Blue cared for in this world, it was his weapons—the ones that were just destroyed. Blue's eyes burned with red flames.

"Oh, I figured you'd be past your security blanket by now, big guy."

He had no idea why he did or said these things,

but he guessed that if he had to die, it might as well be as fast as possible.

Blue's burning red eyes flared, and the beast charged. It was faster than Brian could react. The giant left fist hit him in the chest, and he went flying head over heels down the road, coming to a stop with the help of a parked truck that crumpled on contact. He wiped the blood from his mouth. It wasn't going to be long now.

The beast landed by the car, and the windows in houses around them shattered to pieces. "You wrecked my guns, the only thing I had left, and you had the nerve," Blue said.

Brian spit in his face. "You hit like a wet noodle." Without hesitation, Brian used the hulk of steel he was wrapped around as a bat, spun around, and knocked Blue through a house. He spun again to toss the truck his way, demolishing the house in one go. Then he picked up a long, sharp piece of steel and hid it behind his back.

Still bleeding from the mouth, he knew running wasn't an option here. He had to stand his ground. The beast rose from the wreckage and fire. "That's right, I'm not running. Don't wanna die tired. Let's get this over with," Brian said to him.

Blue waded out of the wreck as if it were nothing more than water, then broke into a run. This time, Brian was ready. The first punch came, and he twisted to the left to dodge it. Then that sharp piece of steel spun and hit Blue in the left eye.

It was the one place on him that could be hurt that Brian knew. Blue stumbled back and started screaming. "What is it with you people and eyes?" Blue screamed and pulled it out. Flames shot out instead of blood.

"We do what we can, noodle," Brian replied, lunged, and hit him in the face hard enough where it should have taken Blue off his feet, but he didn't fall.

He had no idea what he was doing here. Every time he hit Blue, something inside of him broke on impact. Brian was doing his best to fight the pain.

Blue grabbed Brian by the head with his left hand and lifted him off the ground. "Alright, I'm bored now," he said. With that, he spun him into the road below. His body did not stop at the surface. Instead, he was buried as the ground gave way.

It'd be as good a gravesite as anywhere. Brian was ready to die. Then a curious sound made its way through the dark.

Gunfire.

Death would have to wait a minute. He needed to see what was going on.

"What, who's there?"

He had to know, so he pushed off the debris and

dug himself out of the hole enough to see. He couldn't believe what he was seeing.

The people of the town had escaped the explosion, armed themselves, and came back. Stupid move on their part, but now he had a new problem.

"People, I told you to run," he yelled, but no one heard him. The bullets just crumbled against Blue's invincible skin.

"You saved us from the Syndicate. We couldn't just leave you here against this alone!" the priest yelled, and from the look in Blue's eyes, he knew what was coming next. This was what he had to stop. Now he had a new reason to fight.

It was easier to fight for the living than it was to avenge the dead most of the time, at least for him. "Thanks for the breather, but get out, now. He will kill all of you. Run!" Brian said as he tackled the monster just as he started to move for the defenseless people, bringing him to the ground and putting his knee into his throat.

"You won't have them, you won't." A new vigor burned through him, and Blue was shocked because he expected this, braced for it, and was taken down anyway.

"How did you do that?" Blue asked, but Brian let his fists do the talking, and the answer was imprinted on his face.

"Run," Brian yelled again, then gave Blue his answer.

Left and right fists to the face over and over again. Each punch caused Brian more pain than it did Blue, but he was not going to stop. Blue made him stop by grabbing his arm and tossing him to the side with ease.

Brian slid to a stop and got up again just as fast. He intended to fight this thing as long as it took to win or die, but this was when the wind picked up from nowhere.

Both of them noticed it and knew this wasn't natural at all. "What did you do this time?" Brian screamed over the strong winds.

"Don't know. Thought it was you."

The air just a few feet from them began to crack open, and this was where the wind was going.

"A hole in the air," Brian pointed out the obvious. The sky was cracking like glass from a window at a slow pace.

Green light was burning through the portal, and the whole thing caved inward. From the black nothing, Emily appeared. Right behind her came two massive figures with what looked like armor, but they couldn't tell what it was.

One had a flaming sword in her hand, and some kind of cannon in the other. She was six feet tall but showed nothing of what she might have looked like. Just the general outline was that of a female in dark green armor with bright yellow eyes.

The other was a man, shorter than her but not

by much. He was wearing what looked to be normal street clothes, but around his neck hung a faded symbol of some unknown god. It wasn't pleasant to look at for very long.

"Oh crap, how come it's her again?" Brian knew better than to fight this one and took advantage of the confusion to run away. Sure, it wasn't the best move to make, but it was the smartest one. No way would he deal with that again. Blue didn't notice Brian running away.

"You three. You're in the middle of my battle. I don't appreciate it. So why don't you--" Emily glanced at this one and knew she didn't like him. She smiled and raised her arm in his direction. The portal moved from its place and hovered over his head in a flash. He didn't get a chance to say anything as it moved to the ground and swallowed him. Then the portal disappeared.

"Now, welcome to the past. Just as I promised, you'll get to face the greatest, uh, heroes, I guess, who ever lived. Follow me," she said and took to the sky. The other two said nothing, but they followed.

"The hell, enemies from the future now? Somehow this makes perfect sense. Better find a phone," Brian said as he watched the three of them take off to parts unknown. He was also a little thankful she took care of Blue.

He couldn't help but wonder where Blue ended up, or when.

# 50

"Look," Cody said as they hovered high in the air. This place wasn't on Heath's hit list.

"They turned a baseball field into a prison camp. I'm sure there are lots of places like this everywhere," Josh replied. Cody clenched his fist. "Woah, buddy, take a look around. If we go after places like this, we have to stay in the fight," Wyatt said.

"Isn't this the fight?" Cody asked, and the others didn't have an answer. "Well, they didn't seem too interested in fighting back. Why should we help them?" Blake asked, and Cody looked. He had words but realized Blake had a point.

"Just because the people gave up doesn't mean we have to. Who knows, maybe they are all resistance fighters waiting for a little encouragement,"

Cody replied, not what he wanted to say, but now wasn't the time.

"Screw it. Let's go give the power back to the people," Dustin replied. "Fine, what the hell, we're all a little bit rusty anyway, I imagine," Cody said.

"I don't know about you, but I flipped a train. I think I'm good," Josh replied.

"You could have just wrecked the rails," Wyatt replied. "Shut up."

Wyatt laughed a little.

"Are you done? If we kill all the prisoners, this is a pointless mission. This is what we're gonna do. Dustin and Josh, take out the walls. Blake, Wyatt, kill everyone in those towers. I'm going after the commanders. Maybe we can get some information. We attack at the same time, and they won't know what hit them," Cody said.

"Oh, now we have a plan. All hell literally breaks loose and its pure chaos. Simple prison camp, then you have a plan?" Wyatt asked.

"I always have a plan," Cody replied, "just, sometimes it's not that great," he finished.

"Yeah, we noticed," Wyatt replied. "Alright, let's do this," Dustin put himself in the conversation.

With everyone having a mission, they separated.

Josh and Dustin flew side by side. "So, what wall do you want?" Dustin asked. Josh looked at them. "That one. The big one in the back."

"Do you plan on just flying through it or what?"

Dustin asked. "Did you always ask this many questions before?"

"No." Dustin looked at the walls. The others around the field looked as if they were basic steel, put up in a hurry. Good enough for people, but not something you'd want to trust. "I'll get the one on the right. That should be enough. Hope everything goes well," Dustin said.

"Hope will drive you insane," Josh replied and began his attack, diving down. Dustin banked to the right and descended down toward his target.

Josh had no idea how thick that wall he was flying toward was. Since he flipped a train, he was sure that he didn't need to worry. There was always a chance it was more than he could handle.

He crossed his arms and turned himself into a projectile. Ramping up his speed, he made impact with the big green wall. Josh tore through the concrete and steel as if it were paper. Then out the other side, he landed on his feet, sliding to a stop. He turned around to see the debris still falling and the dust still clearing.

There was a big, gaping hole in the green wall. However, with all the wreckage, it didn't look like anyone was getting out this way after all.

"Well, that was dumb," he said to himself and started moving back into the camp.

Dustin moved to his target, lifted his wrists, and used his cutting lasers to slice the steel walls into evenly sized pieces. Then, the sheet metal collapsed into the dirt. The people were watching Dustin work.

"What are you waiting for, run, maybe?" Dustin shouted at the people. Yet, they didn't leave. They looked terrified of something, but Dustin knew it wasn't him.

"Cody, when you find that commander, don't kill him right away. Something's up with the people here," Dustin said into the intercom.

"Got it," Cody replied.

"Six towers, three a piece," Blake said.

"Yeah, but let's be honest here—you could take them all out from here. Josh just turned himself into a battering ram and accomplished nothing. Everyone's distracted. Just get it done," Wyatt replied.

"Not being a glory hound, you must be sick," Blake replied.

"No, just, I don't know. Get it done," Wyatt said. Blake took aim and swept the scope of his rifle over the towers, marking all the people in them, two each, all eyes on the sudden destruction.

"You got the next one," Blake said once everyone was marked, then moved back to the beginning. "Taking out the trash, one bullet at a time." Blake started to shoot. His rifle made no sound, but one by one the tower guards were losing their heads and slumping down.

Wyatt was right about the tower guards being

easy prey. However, after the alarms activated, no one counted on the armored soldiers that came out of the lower doors. There were only four of them.

"Looks like I'll have to work after all," Wyatt said, drew his sword, and shot down to meet the soldiers. The closer he got, the more the armor looked just like theirs did in the early days. "Of course, they did that," he said to himself.

Wyatt landed in front of the four of them, and they pointed their weapons at him. "Now look. I know you have all that fancy armor and stuff, but you have no idea what's about to happen here. You can either walk away, or you can die. The Syndicate doesn't care about you, neither do I," Wyatt said. He had to give them a chance.

"Put your weapon down and put your hands up," the soldier said and took a step forward.

"Goddamned robots," Wyatt said, tightening his grip on his blade. He took a breath and blasted ahead. They had their chance.

This new armor moved so fast the four of them looked like statues. He put the edge of his blade through the neck of the first one. It cut clean through. He ran forward and did the same thing with the man behind him in the opposite direction.

He spun around, behind the other two now. He impaled the blade through the back of the armor all the way up to the hilt and used the momentum to push the rest of the blade into the last soldier.

Wyatt ripped his blade out and slowed down. The heads of the two beside him fell to the ground. Their bodies followed.

The other two collapsed on one another. Blood pooled around his feet as Wyatt's sword absorbed the blood into the metal.

"You should have walked," Wyatt said, then looked at the people staring at him, still confused at what just happened. "I move fast, get over it," Wyatt said to the crowd. They started to cheer as he walked away.

Cody tore in, kicking the door to the command center. These wardens were how he expected them to be—out of uniform and terrified. "Boys, take me to your leader," he said. Someone got a shot off, the bullet deflecting into the wall.

"No, I said take me to your leader, not shoot me. Learn to listen, will you?" Cody asked.

"I'm the warden. You're going to take your team out of here," the man said. Cody crossed his arms.

"Let me guess. You have the switch that'll kill all the prisoners, and if you don't get what you want, you'll be the inhuman monster you dream about and kill them all," Cody replied.

"Yes, I mean, yeah, you need to leave," he replied.

"Something you should know about me. I don't like terrorists," Cody said and walked towards the warden.

"Stop. I'll kill them all, I swear," he said as Cody grabbed him by the shirt collar and pulled him close.

"Go ahead," he said and pulled him back out of the room. "If any of you go anywhere, my friends will kill you. They might just kill you anyway. Best of luck—your boss and I are going for a ride," Cody said. Once they were back outside, the two of them took off.

The commander was high in the sky, holding the warden like a kid with outstretched arms.

"I suppose you know that Mark guy, right? Care to tell me where he might be? I need to talk with him," Cody said. The warden was in full panic mode.

"Hey, buddy, look at me now. Come on. Think—where do you get your orders from? Where is Mark at these days? Someone as low as you on the food chain should know something," Cody said.

"White House. Washington, D.C. Everyone knows that's where he is most of the time."

Cody couldn't believe this. They expected him to believe this story.

"White House, like he'd do that again. One more time. Where in the hell is he? I need to speak with him."

He didn't know anything more. Cody figured that he would have talked if he did. Then he felt a chill go down his spine.

"Ah, soldier man still likes to ask all the questions. All of this reminds me of the old days when you used to show up like it was scripted. Believe it or not, I miss those days," Jake said.

The other man was happy to hear this voice. Cody held out his hand. "Give me the kill switch," Cody said. The warden reached around in his pocket, pulled out a black box, and put it in Cody's hand. "Thanks," he said and turned around to face Jake.

"Old habits die hard. You want your man back?" Cody asked. Jake shrugged.

Cody tossed the warden into the blue void without hesitation. "I have the kill switch. There might be others. Interrogate and kill the staff. 188 showed up, we're going to chat," Cody said into the intercom.

"Done talking to your people yet?"

"Yeah. What do you want?" Cody asked him. Jake just smiled.

"We won. Someone let you out of your cage, don't care who did it. Would you mind taking that armor off before I have to tear it off of you?" Jake asked. His golden eyes flared, and the same color of energy flowed around his clothes as if they were liquid flames.

Cody was always a little impressed at the sheer power Jake had, but he was ready.

"Sorry, wasn't paying attention to your speech.

Where's your boss at?" Cody asked and crossed his arms.

"Oh, speaking of old days, remember when you used to be the boss? Those were some good times. You, calling all the shots, like a boss should. Now you're just, well, whatever you are. All of you and your group have one thing in common. We beat you—all of you. Even killed some of you. Too bad no one stays dead anymore," Cody added.

Jake clenched his fists. There was so much he wanted to say. Anger was rising. Head games, that's all it was. Bait.

"What's the matter, electric boy? Got nothing to say, or what's the deal? Just tell me where Mark is, and we can go our own ways," Cody said.

"Mark, well, you should know there is a new boss. The Syndicate, as you can see, controls everything. Mark is not in control anymore. So, you're going to have to drop the grudge and--"

Jake never saw it coming. Cody's hand was around his neck in an instant.

"Where. Is. He." The commander was face to face with 188 now.

---

"He must have something to prove," Dustin said. All eyes were turned toward the sky. Jake and Cody were having their conversation.

Wyatt stabbed the last officer in the neck.

"It's Cody. He always has something to prove. Our mission was fun while it lasted. Jake's gonna kill us all. We don't have a dimension cannon thing this time," Wyatt replied and pushed the body into the dirt.

"Yeah, but what's left? He saved everything. He always needs to do things on his own, isn't that right?" Dustin asked.

Blake wondered what was going to happen next.

"You two talk too much. Shut up," Josh said. He hated it when they talked like this.

"Well, train gang here wants us to shut up, better do it," Wyatt said, and Josh looked at him. "What? I thought it was funny."

"Maybe a little," Josh replied, then looked back to the sky.

"When do we start to help him?" Blake asked.

"When we need to," Wyatt replied. "In the meantime, we get these people out of here," he finished.

## 51

Jake was shocked at the speed but quick to recover. He knew this armor was special. More intense than the old stuff if the rumors were true.

"Oh, so you can move fast if you need to. Impressive. Bet you're still worthless underneath that suit of yours. Like all the others. Without your armor, you're weak. You'll always be weak. You and your whole team are obsolete. You were the minute you got the job," Jake said.

"Well, this obsolete guy is about ready to break your neck."

The free hand, with no warning, struck Jake in the side of the face, sending him back through the air with trails of energy behind him like a falling star. The sound was loud enough to be heard on the ground.

Cody's armor was a work of art. Now that Jake had some distance, he could see it. It was never meant to show emotions—not anger, sadness, or pain. It was meant to show only one thing: power. The dark midnight blue color of the armor mixed well with the black pieces.

It was ice cold. Jake looked at the thing and felt bad he had to wreck it. He knew Cody would never stop.

He did his best to commit the suit to memory since this was the last time he was ever going to see it.

There were no real eyes here like the last one, just black spaces that seemed to go on forever. The dark midnight blue color of the armor absorbed the light around it, or maybe it was just an illusion. Jake noticed another detail on Cody's hands began to change shape.

"Right, nano armor. Almost forgot," Jake said.

The plasma cannon in his hand turned into something bigger. He didn't know how to describe it, then the other hand did the same.

The beams were brighter than the sun, the noise was the sound of rushing electricity. The dual beams slammed into his body and threw him into the ground.

Cody watched Jake hit the ground. He must have run into something because there was an explosion. He made sure to aim away from the prison camp, hoping the people didn't run in that direction.

"I want answers."

Cody's weapons reformed into his hands, then he shot out of the sky and landed near the crater. Jake was already standing. All of his visible skin had been seared off, his hair was gone, and his left arm was broken, bent backward. Just those golden eyes remained.

Cody ignored all of this, knowing he would be fine in just a couple of minutes.

"Tell me what I need to know."

"Tell you? Why? I like watching you squirm. I like watching you suffer. New armor or not, I know it's killing you inside. The idea that you're going to fail again is priceless," Jake replied as his broken arm snapped back together.

Cody hated Jake. He was sure the feeling was mutual, but his armor started to respond to the emotion.

Those black eyes began to glow electric red just after the last word was spoken to him. He began to walk forward. Jake's golden energy flowed through his hands, and those old beams flew in the Commander's direction. Cody twisted to the side to avoid both of them.

They missed and slammed into the ground behind him, causing dual explosions. "Not possible that I missed at this range."

He was doing an excellent job of hiding it, but Jake was terrified. Something about those terrible red eyes was digging into whatever he had left of a soul, and it threw off his aim. "Answers."

It was all Cody said in the same, cold voice.

He wouldn't miss a second time. He rubbed his hands together and combined them into one golden blast. The golden fire was concentrated into Cody's chest, and the force hit with such intensity that it pushed him back through the burning earth. He refused to fall and tried to hold the energy back with his hands.

He didn't care. His armor was giving him readings, the power was still a threat and he was being pushed to the limits.

Jake was sure nobody could stand against such an attack. Not this close, not this much energy. Jake thought about running, but he hated the commander. This was his chance to get the job done. He started to walk forward.

The heat burned through the armor, but the protection held. Cody didn't know what this new stuff was made from, but it was coming in useful now.

Jake put his hands down, smoke flowing from each of them now.

"Just die, you overgrown Smurf, you can't win."

The earth around Cody was black, ash, and everything around him was melted. "You did not just call me a Smurf, did you."

The voice was angry, different than before.

"No, impossible. Not even you could have--" Cody cut his air supply off with one quick hand around the neck after closing the distance between them.

"Spare me the impossible speech and tell me what I want to know. I know you can't die, but that just means a little more fun for me," Cody held him in place.

"Tell you? All I know is that you'll never find anyone. You'll search for them forever. Theron brought them back, but they are all going to die again. Nothing you can do about it." Jake was scared for the first time in years, but it was the idea that the commander would be forced to fail again. He forced a smile.

"Squad, we have someone who wants to say hello," Cody said.

"See. It'll be like a reunion or something. I am sure they'll just love to see you again," Cody said and tossed him to the side. Jake hit the ground and rolled. "How the hell did you get so strong?" Jake asked.

"I fought the impossible, and I won," Cody replied. He had no idea how he managed any of this, but Jake didn't need to know that.

While he had no real taste for torture, the others didn't mind it much.

"They'll be here soon, Jake. Telling you right now, immortality and an angry Flesh Tearer don't mix. We have nowhere to go until you, you know, let us know where to go. All you need to do is point in a direction," Cody said.

The visions of blood and pain filled Jake's mind. It had the potential to make him wish he could die again.

"Viper, they're on the Viper. I don't know where it is. They don't tell me anything. I was looking for Emily when they told me where you were, God damn." Jake broke, he couldn't bear the thought of pain like that. Cody smiled under his helmet.

"Thanks, that's a step in the right direction," Cody said. "Commander to Delta Squad, we're going for the Viper. Let's find it."

Jake was confused.

"You, you never told them to come here, did you?" Cody almost laughed.

"Of course not. I am the commander for a reason. I just played you, but a piece of advice. Go into hiding, and never show your face again. But remember, you owe me," Cody said with hate in his voice.

He hated him and all of his enemies, but he got what he wanted. Now he was going to do what he said he was going to do.

"If you forget that I spared you today, I'll never stop until I find a way to kill you. Never," Cody said, and with that, he flew off to meet up with the others.

## 52

Adam woke up with a start, some terrible dream he was having, but then the pain of the hangover—oh, that was the worst part. The sun was streaming through the windows, and he got up, heading for the nearest source of water he could find.

"Gotta stop drinking so much before bed, yeah, sure."

He stumbled over to the sink and filled up a glass, took a drink. It was good, cold. He didn't feel much better yet, but it was a start.

He'd have to take it easy for a while. He looked at the desk behind him. The book was out again. He didn't even want to know the things he was reading about last night. He stumbled back to the desk chair and collapsed in it, closing the book.

It was early in the morning, well it had to be, he supposed. The other two were still sleeping. The mind charms were still working as intended. Small blessings.

He didn't want to kill them both, but here was as good a place as any. The ritual to break the nexus barrier around the planet needed the blood of two sacrifices, willing or not, it didn't matter.

There were rules to this kind of thing. He had trained in the black arts for most of his life. There was a problem with this ritual, not because it was dangerous but because of the stars. They troubled him.

He was afraid that if he used their blood, the ensuing result of the altered nexus might break the cosmic lock or help speed up the breaking of it. It was a tough choice to make.

If he died before keeping his end of the deal, his eternity was forfeit. He'd rather go to hell than face a pissed off Bob any day.

"Hey there, you're up early."

He cringed at the voice a little as Lindsey said it. "Yep. The sun did it. Sleep good?" he asked her, but his voice never changed.

"Well, no. Not really. Kept having weird dreams. I think because of all that stuff you said the other day," she replied and sat up, rubbing the sleep out of her eyes.

"I don't know why you stuck with me. You

make this so much easier," he said and turned around.

"Make what easier?" she asked, looking at him.

"There is a ritual I need to do. The barrier around this world keeps the true masters out. We can't have that. I can break it, but I need, well, I need blood." Then he tapped his fingers on the cover of the book. There was silence for a few seconds.

"Blood? I'm off limits. So is Haley. Did you not see those things? They were all horrible. We don't need any of their kind on this planet. We need, well, what we need is someone to kick the crap out of the Syndicate so we can live without being afraid of the nightmares we have now. No more hiding," Lindsey said and crossed her arms about the whole thing.

Adam sighed.

"No, Bob is right, this world needs to end. It's broken, no fix left to it, and the time is here. All of the signs have pointed to it, all things that were foretold have come to pass. I just need to get things back on track. I owe it to the Cosmic Ones," Adam replied, believing every word of this.

"Right, end of the world sounds like a great time and all, but I'm gonna have to go ahead and say no on this one," she replied to him.

"Sorry. You don't get a choice, and today is going to be the day I fix everything." Lindsey just sighed as the necromancer revealed a very long kitchen knife. There didn't seem to be anything special about it.

She didn't care where he got it. Before Adam even had a chance to take two steps, he found that there was a foot slamming into the top of his forehead. He had a second to realize this before he was knocked out, sent end over end across the table and into the wall.

"No choice, right."

Haley was woken up by the noise and rushed out of bed to the source, wearing nothing. "What just happened!" Alert and ready to kill anyone who would be responsible for it.

"Oh, don't worry about it. Adam just had a relapse into his ritual thing again."

"Oh, well, if that's all, I'm going back to sleep," Haley said and turned around. "Looking good, H," Lindsey said. "Bite me," she replied, disappearing through the door.

"Maybe someday. Now I need to drag you back to your stupid chair," she said with a sigh.

Adam had two distinct sides to his personality. One was the necromancer who wanted to kill them for some ritual, the other was a decent guy who knew all about black magic and had a plan to make the Syndicate pay for everything they did.

It was a struggle living with the two halves, but

they managed to do it. She tossed the knife into the sink.

"Sorry about the kick to the head, but I had to act fast. I didn't think it through." She looked out the window. Just to the side of the sun high in the sky was something there. Something metal and black. She knew it was a Syndicate recon drone.

"Damn it, and I was beginning to like this place too."

## 53

Jason found himself in a black place. The last thing he remembered was attacking Bob, searing pain, and then nothing. No heaven or hell, just nothing but the dark. It felt like an instant.

But this darkness had no end. No beginning, it just was. It only felt like a few seconds when the blinding light took him.

Finally, heaven. It was the only thought that entered his mind, even if he knew he didn't deserve such a place. The light disappeared, and at once he sucked in a breath of stale, hot air.

"What?" he asked as the internal lights of the Chaos armor turned on.

"Damn it, somebody must have made a deal. I hate being on a leash," he said as his system booted up to full power, venting the heat. Jason took a look around and the only thing around was blue sky, sand, and the sun.

Jason took to the air and needed information, tuning into the signals.

"The terrorists known as the Delta Squad remain at large—" he shut the radio off.

"Terrorists. Something went sideways while I was gone," he said, aimed himself to the east, and took off flying in that direction to see what he could find.

He woke up. The smell of the ocean was powerful, salt filled air, and maybe some seaweed to go with it. The sun beat down, but it wasn't too hot. "The hell happened," he said, pushing himself out of the sand. Beside him lay his two shotguns. Despite laying in the sand, they were still clean.

Ben struggled to remember. He died on the mountain. Betrayed, maybe. Everything was a blur. A wave from the sea pushed him farther onto the shore. The past wasn't important now. Right now, he knew two things.

One, he was alive. Two, he was pissed. Ben stood up, getting his weapons holstered again. "Gotta find the others," he said and concentrated. He didn't know where he was, but the Zodiac could always get a general sense of where the others were, a direction to go.

Ben looked towards the west, took a breath, and took off into the sky.

Claire opened her eyes, the sun blinding her. The first thing she did was roll to the side to get her eyes out of the light. She looked at her hands. Her body was the same as before. She couldn't remember quite how it went down. Something done with her hands. A monster killed her. The air smelled strange. There was smoke or something like it in the air.

She stood up and found she was high in the air, on top of some kind of tower. "What is going on here?" she asked and walked to the edge of the roof. All she could see before her was buildings, a city unlike anything she'd ever seen before.

"Where am I?" Her brain was jumbled. It was then she realized she had nothing on. If anyone were here to see her right now, they'd die. With a thought, she formed an outfit over her body, a simple green dress.

Her golden sais came with it. They hung on a belt, one on each side. "I almost forgot about you two," she said, running her fingers over the grips. Nothing else made sense, but she could feel the others, a strange pull to the west. "I'll find you." With that, she took off into the sky.

Martin woke up in the middle of a high school football field. It was empty, but there were voices in the distance. It was those voices that alerted him he was alive. The man sat up and formed his clothes as he did.

Black shirt, black pants, and a black hat. There was no time to gather his surroundings, no, he was exposed out here in the open. He got up and ran for cover as fast as he could. There was no telling what was going on.

Men in black uniforms were around the building. Soldiers with weapons. Didn't know what kind of weapons they were, but soldiers never changed. Hostile or not, impossible to tell. Soldiers were always trained to shoot first.

However, he felt as if he needed to take a chance. With a deep breath, he moved forward into the light.

"Hail," he said, the first thing that came to mind, and the men reacted, weapons drawn.

"Put your hands up and get down on the ground now," one yelled. "Wait, I just want to know what's going on. I'm lost," he said, telling the truth.

"Get down on the ground now," the Syndicate soldier repeated himself. Martin didn't take orders from nobodies well.

"I don't think you know who I am, son. Listen to me. I think you need to take me to your leader, we need to talk, and—" the soldier opened fire. Martin was hit in the chest. The bullet hit like a hammer and knocked him to the ground.

"Damn it, call a meat wagon," the other soldier said. He hadn't expected to be shot, most people didn't have it in them. Not a mistake he'd make again. Martin levitated to his feet.

"Boy, I don't know what the hell you were thinking, but you'll have plenty of time to regret your mistake in hell."

The soldiers were shocked. "We got a code fifteen," one said into a strange-looking black box, some kind of communicator Martin figured, but he didn't care.

He rushed forward faster than the men could react. His right palm hit the first man in the face so hard his skull caved in. Then he spun around, with his other hand, the left knife edge of his hand, he tore the head off the other.

"You boys lack balance," he said as they both fell to the ground. "Oh well, if you ever make your way back, I'm sure you'll get it right next time."

Then he felt it. The others were somewhere in the world too, to the north. "I'm on my way." Martin looked at the bodies again, then flew towards the north before anyone else could show up.

The first breath he took was full of dust. He coughed and sat up with a start. "Where the hell am I?" he asked, reaching to the side where his long spear lay beside him. It sparkled in the hot sun. "Diamond, right," he said, trying to remember how he got here or what happened in the past.

"Delta Squad, fight, did I die?" he asked out

loud. There was no reason to be here, and this wasn't hell, breathing, feeling, alive.

Brad stood up, his spear came to his hand on instinct. He leaned on it, still feeling dizzy after the rude awakening. The land was so flat here. "Kansas, maybe?" he asked. With a thought, he formed clothes. Red shirt, blue jeans, white hat.

A grasshopper jumped. He moved the tip of his spear an inch to the left and watched as the bug was torn in half as it jumped into it. "Still got it," he replied, then felt bad for the bug.

"Sorry," he said and felt the others. "You're still alive out there. I hope you know more than I do," Brad said and flew into the sky.

Derek woke up in a forest. The trees were redwood, towering high, blocking out the sun.

"What?" he asked.

Last thing he remembered was dying at the hands of a monster. Now he was somewhere else. "California, giant trees. Bigfoot. Lurkers. Danger," he went through the checklist in his brain and sat up, his clothes forming around him at the same time.

Simple brown shirt, black pants, boots.

"Not safe here," he said, already feeling watched from every angle. "Go away. You don't get to take me, not a chance."

In a panic, feeling under attack from every direction, he shot up into the air and moved above the tree line. He didn't feel safe yet, but it was better. "To me," he said, and his halberd appeared in his hand. It looked nice but nothing compared to when it was on fire.

He considered burning the whole thing down, but there was no time for that. Derek scanned the horizon and felt the other members of the team.

"Thank Theron you're still out there," he said and looked down. Could have sworn he saw shining silver dollar eyes looking at him through the trees.

"Not today, clown," he said and took off to the east.

## 54

Bryan found an abandoned parking lot, some mall outside of some town, no one knew where they were, and signaled this was the place.

"See, I was good," Alex said. Sam dropped him on the cement. "Not that good," Alex landed, laughing the whole time. "What a rush," he said.

"I say we never travel like that again," Brittany said as Ariana let her down. "You can fly Ariana Air anytime, B," she replied. Brittany rolled her eyes.

Matt let Dani down. "We never speak of this again," she said. He nodded. "Agreed."

"Hard to imagine we were just trying to kill one another months ago," Hale said as Tiffany set her down.

"Things change fast. We could be enemies again

in a month, so don't get used to this," Tiffany replied. "Right," Hale said.

"My lady," Bryan said as he set Melissa down as gently as he could. "I don't break, you know, but thanks," she replied, and he just smiled. "Don't worry, I won't tell anyone," he said. "Better not," she replied.

"They'll be here soon," Bryan said as the others spread out.

"The sun is going down, not a soul in sight. It should be fine, right?" Samantha asked. No one dared answer. The universe seemed to be looking for reasons to ruin everyone's day. It was best not to tempt it any more than they had to.

It wasn't long before figures appeared in the sky from all directions.

"All at the same time, I wonder how that worked?" Alex asked.

"Don't know. Time seems stupid these days, didn't you notice?" Dani replied, and Alex couldn't help but think of the Chronovore. What was it doing?

Then, before he could continue those thoughts, the others began to land. "I hope this reunion doesn't last long," Melissa said.

"I hope they don't decide to try and kill us," Hale replied.

"Ben, you're alive again. Claire, Derek, all of

you. I missed you so much," Cole said and dashed across the parking lot.

"Cole, buddy, wait a minute," Claire tried to stop him, but it was too late. The hug happened anyway. "Okay, okay, glad to see you too. Space, please," she said, and he backed off.

"We were all killed by some green eyed maniac, Delta, right? How are we back?" Derek asked, but everything around him was alien. He didn't feel safe here. "They made a deal with Bob," Bryan replied.

All the ones who had just arrived cringed. The implications of those words were devastating. "What the hell were you thinking?" Ben asked.

"I was thinking I didn't want to stay in a dead dimension forever," Sam replied and looked at the ground. No one got upset.

"So, why here? What is this place?" Claire asked, looking around at the abandoned area.

"Welcome to the future," Jason replied, and his helmet slid back.

"Scorpio, is that you? What's with the suit?" Brad asked. "Machines are the way of the future. Anyway, who's in charge?" he asked.

Ben and Bryan looked at one another. "Are you back?" Ben asked. Bryan nodded. "No choice, brother, not anymore," he replied.

"Then you lead, we follow," Ben replied. Bryan

looked at the others who just seemed content to watch for now.

"You all agree?" he asked. The silence of the others told him all he needed to know. "Right. Oh, you should know, the Guardians rose up against the Syndicate, and they lost. They are still out there somewhere, but the order is effectively destroyed."

The Zodiac members didn't know what this meant for the world.

Alex decided that this had lasted long enough. He stepped forward.

"Hey, guys. Remember us?" Alex said, and they all turned around.

"You?" Ben asked. "I thought you died." Ben said

"Yeah, it's me. You've come a long way since I first saw you. Nice work. Let's see if you're any good. After this is all over, you and me, one on one?" Alex asked.

Ben nodded. "Sure, what the hell, old timer, sounds like a good time," he replied. Both of them knew that there might not be an after.

Once that was out of the way, he got to the point.

"We are going to be working together. We all made a deal with the Abyss, and we can't get out of it. Sorry about bringing you back to life and all, but we didn't have a choice. Our end of the deal is to kill the Delta Squad, all of them, I guess. I don't think any of you will have a problem with that, and with all of us here, we should be able to handle it," Alex said.

"We all have a more immediate problem, however," he added. No one talked, so he decided to keep going.

"Chronovore is loose. It's possessed a former Delta Squad member. So, she's part of the deal we made with Bob. We need to start with her. Everything else can wait," he said.

He could see the name didn't evoke the emotion it should have. The twelve of them just stood around.

"The what?" Brad asked.

"Time eater," Bryan replied. "Parasite made by the Guardians and Syndicate to fight Nazis. It was never used and locked away in Fort Diab. Until recently," Bryan replied.

"What's a Nazi?" Claire asked.

"A Nazi is just a catch all term for anyone you don't like these days. Most of the people who use it slept through history class," he didn't want to get into it. "Maybe we can find something at the fort that'll help us. We should go there first," he replied.

She just shrugged.

"Like hell are we being carried again. Get close, form a circle. We got it this time," Hale said.

The twelve of them moved closer together.

"Don't breathe too much. Portals literally suck the air out of you," Alex said.

"Wait, what?" Derek asked, just as Hale put her hands together and closed her eyes. A massive spinning blue gate of energy opened under their feet, and they fell into the light.

"Suck the air out of you, you're mean," Dani said. She laughed and jumped inside. The others did too, and the gate closed behind them.

## 55

The portal dropped them on the abandoned yard of Fort Diab. They all landed on their feet. All but one.

"I can't breathe, I can't breathe. I. Can't. Breathe," Cole was flailing his arms and legs as if someone had dropped him in the deep end of the pool.

Sam took a deep breath and walked over to him. "Hey, relax, we're here," she knelt and grabbed his right arm. He stopped and took a look around.

"Oh, air," he said and calmed down.

"Yes, air. Now get up," she said, and he did.

"Why are we here again? Where is here? What is any of this?" Derek asked, looking around for trouble. "Will you shut up? I'm sure they'll tell us. I'm not sure I want to know that bad, do you?" Martin replied.

"I always want to know. Then I know how to prepare," Derek replied.

"Starting to think I was better off dead," Martin replied.

"Come on, let him freak out. This is kind of fun, an adventure. The air is great," Claire replied, taking a deep breath.

"Scorpio and I are going to go down and see if we can find anything. We'll be back as soon as we can. You guys stay here and be ready to fight. The Syndicate likely knows we're here, and they don't like people messing with their stuff. Good luck," Bryan said.

"Why the hell do we have to go down there?" Jason asked.

"Old times' sake, come on," Bryan said, and he nodded.

"Fine," he replied. Jason walked to the elevator door, put his right hand on it, then pulled it open.

"Welcome to—" the computer said, and the voice twisted, died off. "Charming place," Bryan replied.

"We'll send up a message when it's all clear," Jason said as they walked inside. The doors closed behind them.

The elevator went down.

"Weird seeing everyone alive again," Jason said.

"Weird, but nice, I suppose," Bryan replied.

"Didn't really miss them. They are ten pounds of crazy in a five-pound bag. What are we supposed to do with them? They don't belong here."

"They'll adapt. We need them," Bryan replied.

"Yeah, if you say so."

Bryan didn't have a chance to reply as the doors opened. The command center was full of men with guns pointed at them.

"I mean. Sure, this is dumb. Guys, come on. I have power armor, and we're both above your paygrade. Just leave."

No one budged from their spot.

"Fine," Jason said, his hands lit up with energy, and he fired his rays before anyone could get a shot off. The men were blasted off their feet and into the back wall. Bryan turned his head to avoid looking directly into the light.

A burning heap of bodies was left behind.

"We could have just mind wiped them."

"Could have, but it was better this way." Jason walked over to the closest charred body, picked it up and a half-melted gun.

"The all clear message," Jason said and tossed the body and weapon into the elevator. It closed on its own.

"Gnihton Gnik," Bryan said and waved his right hand over the smoldering bodies.

"Entropy spell, useful," Jason replied, watching the corpses start to dissolve.

## 56

Four minutes later, the elevator came back up. There was a smoking corpse inside with a melted weapon beside it.

"That must be the message," Samantha said. She walked into the elevator, grabbed the corpse by the shirt, and tossed it outside.

"Cole, we're leaving. Let's go," she said and walked into the lift. It was big inside. She wondered how many people could fit in here after all. She bet all of them.

"Ok, Mister Pole. I have to go. But don't forget what I said, ok?" Cole said and took off running toward the elevator, slamming against the back wall to stop himself.

"That was fun. Can't wait to do it again," he said as the others filed inside behind him.

"Please don't do that again," Martin replied.

"I can do what I want," Cole replied.

"Boys, stop it. We just got all of us back. Let's wait a while before we wipe one another out," Tiffany replied as the doors closed.

Cole crossed his arms and glared at Martin as the elevator went down.

Just a few minutes later, the doors opened. Jason was there to meet them.

"Welcome to Fort Diab, everyone," he said. "Try not to touch anything," he added as they came out of the elevator.

"What is all this nonsense?" Derek asked.

"Computers, just complicated machines. Not much we can do about it. At least we're safe for now," Bryan said.

"I am sure we didn't come back to life to be safe. Just do whatever it is you're gonna do," Brad replied.

"While we're here and have access to things, I'm gonna look for my ship. It's got to be somewhere," Alex said

"Ship?" Claire asked.

"It's a surprise. Trust me, you're gonna love it," Alex said and smiled.

"I love surprises," she replied.

He walked to a computer and looked at it. "I have no idea if this is going to do anything at all," he said as he sat down. Claire sat next to him.

"Show me how all this stuff works," she said. "Will do," he said, doing his best to get to work.

"I made the deal. I should be the one to help look for clues," Sam said. Bryan nodded. "Sounds good to me. Let's take a quick look," he replied.

"The rest of you make yourselves comfortable. Sam and I are taking a walk. Do your best not to push any buttons you don't need to, and someone watch Cole, please. Around here the machines can talk back," he said before walking to the doors leading out.

Sam stood in front of the door, and they slid open. The two of them walked through.

The place was pure white and sterile, shiny too. "This place, man, what is it?" Sam asked.

"This is where the Syndicate keeps all their, uh, science projects. No one really knows how deep it goes. I don't want to find out," Bryan said.

"Oh, the professor found a tomb he doesn't want to dig in. Surprising," Sam replied.

"No, it's not that. It's just that, well, it's not a tomb. It's a prison. Best to leave things locked up sometimes. We're just here to look at the Chronovore cage and see if we can learn anything."

Sam smiled. "You make a good professor. All this fighting, I'm sick of it too. I think everyone is. I'd just like to retire, live somewhere quiet. You know?"

He nodded. "Trust me. No one wants to go back

to some quiet temple and keep uncovering all the ancient secrets, just bury myself in the work. I hear you," he replied.

The two of them walked to the second set of doors and opened it to another hall. "Okay, this place is huge. Any idea where the cage was?" she asked.

Bryan looked around. "No, but there has to be a sign. Something we can't miss and—" Then he saw it. A black crack in the wall, thin, but it didn't belong, also, it looked as if it had just gotten old and started to fall apart.

"There's our sign," he said and pointed. She looked and shrugged. "Let's go." They moved through the second set of doors and followed the black line on the wall through the maze like a string. The decay on the wall grew thicker as they moved. They turned the corner and stopped.

The whole section was ruined. The cage was there, but it was covered with rust, the door lay on the ground in front of it. The glass was gone.

"This must be the place, but what are we going to learn here?" Sam asked and started to walk forward. Bryan put his arm up in front to stop her. "Don't," he said.

"There's something inside," he said as he put his arm down. Sam did her best to see into the dark, but for her, it was impossible.

"Humanoid, but I've never seen an aura like that before. Maybe it's friendly," he said.

"It's never friendly."

Bryan took a step forward. "Hello in there, come out, we don't want to hurt you," he said. Sam wasn't so sure about this approach, but he was the leader.

"Your cage can't hold me, Atlantean," the voice from the dark said, deep and not human.

"Atlantis?" Sam asked, confused.

"You are confused. This isn't Atlantis. It's not even the right time. You don't belong here. Tell us how you got here," he asked.

"Atlantean sorcery, green light, pain. Wake up here. You smell like a sorcerer," the deep voice replied. "For Lemuria."

Then out of the dark, an eight-foot-tall armor-clad lizard person revealed himself. He held an obsidian blade in his left hand and a thick shield in the other.

"Lemurian, lizard people. Well, we learned something," Bryan replied.

"Bitch can mess with time and pull things out of history, yeah, I got it. What do we do?"

"We kill him before he kills us," he replied.

The Lemurian attacked. Despite its size, it was fast. That black blade missed Bryan by inches. Sam summoned her staff and used it like a bat against the reptile's face. The thing staggered back but much less than she would have hoped for.

The beast spun around and put the edge of the blade into Sam's stomach and knocked her across the room for her efforts. Her blood sizzled off the edge of the sword.

"Lemurian, time to put you back in the history books." He formed the Soul Saber in his hands out of green fire.

"Magic weakling," it replied and swung again. Bryan stepped back and let the black blade swing past. The second he saw an opening, he lunged his own sword into it, only for the shield to block it. "No," Bryan said and pushed ahead.

His blade tore through the metal and plunged into the Lemurian's shoulder. It howled in pain, rushing to get back.

"Enchanted weapons, zabith, that's all you are," it said, tossing its now useless shield away.

"It didn't have to be like this, lizard."

The warrior took his weapon in both hands and ran forward. Bryan prepared himself. "Goodbye, warrior."

Bryan swung his blade at the same time the enemy did, and the two collided with one another. For a second, then the obsidian blade shattered. The Soul Saber continued on its deadly path and cut the head from the lizard in one swing.

The body fell to its knees, then to the ground.

Blood pooled from the wound as the heart pumped for the last time.

"Zabith, he called us that. What did it mean?" Sam said, just getting back up.

"It means coward, basically. He called us weak for using magic weapons. I suppose he had a point," Bryan said, and his weapon disappeared.

"Could you imagine a whole army of these things?" she asked, looking at the body.

"Yes, the story goes they were wiped out by a red god. It's hazy. The Atlantis records from the war are incomplete at best. Best not to think about it. We need to get back to the others. We need to find the Chronovore because history is full of monsters," he said.

"Yeah, and who knows what the future holds? I don't want to think about what kind of nightmares she could find," Sam replied.

"If she gets her way, there is no future, no past. She's one of those villains who only has one purpose, you know. Destroy all of time, eat it, something. Everything else is secondary compared to her. We need to contact everyone we can. Whatever they are doing now is just a distraction," Bryan replied.

"Why is it always the end of the world with these people?" Sam asked, and with that, the two of them started their way back to the main room.

Three turns into their way back, Bryan's radio came to life.

"Hey, a couple of things. First, I found the Viper. I figured we might need some big guns. Couldn't find my ship," Alex said over the radio.

"Great, and what else?"

"The Delta Squad is heading this way. I don't think they know anyone's here, but I imagine they are looking for the same thing I just found. What do you want to do?" Alex asked.

"We're going to have to meet them. I know there's the whole deal to kill them, but right now, we need them, we need everyone. The Chronovore brought back a Lemurian warrior. We killed it, but damn. It's going to get bad. We're on our way back."

Bryan looked at Sam. "Small favors from the universe?"

"Sure, if they decide to listen," she replied.

Then they continued their journey to the control room, hoping for the best.

## 57

The air around Leviathan had become a storm to hide it from anyone who might be looking.

"Where are we going first? To kill the Squad or the Syndicate?" Chris asked and glared into the storm.

"We know where the Syndicate is. We might as well go after them first. Delta is no friend to us. I think if we leave them alone, they'll leave us alone and won't even look twice if we take down the Syndicate. If we can figure out how they are controlling so many people and knock it out, we'll be heroes again," Aphrodite said and laughed about it.

Megan thought about it.

"The Squad will always have a special place in my heart. We'll kill them later. Let's hit the Syndicate first," Megan said.

"Kill them. Those poor bastards did what no one else could. Maybe we can just hit the Syndicate, maybe not fight. These people made a habit out of fighting literal cosmic beings and winning. I don't know about you, but maybe we should change our thinking a little," Stephanie replied.

"She has a point. Even we have to die, and what if there, you know, there's an after?" Matt said.

Megan crossed her arms. "How many people did the Squad kill? Your parents? Everyone you ever knew? They just get a pass all of a sudden?" Megan asked.

"No, I mean, damn it, they suffered enough, don't you think? I bet they are out there right now hunting the Syndicate down with everything they have, and here we are thinking about trying to attack them. Does any of this seem like a good plan to you?" Skye asked.

Megan looked at her, at all of them.

"No," she replied.

"You have all failed to consider that they'll kill us all. I doubt they are the same people we knew from before. You all saw the news report. They wiped out all the first responders and the soldiers at the building they blew up," Megan said.

"The train thing, too. All those people aren't going to get what they need," Skye said.

"So, you trust the SNN network for your information? The news was trash before the takeover.

Now, it's about as real as a comic book," Chris replied.

"Well, fine. We'll go after the Syndicate, and if the Squad attacks us anyway, we lose our element of surprise and we all die. Well, I'm blaming you," Megan replied.

"You know, we could just take this tub back to the moon, dock up with home base, and go back to what we were doing before. No one knows we're here, and maybe that's okay?" Matt asked.

"I suppose that's an option, but once all the chaos here ends, they'll just come for us anyway. No. We stick to the plan. We kill the Syndicate, then, damn it. I guess we'll see what we should do from there. One thing at a time," she said.

Amanda took a deep breath but decided to keep her mouth shut. Nothing was decided, but an outburst might change the mood.

"Sounds good to me," she said.

## 58

Joey and the Horsemen were ready to fight. The powers of Grandmaster Silence had not left him. Yet another of the Commander's failures to add to the list. Once this fact was discovered, all three of them united against him.

This was too much power for anyone to have.

"Joey, I don't know what you're playing at, but you just took down a whole unit by yourself. I don't think we can trust you. If Silence returns well, we can't do that again. You need to get rid of this," Angel said.

"Power? Look at all of you. I am practically a physical god, and you three are mechanical mistakes. Do you think I would ever give this up to be less in the world we live in now?" He asked, shook his head, and laughed.

"No, I'm the leader. You have a choice: follow me, or we can fight. I don't want to kill you, but I can. I will," Joey said and took one step forward. With this one step, out came the black cloak from nowhere, the hood that concealed everything.

"It's still me, but I like this look. It scares people, and it terrifies them once they know what I can do," he finished.

A storm rumbled off in the distance behind him. The thunder and lightning were a great complement to the look he was trying to make here, but then Joey turned around and looked.

"Horsemen, do you sense something off about that storm?"

Tyler channeled Famine and scanned it.

"You're right, that's the damn Leviathan, and the Olympians are on it. That kind of power isn't easy to hide," he said.

"Yeah. So, what do we do?" Brianna asked, looking into the approaching storm.

"A better question is why is it coming here? They have a whole planet to fly around, and they are coming here?" Angel asked.

"Chances are they don't even know we exist down here. All we need to do is let them fly on by," Brianna replied.

"Well, the Olympians equal bad news, and the Leviathan is even worse, so I say we go up there and break it," Joey said, didn't even think about it.

"Do you have any idea who they are? They can do things, you know?" Tyler said. Even in this state, he didn't want to take on things that claimed to be gods.

"Tyler, you're kind of a wuss. Live a little bit."

"Think about it. If we took this threat out ourselves, we can do anything," Joey finished. "Yeah, but I don't think they are a threat to us. I mean, they aren't scanning us. I'll bet they don't even know we're here. We could just let them pass on by and do nothing. Wouldn't that make sense?" Tyler asked.

"Nothing in this world makes sense anymore," Joey replied and raised his left hand. From it, a bright red bolt of lightning shot and struck the shields, refracting around the whole thing, revealing it for a brief second.

"Great, we just picked a fight with people who think they're gods and can prove it, and they have a ship that's a mile long, armed to the teeth. At least we know there is some kind of an afterlife," Brianna said.

The sound of the cannons powering up was unmistakable. At this range, missing was impossible. "Giant warship cannons, not the best way to start a day," Tyler said. "Shut up and run," replied Brianna and took off running as fast as they could.

"We should suit up, right? Now's the best time for it," Angel said.

"Bring it on, you overgrown flying metal brick!" Joey shouted into the storm.

The cannons fired, light brighter than the sun. The three of them hit the ground, but there was no explosion.

Brianna looked back, and for a second, she saw Joey standing there with his arms raised to the sky. It was all she could take.

Then the energy was thrown back into the Leviathan. The three watched as the bright blue energy rocked the shields. The ship stopped moving forward.

"How the hell?" Angel asked.

Joey was still standing there, his hands smoking, but he didn't move. "See, I'm no pushover," he said, clearly trying not to express the pain he was in.

A black figure left the Leviathan and started to fall through the storm. It was just a few seconds before he stood before Joey. The other three had stood up.

"Hades," Brianna said, knowing the armor right away.

"Who the hell did that?" Hades asked as he landed, staring at Grandmaster Silence and the three people behind him.

"Obviously, you have a death wish. What are you thinking?" Hades asked the four of them and took a step forward.

"No, it wasn't us. It was this idiot," Tyler said.

"Silence, you're working with people now? I thought you were dead," Chris said.

"Did you really think anyone could kill me? Me, Grandmaster Silence? You know who I am. You know where my power comes from. You are afraid. I can taste it." From beneath the hood, the eyes were glowing a bright green. Chris and everyone else knew this threat was destroyed, but here he was.

"I attacked you. Now I will send your body up as a message to the other false gods." Joey was talking in the old Silence voice that sent chills through everyone who heard it.

"Yeah, if the commander of the Delta Squad can beat you, so can we." Chris said and was ready for what might be the fight of his life, if not his last one.

Joey smiled. "Oh, a gambling man. I like it," he said. "Well, then you're going to love this," Hades replied.

Joey saw the chains coming in slow motion, but just seeing these black chains put him into a state of shock.

He was entangled in the chains with ease and thrown a large distance before hitting the ground, cracking the street on impact.

It didn't hurt as much as he prepared for. "My first real fight," Joey said, reached out and grabbed the chains.

"I'm finally important," he said. Then he pulled on the chains as he levitated into the air.

As he did, he watched his enemy get pulled off of his feet and towards him. So, this is what it felt like to be truly powerful. He liked it. Chris, on the other hand, was trying his best to keep this from happening and failed.

Maybe chains were not the best idea. He would need to escape from this and sent this most powerful electrical charge through the chains. This not only made them electrified, but hot as well.

Joey felt the electricity enter his hands. He felt the heat, and both things did hurt, but not enough for him to want to let go. Not yet.

"You need to keep pulling him in, he's as good as dead."

Joey heard this inside his head. It wasn't his voice, but it made sense, so he kept on doing it. Hades expected this to work, but it didn't. This was not a good way to start out.

"Come closer. We're going to have all kinds of fun," Joey said in that sinister voice.

Joey was going to tear the god to pieces, but it was just then when something from above burned into his back and knocked him out of the air, and caused him to let go of the chains.

"Oh Joey, you should pay better attention. The others are coming. Get up, fight them all. Don't be scared, trust me." Joey wasn't afraid of a fight. He spun around to face the Olympians, prepared to kill them all.

Then a problem. He saw Aphrodite and was stunned.

"Wow," is all he could say. It was metal armor, but to him, it was perfect. He'd never seen anything quite like it before.

"No, stop being a damn simp. Pay no attention to her. They all want to kill you, remember," the alien voice screamed at him, but he paid no heed to it anymore. He had to give it a shot. He was a literal god now.

He removed his hood and began walking up to the line of Olympians, up to her. "Hey there, what's up?" he asked nervously. He was shaking for whatever reason. All this power, and he still had to work up the courage to talk to a woman.

She looked at him and shook her head. "Nothing much, but you attacked me. We're not exactly friends, so yeah." She trailed off, clenched her left fist, and put it against his face so hard that he left his feet and flew through the air.

He rolled to a stop at Brianna's feet.

"Women with superpowers, so hot," Joey said and picked himself up off the ground. "We need to take 'em down," Joey said. "I have superpowers," Brianna replied. "Okay, you're an exception" Joey replied. Brianna wanted to punch him, but didn't.

"Why do we need to do anything? The only aggressive one is you," Angel asked.

"Yeah, sure they seem good now. Just wait, they'll get all preachy and demanding, and you'll wish that you took them down when you had the chance. They wanted to take the world over once before, remember?" Joey said, and he had a point.

"Damn it, cloak's right," Brianna agreed with great hesitation.

"That Aphrodite chick, she's all mine. You can have the rest."

"Fine, what's the worst that could happen?" Tyler asked. They stopped pretending there was a way out. "Looks like we have a line to hold," Tyler said and stepped up with the rest of them.

"I hate lines," Brianna replied, then closed her eyes. Black energy flowed around her body, and in an instant, she and the others were in their armor.

"We didn't have to give them time to transform like that. I hope you're aware," Skye said.

"I'm not worried," Matt replied.

"I'm a little bit worried," Chris said.

"Well, guys, the only threat we have to deal with is Silence. Not sure why he's teamed up with those three, but it doesn't matter. This shouldn't take long," Megan said, and her armor's eyes began to glow an electric blue.

## 59

The Angels and the Zodiac stood in front of the entrance to Fort Diab. "This is dumb, we should just bug out," Ben said.

"We outnumber them by quite a bit. They wouldn't be stupid enough to fight us all like this," Bryan replied.

"I don't know, have you met them? Being smart isn't on their record," Ben replied. "We'll be fine, don't worry about it," Jason replied.

"If you say so," Ben replied.

"Haven't seen a Delta Squad member since they killed me. This should be fun," Brad said.

"Do you guys always talk this much? Shut up, please," Alex said, then looked into the sky. There were five points of light in the sky, like comets.

"Not even trying to be stealthy. Great, they're pissed," Sam said as the light came into view.

"Yeah, well, no one's having a good day," Tiffany replied.

"No one's going to have any days left if we don't do something," Bryan replied.

---

"You said nobody would be here. That looks like a lot of nobody," Dustin said. "Yeah, I know," Cody replied.

"So, how do you want to play this?" Wyatt asked.

"I say we kill them all, but that's just me," Josh said.

"We're not killing them all, we're going to need to talk, I guess," Blake replied.

"I hate talking," Josh said.

"We're talking. Shut up, try not to shoot anyone. If they wanted to attack us, we'd be fighting right now. They obviously want something. Let's try to find out what first," Cody replied as he began the descent.

It wasn't long before the five of them landed in front of the group.

"Bryan, what in the hell is going on here, and who are the rookies?" Cody asked the one he thought he knew.

Bryan waved as they landed.

"Long story short, after it all went down, the Zodiac and Angels were banished to the Dead Zone. They made a deal with Bob. He brought the other dead members of the Zodiac back to life. In return for freedom and the resurrection, they have to kill you," Bryan said and sighed.

"Of course, they did that. Wonderful, real high class world thinkers over there," Blake said and began to tense up. Upgraded armor or not, this would not be easy.

Ben stepped up.

"Yeah, he said we had to kill you, but he never said when. The Chronovore comes first. We can deal with one another later. If we don't, nothing will matter anyway," Ben finished saying, trying his best to avoid a pointless battle.

"Emily's still out there, you didn't stop her?" Cody asked.

"No, she's been, well, hard to find. Look at the sky. I think it's been five in the afternoon for the past six hours," Bryan said.

Time was something they didn't notice. Light and dark didn't even care what day it was.

"Professor's right, something is screwy with the time lately. It seems to be slowing down," Blake said.

"If we don't work together now to deal with

this, there is no more tomorrow. No more history. No future, no more life. Nothing," Bryan said.

"Okay, lay off on the sales pitch. I get it," Cody replied.

The tension was beginning to subside when out of nowhere Gemini ran past everyone, swords drawn, and his eyes burning bright green.

"Say cheese, you son of a bitch."

"I got this," Wyatt said, pulled his blade with no hesitation, and charged to meet him.

Cole's twin blades came at him with amazing speed. Even in this new armor, it was still hard to follow. He put his own blade up and blocked both of them. The impact pushed his feet into the ground, but he held fast.

"You're good, but I'm not your enemy right now. Wake up," Wyatt was quick to try and bring this to an end, but it didn't work.

Gemini wasn't interested in words.

The second his swords connected, he retracted, regained his footing, and struck a strange pose with his arms in the air. Wyatt was sure he was just making it up as he went along.

"Anime now, great," Wyatt said to himself, trying to be ready for anything.

Cole became a flurry of blades. His left blade extended out, his right followed it in a downward attack. Wyatt didn't dare block one because he would have to be hit by the other in order to do it. All he could do was keep backing away. He thought he heard Josh laughing at him in between attacks he avoided. "Cole, come on, man, I really don't want to hurt you right now, stop it," he said, twisting out of the way of the right blade, blocking the left with his own, sending deep red sparks as they made contact.

Each attack came faster than the last. Each block sent a shower of deep red sparks. Wyatt had lost his patience, jumped to the side, a fair distance away.

"Come and get me."

"Stop running, Zabith," Cole yelled. Wyatt had no idea what that word meant, didn't care.

"Sorry."

He stood still and waited. Cole attacked with both blades. Gemini charged in his direction. He was sure this was faster than normal people could see, but there were no normal people watching.

Wyatt dropped his blade the second Cole made contact, stepped to the left, and watched him fall forward. Wyatt punched Cole in the face with everything he had. Those micro blades in his armor tore through the skin every inch of the way, sending blood in every direction. At the same time, he was fast enough to grab his blade just before it hit the ground.

Spin with it and bring the edge of his blade deep

into the back of Cole's neck. Gemini hit the ground face first, bleeding.

Wyatt stood over his fallen enemy, blood dripping off his blade.

"Well, nice work, now he's going to hunt you down forever," Ben said.

"Don't care. You don't screw with me like that, or my friends. Now that's over with, what are we going to do next?" Wyatt asked. He could already see the wound healing.

"Don't worry about it, I can distract him from the whole revenge thing," Sam replied.

"We have a ship to find. I assume you want it back?" Tiffany asked.

"The Viper, you know where it is?" Cody asked.

"We do. We planned on taking it for ourselves and using it to wipe out the Syndicate. And you." She replied. Cody looked at Bryan.

"You know, you sure have some twisted friends. All this time and you never even mentioned you were part of the Zodiac, and why is that armored freak show still alive? Bob melted him into nothing." He said, pointing at Jason.

Bryan shook his head.

"It's a long story. Maybe someday I'll tell you all of it. We don't have the time right now. Nobody has the time," Bryan said and looked around. Nothing had changed.

Alex looked at his watch. "Clock still works like

it's supposed to. Says it's nearly midnight. Still looks like sunset. Yeah, this is a great sign," he said.

"Bryan, how much time do we have? How the hell is this even possible?" Blake asked.

"That's just it. It's not possible here. We did something that broke all the rules we knew because of some human threat. Now all of everything is threatened. Ironic, that is irony, right? I don't know, I guess. I'm not much of a writer after all," Bryan said this but found no humor in it.

"The evil men do lives on," Blake said, not sure if he should be frustrated or impressed right now.

"Okay, enough of this, let's get down to business," Cody said. "The Viper is currently over the Pacific Ocean, heading south," Tiffany said and tossed Cody a white flash drive. "That's the last known location off the computer," she said as Cody caught it.

"You come prepared, I like that. Dustin, call it in." Cody said as he accessed the information on the drive. Dustin sighed and walked off. "Yeah, mister communication, that's me, sure thing, boss, call it in to who?" he asked.

"Heath," Cody replied.

"Why?" Blake asked, "Thought we didn't take orders or report to them anymore," he finished. "We don't, this is just, I don't know, fun," Cody replied.

"Fair enough," Dustin replied and made contact.

"Heath, anyone, are you out there or did you die?" Dustin said into the intercom. "Yeah, glad to hear you're still alive out there. Report?" Heath responded.

"Commander wants to go after the Viper to save whoever might still be there and take the ship back."

"Negative. The Viper is not the main objective. The Syndicate is. You are ordered to go after the Syndicate on the mainland. Get the commander on the line, I demand to--" Dustin cut him off. "Wasn't asking permission, just letting you know," he said and walked back to the others.

"Cody, we have a ship to catch," he said.

"What'd Heath have to say?"

"He said good luck," Dustin replied.

"I'm sure he did."

"Right then. Let's go save the world," Jason said, and his helmet slid back up. "We could teleport us there," Alex said.

"Still the rookie. You don't know where the Viper is. If you don't know exactly where it is, we could end up in the Viper walls or just in a random place in the ocean," Ben replied.

Alex shook his head. "Yes, but I was thinking more like Santa Monica Pier or California. We're in the middle of the country, and we shouldn't waste time, you know?" Alex replied.

"Do it," Cody said, no hesitation in his voice.

Alex nodded to the other angels. "Ladies, you know what to do. Let's do it."

"When the hell did we turn into a taxi service?" Brittany asked.

"The world's coming to an end, not the time to complain," Bryan said.

"I hate portals," Derek mumbled to himself as the angels took their places. Seconds later, the familiar blue spinning gate formed under them, and they all disappeared inside. Seconds later, they reappeared on a deserted beach. The sky was filled with alien light, as if the sunset had been frozen and twisted into something sinister.

"I'm the leader, you follow me. If we are to work together, you will follow orders. I don't know all of you. Don't even know your names. This will not be a suicide mission. Any questions?" Cody asked.

No one had any complaints.

"Will there be cheese?" Gemini asked from the back.

"Yes. The Viper is supposed to have three years' worth of food on it. There will be cheese," Cody replied.

"Let's do this," Cole replied, then he picked Dani up with no warning. "Madam, I will be your escort today," he said.

"Just don't squeeze too hard or drop me," she replied.

"Never," he replied. Sam tilted her head a bit and narrowed her eyes. No one else wanted to know why. If Gemini had a reason for everything he did, he'd be even crazier. It was best to just let it go.

Cody and the Delta Squad took to the air. The Zodiac Corps followed.

## 60

"Grandmaster Silence and the Horsemen, it sounds like a band. Not a good one," Athena said.

"Yeah, so? What's your damn point?" Brianna asked but didn't want to start the fighting yet.

"That kinda was, you know what. Never mind," Athena replied.

"Can we just kill these people now? You know they are really getting on my nerves," Hera said and stepped forward.

"Yep, let's get this over with," Megan said.

"Well, looks like that's it then. Remember what I said. We fight together, but the girl is mine," Joey said.

"She's going to punt you into next week," Tyler replied. "I'm okay with that." Joey said.

Joey had become the center of attention he always wanted to be. All the cosmic powers granted to him by the abyss, all the willpower that was his own. He wanted the head of the Olympians and charged for Zeus.

Joey was sure that there would be no mistakes this time as he flew forward with all the experience of a high school kid who might have been in three fights, at the most. Megan lifted her hand and fired the thunderbolt.

Joey didn't even attempt to get out of the way but failed to realize this had the same power as Typhon's blasts. The attack hit Joey in the chest, knocked him to the ground, and knocked him out cold, sending him rolling through the air backward with random bolts of energy still diffracting from his body.

He hit the base of a traffic light, snapped it off, but it was enough to bring him to a stop. A smoking body on the side of the street.

"Well, damn it. There went our best guy," Brianna said sarcastically.

"Really, our best guy? Him?" Angel said just before he met up with Poseidon.

"Shut up and fight me," Matt said, and just before the burning blade came down on him, he formed a shield of ice out of the water vapor in the air, stopping it.

"You're quick, but I can read you like a book,"

Poseidon said while he threw the blade to the side, sending his armored fist into War's head. Angel took the hit but kept his balance, going into a spin with the momentum.

That burning blade came back around and shattered the ice shield. It caused the Olympian to stumble, and that stumble allowed the sword to go over his head.

"Don't worry, I have plenty of fight in me to make up for the lack of yours," War said.

"I'm going to drown you and all your friends, don't waste your breath," Matt replied.

Brianna knew the odds were against them. She looked at the others. "Hell with it, if you're going to die you might as well go out with a bang." She pointed at Hera and Athena. "You two scrubs, let's go," she said.

The two of them looked at one another, then started to fly in her direction.

Brianna fired her cannon, and the intense silver ray shot forward. Athena got out of the way.

Skye raised her right hand, formed a force field around her, and did nothing as the bullets deflected from her. This was pointless.

Athena got out of the way for a reason.

She twisted the cannon to the side. Athena had just stood up when the silver light hit her on the left side. Brianna thought she heard a scream and couldn't help but smile a little.

It knocked her to the ground. Hera intercepted the beam again to block it.

"You do have a weakness, the same one as everyone else." She made a mental note of it.

"You can't break through this. You never could," Hera said and started to walk against the beam. The goddess had a point, this beam would never break the barrier. With a single thought, Brianna's black horse rushed beside her with all the speed of a runaway fighter jet.

The impact shattered the force field on contact, and Hera was knocked off her feet as she tried to spin out of the way.

"I see now," she said and moved towards the both of them.

"You arrogant worm," Hera said.

"Hey, I'm not arrogant," she replied as she put the weapon in her face.

Skye grabbed the barrel and pushed it to the left, and with her left hand fired the prism beam into her stomach, sending her back. It felt like a firehose that burned like acid. She braced herself against the concussion beams, sliding back to where she started. Hera stopped the beam and stood up.

"I'm much more exciting. I took on the Delta Squad. I think I could keep you busy for more than a few minutes," she said and continued, "show me what you have besides the light show. I'm sure you've got something more than just lasers and shields."

Brianna expected some kind of a quick comeback to that. Hera said nothing, just kept on walking forward.

"Well, I guess that leaves me and you three. Better go for the big fish." Tyler said, took one of his sniper rifles off his back, and pulled the trigger. A thin, red beam of light hit Zeus between the eyes and knocked her off her feet, to the ground sending sparks in every direction. Hades and Aphrodite looked as if they were about to attack, but then they stopped. Zeus lifted off the ground like a vampire from an old movie, right back to her feet.

"Joey is an idiot. I'm not quite so bad."

"Maybe not, but so what. You're a better shot. Maybe you can learn to dodge, too. You're all dead and just don't know it yet."

Her eyes began to glow with an electric blue. Tyler didn't move. Zeus let that thunderbolt loose again. Tyler stood fast and took the shot to the chest.

The energy didn't knock him over, instead, his armor absorbed it.

"Hit me, baby, one more time," Tyler said as the energy stopped.

Megan realized her mistake. Famine's frail-looking body crackled with power now. Tyler guessed this is how it felt to be a god. No time to waste now. He ran at the three of them. He jumped into the air, his speed increasing the whole time, and kicked her in the face. Megan didn't fall, but the brief contact allowed him to drain even more energy from the Olympian armor.

"Maybe I'm more of a god than you are after all," he said, turned to Hades, and punched him in the face. He gathered more of his energy too.

Amanda shot into the air before Famine could touch her.

Aphrodite looked at the fighting between the various armored people. None of it made sense. It was as if some kind of madness had infected everyone. She watched as War used his miniguns on Poseidon, and he blasted him in the chest with his own cannon.

Pestilence and Hera were locked in a battle to the death, but Hera was going to win this. It was easy to tell. Athena just watched.

Famine was holding his own against Hades and Zeus, moving faster than either one could react.

"Stop it, stop fighting."

She screamed, but no one listened to her. No one was paying attention to her, nor could they. Her hands lit up with her bright pink and white energy, and she lifted them up. It was easy to see them all from where she was.

"Alright, that does it, you idiots," she said and unleashed a great arc of pink energy in all directions. Nobody was safe as the blast wave extended in all directions. The fight was over between them all as they all got knocked to the ground in the shockwave.

Amanda fell back to the ground but managed to land on her feet.

"You idiots. You want to kill one another when the enemy is still out there. Don't you think that we could maybe use our heads for once instead of killing one another because this prick down here wants a fight?" She pointed at the still knocked-out Joey. "Let's get to the ship and make some kind of a plan. We can't do anything if we are all dead. This is stupid!"

Everyone started to get up.

"It's true, Dwip over there attacked you. It wasn't us. We just wanted you to pass over," Brianna said.

"I am pretty sure we tried to tell them that when it started. Joey, he's the real threat here," Tyler said and helped Zeus and Hades stand up.

"How hard did you hit him?" Angel asked.

"Hopefully hard enough to kill him," Megan replied.

"So, what, we team up with these idiots?" Chris asked. "I don't trust them."

"We were all in the same tournament, we have a history, right?" Brianna asked. "Still don't trust you," Chris replied.

"Enough, stop. We're going to wipe out the Syndicate, and your idiot friend was right about one thing. Once we do, we're taking the power back," Megan said.

The Horsemen looked at one another. "They can't be worse than the Syndicate. We should go with it, at least for now. We can always kill one another later," Tyler said.

"Good point," Brianna replied.

The two groups looked at one another.

"Delta Squad, what are you going to do with them?"

"I don't know. We decided to wait and see what happened and roll with it," Megan said.

The three of them looked at one another. "Well, we won't fight them. They saved all of us, you, everyone. We wouldn't be here if it weren't for them," Angel said.

"Yeah, we kind of thought the same, or, she did at least," Megan pointed to Aphrodite.

"Big softie," Angel said. She just glared, pink glow where her eyes should have been. "Big powerful softie," he corrected himself.

"On the other hand, I never liked the Syndicate. It was them who made these armors. They are responsible for everything that happened to us," Tyler said.

"We can't bring him with," Megan said. They looked at Joey still lying there.

"I want nothing to do with him either," Angel replied.

"We're leaving him here. Get to the Leviathan. We have a world to save from the monsters," Megan said.

The Horsemen summoned their horses to their side and rode towards the ship. "Ghost riders in the sky, man, they look cool," Matt said.

"Yeah, I think so too. Let's go," Megan said, and the Olympians followed.

## 61

Mark walked into the leader's office. He didn't knock.

"Are you aware of the situation? Surveillance is tracking seventeen signatures at least. They left the California coast, coming right in our direction. Someone made a deal and brought the Zodiac members back, too, and apparently, they're coming right for us," Mark said as the door slammed shut on its own.

"Relax, soldier. I've seen all of this take place, it had to happen," the green-eyed man said as he leaned back in his chair, no tension in his eyes.

"What do you mean you've seen this all already? How the hell have you seen it?"

"You want to know all the things. I know you

do. You will when it's time and when you need to. There are just a couple of details that are fuzzy yet, but I am sure they won't amount to much in the end, and believe me, there will be an end. It's been coming for a long time," Mark looked at what the man was looking at, a wall.

However, it appeared there was something more to that wall.

"That's not a very interesting wall. Why don't you just tell me what's going on? My patience with this mystery is wearing thin, and now everything we have built is about ready to be wiped out. A whole group of people **is** heading this way, and each of them might as well be a one-man army. We're screwed if we do nothing," Mark said.

"I know what I am doing. If you question me again, I'll kill you. It won't be a big loss to the effort. Your place in history is limited anyway. Also, learn how to knock. You act like a stupid kid."

Mark glared but knew better. He walked out without another word.

The man at the desk pushed the button on the intercom.

"Solaris, how is the project coming along?"

"Fine. It will be ready soon. If you rush it, well, you know how science is—half art, half precision," Solaris replied.

"I don't care what it is, just have it ready," he replied.

"Don't worry, I got you," Solaris replied, and the communication ended.

# 62

The ocean was as vast as it was horrifying.

Quentin was on the West Coast. He had been brought and imprisoned here. After he was released—he never could get himself to call it an escape—he felt a pull toward the water.

He walked for what felt like countless days, but nothing around him ever changed. The sun never moved. Time was—well, something was wrong with it. The sky seemed to twist sometimes in places. A glitch in reality.

The ocean itself had no waves. Still as glass, like ice. Quentin couldn't help but feel a shiver down his spine as he looked at it.

Everything looked older, more worn down. The sand was faded, too. It didn't make any sense, but even Sparky seemed to be older, too.

The book he held under his arm remained unchanged, but it was old when he got it. He was unsure how ancient this thing was.

Quentin now stood on the shore. He was alone. He looked up and down and realized that, in fact, he hadn't seen anyone. Where did all the people go? He didn't even see any Syndicate patrols out, but he did see their trucks on occasion—trucks that seemed to be rotting where they stood in this strange acceleration of time.

He realized that this was death. Death for everyone and everything but him. Was he immune? Was it the book? He didn't know, didn't care. Then it hit him. The sound of the waves was still there. The ocean was dead, but the sound still existed. Everything was out of sync.

The sound of the waves was all there was.

"The ocean, it's waving goodbye," Quentin said to the metal cat at his side. He took the book in his hands and opened it, starting at page one.

"The book. It wants to go home. That's all it wants. All it wants is just to go home."

Quentin was listening to the voices in the pages. He could hear them speak as he turned them. "The words, what words, where, oh, right. There are the words." Quentin was talking to himself, maybe to the book. He raised his left hand toward the water.

"Xarathan, Turo Noc. Ispep Yondo!"

The words themselves made no sense. Quentin

was just reading them out loud like the book had asked him to do, and they seemed to make sense to him on a deeper level he could only feel. Their meaning, however, could not be known by him or any other human on the planet.

Something understood the words. Something heard them through the barrier the ocean had provided.

The water recoiled from him and the shore as if it had suffered some kind of unknown injury. Quentin watched as the soft earth formed a path down into the darkness. In a moment of sanity, or maybe something else, Sparky lightly put his metal jaws around Quentin's free arm, begging him to stay where he was. Quentin looked down.

"No, it's alright. The book just wants to go home. It just wants to go home, and we can bring it there. Together, you and me," he said to the metal cat, but Sparky refused to go on this path and tried to pull him back.

Quentin pulled his arm free. The metal teeth cut his arm, but he didn't feel it.

"Wait for me here. I'll be back. We're going to win today, you just wait and see. I'll fix everything."

These were the last things he said to the metal cat, and with that, he began his journey into the dark. The second he was under the water, the ocean closed behind him. Sparky lay in the sand, waiting for his return, alone in an alien landscape.

## 63

Paxton shut the car off in front of a dilapidated building.

"Have you seen such an awesome place?" Paxton asked as he got out of the car, but they stood in front of something that was a few degrees south of awesome to them. No reply made Paxton roll his eyes.

"Well, okay, it could be better on the outside. It's what's on the inside that counts, come on. I'll show you."

They began to walk toward the building. There were no guards, and the suspicion that Paxton had lost his mind was easy to believe.

Nate and Lance glanced at one another. "You needed help with this?" Lance asked.

"You never know."

Paxton walked to the front door and pulled it open. "No security, what is this?" Nate asked as he walked in. The inside was different than the outside. It was filled with advanced technical equipment. It was smaller than it looked on the outside.

"Guys, let me introduce you to my newest suit of armor."

He walked in front of it.

"I don't have a name for it yet. Actually, that's what I needed help with. You should help me think of a name."

"I don't know. It looks, well, it looks evil if you ask me," Lance said.

"Yeah. It's something alright," Nate said.

Neither of them knew what to make of this new armor. It looked like a beast. "Call it, oh, I don't know. Infinite Nightmare. Because, well, it's pretty damned scary."

Just looking at it gave them the chills.

"What inspired this monster?" Nate asked. Paxton just smiled.

"The Delta Squad did, of course. I commissioned Mustafa to combine aspects of the Hell Razor and Flesh Tearer armors. He studied both of their old armors, added Blood Wraith to it, and created this."

"Yeah, nice work. I can see that, but, Olympians, Horsemen. Isn't it obsolete already? The Typhon armor is still out there too," Lance said.

"True, but I don't have superpowers like you. I'd rather have something than nothing, you know. Besides, I think this can hold its own," Paxton replied.

"I want a rematch. With this, I can take on the whole Squad. All on my own."

"I don't know about that. It seems like a bit more than you can chew," Nate replied.

"Don't worry, I'll have you as backup."

"The squad kind of fought the devil and all the cosmic things so we could keep breathing. Are you sure this is the best way to say thanks?" Lance asked.

"They'd understand, I think," Paxton replied.

The two of them looked at this armor. It was more bestial than human. Something about the face was wicked, those hollow, black eyes staring at them. Pronounced against the shiny silver metal just made it worse.

"Damn man, you sure have a twisted imagination," Nate said.

"Infinite Nightmare? That's a lot to say each time. Let's call it what it is. It's what Violence would look like if it took a physical form and learned how to walk. It's Violence." Paxton said with a smile and walked toward it, not as if it was a simple armor, but as if it was something alive. The other two didn't feel safe.

They knew how Paxton got when he had power armor on.

"Violence it is," Lance said, and it made him nervous.

They watched as the suit opened up. Pitch black inside.

He turned around and backed into it. The thing, the horrible-looking armor, closed around him, and all was quiet for a few seconds.

Then, it came to life, and the monster took its first, careful step forward.

Nate and Lance never saw the thing move as it was behind them. One hand rested upon their shoulder, each, and their blood froze.

"Guys, it works. This is one of the best days of my life," Violence said in a black, tainted voice. "Now, what do you say we get some practice in? Join me outside."

Before the two could look back, he was gone. The door was swinging open.

"Practice?" Nate asked.

"He's gonna lose it, and we're gonna die. That's what it means," Lance replied.

The two of them made their way outside and looked around.

"Alright. Show me what you can do." Violence was in the sky, looking down.

"Yes, what we can do. Are you ready for us?" Nate asked, but didn't give him a chance to respond because at once Paxton was thrown into the ground with a telekinetic slam.

When Paxton looked up, he saw the car they came in flying at him. It seemed so slow as he leapt into the air and shot in its direction. As he passed over, it exploded under him. Violence was on fire as he came out of the other side.

"Nice trick, Nate, but I'm still fine."

Lance knew he was useless in this fight. Power armor could block his illusions. "I'm not in this fight. You got your helmet on and I'm useless, you know that," Lance said.

It was all he would say before turning around and looking, and all he could see was Violence's horrid face right there, filling his vision.

"You move so fast. You were over there and then behind me before I could turn around. Nice trick, but get out of my way. We're still friends, right?" Lance asked.

Violence nodded. "Of course, besides, you're irreplaceable," Paxton replied and put his hand on his shoulder. It was cold. Lance didn't like it.

"Now that we blew up the car and you proved you're really fast, can we stop this? We both know all the power armor in the world won't help you against me," Nate said. Paxton turned to look at him.

"If you can catch me," he replied.

"I was thinking that if this armor worked out this good, yours will be amazing," Paxton said.

"Ours?" Nate asked.

"You thought I'd leave my best friends behind? Of course not. It's a whole new world out there, and we need to be ready for it. Come on back inside, and I'll show you," Paxton replied, then disappeared.

"This day is something else. Let's not keep him waiting," Lance said.

Nate looked up at the sky. He couldn't help but feel as if something was wrong with it. It seemed frozen to him. There was no wind.

"I have a bad feeling about this," he said before walking back to the building to see what was in store for the both of them.

# 64

The Delta squad, led the Zodiac over the Pacific Ocean along with the Guardian Angels when Cody stopped. The others followed his lead. There in the ocean was something that none of them had ever seen before.

"What?" Wyatt asked.

"It's a giant ship, a floating base, I think."

"Who the hell builds all this trash? Why is this here? So many questions," Dustin said. There weren't any answers.

Cody turned to the rest of the group.

"Well, what do you want to do? Wreck this, whatever it is, or keep going?" Cody asked.

Nothing was supposed to be out here. This thing looked like it was alive.

"I say we wreck it," Gemini yelled out from the back. "I'm with him," Dani yelled.

Bryan shrugged. "Either now or later," he said.

"There might not be a later," Alex replied.

Cody scanned the group. They were all powerful but untested. There was no way to know how they'd work together and they needed a test run.

"Alright. We're going to ruin the Syndicate's whole day," Cody said, and his plasma cannon formed in his hand.

"I was thinking the same thing," Blake said. "Let's say hi," he said, drew his rifle, and pulled the trigger. The bullet smashed against a forcefield.

"Shields, why does everything have a shield?" Blake asked.

"Well, that explains why they don't seem too nervous," Hale said with her cold voice.

"Right, well I say we blast through it and kill them all," Derek said, and Josh, to his amazement, found himself agreeing. Maybe the Zodiac weren't as bad as he thought. Maybe they were worse and more like him.

"Yeah, but the longer we wait, the farther the Viper gets. This base isn't important," Ariana said to them and looked towards the ocean.

"It's not important, sure. I'll bet the Chemical Dragons are here. It would be easier to take them out here, while they are all in one place," Dustin replied.

"Yeah, I'm sure this is their mobile base," Cody said.

"If these are the Chemical Dragons, this is their home base. We shouldn't just underestimate them like that," Claire said, then she wondered. "What's a Chemical Dragon?" she asked.

"Syndicate shock troops. They dealt with the stuff just below Delta class stuff," Dustin replied.

"Arrogant pricks, usually. Not sure why they are working for the Syndicate now but, here they are," Blake added.

"Calm down. We can take them, but the Viper will get away, or get to where it is going. We don't need that," Jason replied.

Everyone was right. Cody made a choice.

"I have to get to the Viper. I'll go on alone. This base needs to be destroyed. Blake, you'll lead the Zodiac into battle against them. Catch up when you can. The Angels and the rest of us will catch the Viper," Cody said.

"We can't fly—oh, damn it," Alex said. "You make life complicated," he reached in his pocket and pulled out a ring with a blue stone in it.

The others did too.

"What's that?" Cody asked.

"Levitation ring. It lets you fly but is kind of a drain on your energy. Let's go find the Viper," he said. The others did the same.

"You want Blake to lead them? What if they just kill him? He's outnumbered," Wyatt said.

"I'll be fine," Blake replied. "Get out of here," he said.

Cody and Blake looked at one another. "Alright, good luck."

"Blake. I'd kill all of these Zodiac people in exchange for you. Don't trust any of them. Watch your back," Cody said this over the intercom.

Blake didn't trust the Zodiac—not the new ones, not Bryan, not any of them.

"Thanks, I hope I won't need it," he replied.

With this, the Delta Squad and Angels shot off into the distance, leaving the base behind. Then he turned to face the Zodiac.

They had to be up to something, but he didn't care.

"Thanks for being so agreeable. Remember, you're all powerful, but the Chemical Dragons are likely filled to the brim with Crimson Eye and top of the line weapons, who knows what else," Blake warned them.

"Thanks for the pro tip, but what's the plan?" Tiffany asked.

"I'll start the party. Bryan and Ben, you're with me. The rest of you stay out of sight until you get the signal. Someone keep Gemini in place, we'll need him. Until I get back, Samantha is in charge. Woman, you better be patient, alright? Do not do anything until you get the signal," Blake said. "Sure thing," Sam replied.

"So, what's your plan?" Bryan asked.

"If your blade can cut through reality, this shield should be no problem, right?" Blake asked.

"Who told you what I did?" Bryan asked.

Blake wondered how he knew that. Now that he said it, he had no idea. "I don't know, but I feel like I'm right," he replied.

"You are, and I can."

"We're going to sneak in from under the sea," Blake replied.

"But you shot them, they know we're here," Ben said.

"Listen, look at the shield, things are falling into it all the time. I doubt anyone noticed us. Their radar isn't looking for people," Blake replied.

"So, why am I here?" Ben asked. "Because I don't trust you," Blake replied.

"You open the shield. Ben, give me your weapons. I'll shut the shield down and that's the signal, got it?"

"I am not giving up my weapons," Ben said.

Bryan's eyes shot in his direction. "The man needs firepower. Give it up," he replied. Ben rolled his eyes but gave the weapons to Blake. Blake tested their weight to get a feel for them.

"Well, thanks for the vote of confidence. Don't

trust me but want my weapons?" Ben asked. "You want trust, you earn it. Let's go," Blake replied.

The three of them disappeared under the waves. Blake led the way. From there, the shield in the water could be seen with a clear outline. Blake got close to it and motioned Bryan to do his thing. He summoned his blade, not knowing if this would work at all.

Bryan plunged his blade into the barrier, and it created an electric discharge. Bryan pulled the blade down and created a narrow gap.

Blake slipped through the opening. The second he was through, Bryan pulled his blade back, and the shield closed. He gave them a nod and watched them retreat.

With a mystical shotgun in each hand, he was ready to get to work.

## 65

He remained motionless for a short time. Some of the people below were looking up at the disturbance, into the water. He was sure they didn't see anything.

Blake's armor was like a mirror, and now he was the same color as the ocean. He moved up and slid out of the sea the second those people disappeared over the side. His cloak engulfed the shotguns as he rose through the air.

Blake lifted up and above the base.

He looked down, his eyes were scopes, and he could see everyone's weapons, their faces. They were Dragons alright, and their eyes were blood red too. Not a sign of Crimson Eye, he hated that stuff. Elevated heart rates, people rushing around. He wondered what was going on.

He needed to make a good entrance. He was looking around, and soon he saw what he needed.

"Armory, perfect."

He then moved to the roof of the building. There was no way he was getting in from up here without making a whole lot of noise.

He'd have to get in through the front door. He walked to the edge and looked over it, two guards posted at the front, a DNA lock on the door. Couldn't move yet. Patience was the key here.

Blake switched his vision to thermal, and it revealed hidden cameras, giving off the slightest heat on the walls. He was sure no one was watching them right now. No alarms were a good hint, but all the same, this could have been a trap.

There was a choice to make. He thought about it for a few seconds and made it, setting the weapons down. From the top of his wrists launched two zip lines, with blades on the end of them. These two sliced through the backs of their necks and into the metal floor at the same time. On impact, he pulled the two bodies back up to the roof, and the zip lines went back into their places.

Blake looked at the shotguns, picked them back up. He put them on his back, crossed them together, and his armor adjusted to hold them in place.

He soaked his hand in the blood of the guy on his left side and jumped to the ground, landing with no noise. No alarms yet. Someone was either sleeping on the job, or there was something more important going on. He put his bloody hand on the lock. He had no idea if this would work or not. He waited.

"Access denied," the computer voice said.

"What, are you kidding me right now?"

Inspecting the door, he found the seam and put one hand on each side.

"Fine, here we go. Look at you, Mister strong guy making his move for the whole world to see," Strom said out of nowhere.

"Yeah, you're the last one I need right now. Make sure to tell me if anything is coming, if you're useful at all," he said to his ghost. He was never sure if he was just going insane or if it was a real ghost.

"Oh, you mean, like them?" Strom pointed, and Blake looked to his left, and sure enough, four black armored soldiers were coming right at him, four from the other direction.

"Josh gets to take out a train, and I get stuck with these losers? Just my luck."

He turned visible, and they stopped from both sides.

"Hey guys. What do you say that this never happened, and everyone can go their separate ways?" Blake asked.

Nobody moved.

"Well, what is it going to be?"

"Alright, sir, just let us go, and we won't tell anyone you were here," one of them said. You could hear the terror in his voice. It made Blake even more sad. This place was going to become a war zone in mere minutes, and he couldn't tell them that, that and how pathetic they were. Maybe they weren't working for the Syndicate at all.

Figured he'd ask.

"Who do you work for these days?" The eight looked at one another.

"The Syndicate," someone on his right side said. It was all Blake needed to know.

Nothing was right about this.

This place should have been crawling with enemies right about now. Where were they?

Then it sounded as if the sky was being torn apart. The men looked up. Blake did too.

"Well, look at that. The party is starting early today," Strom said with a laugh and pointed up. "Look there, what do you see?"

The blue sky was consumed with bright green flames, and the shield was dissolving.

"It can't be," Blake said and got a sudden sense of terror in him. He never feared any human, but he's seen enough of this stuff to know nothing human did this.

"What are you waiting for, call the others, tell them Emily is here," Strom said and walked off laughing, fading away into nothing.

"I know, ghost," he said, then turned on his intercom.

"Cody, listen. Emily is here. She's attacking the base. I can't see her, but the sky, it's on fire. If you can hear me, this might be our best chance to stop her. We have an army. It'd be stupid not to use it. I guess I'll know if you got this message or not. I have to go in without you," Blake said to the intercom and took off into the sky. It didn't take him long to figure it all out.

This base was here for the Chronovore, that was their target, this meant she was following the Squad the whole time.

Emily came down from the green flames and landed on the steel. Two others were with her, people Blake had never seen. He turned invisible again, hoping it would do some good and wondered where the Zodiac were. He hoped they were smart enough to hide, too.

The alarms started to blare.

Soldiers came running out to meet her. Two miniguns raised from the floor and opened fire. The soldiers did the same. The trap was good enough, but Blake was sure that bullets wouldn't quite be enough here, and he wondered why they thought it would work.

He watched as Emily and her two mysterious companions stood there. The bullets never even got close to her. They turned to dust as they did.

She raised her hand. A strange green light washed over the attackers, their armor rotted away to nothing and fell to the ground with wisps of dust coming out from the cracks. The miniguns turned to rust, screeched to a halt before crumbling.

Blake didn't want his armor destroyed just yet. She had to remember him, right? He flew towards her as fast as he could.

"Emily, can you hear me?"

At once, she looked at him, those burning green eyes turning human again.

"Yes, I can hear you. You're right there."

"Are you following us?"

"Yeah, I am. You move so fast, what's the hurry?" She motioned for the other two from the future.

"Let me introduce you to April and Josiah. A couple of very upset people from the future. Oh yes, Blake. I know what you're thinking. If there is a future, then you must win the day. I'll let them explain."

She laughed. It was hideous and sounded nothing close to human.

The man came forward. "Delta, you just couldn't give up the fight. At any cost. Your victory shattered the whole world, forever. The human race is dying because of what you did. We've cursed the name Delta ever since that day."

He held the symbol around his neck in his hand

then. Blake was confused. Then the woman moved up.

"That's right. Your reckless victory killed us all. It's a slow, lingering death. The so called 'legendary' squad, their legend will be one no one will ever forget. They'll recite it on their deathbed. Parents will tell their children why the world has been decaying for their whole lives. Yes. Your story will live forever until there is no one left to remember it," April said, and he couldn't believe this.

"She, this miracle, came to us and offered us a chance to save the future. All we have to do is stop you." She finished her generic speech. Blake was bored with this 'kill the Delta squad' business, no matter the reason.

"Yeah, that's great, but you know what? You're far from the first to try, and you lose. Do me a favor and go home already." Josiah's eyes ignited a very familiar, bright gold.

"Cyranthis' power still exists in the future? Of course, it does. Who found the stone this time?"

"You don't need to know anything. You don't deserve to know." Blake could sense the anger in his voice. This wasn't fair. Being attacked for something they haven't even done yet was a new one. None of that mattered. He knew her armor had to be something wicked. It looked much like Jason's armor, only made for a lady.

The guy, he couldn't tell. But if it was anything

like Jake, it should be easy to deal with. Underestimating the enemy was the main reason most people died in a battle. He couldn't afford to die yet.

"Alright, kids. Let's play nice, ok? Killing me won't make a difference, and besides, you don't have a chance. Let's work together, and maybe, just maybe, we can change the future the easier way?" Blake did have a point, but they didn't seem to believe him.

"Nothing but liars and killers, just like the legend always said. Let's kill this one and make an example out of him." She raised her flaming blade. This sword looked familiar to him, but he just couldn't place it. He didn't have the time.

April attacked with speed that even with this armor was hard to track. He knew it would be advanced, but how much, he had no idea.

As he avoided this attack, the other one fired golden beams from his eyes. Blake saw them coming but couldn't get out of the way in time.

This attack hit him, and he was thrown from there into the ground. "Ouch," was all he could say. The armor had protected him, but it did suffer some damage at the impact point, superficial, for now. They must not have known who he was.

They must have had some kind of history failing, keeping this one, out of all of them, at a distance was one of the absolute worst things anyone could have done.

Josiah smiled at this accomplishment. He didn't think it would be so easy. His smile disappeared once the bullet tore through his neck. His hands went up to the wound. It was already beginning to heal, but the shock alone was more than he had expected.

The blood sprayed and covered his strange medallion and his blue shirt. April didn't even know what happened. It was all so fast that all she could do was try and track the bullet path.

Blake was gone without a trace.

"That's impossible. How can he hide from me?" she asked.

"Don't underestimate this one, or any of them. They are remembered for a reason. Only they could have done what they did. These are not normal enemies," Emily said.

April felt a bullet slam into her stomach, but it didn't bounce off.

"What the?" was all she got to say before her armor had a casing of ice over it, and she fell. "Oh my. Ice bullets. Haven't seen those in a while," she said and watched her fall.

April broke out of the ice. Blake was still missing.

"Come out here and fight us like a man, you coward," Josiah screamed.

"Hey, geniuses. The guy is a sniper. This is how

he fights, but if it's a knock down, fistfight you want, I'd try for one of them." Emily said.

She pointed to her left, and there was the rest of the Delta Squad. The Zodiac stood behind them.

"They came to us, perfect," April said, and the two of them seemed ready to fight everyone.

"Blake, I can't leave you alone for a second without you needing me now, can I?" Cody asked.

"Well, maybe a second, not much longer. I'll end up doing all the work myself if you don't keep up with me. These two aren't so tough. It's Emily we need to—well, you know how this goes. Same as it ever is," Blake replied.

Cody looked at the two of them. They had confidence and power, but they were wide open to attack.

They were inexperienced, he could tell just by the way they were standing.

"Alright, you two morons obviously have some kind of issue with us, let's get this over with. We do have things to do today." Cody addressed these two with a dismissive tone.

"You will not speak to us that way, World killer. We will have our day. We will have our justice and —" It was then a blade struck them down. One sliced through the flesh so deep that it cut the man in half at the chest. The woman's armor was torn open, blood splashing onto the metal. Both of them fell to the ground in pieces.

"Wyatt, in the middle of their speech, come on now, that just wasn't very nice," Dustin said and shook his head.

"Yeah, we should have broken them before they had a chance to start," Josh added.

"Well, yeah, you talk too much, then you die," Wyatt said and wondered if they'd get back up. Sometimes these people didn't know how to stay dead.

"Well, that didn't take long, a little disappointing actually after I went through all the trouble," Emily said, looking at the bodies.

"Anyway, I like your new toys. I bet Erin worked really hard on them. I have so many tricks. I want to play a game with you. Interested? I know I am," she said with a smile, and continued, "if you win the game, you get one shot at me. If you lose, well, you'll never ever see this time period again," she said, then looked to the others.

"As for the Zodiac and the Angels, while they are gone, you and I can wrestle. See who's better, an old Delta member, or all of you?" she said.

"Why in the hell does this always turn into some kind of a game?" Josh asked. She waved her hand, and at once all of them disappeared in green flame.

"Now, who wants to go first? Ben, Bryan, I guess it doesn't matter? I'm going to see you all burn, everyone, everything. You'll all make nice meals."

As she said this, her fire began to swirl around her body, and the sky began to twist violently above her.

"That bastard disappeared with my weapons. I knew I shouldn't have trusted him," Ben said as the world around them began to crackle with energy.

## 66

They looked at their suits of armor as they stood there in their energy sealed containers. "So, guys. What do you think?" he asked them and put his armored hands on their shoulders.

"Thanks, I think they are great, but I think I speak for both of us. We got out of this battle—no, we didn't get out, they let us go. The most powerful fighting force in the whole world just let us walk away. I think it would be pretty stupid to get involved in anything they were doing," Lance said.

"Yeah, I don't think I want to get involved with them again. We're alive, and the only thing we can get by going back is killed. If you want to go, that's fine. I don't want to risk it," Nate said and looked away from the armors.

"The squad is on a whole other level. There's no

way, even with this armor, we can win. Not that I'd want to. Think about it, Paxton. They are in no mood for this. They will kill us like any other enemy. Besides, we owe them that much to stay out of the way," Nate finished.

Paxton shook his head. "No, you guys don't understand. We can help them, then we can join them. Make up for the stuff we did." As he said this, the two of them looked at one another. "Paxton, I, um. I think if the world needed our help, it would have asked. I don't think we should be getting involved anymore. In fact, I won't do it," Lance said and began to walk away.

"You two really don't get it. The whole world is ending. If you haven't noticed, time is messed up. The Chronovore is out there, and she is going to kill everything. There will be nothing left anywhere. I don't know about you, but I live here too, and if we can even buy them a second, a minute, it might be enough for them to win the fight. We have to try. We have to do something. The armor is time-locked, see? I've been working on it. Our armor and the people inside of it will be unaffected by her time altering ways. We can make a difference this time," Paxton said, pleading with them.

"You tell one hell of a speech," Lance said and turned around.

"Damn it, fine. We'll wear the armor and see what we can do, but seriously. If you get me killed,

I will chase you through the rest of forever, understand?" Nate said. Paxton gave him a thumbs up.

"The one on the left is yours, Lance, a mix between Flame Genesis and Dead Eyes. The one on the right, well, I ran out of ideas, so it's a mix between Venom Sting and Chaos Specter."

They couldn't see his face, but by the sound of it, they could tell he was proud of himself.

"Mine is called Violence. Name your own if you want. I don't care. The sooner you get into it, the better you'll feel. The time is already slipping away from us. Get inside and stop that," Paxton said to them.

"How did you manage a time lock? That seems kind of, you know, advanced," Nate said.

"Syndicate has always been very interested in the concept of time. As you know, 188 did manage to make one time machine. It's all touch and go, but you know what? They did manage to learn how to freeze time around the same period they created the Chronovore. It was how they kept it locked up. Outside of that cage it was in, it was still the forties until Emily opened it and, well, you know the rest."

"These armors will protect us from at least that. She's still human on some level. The monster needs a host to keep on living. If we can kill the host, we can kill the monster too."

Paxton had all of this stuff planned out already.

"Nice plan. Can't wait until everything goes wrong," Lance said.

"Hey now, who do you think is leading this operation? It's not the commander of the Delta Squad. I'm pretty sure our chances of success are high," Paxton said with a sarcastic laugh. He knew they'd do everything they could to save Emily from the monster, but this tactic just didn't seem to work out for them in the past. Maybe they didn't have the heart to do what needed to be done, or maybe it was impossible for them to take down a former friend.

They would not share the same problems or issues. Paxton watched as the two of them entered their armor. "Thanks. You guys won't regret this."

## 67

Joey woke up alone.

"You see now? You will always be alone. All you'll ever have is me. I'm not sure what that pile of a commander did, but I'm stuck in here, and you have all of my powers. It's a shame." Joey heard the voice but was used to it by now.

"Well, how do I get rid of you then?"

"You can't. Look into my memories and see for yourself. I've been on this miserable planet, world, whatever, long enough. The only way I can go home, Joey, is if someone kills you. You see, that commander didn't have it in him to kill anyone. I did try to take him instead, but that pest Cyranthis did something—that true power made us switch places, Joey. Now you're in charge. You could have taken them all out on your own if you wanted to.

Why didn't you? What was holding you back?" Silence asked him in a demanding, angry voice.

"I was scared of them, and then I saw that Aphrodite. The name fits. I couldn't just kill her, you know?" There was quiet for a few seconds.

"What? You're kidding me, right? Oh, you are so pathetically human. Sometimes I have to wonder why the Abyss gets all the stupid people to accept his deals. Out of all the people in the world, why did he have to ask you, and why were you dumb enough to accept?" Silence asked.

"I wanted to be special, is all. Important."

Silence laughed a second after this was said.

"Kid, you have no idea just how special you are." Joey narrowed his eyes and looked at the sky.

"Shut up. I'll show you and everyone I can do this. I'm worthy of power. You'll see. Everyone will see." Silence didn't respond to this, and Joey took off, but he had no idea where to begin to start looking.

He thought of all the people who had tried to kill him. Nobody wanted him around. The lines between being the hero and the villain were so blurred at this point that anything could be happening, all around him, all the time. It seemed that there were no more sides. No more heroes or villains. No, the world had moved past all of that good and evil stuff. Now it was about staying alive.

This world was on the brink of something horrifying, and he could feel it getting closer. The most troubling fact was he could feel it on a level that was more than just an instinct that something was wrong, more than just a bad feeling. It was chilling the air. It was easy to see that the whole world was decaying and dying around him faster than it should.

He didn't know what to feel about this. Silence? Well, that was easy. That thing wanted to kill everything just like the one who created it did, but Joey liked the world—not as it is now, but as it was, back to normal. It looked like he would have some time to think as he sailed through the air. He'd have to pick a side now. Life or death.

It wouldn't be an easy choice. Part of him was okay with dying, too.

## 68

Quentin was going down a forbidden path. He could feel that none were supposed to ever walk again. No person was supposed to be here.

It wasn't entirely his fault. Who could blame him? He had read the books that were provided to him. The words got into his mind. They revealed things—impossible things that made no sense but still worked. It shook the core of everything he believed in, the reality he thought he knew. He wondered how much was real, and how much was the product of his delusional mind.

The stairs, he couldn't see them very well. They felt like they were made out of solid bone and were just as white as well.

A mysterious light was shining through the wall

of water that surrounded him on all sides, but there was no way it was the sun.

He soon entered a chamber. The water formed a dome around this room. He looked up and around. There was nothing in here, and it was obvious that it had remained this way for a very long time.

Before Quentin was a massive doorway. It was made out of some unknown, smooth black wood. It towered over him, and there was no handle.

"This is the first gate. It says so in the book."

Quentin had expected this. So far, the book and the path matched up perfectly. He looked at his book and lifted it with both hands, opening it up to the page that matched.

"The first gate, the last seal to the way home. The seals were set up by the Tyrant." He read the words out loud. He had no idea who or what this tyrant must have been. All he knew was that he had to break the seals. They could only be undone from the outside in.

Never from the inside. However, the way to unseal it was not revealed in the book. Either the writer didn't know how to unseal it, or it was hidden in the book somewhere. Quentin wasn't going anywhere for a while, so he began to look through the book for something he might have missed. The pages—he'd seen them all before and looked at all of them one at a time. Nothing had changed.

Was it some kind of trick?

No, he hadn't come this far to stop now. He looked all around the room but saw nothing. He was in the wrong state of mind to be doing this right now. He walked to the gate and stared at it.

"You won't beat me. You won't."

He slammed one fist against the door, and the other hand held the book. They connected at the same time. He drew back, but the book stuck to the surface of the door. He took three steps back as the doorway began to shimmer and crackle where the book was, and it was spreading.

"Yes, that's it. It makes sense now."

It was an accident, but he figured it out. Nobody had to know how. He walked to the door and tried to touch it again, but his hand passed right through the surface. He caught the book with his other hand as it fell. Its work was finished.

"One down, six more to go," he said as he stepped into the black entrance.

## 69

Emily saw the impressive force led by the Commander, and something inside her couldn't just kill the five of them off. Instead, she sent her five former friends into the past. She didn't care where they went, and she didn't send them together.

The Delta squad would never see one another again, forever separated in time and space, each not knowing where the others were. She sent them away and granted them the one thing they could never find on their own.

Peace, or at least that was the plan.

Wyatt had some experience traveling through time before, but this was different. It was a bright green flame. His whole body was on fire, and everything hurt. It only lasted for ten horrible seconds.

The green fire disappeared.

Wyatt found himself falling through a frozen sky. Everything was white, and it was snowing. The air was so cold that ice was forming around his armor as he fell. He could see a vast snowfield below him. To the north was a black mass of humanity, raiders armed with axes, torches, and many other kinds of sharp things.

They reminded him of barbarian hordes he had read about as a kid in fantasy tales of high adventure. These guys looked like the primal bad guys the hero always defeated. He loved these stories. This horde was coming towards a village that was below him. This place never saw it coming. The snow kept them inside. Maybe this place was meant to be destroyed by the horde, lost to the frozen wastes of history.

"Not today." Wyatt took control of his fall and began flying towards the barbarian horde.

He was about to make his own legend.

---

Blake woke up under murky water. He was in a swamp. He broke the surface of the water and could hear voices in the distance.

In the distance, there was fire, there were people

here. Shouting things. Saying things that didn't make any sense. Not at first anyway. The shock of time travel messed with his head, but it cleared up.

He heard preaching, but it had nothing to do with religion.

He waded through the water, towards the firelight and the clearing in the distance.

He turned invisible just to be sure he'd remain hidden, but they were too focused on the red ghost. He was talking to hundreds of white ghosts. After each sentence, they cheered him on. Blake narrowed his eyes, it had to be sometime in the twenties.

The Klan, just his luck. He hated racists, he hated people who dressed up in stupid white robes, if they had any real thoughts in their head at all they would use black because it hid the stains better. White, well, everything showed up on white, and when you wore it, it was a promise you'd always get something to spill on it.

He hated these guys, sure, but now he had a choice to make. Change history, or sit and watch. For now, he would sit and watch. No need to reveal himself just yet.

---

Dustin opened his eyes. He was in a trench of some kind. There was screaming going on, horrible sounds he tried to block out, but couldn't. He sat up and looked over the wall. It was a battleground. It was a terrible sight. The sky was a sick color of green, and the fires in the distance raged for miles. The bodies of the dead were in piles.

Dustin couldn't see any enemy.

"Look what we have here," someone said from behind.

He turned around to see Will, an older version but still him.

"You're dead. I watched you die, we all did. How did you get here?" Will said and took a step back. "Don't ask me, Will, General. Emily zapped me through time, and I don't even know where I am now or when," Dustin replied. Something exploded in the distance.

Will took a second to gather his thoughts. "Screw it," he said.

"Ten years after the final battle you die. You all died. It was an intense battle to be sure, but it wasn't enough. The Chronovore lived despite everything you did to it. I met myself sometime back, told him to go back and stop this. Since all of this is still here, I can only assume I failed too." He laughed then.

"The whole world is dying, dead, and it's all your fault, well not really, I guess even the Delta squad has their limits I suppose. It was just a shame that this was the result of all that effort." Will was saddened by these memories.

"I can stop this. We need to send me back," Dustin said and grew a bit frantic. "Yeah, any suggestions on how?" Will asked and shrugged.

Dustin looked to the ground. The mud was soaked in blood that was oozing up under the weight. "No," he said.

Will looked at him. "Son, there might be a way, but it's dangerous," he said. Dustin scoffed. "Dangerous, we're all dead, if there is something we can do now's the goddamned time to spit it out," he replied.

---

Josh woke up in a different world. It was still registering as Earth on his armor. He had no idea where he was. He got off the ground and looked around. There were no people anywhere he could see.

"Well, she sent me nowhere. Now I'm mad. I'll find her, and kill her. Twice."

Then the earth began to shake, not constantly. They were footsteps. Josh had no idea what could cause that and be alive, so he turned around and looked up.

"Oh," he said as the shadow of the Tyrannosaurus Rex covered him.

It roared at the intruder.

Josh didn't like being roared at. He took to the air and slammed his right fist into the nose of the beast, and with one punch, knocked it to the ground. "Bad fluffy. Very bad. I have more punch than you do." The beast managed to get up and spin around. Josh didn't know much about giant reptiles, but he saw it coming, yet he took the hit from the tail anyway—after all, how many people could say they were hit by a dinosaur?

The tail slammed into him with way more force than he expected, and it knocked him out of the sky and back into the dirt.

"Well, okay. You've got some spark. I like that," he said to the beast, then realized he was talking to a dinosaur and decided to stop. He was ready to kill this thing when something else ran into him from the side it didn't knock him over or break through his armor. It just fell to the ground. When he looked at it, and it was a spear.

"What the hell is going on here?" The beast charged him, but he turned to look at it, and his eyes flashed blood red. This was enough to stop the T-rex, now known as Fluffy.

Well, he thought it was him that scared the thing, but it was something else. Something that the dinosaurs feared was near him. Josh looked around and saw this thing, and he had to take a second look.

"What is this, what are you?"

"I am Xulthal, I dwell in the city of Ib."

"Ib? What the hell is Ib, and where am I? What are you? No, you know what. My name is Josh. Take me to your leader."

The snake woman recoiled in horror at the name.

"You've come. The great destroyer, the wound that walks. I thought you had to be him when I saw you take down the beast like that, and the spear bounced off your skin! Is it time? Is the disaster upon us all like the God said?"

She was in a panic, no matter the species he knew the look of fear. She was wearing what looked to be dinosaur skin.

"Tell me more about this god of yours."

Josh knew something was wrong with all of this. The woman with the skin and black eyes of a snake tried to relax.

"Alright, if it keeps me alive a bit longer, I'll reveal to you everything you want to know," she said in a shaking voice.

---

Cody woke up, the sun was shining. He could smell the ocean. For a minute, he didn't know where he was or what he was doing, but it didn't take long to realize where he was.

"It can't be," as he sat up and looked around. "No, this isn't happening,"

But then he replied to himself.

"Yes, it seems to be the case. You look like I do, but you look different. Who are you, one of 188's men, some kind of cheap copy or what?"

Cody heard the old sound of the plasma cannon powering up. It was his. "I forgot. I completely forgot this."

Cody turned around, and he was looking at himself, in the old armor.

"Forgot what, your name? Happens a lot when people see me for the first time. Usually, they don't get the chance to remember. It's been three days, but I don't remember seeing anyone like you. I'd tell the others about you, but I think I can take you." Future Cody looked away.

"You think you can take me I know, but you can't. I don't know what I am doing here. I can't tell you anything."

Cody hated time travel so much right now.

"Tell me what, oh you know what. I have a mission to complete. Coral island is going down. I'll see to it this weapons base is finished," the younger version of himself said and at the same time decided that this copycat was no friend. He went into an attack stance. Cody knew this better than anyone else would have.

"Wait, listen. I'm you. Sent back through time,

not sure why to right now. I don't know how it works, but I was sent here. I don't want to be here, but I have no choice in the matter. Look on the bright side. If I kill you now, none of my future would have ever happened. Believe me. It's nothing you want to see." Cody said and copied the attack stance.

"If you were me, anything like me you'd know that if there is even a chance at winning it's worth risking everything to take it, whatever happens to me from here to now must be bad because you're emo as hell, I won't listen to this crap anymore. I have some spare time. Let me show you what a real commander can do," Venom Sting said.

Cody's eye twitched under that helmet of his as he heard himself, now his memory was coming back, all of it.

Nothing more had to be said about anything. The two commanders charged one another. Cody had the better armor, more experience, and less tolerance for anything. That first punch missed. He watched as the other blue fist put itself against his face and knocked him into the air. Followed by a plasma blast, a direct hit to the chest put him back down into the dirt. Cody felt no pain and wasn't damaged, but how did this happen?

His suit was so far advanced past the first armor that there shouldn't have even been a real challenge, but here he was, on his back, in the dirt.

"What's the matter? Is the commander too tired to get up? Good, makes it easier for me to do kill you, pale imitation, to think you had any chance at all against us. I might have been able to forgive you if you say, brought your own armor, but you copied mine of all people. You really don't know who you are screwing with, do you?" Cody heard these words and tried to sit up, but then a foot came down on his chest, that barrel was all he could see.

"Ranger, Army Rangers. We were in that before we became Delta. All your service records were destroyed after the Island chose you. Remember? Nobody else could know that. I know your name. I know what you think about in the dark. I'm you, and I'm not going to let you kill us both to save the world from all this disaster that I caused!" Cody said. Then he threw the younger commander off of him and stood up in one fluid movement.

"Well, you must be a big pile of fail then if you destroyed the whole world, what'd you do, push the one big red button or what?" Venom sting asked.

"No, I thought, you know what it doesn't matter what I think." Cody charged him but the commander blasted the ground in front of him and created a ridge. Cody's feet hit this in mid-stride, and he lost his balance and fell face first into the ground. He didn't want to mess up and kill himself on accident here.

"You destroyed the world, you? Now that I'd like to see. You can't even take me down. How can you take the whole world out? You suck."

The commander laughed at this one who claimed to be his future self. Cody remembered all of this. It had to play out, didn't it? Just like before. Anything he said or did differently would destroy everything he knew in the future.

"You're right. I failed. I did horrible things." Screw the future, he was gonna change it up a bit. "What do you mean, did horrible things?" The commander asked and pointed his weapon at his double.

"Yeah. Made deals, made promises to monsters that at the time, and they still don't make any sense to me." Cody looked into the ground.

"Explain, we have time and you're not in a—" Cody then surprised his younger self and shot into the air, over the gun and lunged forward, putting his hands around the younger commander's neck.

"Oh, but I am. I won't let it happen. It all ends today," Cody said but he did the one thing, made the one mistake that he never should have.

He underestimated himself in battle.

He got too close and the plasma blast that hit him sideways proved it. It wasn't anywhere near full power but he counted himself lucky, he was just thrown away and didn't get vaporized.

"You went up close and personal with a guy

with nanite armor and a plasma cannon. Wow, you're the sniff and scratch at the bottom of the pool dumb." Cody was already getting back up. "No, I'm not that bad. I just didn't want to put that much effort into it," Cody said and continued, "I know you don't know who Bob is, but you understand, it will look like you'll get out of this deal, you'll never tell anyone how you do it. Not until whenever the time is right. Do you want to know a secret?" Cody asked and laughed, he wondered how this would change things.

He didn't want to kill himself.

"Sure. Tell me a secret."

# 70

Wyatt landed in the path of the raiders. He stood motionless, a statue in the falling snow. The war party started to filter through the trees. Still, he didn't move.

There must have been about two hundred of these people. As they approached, he did not move an inch. Then, as they got closer, the leader took notice and gave the signal to stop. The group didn't seem too happy about it, but they did.

"What are you?" the leader demanded.

Wyatt didn't care who he was. "I am Wyatt."

The leader drew his blade. Wyatt looked at it. It was impressive for its time, but it didn't compare to his own.

"Yit? Yit, what sort of being are you? A knight of the Old Gods?" The leader asked, this time with some amount of fear in his voice. Wyatt forgot how his armor must have looked to them.

"Yes, I am. The old gods protect this village from all attacks," Wyatt replied.

"The old gods haven't been seen in ten generations. Why would they show up now? It's just a demon of some kind. We can kill it like anything else," the leader said with a laugh.

Wyatt drew his blade as the leader laughed at his own claim.

"Alright, time to make a point."

He lunged at the leader. With a single stroke of the blade, his head leapt from his neck. The blood sprayed out as he hit his knees and fell into the snow. Nobody even witnessed it happening. "Your leader is dead," Wyatt pointed at the guy next to the body.

"You're in charge now. What's it gonna be? Attack or do we find another leader?" Wyatt asked.

"We leave, but you have to understand, this land is harsh. They live by the sea and have food. We've asked them to share for the winter, and they didn't bother to reply. Our people are starving to death in this cold, great knight, if you are of the old gods. Help us too. We'll starve in a week for sure."

The other men nodded, getting a better, closer look at them. He could tell they were starving and weak. Now he felt bad about killing their leader, not that he could show that.

"Wait here," he said and turned to walk into the village.

The place was quiet. He wondered where they would keep their food. All the buildings looked the same.

"Halt there, stranger. What do you think you are doing?" Wyatt stopped, turned around. The voice was strange. Seeing someone in armor like this should have scared anyone. It was snowing, maybe they couldn't see. He didn't care. They asked, he'd answer.

"Where do you keep the food? There are men outside who are going to bring back food to their village, and you're not going to refuse, are you?" Wyatt asked. The man got a better look, and his whole attitude changed as he stumbled back.

"Yit, it's Yit. You've returned to us like you promised."

Wyatt raised his eyebrow then. Just what in the hell was going on here?

"I have returned like I said I would, but now the food for those others out there. Where is it? It's cold out, and everyone should get to eat." The man began to stumble back.

"The elders said the hordes deserved to die out there. Maybe it's for the best we listen to them." Wyatt put the tip of the blade to this person's neck. "I'll deal with them myself later. Food first, elders later, what part of that do you not understand?"

There was a brief silence as the man thought about it.

"Yes, of course, this way."

Wyatt put his blade down, and the cloaked figure began to lead him in the right direction.

"Much has changed since the dark days, Yit. You promised to return, but you never did. We gave up hope. The strange missionaries came from their boats and told us of their one God, and all the promises they offered. Not to mention all the free stuff they gave us in return for our temple to bear their symbol. It is but a simple cross. It seems so meaningless to me."

Wyatt glanced at the cross and shook his head. So many things were wrong with this, but now wasn't the time. "Well, we will have to see what's what, but first, business. Go to the horde that waits outside, tell them to send in fifteen or twenty guys to take what they need. Make sure you mention if they hurt you, they die, just to be sure."

The man ran off into the snow. Wyatt knew someone else was watching him. There always was in this situation.

Wyatt turned his head. "Come on out. I know you're there." It was then an old man came out of the shadows. He looked old, but his eyes looked downright ancient.

"You're not 'Yit.' I knew him. Darius's armor

was much bigger. He was much bigger than you were. My name is Stratos, who are you really?"

"My name really is Wyatt. I am no god, I am not Darius either, but I was sent back through time, to here, whenever here is? I have no way back."

"I can smell the power of Cyranthis in you, but it's weaker than it should be." Wyatt shook his head a bit.

"You wouldn't know of a time traveling spell or something like that to get back, would you?"

Stratos looked at the cross.

"The gods are gone. The cross talks a big game like a God should but doesn't do as much as people say. People will believe anything. We sure did back then," he said and smiled.

Wyatt was hoping for more mystical secrets and less memory lane.

"Boy, you're welcome to stay here as long as you want. The elders are cowards and kept all the food for themselves. They won't stop you. They fear your name," Stratos chuckled a bit. "It's almost like he knew what was going to happen." Wyatt could hear the others coming and turned to look. Once he looked back, Stratos was gone.

"Great, he's Batman," Wyatt said under his breath, then moved to the approaching group.

"You there, the food is in that building. Take what you need and leave, but don't come back," Wyatt said.

They said nothing, and he took that as a sign of agreement. The snow was beginning to get worse, and the sun was already falling out of the sky, but the men worked still.

Wyatt had no idea how much they needed, but they seemed to think he did. They could have gotten away with so much more. Wyatt said nothing, but he watched every move they made.

They worked fast. Wyatt took a step forward. "Hey. I'm sorry about your leader," he said.

"One less mouth to feed back home," the man said, and Wyatt nodded.

"Go home," he replied. The man turned and moved back towards his group, and they left the village. The snow was getting worse. He wondered if they'd make it back home.

Footsteps behind him from the snow. He snapped his head towards the source.

"Come on, we have to tell everyone you've returned!"

The kid in the cloak again. If he was some legendary being, he decided to show off a little and floated a few feet into the air, and the kid was spellbound at this.

"You can fly. You truly are a god. This way. I know you know the way, but it's this way, please allow me to show you this," he said, voice trembling.

"Yes, show me."

At a slow pace, they moved forward to the temple. Wyatt landed before the kid opened the doors.

The two of them entered, and there was some discussion going on, Wyatt didn't care about any of it. The second he came in, everyone shut up and stared. Wyatt saw Stratos there at the head of the Elder's table and figured that this imitation game was over.

Stratos stood up with a smile.

"Behold the return of Yit. The promise has been delivered upon even if we have abandoned the old ways."

"He can fly too. I've never seen anyone who can fly before. It has to be Yit." This kid was all about the god angle, seemed to feel special to bring him in to the others.

"Yeah, but we have a new God now, a better one. The one who died for us and--" Wyatt raised his blade at the random council member.

"If your new god died, then this is no god at all. You've been tricked into worshiping a useless corpse. I am not dead. I am here now. I have returned." As he spoke, the volume on his armor turned up, and his voice shook the walls as if it were thunder.

"Alright, please don't scream, Yit, please, forgive us, but understand you never came back, you never did. We are only human, and our faith faded."

A man who wasn't Stratos said this, and it gained his attention.

"Faith can be rebuilt, in time. I'll prove myself. Don't you even worry about it," Wyatt replied. "Oh, if you know of any time magic, speak up now," he said. Hoping someone might know something, or at least ask why.

The people looked at one another in confusion. Wyatt waited, but there was no answer. None but the ancient eyes of Stratos staring at him, something about those eyes made him feel insecure about his place in the world.

"Well, I'm going to wander outside. You can come up with some ideas. I feel like you'll think better without me in here," he said and walked back into the snow.

He looked at the snow covered cross.

"I don't suppose you have any suggestions."

There was never any reply. Not that he expected one, he was sure something had to be up there. He saw Lucifer, so now it just made the silence all that much worse. God just didn't care. None of them did.

"I didn't think so. You never do." Wyatt figured if he was stuck here, he'd be a better God than the one they worshiped now, at least. It was the least he could do for the people.

He did his best to not think about what this

might have meant for the future, too. If one still existed anymore.

## 71

Dustin was stuck at the end of the world. He could see it from here if this wasn't it.

"Will, if you know where 188's time machine is, now would be a great time to tell me."

Will looked at him.

"Oh, you don't think that was the first thing I tried to do? I would have been happy sending myself back centuries to get away from this, but it's gone. Nobody knows where it is. The one who can mess with time is that monster. If you want to go back, you'll have to ask her. That's the only chance you have. It won't work either. She kills everyone who goes up against her. The only defense we have are the old Syndicate weapons we could find," Will said.

"She thought it was funny to take random

things from the past and future and use them as weapons. Machines, you remember them. Some of them are here. Other things we've never seen before. It's all chaos. We're all dead soon enough, it's just a sadistic game to that thing," Will said as he put his back against the earth wall of the trench.

"You said this thing is my chance. Well, I'll fix all of this, I promise." Dustin flew into the black and green sky.

"Wait, Dustin, don't," Will thought about it. "Maybe he's the smart one. Get it over with quick."

He watched Dustin fly off towards the green horizon, disappearing into a broken sky. Will expected everything around him to change. For the worst timeline to end, but nothing happened. "I didn't think so,"

Dustin didn't know what to think.

He gazed at the ground below him, and it was hell on earth. There was nothing that was untouched. Horrible things that hurt to look at slithered down the streets. They didn't notice him. They were mindless, things of pure instinct. He wondered where they came from, who or what was responsible for these things?

He could see the green everywhere, but no Emily.

"I know you're out here. Show yourself. You sent me here. I don't know why you sent me to the future, but it really sucks, and we need to talk, now."

"Yeah, that was my bad. I meant to send you back to the old west, you know? Something went wrong and you were sent here. I should fix that mistake now." Dustin turned around.

"Oh, you just wait a minute, we need to talk." She looked at him. There wasn't much Emily left. It was her shape but everything else was transparent. As if she were made of green fire now.

"This world is dead and you want to talk, typical," she said and floated closer to him.

"I know you, the human part of you. I don't think you wanted any of this. You didn't allow us to fight you, send us all back, we can help you. We can save you from this, the world from this and everything else. You have to send us all back. Give us a chance to put things right."

She considered his words carefully.

"Fine. I'll send you all back minutes after you left. Then you'll all die. I tried to give you all peace you know? Of course, you're Delta. So eventually you'd all just make it back here anyway. Life is violent, and chances are not all of you will be making it back to this point. You'll be born, you'll do what you did. Then you'll be sent back to where I put you. I put you in an eternal time loop. I am sure that you'll want to keep it all the same when you see that. Life isn't too bad, violent, sure, but not too bad. Time is all very confusing, but let it be known that you'll always end up here, now. Time is a funny thing, but for you, I'll grant you your final battle."

She smiled, it looked like a smile to Dustin anyway.

The only thing Dustin got out of all of that was that new Emily sure liked to talk a lot.

"Thanks, I think, actually, time loop, that was confusing. I'm not sure I got it all," he said as she moved closer.

"Oh, where did all the creepy things come from?"

"Well, they came from Fort Diab. I let all the monsters out. I just opened the door. You can thank the Syndicate for that one, too."

She put her left hand on his shoulder.

"Goodbye, Dustin, I always liked you," she said, smiled, and all Dustin could see was green fire again.

Once the green flame faded, Dustin found himself not where he was, but where he was supposed to be all along. He was just outside of some little town called Sunset. At least that's what the sign said on the post.

"The bitch, she lied to me."

His armor would attract some attention. With a single thought, his armor retracted and disappeared. Dustin didn't feel any different, but he was surprised.

"Where did it go?" he asked.

He was in his street clothes. His twenty first century street clothes. He was sure that nobody would notice. If anyone cared he'd cross that bridge when he came to it. With a deep breath to calm his nerves, he began the trek into town.

He had no idea what he was going to do next.

All he knew is it was very hot and sunny out here and to him it felt like he was walking right into a western.

"Could have used a hat."

# 72

Blake couldn't take too much more of this mindless dribble. It was a different time, but hate was still hate no matter the era.

He was about to stop all of his when a hand came down on his shoulder and he jumped, almost fell backward, but the hand kept him steady.

He turned to see, of all things he never expected to see today, Nero Delacroix.

"Had enough fun yet? You're stuck here in the past. Can't we call it a day and go home now? I do miss you," she whispered to him. "The world is going to end, and how did you find me?" He already knew the answer.

"Just a little trick I picked up from my dad. So, can we go now?" He smiled under his armor, she knew it too. "Yeah, if we can get the others back too. I can only imagine they are not happy about being lost in time." She shook her head.

"They could be anywhere. That's a lot of history to cover. I had a lock on you. I was watching you. Them, well I do have my limits."

"It shouldn't be that hard, just connect with their true power, wherever it shows up and get them that way?"

He asked, trying to think of anything to save them.

"I suppose I could try. It won't be easy." This feat worried her a little.

Blake looked over and saw that someone was coming.

"Look there. It's a raid." Blake stated the obvious, but when he saw Abdul charge through the trees, then the others.

The Red Grand Wizard revealed himself by taking off his h. It was Demarcus. All the others did as well and it became apparent that this wasn't about race or genetic purity. Color didn't mean anything here.

Demarcus was always after one thing, power.

The 'Klan' members were all races hidden under the banner of the ghost to be protected from anyone who might show up. Nobody questioned the Klan.

"That rat bastard," Blake said.

Nero just laughed a little bit. "It was a good trick, very committed to his role."

"I guess."

The Delta Squad of the past charged into battle, fearless as any squad was expected to be. "That's right. I remember reading about this in the history files," Blake said and continued. "There was no mention of an armored squad member and his hot, yet mildly psychotic, cosmic and possessive girlfriend showing up to turn the tides."

That earned him a slap to the back of the head. It was light to her but it was enough to knock him off his feet and to the ground.

"I am not psychotic. Not even mildly."

"Oh, my mistake. Not psycho at all."

Shaking his head. "That hurts by the way. I'm not cosmic like you, so please don't kill me on accident. I would be disappointed if you accidentally killed me."

She smiled. He could feel that smile and it was a bit chilling.

"Well fine, my suggestion is to not get in the way of this mess, you've got nothing to do here."

"True. You're right, you usually always are," he replied and pulled his rifle out.

"Oh, what the hell, take the risk. Who knows, maybe you change everything with a single shot and make it all better. Because everyone knows when you change the past, the world gets better," she replied.

Blake fired a single shot. "I never read the whole file anyway. Maybe this is how it's supposed to go down," he replied.

One of the squad members was deep in battle. It had to be a Flesh Tearer. Only they'd be dumb enough to get this deep into the enemy ranks so fast and the guy didn't have a sword. Blake's bullet tore through the back of a nameless fighter, dropping him to the ground, saving the Delta team member from getting an extra hole in the back of his head, too.

"What did you do?"

Nero stared at him with a dangerous, and cold stare he could feel.

"Delta takes care of its own."

It was the only response he could come up with. "You're going to be the death of me yet, Blake. Let's get out of here and find your loser friends who can't seem to stay together." He put his rifle away.

"I hope you don't plan on shooting anyone else?" Her cold stare faded just as fast. She couldn't stay mad at him for long.

"Well, if we could make a stop in thirty-three, I could make use of a bullet or three," Blake said, and Nero smiled. "I bet you could."

She walked to him and wrapped her arms

around him. She was warm, even through the armor. "Thank you," Blake said.

"You never need to thank me for anything, let's go find your idiot friends if we can," she said, and the two of them disappeared.

## 73

"A secret like that, how could you make that kind of choice? Life must not be easy in the future," the younger commander said and looked away, understanding everything now.

Cody knew all of this. He got so caught up in the process of events back then that he forgot this whole conversation, and now it was happening just as he remembered it. How in the world did he forget something like this?

It was as if something made him forget, maybe it was a time travel thing.

The secret he couldn't tell anyone, not now, not ever. So much had happened that he forgot, and he would forget again. This version of him would change into the present day. Not that it made any difference. This loop had been closed.

"You have no idea. Now you need to go do what you are supposed to be doing. Just remember what I told you. I planned it all out. I knew once I'd be back here. I never knew how to get back then, like you didn't. This time I remembered to tell you. You have your mission now. Get it done. Tell no one, or everything could be for nothing," Cody told himself and looked around the island.

Lost in a memory, a painful one. He remembered this place and knew what had to be done.

"Fine, won't tell anyone, but you and me, we're not done. You can't be this pathetic in the future, or it's all pointless. Show me some of your true power, show me something that can make me feel confident this isn't all just a waste of time. That new armor of yours must be special somehow. Prove it. Fight me and show me, or otherwise, I'll just quit now." The younger commander took a fighting stance again.

"There is no talking you out of it, is there?" Cody said and took a step back, his eyes beginning to glow.

"You've been told, but now you learn just what you have to look forward to, come get me," he said and took a very similar fighting stance. The younger commander leapt at his future self. Right fist primed, moving faster than any human on the planet.

At the last second, Cody grabbed his fist,

twisted it around with so much strength the younger version was taken off balance for a brief second. One foot forward, and to the inside, the free hand proceeded to slam him into the ground.

"Remember what I told you. No matter what happens, it has to be how it plays out. Don't try and change it. Oh, now I remember why I lost so badly that one time. It was because of this," he said with a slight laugh before backing away.

"Damn, my armor is damaged. You're still good. Or I am? It's all confusing."

He stood up, fighting the pain that was fading in the process.

"Sorry about the armor, I really am. You go now, do what you were meant to. I have one thing left to do. This armor is so powerful that anyone looking will be able to detect the massive energy spike. They won't know it's me but they'll notice it. Just make sure you're off this island at the right time."

The commander nodded to him and turned, walked away to his post once more, didn't even look back.

"That's right. Now I wait." Cody was alone.

Day turned to night.

He expected the sounds of battle to start soon. He couldn't remember exactly when the battle took place. Eventually, they began. No part of the island was protected from those sounds, all the screaming. The battle ended and soon that thin gold beam that let Paxton escape the jaws of death was there.

Cody wanted to mention that, but things needed to happen in the course of events.

Cody's armor worked out the beam's frequency and the answer shocked him. They never found out who saved Paxton all those years ago. They always assumed it was 188. According to his armor, this beam was generated using Syndicate technology. Everything Cody believed changed.

"How long have they been in on this?"

The answer only could have been that it was from the beginning. Everything made sense now. The battle was over, and barely an hour in, the Syndicate forces were giving an extraction for the squad. They would never see him and they wouldn't search the island yet.

Coral Island was a weapons development lab, and they'd always assumed it was 188's lab and stuff, but it wasn't.

He waited until the black helicopter taking the squad was out of sight. "Better days," he said as it left.

"Right, goodbye Coral Island."

With that his armor turned on, it glowed an intense blue around his hands, bright electric arcs of power jumped from the ground into his armor and back down again and the wind started to pick up, too.

He was going to kill everyone on this island, nothing would be allowed to leave from it. The Syndicate would pay for this betrayal, but he wondered just how many people were to be trusted, and how many people were in on this whole thing from the beginning. The power he generated was more than enough to destroy the whole island.

A hand came from behind, landed on his shoulder.

"Thanks for the flare, it was hell trying to find you," Nero said.

"Move it, get away from here," Cody said and took to the air. He let his energy loose into the island and the three of them watched as a chain reaction started over the surface.

Soon, the whole place was on fire.

"It looks nuclear, but there's no radiation," Blake said and looked at Cody,

"How are you doing?" he asked.

"I'm better now, but listen. I found out the Syndicate has been behind pretty much everything since the beginning. Chances are everyone is involved. We can't trust any of them."

Blake heard this and shook his head.

"Figures as much. I believe you two already know one another?" He pointed between them. Nero smiled.

"Nice to see you again, Commander. We need to get the rest of your team. You were easy because you were sent back so few years. The others are going to be harder to find. You keep up, this rescue is a one time deal. If you get lost in the time stream, I don't find you again. Simple as that. Let's go."

It wasn't complicated. "Well then, ladies first," Cody said, and she smirked. "Yeah, like you can open a hole in time." She laughed, and then the three of them faded from sight.

## 74

Dustin didn't like this place much, but it was home now he supposed. It didn't even have electricity. He had nothing. No money, no place to sleep. It was like being behind enemy lines without a gun. He walked to what looked like a bar. It had the most people around it, in it.

The sun was beginning to go down and he figured this is what people did back then. He needed to know at least where he was, when, and what was going on.

He walked to this place, walked right in, and didn't bother looking at anyone, but everyone was looking at him.

"Stop, I was thrown through time to get here. I don't like it any more than you do. I'm having a bit of a bad day right now, so do me a favor and go about your own business."

With that out of the way, he walked up to the bar and sat down.

"What does a time traveler get these days?" he asked the guy behind the counter. "For a story like that, you can have anything you want, on the house," Dustin smiled. "Something strong, I can handle it."

The bartender walked away then. Dustin had no idea what he was going to do for the rest of his life. He'd never stop looking for a way back home.

Someone sat next to him. He did his best to not think about it.

"Time travel, it's a funny business, isn't it?" The question got Dustin's attention and snapped him out of his thoughts. The Scottish accent did too.

"Yeah, it's downright comedic, who are you?"

"I'm just a doctor. I know a bit about time," he replied and smiled as the tender brought him back a glass with something clear in it. It smelled terrible, it was perfect. "Thanks," he said as the man walked away again.

Dustin wasn't interested in the story or the conversation, but didn't have much of a choice.

"Okay, Doctor, what do you know about time that might be useful," Dustin replied.

"It's eighteen and seventy-four. You are in the western part of America, some boom town not destined to last much longer. You're obviously not from around here, you and that armor of yours. Pretty advanced, even for earth tech," the man said, and Dustin took his shot, then turned to look at this person.

He had Dustin's interest.

"So, Doctor. Doctor who, exactly?" The doctor just smiled.

"It doesn't matter. Just wanted to say hello to another legend is all."

Dustin rolled his eyes. "You're crazier than I am."

He motioned to the bartender for another. It tasted a lot like gasoline than anything else, but he needed something to get his mind off the situation that he was put into.

"Maybe, but I know things you don't. In an hour from now, this whole town is wiped off the map. Nobody knows why, wouldn't it be interesting to find out?" The doctor asked.

Dustin didn't react to this.

"There is always a town somewhere about ready to be wiped out. Maybe this is how I end. A forgotten footnote in history."

The doctor nodded.

"Maybe, but if that's true, you have nothing to lose by helping me." The stranger had a point. "Yeah, I have nothing else to do, what do you need?"

"Alright, finish your shot and I'll meet you outside. We'll talk," he said, got up, and walked out. Nobody seemed to notice this guy. "What god is it this time, magic nonsense," he said and drank the second glass. It burned again.

"Thanks, say do you know anything about that Doctor guy?" Dustin asked, and the bartender looked around.

"Just been you here, thought I heard you talking to yourself a bit, but I didn't want to intrude. It looked serious," the man replied.

"I'm sure. Thanks for the drink," Dustin said and stood up to meet the mystery doctor outside. He was there, still in his brown overcoat, and a bowtie. Dustin almost laughed.

"Okay, what are you? God, ghost, mage?" Dustin was going to get right to the point.

"No, none of those. Just a doctor. I've been waiting for you," he replied, and Dustin rolled his eyes.

"To the point, doctor, please. I just want to find somewhere to sleep," Dustin replied. The man's eyes, along with the rest of his face, turned serious.

"I lied," he said.

"I kind of figured out you're not a doctor," Dustin replied.

"No, I lied about not knowing why this town gets wiped out. Look up there," he said and pointed towards the sky.

It looked like a comet from here.

"You literally can't be here, come with me," the doctor said, but he didn't feel too rushed.

Dustin winced when he saw the thing.

"Shouldn't I do something?" Dustin asked.

"Can't, history says this place is wiped out. That sure is a shame, oh well, we better get going."

"Well, screw history."

Dustin ran, leaped into the air, and took off as the armor reappeared around him. He was flying towards the comet, his power burning through the armor, leaving a trail of white fire behind him.

"Well, I may have made a couple of things up," The doctor said as he took a couple of steps forward to watch.

Dustin collided with this thing, and to his surprise, it was metal. He expected it to be a rock, he'd worry about that later. This thing, it wasn't that heavy, but it was still going too fast. He wouldn't be able to stop the crash, but he was able to offset it. The landing would not be in the center of town.

He watched the town fly under him in just a few seconds. Once he was sure everything was going to be alright, he spun away and let the thing fall away from him. "I hope I didn't ruin the world for this town," Dustin said and watched the thing carve a deep trail into the earth, leaving fire and dust behind it.

He landed beside the craft. It was an alien ship. "Aliens, again?"

The doctor was beside him, staring at the wreck.

"Earth equivalent of teenagers taking their parents' car for a joyride while drinking. Oh, I lied about the whole town destruction thing. Do you really think I would have ever let the whole town be wiped out? Nah, just wanted to see how you reacted, just as I knew you would. Now. I'll take over from here. Thanks, oh, and by the way. I'm sorry," he said and bowed his head a bit.

"Sorry for what?" Dustin asked, confused.

"You'll understand later. Go back to town and wait. Your ride is coming. They'll need you. Go now. Oh, and don't make a big deal out of this alien thing, either. Just go on and finish this."

Dustin didn't make sense out of any of this, but he felt he could trust this guy. He began to turn around to walk away.

He looked back when he heard a strange pulsating sound in the distance, but nothing was there.

"So weird."

He turned to walk away. The town itself was in a panic. It was understandable. Something did just come out of the sky and try to wipe it out.

He didn't get ten feet.

"Dustin, what the hell did you do? I leave you alone for five minutes and you almost blow up a whole town?" Cody said.

Dustin jumped and spun around.

"The hell, how did you get here?"

He saw Nero.

"Oh, right. Well, thanks for the rescue."

"Super easy, barely an inconvenience," Cody replied. Dustin didn't think this would happen. Now that he had to leave, he kind of wanted to explore the old west a bit more. Maybe he could go back someday.

She just nodded to him, didn't say anything.

"This time travel thing isn't easy, is it? I can tell. Three of us here and two more to go. Can you handle it, or is this too much?" Dustin was always the one to worry about things. She walked up to him, put her hand around his neck, and lifted him off the ground.

"Bitch, I can handle it. Don't ever question my skills. Be ready to keep up," she dropped him.

"Fine, alright. Sorry for asking, but keep up how?" Dustin asked, "and did anyone else see that weird doctor guy?"

Cody just shrugged. "Doctor who, now?" he asked as they disappeared into the growing night.

## 75

"It was all a horrible mistake," Stratos said.

The two were alone in the chamber. Wyatt had gotten annoyed with the uselessness of the people, so he kept them out. He only allowed Stratos to visit now.

There was little to do but watch the snow fall as the months passed, eat questionable things, and do his best to not kill anyone while practicing in silence. Because he was some kind of a god now, he couldn't ever fit in with society without everyone acting weird.

Life in the old days was nothing like the stories he read about. Stratos was the only one he could talk to, and right now it felt like the old man had a story coming on.

"Mistake. How so? What are you talking about?"

The old man looked at him with dead eyes. "Christianity was a mistake, overall, the way people believe it today. Let me tell you a story."

Wyatt shrugged. "Sure. I could use the history lesson. Not doing anything else."

"That poor boy was never supposed to die on the cross for anyone. About nine hundred years ago or so, a group of us were supposed to, you know, provide the planned divine intervention. You see, those pesky Romans, that's how they lived. Their way of life was war—go out, beat the hell out of someone, and take over. They were pretty good at it too. When this character shows up claiming to be the son of a peaceful God, to make friends instead of war. Well, he got some attention, but not from the people you'd expect." Stratos laughed at this.

"Okay, so, whatever, keep going," Wyatt said. Most of the story he got, some was new.

"The peace and no war thing made sense at the time. The Romans just weren't that interested in it, but worse, the Jewish leaders hated it. You see, there was power in being oppressed. The Jews were fourth-class citizens, but their idiot leaders got the scraps the Romans gave them. That power went to their heads," Stratos said, staring off into the distance as he talked. Wyatt wasn't sure what he was looking at.

"Okay, I'm with you so far. Romans were power, Jewish leaders thought they were powerful, got it," Wyatt was ready for the part he didn't know.

The Romans didn't like Jesus, but he wasn't a threat. All he taught was peace. It was a nonissue overall. The Jewish leaders couldn't have the Romans look at the Jews as equals, you see? If they did, they would become equals, and their power over their people would be gone. This terrified them, as losing power always terrifies people who think they have it," Stratos said.

"Makes sense so far."

"In a horrid act of betrayal, they took this guy down and put him on the cross. Called him a false prophet, sinner, all the horrid things, beat him down. The one guy who tried to do the most to help them, the leaders put to death."

Wyatt nodded. "Seems to be one of humanity's defining traits, attack the person who wants to help the most. Nothing's changed."

Stratos looked down at the floor. "That's sad," he replied.

"Yep."

Stratos took a breath. "None of that was supposed to happen. God, well, this one, is powerful, but there are reasons he channels his powers through humanity. He came to Darius and asked him to find his best Guardian to save his earth-bound son. Long story short, Darius picked the best guardian and sent him to rescue him," Stratos said.

"I never understood that. Couldn't Jesus just magic himself away? Why stay on the cross?" Wyatt asked.

"Miracles are powered by people who believe in them, plus he didn't want to be like his brother," Stratos said.

"Brother?"

"Lucifer and Jesus have the same father after all, they are related," Stratos replied.

"I guess I never thought about it like that," Wyatt said. "Humble idiot until the end."

Stratos chuckled. "Yeah, humility was one of his things. All that power in his blood, and he just wanted to help people find redemption, go figure."

"Obviously, things didn't work out," Wyatt said.

"No. The Guardian was captured by Necromancers. He was, uh, sleeping too close to the road, and they got him. That was a stupid mistake. Anyway, the execution went as planned, and there was no intervention. Everything happened just as everyone knows it today."

"Was there a point to this story? Someone screwed up, it happens. Sometimes even the gods get disappointed." Wyatt wasn't impressed yet.

"Well, the guardian escaped too late and heard of the event. Jesus died on the cross. It was a spectacle. Not every day you get to see divinity die after all."

"Determined to make things right, the guardian did some capturing of his own and forced the necromancer to the site. The tomb was under guard because you know how people get, so the necromancer magicked the two of them inside."

"The two of them did a resurrection ritual. They got the divine soul back into the body. The Guardian did what he was tasked to do. He saved the son of god, and then they got out."

"Necromancers are just healers who came late to the party, anyway, right?" Wyatt asked.

"I guess if you put it like that, kind of, yeah," Stratos said.

"Trouble is, that wasn't the plan. The followers started spreading the message of 'he will return' and they created a religion, an unintended side effect that's been causing headaches for everyone ever since."

"I'm not sure if it's ironic, but they took the symbol of the thing their savior died on and turned it into their holy symbol, like anyone else who was ever crucified was useless and forgotten. Now everyone is waiting for their savior to return. I wonder how they would react if they knew that he wasn't ever coming back," Stratos looked at Wyatt and shook his head.

"Great story, how do you know any of this?"

"I was there. That's how I know. I just thought you should know, that someone should know before I pass on."

"That was nine hundred years ago, right? You're still alive, explain."

"Darius was disappointed in me and granted me a long life, so I could think about what I had done and how I messed up," he replied.

"Oh yeah, living a long time. What a punishment," Wyatt said and continued, "actually that makes a lot of sense, I mean what are a few miracles compared to creating the universe anyway." Stratos stopped him.

"No, all the gods that are, lesser or greater status, were created when the Abyss and its 'brother' fought for the first time. The aftermath of that battle created reality as we know it. The whole realm. We are a tiny speck in the whole of reality. We just happen to be one of the main points of the Nexus, making us special," Stratos said and coughed some.

"Makes sense."

This story made him feel small. Now he kind of felt bad about a few things, but was this the truth or was the old guy just making things up? There was no way to be sure.

He kind of wanted to keep it that way too.

"Thanks for the story, but right now we have bigger things to worry about. The news that the old god has returned has spread throughout the villages over the past couple of months, and now that the winter is fading, they'll want to come and see," Wyatt said with a dejected sigh, hoping to get out of this mess before then, but nobody was coming to the rescue this time.

"Wyatt, it's too late for that, they're already outside. The tribes have not only heard this news, but they have come to challenge the new God. There is no better way to prove the new ways like doing your best to kill the old," Stratos said, and Wyatt just sighed.

"Yeah, I guess we better go say hello to the adoring fans." Wyatt said and stood up, stretched out.

"None of this is fair. Trial by combat, you with your god armor and stuff," Stratos said. Wyatt shrugged.

"Life isn't fair," he said and put his thick fur cloak on. It was itchy but it kept him warm enough. He walked outside, and Stratos followed him.

Wyatt didn't know what to expect here, but there were only a few fighters, and each had a couple of people with them. He wasn't sure who the fighters were and the escorts. They were all watching him. Wyatt did his best to remember the language. He didn't want to suit up just to talk to them.

"Hey, I know you all seem to think you have something to prove, but I don't think you want this," he said, hoping he said everything right this time. The fighters laughed. Seeing this God in the flesh, they were unimpressed.

Then, from across the way, a big man hurled something long and sharp at Wyatt's head.

He moved to the side and caught it. This thing was heavy. "Did you cut down a whole tree for this thing or what?" he asked under his breath.

"A spear? Are you trying to see if a god can bleed? Well, let me show you that it is true, even the gods can bleed."

He sighed and put his left hand around the sharp stone and slid his hand over it. Wyatt did his best not to wince, and the blood did come just as it was supposed to. The wound was deeper than he intended.

Then he held his hand up to the crowd, and they watched as the flesh pulled itself together.

"See. I just heal faster than the average person," he said and tossed the stick to the ground so hard it broke in half.

"You still want to do this?" he asked in their language.

"Surely the one true god will give me the power I need to beat you."

This big guy walked out of the crowd. He had the cross around his neck, it was silver, he was dressed in the traditional cloth of a priest of the day, but this man was a killer, Wyatt could tell just by the way he moved.

"Are you willing to bet your life on that? I don't show mercy. Are any of you willing to die for what you believe in?" Wyatt already knew they were. No one was backing down.

"Alright, Christians first, and older religions, the older it is, farther back on the list you are. Those who are about to die for a god or gods who don't give a damn about you, prepare yourself."

"You have fifteen minutes," he said as he walked away from them all.

"Your arrogance is godlike, but don't underestimate them. I saw some of the ancient orders in the crowd. They were stories when I was young and only existed in the dark places of the world, if they are here, they will surely fight in their god's name. The ripper of flesh, or the walking wound," Stratos replied.

"Wait, Flesh Tearer? What order is that?" Wyatt stopped walking.

"The ancient Lemurian religion, they say this being, this god, was real, and it was told that he grew angry with them, so he summoned the power of the universe and destroyed the whole of Lemuria and Atlantis with a devastating attack. He dropped the sky stone onto the earth and killed nearly everything in a fit of rage, others contested this theory. Saying some kind of alignment was broken ages ago. The truth may never be known. But still, you should watch out for those ones."

This brought a smile to his face.

"So, that's where he went."

"I'll be fine, old man. Don't you worry about me." The fifteen minutes flew by, and now it was time to get on with it.

"Alright, all you losers and hypocrites, the time is now. All at once or one at a time. It's up to you. Anyone who isn't here to prove how strong their god is or isn't, stand back now."

Wyatt returned, all those who wanted to see tomorrow did back off, leaving those who came to fight. There were eight.

They had come prepared for battle. They had their armors, their weapons, and their faith with them.

"You mortals have your weapons. I have mine."

Wyatt walked forward, and his armor formed around him in an instant, and everyone gasped at this. They'd never seen anything like it. "My blade." A priestess walked forward with a long black box. She opened it. He pulled Hell Razor out and stared at it for a second like it was an old friend.

"Now, who's first again, oh right, the peaceful ones, let's do this. Alright. You're up first." Wyatt didn't know his name. He didn't care as he pointed the blade at the warrior priest.

This person seemed to be so confident in his ability that there didn't seem to be a worry in the world. The crowd seemed as if they chose their champion as well. This man had a hammer as a weapon, it was massive, and it looked scary at least.

Wyatt saw the man talking, something about how divine justice was coming on him, something, he didn't pay attention to it. The hammer came at him, the swing was arching overhead. It was slow, wide.

Wyatt didn't want to make a show out of this. His own blade came out and sliced through the hammer and through the arms of the man who held it in one easy strike. He stood there for a second, then fell to pieces as if he were always just a puzzle. This silenced the crowd. God's supposed champion was beaten in one strike.

"You can all go home now if you want. I don't want to kill anyone else."

Nobody wanted to go home now. They wanted to see a god in action. Today would become the stuff legends were made from.

"I am Theros, son of Ares, and here, with me is my cousin, Bront, grandson of Zeus. We are the last remaining in a line of heroes of the ancient past. We are the strongest. We invite you to stand down, armored one. You may be strong but inside of us is the blood of the Olympians."

The two men came forth. Wyatt looked at them,

and the way these two looked, they could have been telling the truth. Wyatt rolled his eyes, however. Even way in the past, he couldn't get away from Olympian wannabes.

"Olympians, you say? Where did they run off to? They left you here all alone to fend for yourselves. Parents of the year, maybe not. If you are who you say you are. You might have a chance. If you are lying. You'll be dead, just like this one. I am standing in his blood. Take a good long look at it, then tell me if you're ready."

His eyes flashed just for a second. The two of them looked at the body cut to pieces.

"Your future could end right now. Interested in that chance? Live or die, I don't care."

These words were enough to make them rethink their approach.

"No, you're right. We don't belong here. We'll be leaving now." The boasts turned to fear, and they turned to run away. The crowd almost started to laugh. Wyatt wouldn't have that either, turned to face them.

"There is no shame in running from me. The first one to laugh at anyone who chooses to not fight takes their place. No exceptions. Nothing wrong for wanting to live." This killed the laughter in the crowd.

The other ones who were so eager to fight couldn't seem to find it in their hearts to go up against a god who seemed to respect life, give choices. All of them but one.

"I'll face you. I know exactly who you are," a cloaked figure said and stepped up. The voice sounded familiar, not quite known but like he knew it.

"Who are you?" he asked this person and waited.

"I am from an ancient bloodline. These frauds here, they don't know anything about what it is to be related to a true god. In Lemuria, there came a god, two of them, real ones. One was a king, the other was a destroyer. Before the rage took over, he started a bloodline. It continues with me." The cloak was removed. It was a lady.

Wyatt noticed her eyes first. They were not human. They were the eyes of a snake. Stratos took a step back.

"Serpent race, Lemurian. After the great disaster, their race devolved into a savage people. We encountered some, Darius and our friends. They were basically monsters by that time. No choice but to kill the ones we met, but they were few. Legends of a hybrid race existed. We never met any. Didn't want to," he said and coughed some at the sight of her.

She removed her cloak, and was in full armor, it covered every inch of her. It looked exactly like

Josh's armor, in style anyway. There were black symbols burned, or carved into it. He couldn't tell.

Wyatt saw this and stepped back, but he had to laugh.

"Well, at least I know what happened to him. It'll make doing this that much harder. What's your name?"

She looked at him. "I wasn't given one. They hunt us down, killed families. Called us monsters. Our kind has what you call a genetic memory. Our history is born with us from one generation to the next. We never forget who killed us, who hunted us down and most importantly where we came from. Our race, well, we had to get brutal to live. I think I am the last one left. Humanity will pay for what it did. I'll start with the one who claims to be a god to show everyone just what it is I can do." Wyatt sighed.

"Listen lady. I'm not interested in your revenge story. I can't change what was done to you, but if you want to live here with us, you can. We're pretty much family, it seems. I'd hate to have to kill you. I really would."

He knew this wouldn't work.

He could feel the rage, it had trickled down through the infinite ages of time, but it was still here. It was unmistakable. She roared, and her helmet slid up over her bright red hair and blood red snake eyes.

There was only one way to talk to anyone like this. She attacked, leapt into the air with enough speed to make him worry about it. She hit the ground with so much force that everyone watching this nearly lost their balance. Wyatt knew better than to be standing there. The edge of his blade struck out across her armored face. It didn't cut through, it made sparks and left a scratch. She didn't seem to notice, and when he tried to draw back, she grabbed onto his blade.

She twisted it and stuck the end into the ground. With the other hand, she made a fist with a fair amount of force, put it into his chest, knocking him back off of his feet and into the ground.

"That power, good to know it's all genetic, and your temper is just as bad, you fight like him, too." Wyatt knew this could be trouble if he wasn't careful enough about how he did things from here on out. He took off into the air. He felt that attack but it didn't cause him any real damage.

"Alright, Kid. Let me show you how your relative fought. I knew him well. Let's see if you measure up."

She went right for his head in a blind rage. He watched her coming in slow motion. He was already out of the way. He put his fist into her stomach and watched her buckle over, her armor caved in with one attack and she was done.

"Girl, like I said, I don't want to kill you. I don't

want to fight you," he said to her as she fell to the ground.

Not taking any chances, he put the sharp end of the blade against the back of her neck. Emotion didn't play a part in this at all.

"I know who you are. I remember all the stories. I remember," she said, trying to breathe.

"Then you'll remember that I am one of the goodish guys and stop trying to kill me because obviously, it's not working out so well for you."

"Yeah, you just happen to be in the wrong place at the right time. I can take you down, Wyatt." She said his name, and it made him flinch. She said it with all the rage Josh would have. This flinch was all it took. She rolled into him away from that blade and managed to kick him in the back of the knees.

The power behind that kick was enough to make him fall to the ground. She grabbed the hand with the sword in it, stopping it from taking her head off, and pushed Wyatt to the ground. "I have you now," she said as he grabbed the blade away from him.

He rolled over onto his back and was laughing.

"You sure would make him proud, you know that? You got all that power and rage, but you also got his weakness."

Wyatt laughed even harder. This only enraged her more, and everyone left watching didn't understand what was going on. She raised the blade, going for the killing blow.

"Flesh Tearer, well, he was never that bright."

Wyatt lifted his right hand and fired one of his throwing knives. It tore through that armor, into her side, and blood began to leak around the edges.

She tried to pull it out when the electric shock burned into her armor and her flesh, and sent her back to the ground, dropping Wyatt's blade.

It stuck into the ground beside her.

Wyatt got up and pulled his sword out of the ground.

"I know you'll never stop. Next time you might get smart and use people against me. I can't have that." He swung the blade towards her neck.

A blue hand caught his own mid swing.

"You don't really want to do this, Wyatt. She is family after all."

Wyatt didn't move for a second. "It can't be." He jumped away and looked at the others.

"Hey there, buddy. How's it going?" Dustin asked with a wave.

"Yep, it's us. Just when you thought it was safe to play God, we show up," Blake said. "Cody, what —well, you know. Explain. Now." Wyatt was still trying to wrap his head around it.

"Simple. Blake's cosmic girlfriend offered to save us. Not sure why, and sure we'll have to pay for it later. This is how these deals usually work. So, business as usual. You know how it is," the commander said.

The fighter began to stir, Cody sent a weak plasma charge into her armored head and knocked her out again. Wyatt recalled his blade.

"Yeah, business as usual. You seem changed. I like it, I think." Wyatt said and laughed. "What do you want to do with her?" Cody said and looked at her.

"No idea. She'll kill everyone if we leave her, on the other hand maybe not. Who knows? I say we kill her anyway and get it over with," Wyatt said.

"I don't think that's the right move here," Cody replied.

Wyatt decided to do something.

"Nero, I know you've done a lot for us, but can you send this one someplace where she won't hurt anyone? I'd rather not kill her, you know. If you can't, I guess it's back to plan A."

Wyatt turned and looked at her, but she wasn't in good shape. All of this time traveling was taking its toll on her, and she was out of breath.

"You want to save the life of one mistake, why?" Nero asked.

"I have my reasons. If you can't, don't try. I'll understand," he replied.

She closed her eyes. "Fine. I have a good spot all picked out." Nero pointed at the fallen fighter, and she disappeared.

"There. Done. Can we go now? The sooner we get this over with, the sooner I can go home and sleep. I'm not used to all this time jumping."

"Oh, Wyatt. When we find Josh, I'm gonna tell him what you said. I'm sure he'll be thrilled to hear you think he's an idiot," Cody said and laughed as Wyatt put his blade back.

"You wouldn't do that, right?" Cody just crossed his arms.

Wyatt turned to Stratos, who was just as stunned as the rest of the crowd that had watched this entire time.

"You're in charge again. I'm going to save the future. Build a statue of me or something if you feel up to it. Most important, remain free," he said. Then he turned to the others. "If you join forces none of you will ever go hungry again. If you fight one another, you'll all die. Choose wisely," Wyatt said. Hoping that'd be enough to end the raids.

Stratos waved, nodded. Wyatt waved back as he and the others disappeared.

## 76

Josh was led into the ancient serpent city of Ib. Most of the buildings were constructed with large blocks of stone stacked on top of one another, at least that's what it looked like to him. There was a word for that he heard once. Cyclopean, he thought.

The snake guards were quick to surround them. Their obsidian spears pointed at him. "What is this thing, why have you brought this here?" They were going to kill them both. Josh didn't know if they were speaking English, or if the armor was just able to translate it.

"This is the one from the sky, the red God. I saw him appear out of the sky. He seeks the King," she replied.

The guards weren't having it. "This is Atlantean

trickery, there is no way we are letting this thing into the keep," one of them said.

Josh grabbed the end of the spear closest to him and snapped the tip off with one hand. "Bring me to your leader, or I will kill all of you," Josh replied, doing his best to not lose his temper and do it anyway.

The reptilian guards could feel his rage. At least that's what it looked like to him, and they backed away. "Come with us,"

Josh was a little thankful he didn't have to start killing everyone, at least not yet.

The group moved to the black castle in the distance. To Josh, the thing looked like a predator stalking the town, a living shadow. He wondered how they made so many things out of materials like this. He'd never seen anything like it in his own time.

The King sat on the throne, as a King is expected to do, then he stood up the second he saw this thing enter the court. This thing didn't look like the rest of them. It was taller, looked more like a dinosaur than a lizard. Some kind of mix, Josh didn't know, didn't want to ask.

"What is the meaning of this?" he asked. The second he spoke, Josh knew why this one was the leader. Josh decided to get to the point.

"I don't belong here. I was torn through time and just want to get back. You wouldn't happen to know of any magic users, would you? Mages, something like that?"

The king looked the armored one up and down. He believed him.

"We do, but I don't know if they can help you." Anything was better than nothing at this point.

"Thanks." Josh didn't know what else to say.

The guards relaxed. "No, he's lying. I saw him come out of the sky, he's the one. The one that's going to lead us against Atlantis, he's the chosen one," the woman said.

"No, I'm really not. I promise it's just a mistake, whatever stories you have or predictions, whatever, it's not me. Did you say Atlantis?" Josh asked, trying to get his head around all of this.

Then a large bell began to chime. Josh knew that was a warning.

"Atlantis attacks again," Xulthal said, and the guards rushed out of the court. "They want to kill us all."

Genocide. It was always that with the enemy. He had no idea what started the war, or who, but these people, lizards, whatever, didn't deserve to be wiped out. Then he made a choice.

"Take me to the front," Josh said.

Xulthal looked at him. The King looked at him too. "If you want to fight, follow the guards, they are heading there. Good luck, stranger," the King said, then turned to walk away.

Josh looked at Xulthal, then he lifted to the air and flew out the large black doors. The second he did this, the King looked back just in time to see him disappear.

Josh flew over the city. He knew people were watching him. He didn't need to follow the guards. He could see the problem from here. Atlantean ships sat in the ocean. He knew it because these people were just as human as he was.

The ships were firing bright yellow orbs of flame into the walls of the city. It was not the first time this had happened. The whole beach was covered in scorch marks from the past. Meanwhile, smaller boats were racing towards the shore, each one filled with fighters.

The lizard people had done him no harm, and he wasn't about to let them die. One of the projectiles was going to make it over the walls. Josh saw it and veered to the right. Before it could do anything, he flew through it, and it exploded over the beach.

The smaller boats weren't going to stop. He could see the lizard people start to man the walls, archers. This was a bloodbath waiting to happen, all the ships had to do was keep shooting. Another explosion against the black wall—the flames died out. It was time to make this quick.

His miniguns on his wrists popped out of his armor and started to spin. "Whatever," he said and started shooting. Starting with the boats closest to shore, he watched as the bodies fell into the ocean. The boats were made out of wood. This kind of force was tearing them to pieces. It only took a few seconds to wipe out the people in each boat, and soon the ocean was littered with blood, dismembered bodies sinking due to the armor they wore.

It didn't take more than two minutes before the forces farther out to sea turned back on their own. Josh made sure that anyone who managed to make it to the shore wouldn't live to talk about it.

Once he saw they were in full retreat, he stopped shooting. Those three ships in the distance —he couldn't let them all get away. He took a breath and charged out to sea. It was less than ten seconds to close the distance.

The ship on the right was first. He turned into a living battering ram, smashed through the left side of the ship, and made his way through to the other side. The ship was going to sink, but Josh didn't stop to think about it as he did the same thing to the next ship, leaving a gaping hole in it.

The last one he stopped, flew to the deck, and landed on it. A quick scan told him who the captain was—the one staring right at him with the fearless look in his eyes. Everyone else was terrified.

Josh walked to the man.

"Got a message for you. Don't come back. Leave the dead. Take the ones who lived with you. Understand?"

The captain stared at him.

"You're a warrior. You know I control nothing," he replied. The man had a point. "I know, but if you tell them what you saw here today and only one ship comes back, your, whatever makes the idiot decisions, might pay attention. Maybe we can bring this war to an end early," Josh said.

"An early end to a war? Nothing would make me happier," he replied. "Me too. Best of luck. I hope the next time I see you, it's for a peaceful reason. I think we could be friends," Josh said. Before the captain could say another word, he flew off into the sky, heading back to the shore.

Josh didn't bother with the retreating forces at the wall. Instead, he moved right to the castle. The closer he got, the more he could see something was going on.

He landed in front of the doors, walked in, and it was chaos. The guards were holding back a crowd. Josh lifted into the air, no one noticed. In the center of the madness, there it was. An assassin was impaled, dead, but beside him lay the King, skin charred black. It all made sense. It was a distraction at the gates to get this job done.

Josh didn't like the Atlanteans before, but now he hated them and was tempted to go back to finish the job he started.

Xulthal's face and left side were burned too. Others around had died. The throne was still smoldering. Josh had no idea what caused this. There was a Lemurian in a cloak standing towards the back. He had a long stick in his right hand that had a gem on top. Josh knew a wizard when he saw one and flew over the crowd to land beside him.

"You must be the mage the King spoke of," he said. The wizard just nodded but was too distraught to speak.

"Can I get home?" Josh asked.

"You could." Josh knew the tone of that voice.

"Walk with me before you say more," Josh replied and turned to move towards the back of the room. The wizard followed.

"This isn't my fight. I don't belong here."

The saurian looked at him. "We're all soldiers now," he replied.

"No, you don't understand. I'm not like you. I'm, well," he didn't know how to say it, so he just slid his helmet back, revealing his human face. "I'm like them. You're smart, so you get it, but the average, uh, whatever you are, won't. I know how this goes," he replied.

The wizard smiled. "You defended us. Everyone watched you defend the wall. You're one of us. Doesn't matter what you look like," he replied.

"I don't know how this war ends. Well, okay, there aren't any lizard people running around in my time, so I suspect this is a war you lose. If I help, I could change everything."

"Do our lives not matter in the here and now? Would you just let us die? Is it in your heart to do nothing?"

Josh looked back at the crowd, their dead king. The misery. Human or not, he could feel it.

"No, I can't just do nothing." He hated that answer, but it was the truth.

"My name is Quarl," the wizard said, and Josh didn't care. "I am in charge of choosing the new leader of Lemuria."

Josh froze. "Wait, hold on a minute," he said.

Quarl looked at him. "You come from the sky the day our leader is murdered. Slaughter the enemy. You wear the armor of a God, and your soul burns like I've never seen," Quarl said.

"No. Don't you dare do it, lizard wizard," Josh said.

"I choose you to lead us in the war. Once the war is over or victory is impossible, then I'll send you home," Quarl said.

"I hate you so much right now. I don't know anything about any of this. I'm a terrible ruler. I don't even know the laws. Anything."

"You'll be the literal King. Who cares what the laws are? Change them, it's your job. It's good to be in charge. I will inform the people in a few hours."

"Yeah. I'm just sure this won't have anyone pissed. What could go wrong?" Josh couldn't believe how this was turning out. All he wanted was normal. He kept getting thrown into all the odd. Time eating monsters on one hand. Ancient wars and lizard people on the other.

"Everything could go wrong, we could all die, so there's that, I suppose," Quarl replied.

"Sarcasm must not be a thing yet." The wizard ignored him and walked towards the still smoking body of the King.

"Today is the first day of the rest of your life," Josh said to himself as he did his best to come to terms with his new reality.

## 77

Josh's ascension to power became a distant memory. The destroyer made King took the throne. Everything changed.

The war raged on through the decades. Some battles they'd win, others they would lose. With each passing generation, the word Josh became synonymous with King.

It had been one hundred years of constant war, death, and misery since he had arrived.

He didn't have anyone to talk to. Everything was just war plans, orders, daily violence, and a daily number lost, to their best estimate. He sat upon his throne, which was now constructed from the bones of the generals of Atlantis. He had killed thousands of soldiers, officers, children—anyone who dared wear the colors of the enemy.

This fight would have been over ages ago if not for the magic, but he'd seen it work. Strange liquid light burned the flesh off of soldiers as they stood. Black rains fell from the sky and made armies fall into chaos. The magic of Atlantis was vicious, but so was he.

"Sir, we have a grim report."

Josh looked up, tired eyes. There was a grim report every day. This was nothing new. "Report. What is it now? What beast do they bring this time?" He was more than ready to slaughter everyone who dared come to his shores. He was king for many different reasons.

"No beast, none. The seas, Sire, at sunrise upon Morgrath Point. The seas are filled with an invasion force the likes of which we have never seen."

Josh felt a bit of a chill run down his spine. It was strange.

"I'll go to the point and see for myself," Josh said and stood up. His armor appeared around him, and he took off into the morning sky.

The point wasn't far. It was one of the scary places they talked about in their religion—some kind of old thing lived under the mountain, he never saw any evidence of anything horrible in all this time. That wasn't important now.

It only took a few minutes to get there at these speeds. He landed on the peak and looked out towards the ocean. It was black with ships. His armor did a digital scan and estimated their numbers to be at least a million soldiers.

A million genocidal maniacs coming this way. It must have been the entire army picking up a blade and coming after them. Josh knew defeat when he saw it, and this was it.

He knew every living thing on this land was going to die.

"Why now?" he supposed it didn't matter. He could never go to Atlantis because it'd leave his kingdom unprotected. Now Atlantis was coming to him. Small favors, he supposed.

He couldn't stand the thought of everyone dying. With no more time to waste, he flew towards the castle and made the trip in half the time. The castle was buzzing with activity, but he ignored it all and made his way to the war room.

The four generals were waiting for him there already, arguing with one another about what to do, each voice louder than the next.

"Enough," Josh said as he landed. The silence was immediate.

"It's true. The last invasion of the enemy is coming with everything they have. We won't live through this. We'll die fighting, protecting our homeland to the last man, and make no mistake about it. I've known many men. There is not one among you who is any less human just because of what you look like. I'll fight with you to the last man. If you want to run, you can. There are no bad choices here. I have nowhere else to go. What is it going to be?"

Josh slid his helmet back.

"We'll assemble the army." Josh looked at his officer and almost smiled.

"You have less than an hour to prepare. Meet me at the beach. Bring as many as you can find."

"We're already on the way. The captains are giving all the speeches they can right about now, I'm sure," the general replied.

"Right. See you there. Don't be late, don't leave anything behind," Josh knew where he wanted to go next and took off again.

The trip to the plains didn't take long. They were there waiting for him too. Fluffy the Fourth was being used as a pillow by the little ones. He landed. "Quarl, Endol," Josh called their names. The queen moved towards him, graceful as ever.

"Quarl, I need you to get the Queen out of here. Take Brok and Ollie out of here too," he said. They started to protest.

"Listen. They are going to kill everyone they can find. They've taken enough from me, from this land. They can't have you. I won't let them," Josh said.

Endol crossed her arms, and those yellow snake

eyes glared at him. "I am a fighter. I will fight for my land, for the kids. Why would you want me to run?" she asked.

"There are a million fighters coming, maybe more. We don't have a chance. I mean it—not even a little one. You need to take the boys and have Quarl get you someplace, anyplace else. Today could be Lemuria's last day, and I want you to see tomorrow," he said.

"Sire, I am better suited on the battlefield. Perhaps a spell could turn the tide," Quarl replied. He was ancient now, gray-scaled and tired. Josh knew he meant well, but his magic had been faulty in recent years.

"You've been wise counsel this whole time. I owe you everything. Let me repay you with the rest of your life. Take them away from here. Please," he said, and the sound of his voice softened just a little.

Endol looked away.

"We'll find one another again in the next life, no matter how long it takes," she said, and he smiled. It hurt to smile these days, but he managed it.

"Yes, I promise."

"Well, hug her, you big idiot," Quarl said, and Josh ignored the language. No one was watching. Usually, royalty had to be official and proper.

The two embraced in a hurry. Neither one

willing to shed a tear, only a few seconds before taking a step back.

"Boys, come here," Josh said. The hybrid children lifted themselves off the dinosaur and moved to him.

"Guys, you need to—well, you're going to need to grow up a little faster than I'd like," he said, and they couldn't keep eye contact.

"Hey, look at me." Josh didn't have much time, but he didn't want to lose his temper with the kids, either.

The two of them did. "Will we see you again?" Brok asked, and Josh just smiled. "Someday. Just like your mom said. No matter how long it takes, we'll find one another again."

It didn't make anyone feel better. They knew what it meant and started to cry. "Hey. You know the rules. No crying until after the bad thing happens. Not before. You never know what might happen." Josh wiped the tears from their eyes, then pulled them both close.

"Take care of your mother for me, until I get back," he said, then stood up.

"Quarl, take them out of here. I don't know where safe is anymore," he said, and his helmet slid up over his head.

"Yes, I will," Quarl replied and moved to the rest of the family. Josh watched as the old wizard lifted his staff and put the end of it into the ground.

They all disappeared in a burst of black flame. Then he was alone with the Rex.

"What do you say, Fluffy? One last time?" he asked, and the dinosaur stood up with a light growl. "I thought so," Josh said as he levitated beside the beast, then the two of them moved in the direction of the beach.

## 78

The trip to the beach was short. The Atlanteans were already coming ashore in droves, setting up their bases. The Rex with the Red King beside it was an impressive sight. Josh decided to try words first.

"You have one chance to leave this land forever. If you don't, I swear you'll never see home again." Short and to the point. It was the best thing he could do. He almost laughed at his speeches from ages past—so many words, embarrassing.

"The time of the Bloody Bastard is over. Take your overgrown lizard and run back to your pathetic Queen," someone in the crowd yelled. Josh was too slow to notice who said it.

There was no way he was going to kill them all.

Then Fluffy swung his head to the left, a sound. Then Josh heard it.

After a few seconds, everyone heard it.

The wave of fire came from the left and was spreading down the beach. The Atlanteans were screaming as the white fire ate their bodies.

"What the hell is this supposed to be?"

A figure walked out of the fire. A person that looked like he did. Josh knew this person, but the memory was so distant and broken that it was just a feeling. Chills ran down his spine.

More walked from the fire. "What in Ktulu's name is this?"

"Hi, Josh. Did you miss me?" The figure asked as he flew in his direction.

It was now he figured he had lost his mind under the stress. Right now, he was sure an arrow had broken through his armor and he was bleeding out in the sand. This was just him, dying.

"Looks like trouble to me," Cody said and was right beside Josh. He turned to look at him. "Am I dead?" Josh asked, "Are you here to bring me to the afterlife?"

Cody put his hand on his shoulder. "No, brother. You're not dead. We've looked everywhere for you. You were thrown so far back that it was nearly impossible," Cody said. Josh didn't understand what was going on, but his memories were starting to fire. Things he had pushed away for over a century.

"How? I haven't seen you in a century. How did you find me?" Josh said and looked around at these people then, like seeing them for the first time.

"Cosmic Girl brought us through time to collect us all. You're the last one. Now we need to go home and save all of time and put an end to all of this once and for all," Cody said, but didn't take his eyes off the massive invasion force.

"Well, but I have a fight on my hands. I can't abandon my people."

"Your people?" Cody asked.

"I'm King. Have been for a hundred years. Long story, I might write it down someday," Josh replied.

Fluffy roared. "I have my own dinosaur. He's called Fluffy."

"Like your lizard," Dustin said and gave a thumbs up.

"We may not have a choice but to stick around. Nero's out cold. I think she overdid it," Blake said as he walked to her. She was lying in the sand, looking just like she was sleeping. He couldn't help but admire her for a second. Then he knelt down and picked her up. "I'll get her out of here," Blake said and took off.

"Isn't it weird that this happens now?" Josh asked.

"Yeah, seems convenient that we show up just

as you need backup the most," Wyatt replied. "Almost as if there is a higher power pushing things along a bit, writing a story," he finished.

"Well, we'll have to worry about that later. We have about a million angry Atlanteans coming to kill us," Josh replied.

"This is your show. Any suggestions?" Cody asked.

"Just one. Don't let any of them live. No need to hold anything back. They've earned this a thousand times over." Josh had a new kind of tone in his voice. This was personal.

"Death to Atlantis and all who live on it," he shouted, then flew through the fire into the horde at sea.

"I mean, I get the anger, but all of them? Seems like a lot of work to me," Blake said as he returned.

"Go for the ships," Wyatt replied.

## 79

The rest of them took to the air and shot through the wall of fire, over the ocean in seconds.

Wyatt's blade burned with red fire. This was a target rich environment. Almost felt impossible how vast the fleet was and how far it stretched. All he wanted to do was stare at all of this forgotten history, not wreck it.

As he burned through the air, he extended the blade out to the left and cut a jagged gash through the hull of the first ship he reached.

It was enough to cripple the thing. The ocean spilled through the damage, and the boat started to list to the side. The soldiers just jumped off the side and started to swim toward the beach.

"Of course, they can swim," he said, but there

was no point in worrying about that. The ships were more important—at least they wouldn't get home. He ignored the survivors and moved to the next ship. His actions didn't go unseen.

At the last second, he rolled to the left as a large spear hit the water. "I think that used to be an entire tree." Wyatt was a bit impressed with the accuracy at these speeds. On the other hand, he didn't want to get hit by the tree spear, or javelin. He was sure it had a name, but now wasn't the time to worry about it.

Wyatt flipped through the air and moved to the deck of the ship that shot at him, landing in the center of it. "I really hate it when people attack me with trees," he said and didn't wait for them to get into a better position to attack.

His black and gold armor turned into a blur as he moved ahead. In less than a second, he was on the other side of the ship. He stopped and turned around. The eighteen heads of the Atlantean sailors fell off. Their blood covered the deck as they fell.

Wyatt noticed that these ships didn't have sails. None of them did. There were purple crystals by the mast. They had a dull glow to them. Wyatt walked to the wheel and spun it to the left. The whole ship followed. "Ramming speed."

Wyatt took to the air without looking back. All he could see was an ocean overcrowded with ships. The outcome of this battle was easy to predict.

Blake didn't know what to do. Well, he did, but it didn't feel like a good use of his talents. Like shooting fish in a barrel, this was not his idea of a good time. He took aim through his scope and looked for a better target. It didn't take long before he saw glowing purple crystals. Those would work. He adjusted his aim and pulled the trigger. The bullet hit its mark, and at once the whole thing blew to pieces.

The whole ship went up in flames, and he was sure everyone on it died screaming. "Better." Blake moved to the next one and fired. Another explosion.

"Guys, aim for the crystals by the mast. One good hit, and the whole thing goes up in flames," Blake said to the intercom.

"Got it," Cody replied.

"Makes sense," Josh said.

"These things really have a video game boss weakness? How lucky can we get?" Dustin asked.

"Shut up, Dustin," Wyatt replied.

"I don't like our odds here, guys," Dustin said. "No one likes the odds, but we're here for Josh, so shut up and kill as many as you can," Cody replied.

"Hey, stop telling me to shut up, I don't like it," Dustin replied.

Radio silence. "Guys?" Dustin didn't like it. He was on the goddamned team, right? Yet, still, they never seemed to appreciate his ideas.

He looked to his left and saw another explosion. The firelight was dark purple. Here in the sunlight, it almost looked black. "Tell me to shut up one more time," he said to himself. He flew over the ships, lifted his arms, and fired his red cutting beams as he passed over the ships. He aimed for the purple crystals.

Sure enough, just like he said, the things started to explode, one after another. Dustin created his swath of purple flames. While he enjoyed his work, it was just a drop in the bucket. It changed nothing.

"This is stupid. We can't win here. They just keep moving towards the shore."

"I agree, this is unwinnable, and we literally are running out of time," Cody said in between plasma blasts.

Dustin got an idea. "Might as well," he said and flew down to a random ship and landed on the deck.

The crew surrounded him with spears. Someone shot an arrow, but it just bounced off his chest. "You, where do you keep your ale?" he asked. The men looked at one another.

"The galley. Why?" the captain asked, and Dustin looked down, then stomped his foot, shattering the wood to pieces and making his way down a level. Sure enough, the galley was easy to find, and there were six barrels attached to the far wall.

He walked over and punched a hole in the top of the first one. The precious liquid started pouring onto the floor. He tore the barrel off the wall with one hand and lifted it above his head, opened his mouth, and drank as much as he could.

This was just how he remembered. He could only drink so much before having to catch his breath.

"I needed that," he said.

Then he analyzed the ale with his armor. The nano system copied it. "Perfection," he said, then lifted the barrel again and drank again. It was enough.

"Gonna take this back home, make all the money once we deal with the end of the world," he said to himself, tossed the barrel to the side, slid his helmet back up, and then set fire to the whole thing. "This is fine," he said, surrounded by fire, then flew out the side of the ship to continue the fight.

Josh knew it was a pointless battle. There were no Lemurians in his time that he knew of. They all died after this invasion, one way or another. He didn't want to lose after everything. He didn't know what to do. He looked around at all the fighting.

This wasn't going to play out like history wanted.

Josh had one more idea. With no warning, he shot into the sky as fast as he could go. Everyone watched him, only for a second. Cody blasted six ships into burning timbers with his plasma cannon, then wondered what he was doing.

"Josh, what are you doing?" Cody asked, no answer. "Great," he finished and blasted another ship to pieces.

Josh traveled far into the sky as fast as he could go, and soon the blue gave way to black and the stars. "Suggestion. Prepare to leave as soon as you can. Things are about to get messy." He sent the message to all the Delta members below. If they could still hear him, it would be the only warning.

Josh saw his weapon in the distance. There were questions. Why was it there, so close? He flew to it. Deep in the dark, he thought there was a man standing there. A man dressed in black, it looked like he waved, then he was gone. Maybe he was never there.

The stone in space was massive. Josh didn't know how big this rock was or where it came from. He put his hands against it, and his armor exploded with his true power and everything else he could summon. The rock didn't move an inch.

"Come on, you bastard, move." Josh pushed again. The space mountain started to move.

It was going to be Atlantis's last day one way or another. Josh had gone farther out into space than he had planned to.

It wasn't long before the atmosphere of the earth

was trying to burn this mountain up to protect itself. It would have to take this bullet.

"He's killed us all," Blake said as he watched the meteor burning through the sky. "Blake, how's Nero doing? Please tell me she's ready to go," Cody said as he watched the burning mountain fall through the sky.

"I'm fine, you blue weirdo," Nero said. She was standing behind him. Cody jumped and turned around. She looked weak, drained, and pale. "You look like hell," Cody replied.

"Everyone on me, now."

"We need him. What are we going to do?" Blake asked.

"I'll get him," Wyatt replied, unsure of what he was about to do, and flew as fast as he could towards the burning mountain in the sky. It was still far away but huge. Time was running out.

"Josh, seriously. Anger management class for you when this is all over," Wyatt said as he sped towards the end of the world. He could see Josh pressed up against the massive rock. "We need to go, now," Wyatt said.

"I need to be sure this works. I have to guide it down." Wyatt cringed. Josh had lost his mind. There was no reason to guide this monster anywhere now. "Listen, this is not going to be something any of us can live through. Come with me now. If you don't, none of this is going to matter anyway. The Chronovore will come back here. Hell, man, I don't know how any of this is gonna work." Wyatt didn't want to lie.

Josh knew Wyatt was right, pulled his hands out of the black stone and blasted away from it.

"You just ended the world. Thanks for that, by the way," Wyatt said. "I think that was my purpose," Josh replied.

"Right, let's go before we get ended with it."

The two of them blasted towards Cody, away from the destruction.

"Alright, Nero. One last trip, and then this is all over. You can do it, right?" She glared at Cody. It was enough of an answer for him. Josh took one last look around his homeland and didn't quite know what to think about this. It was all happening so fast.

Josh watched as the meteor hit.

There was a great flash of light. The shockwave looked like a solid wall racing towards them. Josh wondered if he just killed all the dinosaurs and thought about everyone he'd never see again before they all disappeared.

The six of them reappeared somewhere else. It was cold, and they were in a forest. It was black, night, but there was a light in the sky. When they looked, it was easy to see that there was a big alien ship in the sky that was giving off its own weird light. Almost white, but there was something else mixed in with it that blocked out the stars.

"Where, when, in the hell are we now?" Cody asked and looked at Nero.

She just shrugged.

"The impact must have messed with our landing. No idea where we are, or when. I have more bad news. We're stuck here because that last bit was my last shot of power. Well, when it comes to time traveling for a bit. So, you better see just what's going on here, I guess. That ship up there doesn't seem like it's too happy to see anyone," she said and collapsed, passing out on the spot.

Blake caught her. "We need to find a place to keep her safe," Blake said.

"You do care for the cosmic horror, cute," Wyatt said. Blake ignored him.

"Well, he has a point," Cody replied and looked to the left. There was an abandoned trench. "A trench? What is going on?" he asked.

Pointing at it, Blake caught on right away, moved her in that direction. It would have to do for now. The others followed. No one noticed them.

"Well. Let's see just what it is that's going on and if there is anything we can do to help, I guess," Cody said, looking around. They had jumped from one battle to another.

"Help? What are you even thinking right now? We should stay right here, wait for her to get better, then leave. We don't know what's going on, and it's not our problem. We have one. This isn't it," Wyatt replied.

A ship flew overhead. The sound it made wasn't anything they recognized. "Must be an alien invasion," Dustin said as if it were the most normal thing in the world.

Cody was conflicted. Wyatt had a point, but on the other hand, he wanted to know more.

## 80

It was still night, but the alien ship in the sky was giving off plenty of light.

He didn't remember anything like this taking place. "Do you think we're in the future?" Cody asked.

"Maybe a different timeline? Maybe everything we did in the past led up to this, and the Chronovore isn't a thing anymore?" Blake replied.

"We don't get that lucky," Cody replied and looked into the distance. He was bored already. The others seemed content to stay here. "I'm going to go see what this is all about."

"Damn it, man, stay here. Nothing but trouble we don't need out there," Wyatt replied. Cody just smiled.

"What's the worst that could happen? Just stay

here." Cody stood up and flew to the top of the trench, walking out of sight. The blue armor retracted, and his clothes were still clean, but not suited for this weather. It was cold out here.

He moved towards the closest thing that looked like an outpost to him and was stopped. "Who are you?" a deep voice asked.

Cody stopped himself from saying Commander of the Delta Squad. Instead, he stood up straight and saluted. "Got lost, sir. L Company got hit with something, I'm not sure what. I woke up, uniform torched," Cody said, looking at his clothes.

The man looked at him and put his gun down.

"God damn, son. L Company got wiped out. What do you remember?" he asked, and Cody shrugged.

"Brain is Swiss cheese, sir, a refresher would be great." The man nodded, then saluted.

"You there. It's about time you showed up," Cody heard a voice behind him and turned around to see another commander. Not Delta, Chemical Dragon unit instead. Now Cody was confused.

"Showed up? What do you mean?"

"Yeah. Agent J briefed us, said that the Syndicate's golden boys would show up to help clean up this mess. Actually, he said you'd show up just before the sun came up, so you're right on time," the commander said. Cody wished he would have just stayed in the trench. This had to be some cosmic being's idea of a joke at this point.

"They said the Delta Squad would be here?" Cody asked, still trying to grasp the situation. It was a lot to take in.

"Delta, for this little mess? No, Delta only handles the big threats. Global security is our thing. Those Delta bastards don't even get out of bed for anything less than a personal request from the top, or when the world is about to end. You and your team are the Syndicate's experimental weapons, right?" Cody nodded then.

"Yes, we are. What's the situation? Give me a full update." This is what he came looking for. How it was all lining up like this didn't make any sense, but he was sure this was just some cosmic game and he was about to learn how to play.

"We are in Siberia. The Valimen have requested a chance to invade ever since we made contact with them ten years ago. The Syndicate has obliged their request, under one condition. Each side was able to bring five superweapons to the table. They agreed. These aliens are obviously stronger than humans are, but get this: If you surrender, they won't finish you off. If you drop your weapon, they'll do the same. They are honorable to a fault, and in order to avoid injuries and death, we have agreed to be the same. I don't understand it either, but that's the story they aren't telling people in the news. I'm sure you knew that, but consider this a reminder."

Cody almost laughed at this insane story.

"So, when do we start?" Cody was playing his part and wondered just how long he should do it.

"Anytime you and your team want, all you have to do is formally announce your intentions and start fighting, but please, try not to kill any of them. We've lost a few men already, but that's because they were stupid enough not to give up. It's strange—they seem nice, almost. I don't understand it. This was their request. Don't underestimate them. They are strong and fast. I'm not sure if that means anything to you," the General said and looked at the battleground around him.

"You have a name?" Cody asked.

"Yeah. Neil. What's it to you?" the man answered.

"Just wondering. I'll get the guys together. This will be over soon enough," Cody said and began to walk back to the others.

## 81

Josh hadn't seen Wyatt in one hundred years or so. It wasn't enough time. Josh had a surplus of rage built up over the last century, and now he had no one to take it out on.

"What was that whole thing about?" Wyatt asked.

Josh was snapped out of his thoughts. There was so much he was never going to tell, where would he even begin?

"Not important anymore," Josh replied.

"How long were you there?" Wyatt asked. Josh looked at him. "I don't know."

"Come on, man, you got to open up. Might as well be now," Wyatt said.

"Four hours ago, I was the King of Lemuria.

Now I'm in a trench I wouldn't let—" he trailed off and looked away.

"King, sounds pretty important. I suppose I should tell you. In my personal adventure through time, I met someone who had to be related to you. She had lizard eyes but was human enough. Hated humanity, wanted to kill me. Even wore something similar to your armor too," Wyatt said.

Josh snapped his head in his direction.

"Did you kill her?"

"Almost. Nero put her somewhere safe. Didn't ask where," Wyatt replied.

It was clear Josh was interested now. "Tell me everything," he said, and Wyatt drew back.

"What, you want me to talk when you won't? No way. Give and take kind of thing here."

Wyatt thought he was being clever. Josh snapped, charged him head on. Wyatt took to the air as fast as he could.

"My mistake, the King has a royal fit instead of using his words. Nothing's changed," Wyatt said. However, something had changed, and Wyatt was quick to notice.

Josh hadn't said a word in anger.

"Do you think we should tell Cody?" Blake asked.

"Nope. Let them work it out. I'm sure it'll be fine," Dustin replied as he watched the two take off.

"Josh, it's not like you'll ever catch me. You're

too slow, you've always been too slow." Wyatt looked back just in time to see Josh tear a tree out of the ground and throw it at him like a javelin.

"Oh, yeah, I suppose that might have worked years ago."

That tree missile was avoided and landed on the ground with a loud thud. Wyatt knew better than to get too close. There was no way he could take him.

"Lycin," Josh said, and Wyatt didn't catch the word. He didn't have time to ask because, in a second, Josh was behind him and had his left arm around his neck.

"What the hell was that?" Wyatt asked before the pressure was applied.

"Just a kind of magic. Tell me what I want to know, and I won't kill you. You think you're the first ally I was forced to kill? Think again."

"Oh, you forgot who you were screwing with. Josh's armor and strength were like trying to remove a rusty car bolt, but he pushed up and managed to pull free. Not wasting any time, he spun and kicked him in the stomach.

It was like kicking metal. Josh slid back a few feet, but that was it.

Josh's miniguns raised from his wrists. "Oh, you want to get serious about this? Fine, let's get bloody if we have to." He pulled out his blade and prepared himself, wondering how far he'd take this.

"Stop it." Cody moved between them. He

grabbed Wyatt's wrist, held Josh back, and pushed that minigun into the air.

"I can't leave you idiots alone for five minutes, and you want to kill one another. What the hell is wrong with you?"

Wyatt pulled back. Josh did too.

"Just a friendly conversation that got out of hand is all," Wyatt replied. Josh retracted his weapon. "What he said."

Cody looked between them.

"Alright, I get it. You have some time to make up for now, don't you? I found us something to do," Cody said.

Wyatt groaned. "What mission? Where are we? All you had to do was nothing. Was that so hard?"

Cody just shrugged. "Yeah. I get bored."

"Anyway, we're in Siberia. There is kind of an alien invasion if you can believe it. So, let's get it together for five damn minutes and save the world from aliens, alright?" Cody asked and walked away with no promises that as soon as he turned his back, they wouldn't start right back up.

Josh and Wyatt looked at one another.

"I won't kill you today," Josh said. "I'll hold you to that," Wyatt replied, and the two of them started back to the trench.

"What the hell, Cody?" Wyatt said and stood up.

"Hey, the world is being invaded by aliens. Who knows? Maybe we save the world, and that's why we're not all alien food, because we did things instead of not doing things," Cody replied.

"I hate time travel," Dustin said and got out of the trench. "Nero's still sleeping. I guess we might as well shoot some aliens," Blake said.

"I'm tired," Josh replied. "It's been a long century, and I just want to take a nap," he said.

"No rest for the wicked," Wyatt replied.

"Yeah, I get it. Let's go save the world or something," Josh replied, tired. "That's the spirit. Let's take a look at what kind of aliens we're dealing with," Dustin said and took to the air. The others followed to get a better look at what was going on.

This battle was almost a parody of how it was being played out.

"They look like lasers, but obviously they aren't. If they were moving at the speed of light, we'd never really see them unless it was a solid beam. Projectiles of some kind, slow too. The people aren't too shaken up over them," Dustin said.

"Thanks for the science lesson," Wyatt replied.

"Check out the aliens. They have to be seven feet tall. I haven't seen a single one shorter than that yet. Energy weapons against obvious early twentieth century weaponry, we're still in the past," Blake said.

"You idiots are all in super power armor, and none of you bothered to check the date?" Cody asked, turning to look at them.

They all kind of shrugged. "Way to go," Cody replied and looked back at the battle. "Surrounded by idiots."

"Once this is over, we can kill him," Dustin said. "For once, sounds like a good plan to me," Josh replied. "You can try," Cody shot back. "For now, let's deal with the, whatever this is."

"Speaking of, why does it look like laser tag, but they are taking turns shooting? What is going on?" Wyatt asked.

"Oh, yeah. They asked permission to come fight. They have rules. I know it seems counterproductive, but that's the way these things work. If you kill one when one begs for its life, I assume that all rules are off. Same goes for you. If you can't beat them, just quit. They won't stop as long as you do. Don't shoot them down after you've convinced them. This could be one of the toughest things you've ever done," Cody said.

"We could do a recap of things to compare," Blake replied. "You know what I mean," Cody snapped back.

"Alright, let's do it," Wyatt said. "Try not to lose control of that temper of yours. Wouldn't want to accidentally get the world blown up, right?" Josh glared through Wyatt. One hundred years of being a leader taught him that having a tolerance for stupidity was a bad idea.

"Wyatt, shut your trap." Cody didn't want them killing one another again.

Cody led the group back to the ground just inside the tree line, then, in full armor, walked out of the dark.

"Let me do the talking," Cody said. "You always do all the talking," Wyatt replied. Cody made sure not to react as Neil came running up to them.

"Guys, welcome to the fight. They won't attack you until you attack them. This is the best battle. I wish people were like this," Neil said. They could tell he was excited to face an enemy he could talk to and not be afraid that they'd just stab him when he wasn't looking.

"Right, show us where we need to go and let us do our job," Cody replied.

"Oh, yeah. They are waiting for you, beyond those trees there. Good luck, guys."

They started walking and made it to the front. Dustin looked at the weapons as they walked by the human side.

They were never once shot at. It was weird to not be shot at in the middle of a battlefield. They walked through the trees, and there before them stood five seven foot armored beings.

"Great. How come we never get little enemies?" Wyatt asked, being the shortest member of the team, although not by much. "Oh, they all seem little to me. All you need to do is stand up once in a while. Wait. Never mind," Josh replied with a laugh. Wyatt grumbled under his helmet.

"What's that? Didn't hear you down there," Josh replied.

"What I don't get is why the enemy is kind of like us? I mean, there should have been a blob monster or something. Instead, it's just like looking into a mirror. These are not like the aliens I saw last time," Dustin said.

"Last time?" Blake asked.

"Uh, never mind. It's not important," Dustin replied.

Before Blake could press the issue, a spotlight that didn't seem to have an origin point shined on all of them.

"You five are the chosen?" the voice crackled through their intercoms. "We are," Cody replied.

"You are aware of our agreement?"

"We are."

"Very well. The battle begins. Valimen Elite, you know what to do." Cody assumed this was the same thing everyone was hearing. Then their intercoms returned to their control.

"Weapons?" Wyatt asked.

"Do what you think is right," Cody replied as

the five aliens started surrounding them. "This is still like a game, war isn't a game," Josh replied.

"We still have to play. Spread out, do your best. Don't kill them, and good luck," Cody replied. With no preference on who they fought, each squad member paired off with an alien.

# 82

Dustin decided that if he had to do this, he might as well try to make it quick. Lifting his weapon, he sent a stream of fire over the silver one. The flames burned for a bit, but then they just went out.

The alien was just standing there, unharmed.

"That didn't hurt. Was that an attack?" it asked, confused. Dustin sighed.

"Well, it was supposed to be. I didn't know you were fireproof."

The alien's head tilted a bit.

"Oh, well I am. You should have asked. I would have told you," it said, and without missing a beat, a blade of pure energy appeared from its left wrist and swung at Dustin's head.

Dustin's instincts kicked in. He wasted no time,

stepping to the side. Taking hold of that arm, spinning around, and throwing the alien. It looked heavy, but Dustin was surprised at how easy it was to toss the thing.

It hit a thick tree in the center and slid down, snapping branches as it did, shaking the snow to the ground.

---

The one facing Wyatt watched Dustin throw his teammate and laughed.

"Nice one. This will be a great battle," it said, and Wyatt wasn't sure what to expect.

Wyatt attacked first. His blade hit the strange armor and stopped on contact. The alien looked at his right arm, then pushed the blade back a few inches.

"Do you quit yet, human?"

"No. Not just yet, I have yet to begun to fight, or, something," he said, pulling his blade back.

"How about you? You can stop now. You have no idea how screwed you are."

"I didn't understand any of that, but let's fight, little guy."

"I'm not that damn short," Wyatt replied. He had no idea why this was getting to him now. He blamed Josh.

"You are to me." Wyatt did his best to let it slide and got ready for whatever was coming next.

---

Josh didn't let the enemy do anything. He stepped forward and put a left uppercut into the alien's helmet.

The alien was taken off its feet, thrown through the air, snapping tree branches the whole way.

"These are my weapons. I am a weapon," Josh said and wasn't going to wait for the enemy to come to him.

"I am glad you're a weapon. That makes my job so much easier." Josh didn't care. The only thing he wanted was to make the enemy give up. In the back of his mind, he was forced to remember not to kill this thing. Right now, it felt like he could have done it on accident.

Also, he was going to punch Cody in the face until his arm got tired for getting them in this mess to begin with.

---

Blake still had those shotguns on him, and he was way too close for anything else.

"What are you supposed to be?" Blake didn't understand the question.

"Just your typical guy with power armor and magic shotguns, I guess," he replied and disconnected them from his back.

"Typical guy," the alien said and took a step forward.

Blake pointed the weapons, but the alien wasn't stopping. It was clear he didn't know what they were, or didn't care.

He pulled both triggers, and the blasts knocked the alien off his feet to the ground. They were more effective than he thought they'd be.

"Strange energy, those weapons. Can't scan, are you cheating?" the alien asked while picking himself up.

"No, you can trust me. I don't cheat," Blake said. He lied. Of course, he didn't know you could cheat.

"Remember that time we played Dish Wars on our way to the fourth site? I think we have that kind of situation on our hands," Blake said into the intercom.

"Thanks," Cody replied.

"Hey you son of a—oh, wait, yeah, I remember," Wyatt replied.

"Got it," Josh said.

Cody fired his plasma cannon, nowhere near full blast because, well, he wasn't quite sure how much it could take. He sort of liked these aliens and didn't want to kill them.

The alien took the blast, and it made him slide back from where he stood. The energy crackled off of his armor and faded around the edges as it fractured.

Once the sliding stopped, the thing started to advance through the beam.

"You can walk through a plasma stream. You don't want to make it to the finish line. This is my only warning," Cody said. There was no response.

He leapt into the air, out of the beam, and attempted to land on the commander, fists first.

Cody flew up, avoiding the falling enemy and grabbing him by the back of the neck.

"You can fly," the enemy said, shocked, watching the commander and himself lift into the air.

"Yes, can you?" Cody asked as he ascended into the black sky.

"No. I can't fly."

Cody just smiled.

"Well, looks like we have a bit of a problem, because you're getting heavy. I wonder if you can live through a fall like this."

Cody was sure the alien would beg to surrender at this point.

"Me too, drop me and let's find out. I'll tell you when I hit the bottom!" The commander looked down then. "You're insane, aren't you?" There was silence then, for a few seconds.

"Don't know. What's 'insane' mean? Hurry up and drop me. I can see the whole battle from here."

Cody let go. "Alright, see you down there." He watched his enemy fall. "Crazy aliens. Maybe this means I won?"

## 83

Wyatt was not having a tough time with his enemy. The alien was clumsy, slow, and it didn't make much sense.

For the fifth time, Wyatt knocked the creature on its back. However, his blade never scratched the silver surface.

"Alien guy, no offense, but you'd better quit. I am too fast for you. You don't stand a chance. Quit now while you still can."

"Too slow, me? I was giving you a chance. I figured before I killed you, I would make you feel good about yourself." Wyatt took a step back.

"Really, because I thought you were just about to lose. But if you think you have what it takes to run with me, let's see it." No sooner had Wyatt finished saying it, the Valimen was behind him and tapped his shoulder.

"Fast enough for you that time, or should I do it again?" Wyatt didn't see anything at all.

"The hell, how'd you do that?"

When he turned around, the alien was gone.

"Ok. I take it back. Go back to being slow," he said to the alien, wherever it was. Something slammed into the side of his head and threw him into the ground. Wyatt never saw it coming.

"Alright, you want to play like that? I can play like that." Wyatt turned his armor up to the normal levels then, as he hadn't needed them anywhere near here for a while now. He spun around and blocked the alien blade just before it hit his neck.

"Alright, now we can continue."

The two had their blades in a deadlock, neither of them moving. "Oh, good. The Earthling finally showed up to the party. I was wondering when you would."

---

Dustin was seldom lucky in combat.

He either got into the worst situations or put himself into these places by accident—or on purpose without thinking. He didn't like fighting with his hands if he could help it.

The alien armor was a sponge. Fire, chemicals,

bullets—nothing fazed the thing, and it just kept walking through all of it.

"Wow, when this is over, I want a sample of your metal. This stuff is epic."

"It can take the intensity of space. You think anything you have can break me, human?" Dustin shrugged. "I thought I did. I guess I don't. Weird how life works out sometimes," he replied.

"Life is funny that way," the alien replied. Dustin wondered how different they really were.

He had no choice but to go to physical combat with this thing. The alien started to run in his direction. Without thinking, he fired his red cutting beams mounted on his wrists.

The enemy tried to get out of the way. The burning light burned through its arm, and the alien let loose an inhuman shriek as if it were a mortal wound, stumbling away.

This didn't make sense.

He walked toward the fallen enemy, and as soon as he got close enough, his armor was telling him to back off. Radiation warnings—worse than he'd ever seen anywhere on the planet. The grass around the thing was turning black, and the circle was spreading.

"What the hell is this?" He had to warn the others.

"Guys. I don't know what you're doing right now, but listen up. Don't crack the armor. Inside, they are filled with some of the most intense radiation I've ever seen. Not sure if you can hear me or not, but whatever you do, don't open them," he said and backed off.

"It's like a nuclear weapon or something. Worse, maybe," he said, looking at the alien suit. It wasn't moving anymore.

"I must have killed it," he said, thinking he had won.

"No, I'm not dead. What you call radiation is our true form. We have found a way to live forever inside our suits. You did win the fight, but now I am a danger to everything on this planet. You need to help me."

The voice came out of his internal communicator. It was a bit disturbing, but nothing he couldn't handle.

"Tell me how."

"If you seal the armor, it will automatically pull me back." Dustin hesitated. He knew that radiation would burn through everything here, maybe even him, in minutes.

"Damn it, fine, don't say I never did anything for you."

Dustin ran into the radiation field, knelt down to the armor, and turned it over.

The alarms were not helping either, telling him every fifteen seconds that his armor needed to run the hell away and that it was on the verge of breaking limits. This was unlike anything on the planet. He made sure to record all of this.

It didn't make anything any easier.

Concentrating, Dustin heated both sides of that metal and pressed it together with his hands while his screen started to black out, and he couldn't see.

He felt his skin start to burn, his blood boiling. With one last effort, he pushed the armor back together and sealed it.

The armor shut down, and Dustin collapsed under the weight of it, passing out.

## 84

Josh got a garbled message. He was too busy fighting with an underpowered alien thing to worry much about it.

Some kind of warning, maybe.

He was having too much fun with the punching bag from space.

"How many times do I have to hit you before you give up?" Josh asked and punched the thing in the face again.

The Valimen didn't answer.

Josh threw a left punch, and the fist was caught and stopped in place. The alien, all of a sudden, became much stronger than it was before. This didn't surprise Josh. He expected something like this.

"It's about time you showed up to this fight. I

was beginning to wonder if you really were that pathetic." The alien said nothing.

The other fist came up and put Josh into the ground after a punch came at his head. "Yeah. That's more like it." Josh got to his feet with levitation. He was so ready for a fight.

"Are you stronger than a train?" he asked.

"Train. I don't know what this is. Is it a fish?"

"Yes, it's a fish."

This answer, and the question, just made him even more enraged. So many things didn't make any sense.

One hundred years out of the fight, and now here he was, back in it. Nothing had changed. He nearly forgot what this was like. He didn't even know if he wanted to do this anymore. So much had happened and gone by that none of this was that important to him anymore.

He understood the threat of the Chronovore. It was the only thing that kept him from taking this armor off and walking away.

Maybe if he was lucky, Emily would be kind enough to just end him. The thought ran through his head, but he wasn't sure why. Just tired, he supposed.

Now he was stuck in time, fighting an alien who thought a train was a fish. It all seemed pointless, and this only fueled his rage further. He turned his armor up as high as it could go without getting into hyper mode, and he screamed as it all hit a boiling point.

The alien heard this and backed off.

"Wait a minute. What did I do? Are you ok? Is this pain? Are you quitting?"

Josh had no more patience, no reason to hold anything back. The very idea that this thing was asking him if he was quitting was, well, it was just too much.

Josh flew at the alien.

The punch ripped through the alien, cutting it in half in one attack. Seconds later, the alarms started going off. The radiation poured out of this empty suit.

"That's what Dustin was trying to say. It all makes sense now." Josh couldn't stay here, and he flew up to escape.

"Oh, what's the matter, human? Didn't like what you saw in the armor? I'm insulted you didn't stick around to die." It was a female voice that came through his intercom. He didn't want anything to do with that radiation. It was eating through his armor the second it touched it.

"No, what in the hell are you anyway?"

"We are what you would call radiation. You really did a number on my suit. I wasn't expecting that. Now I am kind of stuck here on this planet with you. Thanks for that. I appreciate the help," the voice said, and it seemed sad.

Josh rolled his eyes, the rage broken.

"So, buddy. What do you suggest we do now? Do I come up there and get you, or should we figure out a way to get me back on my ship? I'd like that," the voice asked. "You sound like a chick. Are you?" Josh asked.

Silence for a bit.

"If you must know, I was female before the transformation. We didn't want to be radiation by choice. The problem is I am, well, how would you say it, stuck. Alive, but with no way to do anything on this planet. I need something to move in. Hey, can I use your armor for a while?" she asked.

"No, Dustin's might be open. Listen, you don't seem all that bad, so I'll try and find something. Don't go anywhere," Josh said and flew off.

"I'll be right here. Unless, of course, the wind blows or something. In the meantime, I'll just kill everything in the area. Take your time. Everything should be fine."

"Great. A sarcastic alien. I hate sarcasm." Now he had to find something for a talking radioactive cloud to use as a suit.

---

Wyatt and the alien were fighting at blazing speeds. Each swing of their blades would carve through a tree so clean that the heat from the attack would fuse the pieces back together if they didn't knock it over.

Wyatt hadn't had a challenge like this in quite some time. He was enjoying it, even if he knew he could win the fight if he wanted to, but there was no reason to put an end to a good time so soon.

The next attack came at his head. Wyatt spun out of the way, put the blade down on top of the incoming attack, slamming the arm to the ground. Then, without stopping, the blade slid up to the silver neck.

"Wait, stop. Don't do it. I'll surrender," the Valimen said, and Wyatt stopped his blade, resting it against the metal. "Well, alright. That means I win."

He withdrew his blade.

"Tell me, why here? I mean, is this what you wanted? You seem so nice, not warlike, to me." The other powered down and took two steps back.

"Humanity is the most violent race that we, or anyone, know about. We figured that if we could take you down, we'd be feared. We know humanity likes to fight. The idea was if we respected you in combat, we'd have a chance at winning because the more violent we got, we knew you would just match and destroy us. Earth is also a prison for so many bad things. In our scan, we found horrible things. We didn't know what they were." Wyatt put his blade away.

"Horrible things like what?" The alien looked at him in what Wyatt could see as confusion.

"We don't know. We've seen other things like them. On other dead worlds, they too were sleeping or locked away," the alien said and looked away. "This planet is something of a miracle, you know. Humans have spent thousands of years killing one another, and you never stopped to ask why."

"Why do we fight?" Wyatt asked.

"It's practice. The real fight is coming. Our psychics tell us the Earth will be a focal point in some horrible battle. You see, humans have been fighting all this time as practice for the real thing that is said to come. We don't know when. We didn't believe it until we got here. Those things we saw that sleep under your oceans. Vast things in waiting, not sure for what. The generals figured they'd never wake up as long as we left them alone. Something beyond the Earth is keeping them in stasis."

Wyatt didn't like any of this information.

"Your psychics, can't they see these sleeping things?"

The Valimen crossed his arms. "Yes, they tried many times. All have gone insane. Had to be isolated in containment chambers. We stopped trying to look."

Wyatt just kept on disliking this information. "All the terrible things are real," he said but decided not to dwell on it.

"Well, now that I win, what do I do? Just wait here for the others?"

"Do whatever you want. I'm going back to my ship. When we give up, we return to our ship. Once all five of us return, it's over. I want to go back home anyway, so tell your friends to win. Oh, and don't open the armor. We are pure radiation and will kill just about anything living on this planet. It's a strange story, too long to get into now. See you never if I'm lucky."

Wyatt was going to say something, but a blue flash took the other fighter away.

"Guys, all you gotta do is win, and the fight is over. Guess who just won? That's right. Me. You guys suck," Wyatt said, but there was only static. He wondered why.

## 85

Cody knew something wasn't right. The aliens didn't seem much like fighters. When he landed, the enemy was unharmed.

"Well, at least I can live through that much," it said as it stood up.

"Cut to the chase already. I'm not as stupid as you think I am. What's the plan?" Cody said and landed on the ground.

"We need to kill you all. This is a prison planet. You see, you humans were supposed to be its keepers, but you're the most violent race anyone has ever known. We are afraid of you. Parents tell their children of the horrible things you've done for no reason. The only thing keeping us safe from you is the vastness of space."

"We scanned your planet some time ago and realized two things. There are monsters here, and there are people here willing to do anything for power. We have to destroy you all. This planet is a paradise. It doesn't deserve to have parasites like you on it."

Cody had heard the end of this speech before.

"However, we will not escalate in combat. If we do, you will wipe us out. We want this planet, and to lose means death to the whole world. We are living radiation under this armor. If we are hurt, we will spread with the winds, killing every living thing we touch. So, we'll fight, we'll play by the rules, and gradually step up our attack. Humanity, well, they won't even notice until it's too late. It's the perfect plan."

Cody took in every word of this and shook his head. He wondered if telling the enemy their whole plan was a universal trait or not. It seemed stupid to just lay it out like that.

"It would have been perfect, but you're missing one important detail," the commander said and looked up at the ship. It was half the size of the Viper, but it was a giant circle, just what you'd expect from an alien invader.

"Forgot something, human. What do you think I forgot?"

"You forgot me. Squad, listen up. The aliens are hostile. Living radiation, threat level three. You know what to do. The ship is likely a Zylon class, B. maybe

C. The countdown is in one hour from now," the commander said and looked at the alien. "You see, I don't know jack about that ship. That light there is anti gravity tech, the same stuff we use to fly in our own armor, or the same idea anyway. You have two choices right now. You leave, or we make you leave."

"Humans lie. I don't believe you. You and your team can't change anything." Cody almost laughed.

"Oh, I don't know. We've taken down some pretty big players in our time. Do us a favor and tell your people to fight back. I'll be seeing you soon. Fifty-seven minutes."

Blake was none the wiser, but the plan came to him. He stopped his battle and just stared at his enemy. This was a stall tactic, and it all became clear.

"Thought you were clever, silver man. I understand now. Wait right here, I'll be back."

"Wait, does this mean you quit? Where are you going?" the alien looked up as he disappeared. "I guess I'm not getting an answer, weird."

Alone with nothing to do, he just waited for orders, admiring the grass and the trees.

Dustin woke up to the transmission.

"What the hell? Zylon class? Level three. I should have known better." Everything hurt, and he felt as if he had the world's biggest hangover, struggling to get up.

The alien in the armor took a step back. "You

saved me from being radioactive dust in the wind. You didn't have to save me and every living thing in the area. You're nothing like what the stories say," it said to him.

Dustin shook his head.

"Listen. One time offer. You need to run as fast as you can from here. Pick a direction and go as far as you can. You could have killed me at any time when I was out, so I know you're not evil as Cody says, but run, hide. Don't come back until everyone is gone."

Dustin didn't have time to find out if it ran or not as he flew off into the first rays of the morning. The alien didn't understand, but it took off running, not once looking back.

Josh watched as the radiation levels fell as the energy being pulled itself inside a grenade.

"This is terrible," she said, and Josh looked at her. "It was the best I could do, come on," he replied and walked to the armor.

He tossed the explosive inside the top half and smashed the suit together. "Surrender and go back to the ship, that's the deal, right?" he asked.

"Yes, human, thanks," she said. "I quit." As soon as she said it, the suit disappeared in a blue flash.

Then Josh got Cody's message. "Hostile aliens, kind of stupid maybe but not a threat. Do we really need to do this?" Josh asked. "Trust me," Cody replied.

"Because nothing bad has ever happened when you said that in the future," Josh replied. "Trust me," Cody said. "Fine, I'm on my way. I won, if you cared at all." No reply.

Josh took to the air and flew towards the battlefield.

When he saw it, the aliens were winning the battle, or at least advancing. It was all a trick. Normal people didn't stand a chance. Their bullets were just bouncing off the armor, but the illusion of honor kept all of this going.

He dove out of the sky and landed in front of three of the aliens with so much force that it knocked them down as the earth moved under them.

"Alright, aliens. New plan, you're coming with me like it or not." The soldiers stopped shooting then, everyone did.

"What is going on here? I demand answers," Neil demanded with a fierce voice. Cody landed next to Josh.

"Hate to tell you, but this is one of those world ending events. Don't worry, let the professionals handle this," Cody said.

"You can't do this. If we break the rules, they'll kill us all," Neil said, but the commander fired two plasma blasts, knocking two silver-armored warriors to the earth.

Cody took off towards the ones he had just knocked to the ground and threw them deep into the trees.

"They plan on doing that anyway. Look, it might seem like a bloodless battle, but they won't stop moving forward. Take a look around. You never had a chance playing by their rules. It was rigged from the beginning," Cody replied.

Neil looked around and saw the stranger was right. It was bloodless, but they were still losing ground, just at a slow pace. So slow it didn't even occur to him what was going on.

"Well, son of a bitch," Neil said.

"Yeah, that's what I thought, too. Get your people out of here," Cody replied. Neil blew the whistle to sound the retreat.

# 86

"Guys, I'm sure you all know by now we can't tear their suits open. Keep them down and back for now," Cody said.

"How many of these things are there?" Wyatt asked.

"I count thirty-two on the ground. The ship has more, invasion force worth for sure. We should assume that, anyway," Blake replied.

"Thanks, that was all I needed," Wyatt replied and took off into the dark.

"Good luck, Josh, go with him. Dustin and Blake stay with me," Cody said. Josh shrugged. "Fine," he said and took off.

Josh knew they weren't all terrible. They couldn't have been. They hadn't even killed anyone yet. It was difficult to be mad at them for anything, even if they were playing the long game. He found a group of six of them advancing while Neil's men retreated from the fight.

He landed behind the aliens and grabbed the one closest to him. "Hi," he said and tossed the thing back into the trees.

"I know you're not stupid. You know what I can do, I assume. Run."

One of the aliens on the left lifted their weapon, and before he could fire, Josh closed the distance between them, took the silver weapon in his hand, and pulled it from the alien. He took the thing in both hands and snapped it in half. There were bright yellow sparks for a second, then he tossed the pieces to the ground.

"Next one is going to be you," he said.

"You can't kill us, human," the one in the middle said.

"Fair point," he lifted off the ground a few inches. "I can break your suits open in outer space, then you can live forever out there, alone," Josh replied.

"You wouldn't."

"Of course I will, I'm a human. You know what I do to my own kind, Imagine what I'm going to do to you. I'll even think it's fun," Josh replied.

The remaining five Valimen looked at one another.

"Zabith we may be, but it's better than drifting

in the void. We're leaving," the one in the middle said, and they all disappeared.

Josh knew that word. He didn't know how a bunch of space aliens knew it too. Maybe something he did had an effect after all. Maybe. He shut his hope off. It was pointless to think about it now.

Wyatt stopped in front of a group of three Valimen. "Go back to your ship." Wyatt crossed his arms as he said it.

"Get out of our way. You can't stop us," the one on the right replied.

"Yeah, I can stop you all day long, but you don't have that long. Something bad is going to happen here, and trust me, you don't want to be here when it does. Get back on your ship," Wyatt replied.

"They are humans, maybe they figured out the plan?" the one on the left asked.

"No need to speculate. We figured it out, and we're pissed," Wyatt replied, and the three took steps back, "however, since you didn't kill any of us, we decided to warn you. Go back to your ship and tell your leaders to go home, wherever home is," he said.

The three of them looked at one another.

"Fine," the one in the middle said, and the trio disappeared in bright blue light. Wyatt sped off to find more to convince.

Cody watched bright blue flashes happen all around him.

"The retreat is going well," Cody said.

"How's the plan coming along?" Cody asked. "We're all doing fine. Does anyone happen to know where we are, what year it is, anything?" Blake asked.

"Yeah. I know exactly where and when we are," Dustin said. "1908, Tunguska event. According to history, it takes place in minutes from now. About 7:18 in the morning, June 30th. Commander, I think we cause this," Dustin said.

Cody looked up at the alien ship.

"Why is there snow here in June?" Cody asked as Wyatt and Josh landed close to him.

"I think we chased them all off," Wyatt said.

"Why is there snow, that's your question?" Dustin was annoyed.

"That was, will be, one of the largest explosions on the planet. It knocked people over a mile away. Cody, this plan of yours is going to kill us all because we have to be here when it happens. I doubt our armor can take that," Wyatt said.

"Guys, listen. We don't die here. This isn't how we go out. We're not done. Trust me and stand your ground. Whatever happens next, we'll be fine. I'll be there in a minute." Cody said and took to the sky. He knew that those soldiers wouldn't live. Knowing what he knew about the Syndicate now, he didn't feel so bad.

"Well, I guess this is a good death, too," Josh said.

"Yep, sure is," Wyatt replied.

The sun was visible now. Cody flew to the ship. It was round, and he wasn't sure where the front of the thing was. He'd improvise and figured if they could hack in, they could hear him.

"Attention, radioactive windbags. You are no longer welcome on this planet. You will never come here again unless you are invited," Cody said as he checked his time.

One minute to go.

His plasma cannon formed in his hand and pointed it at the ship's engine. It looked like the source of the light.

"One anti-gravity super vortex coming right up." He fired a solid beam of bright blue energy into the core of their ship. It was almost brighter than the sun when the ship and the plasma reacted. Cody had to look away as he raced back down to the others.

The ship reacted like he knew it should. This much power into an energy core like this caused a reaction, and the ship fired two beams, one up into the sky, the other into the ground. It turned into a twisting vortex of blue power, forcing the ship away from the planet.

The sky looked as if it was tearing apart. It was clear that as soon as the ship was gone, all of this spinning energy was going to have to go somewhere.

"At least we get front row seats," Wyatt said as the spinning vortex of energy burned brighter and spun faster while it came together.

"It sounds just like a tornado," Dustin replied. All of them were transfixed by the intense energy storm.

"Guys, you're too damn close. Run, I'm getting you back home," Nero's voice said through their intercoms, distracting them from the incredible noise of the tornado thing.

"Squad, we are going home. Fall back. Mission accomplished," Cody said, turned, and started to run away. The intense gravity was making it hard to do anything. All the trees were bending in the direction of the energy storm.

It was too much. The gravity was dragging them back. "We're not getting out of this," Wyatt said, doing his best to just stand up.

"Why not, we have Blake's cosmic girlfriend to help out. We'll be fine," Dustin replied as he braced himself against the gravity winds.

"Hell yes, you do. Think I'd just abandon you here at the end? As tempting as it is to let you all get blown to bits, not today," she said and was standing there in the center of their group. She closed her eyes, and the winds died out. "Come close, gentlemen. We wouldn't want to waste any more time," she said, and the group nearly fell over when the winds died.

They wasted no time in getting close. Cody took one last look at the violent storm in the distance. "Let's go," he said, and the six of them disappeared.

## 87

Ben's body was broken and half buried in the wreckage of the sprawling base. All he could feel was pain as his shattered bones struggled to heal.

Emily wiped the blood from her mouth.

"They put up a good fight."

"None of you are dead. That's impressive," she said, scanning the wreckage.

"We're not so easy to kill. Why are you impressed by that?" Ben asked as he tossed a slab of concrete off his arm with his free hand. She smiled. "You made me bleed. That'll do it."

"Alright, round three," Ben replied.

"We won't give up. None of us will," Claire said, standing up.

"Unless you die again," Emily replied. Claire

was in pain, but that was more than enough to make her want to attack.

Ben was surprised to see his shotguns fall to the ground in front of him.

"The hell?"

He looked around but saw nothing.

There was no indication that their enemy saw anything either. He grabbed his weapons, and they were real. They felt good in his hands.

"Just stay down and witness the end. It is my gift. You've done more than you ever thought you could. I won't eat you. If you don't stay down, I promise you'll die here," Emily said.

"Some gift. Watching the world end or whatever? Sounds great if you're into that kind of thing. Take her down," Bryan said as the others got themselves out of the wreckage.

Nobody noticed that Ben had his guns back.

Gemini was the first one there. He was always the first one there. Those dual blades went for the neck, but she caught them with her hands. "Oh, you're so fast, but you know what, you little psychopathic freak show? I'm always going to be faster."

Her hands were being cut into by the blades. She threw them to the sides and kicked Cole in the head, sending him back into the wreckage.

Two beams came out of her hands and knocked Ariana and Brad out of the sky. They tried to avoid the attack, but the beams twisted and turned as if they were alive and homing in on their targets with no mercy. They both started on fire as they crashed into smoking rubble after being hit.

"Insects, that's all any of you are, but still, I can't drain the time out of you morons, why is cosmic energy such a pain?" Emily was annoyed, but she did notice the guns.

"How did you get them back?" She narrowed her eyes and summoned bolts of bright green energy in all directions. The Zodiac Corps were struck down by the intense attack, but they were not her target.

"Come out, wherever you are."

"Emily, who are you talking to? What's the matter?" Dani asked after dodging the beam by mere inches. She looked at the Angel and smiled a little.

"Don't you feel it? Someone is screwing with the plan," she replied. Emily was an abomination in nature, a walking wasteland.

The longer she stayed in one place, the worse the weather became. Bright red lightning flashed across the sky, and the ice cold rain fell from the bleak and broken sky.

## 88

"Well, you're home," she coughed and leaned against something that used to be some kind of wall, now just a ruined heap of metal, and wiped the black blood from her mouth.

"That time trick, it'll only work once. You'd better earn this. You'd better win or at least do your best to try. I have to go, you know. Recharge or whatever. I'll be watching."

The Squad watched Nero fade out of reality.

"You heard the lady. Let's move out," Blake said and was going to fly out to meet Emily head-on. Cody stopped him.

"Hold on a second. You saw what she did to the Zodiac just now. Without a plan, we'll end up back in the past or worse," Cody said and thought for a second. "This is what we are going to do. Stay with me," he said.

The monster knew something was wrong.

"Really? I don't like these games. Cody, I know you're here. I don't know how, but I can feel you. Come out already," she said, and her suspicions were justified when she looked up into the black, cloudy sky, and in an instant, the whole thing was on fire.

"Well now, dinner and a show. At least they know how to act around a lady."

The rain had been set on fire and was coming down in lines of bright blue. "Distraction."

Emily grabbed the blade as it tore through her stomach, and she saw Wyatt there on the other end. "You," she said in a great deal of pain, doubling over, grabbing the blade and trying to pull it out of her stomach.

"Not today," Josh said, grabbed her shoulders, and tossed her to the ground. Wyatt moved with her and plunged the blade into the mud, burying the hilt to her skin. Emily screamed. "Oh, just die already," Wyatt said and started to push the blade up through her flesh inches at a time.

"You should have gone for the heart," Josh replied.

"Doing that now," he replied. Her flesh was like iron.

Then Emily's eyes went solid green, a pulse exploded from her body, and knocked the two of them away. Wyatt was thrown through a ruined tank. Josh was pushed through a smoking pile of rubble. She stood up, her teeth were razor sharp, and her skin had black cracks in it. Her clothes crackled with dark green energy.

"You just couldn't stay away," she screamed, and her flesh pulled together.

Dustin shot out of the sky and put white fire on her form. She flew up to meet him, grabbed him by the neck, and threw him at Wyatt.

"Should have just broken your neck," she said after letting go.

Wyatt lowered his sword just in time to avoid Dustin getting impaled through the back and took the hit.

"You alright?" Dustin asked. Wyatt's helmet lifted and he coughed up blood. "Will be fine. Get off me," he replied, coughing some more. Dustin lifted into the air.

Emily hadn't moved from her spot as the Squad gathered.

"Great plan, Cody. Now what?" Wyatt asked.

"No idea," Cody replied.

"I say we just tear her apart," Josh said.

"Listen, the reason we're not dust right now is because something of Emily has to still be in there preventing it. We still have a chance," Dustin replied, "a small chance, anyway," he finished.

"No matter. I can take you all the old-fashioned way. It's no trouble," she said with a special kind of hate in her voice.

"You'll try," Cody replied.

Wyatt looked at him. "You'll try? Really? We need to work on your comebacks when we get done with this."

"Never took you for an optimist. Who says there is an after?" Cody asked.

"Fair point." Wyatt spit out the last of the blood and put his helmet back down. She fired those bright green homing rays from her eyes.

Unlike both the Zodiac and the Guardian Angels, however, their armor saw this attack from when it was used before and devised a way to beat it.

"Wait for it," Blake said, making sure nobody jumped. "Now."

The five of them waited until the last second and changed places. The beams followed them and slammed into one another, destroying themselves.

Then they rushed in her direction.

Josh reached her first. He ignored his weapons and was going to tear her apart. He reached for her arms but wasn't fast enough. She flew out of range and punched him in the face. Josh hit the ground and slid through the wreckage. He expected to die, armor ruined at the least, but no, neither thing happened.

She was still holding back.

"I'm too fast for you," she said.

"Not too fast for me." Wyatt came up between the two of them and sliced his blade across her face, sending human blood in a spray to the left. She screamed, stumbling away.

"Thanks." Josh said before flying after her again.

"What do you say, Commander? Can we kill this thing or not? Sure, it's Emily, but we can't save everyone and she deserves it. Your call. Just don't take too long." Dustin said as he unleashed streams of flame at her. She blocked this, or maybe the fire died out before it got to her, he couldn't tell.

Cody was conflicted. He didn't want to kill her, but part of him knew she deserved it at this point.

"I know. I'm thinking. Keep her busy. I'll go see if there is anything we can do for her. Only one person can help make my choice."

He looked down toward Bryan. "I'll be right back."

"Did he really just say keep her busy? I hate that guy," Blake said and fired. The bullets crumbled to dust before they reached her.

"This is stupid. Why do some things work and other things don't? Who's writing the rules to this nonsense?" Blake asked, then he considered using something a little stronger.

"Make it quick, Cody," he said.

## 89

Cody flew towards Bryan, the only person who might know a solution to this madness.

He reached down and pulled a large chunk of metal off of him.

"You were there when this thing was made. How do you turn the monster off?" Cody asked as he grabbed him and pulled him up. His face was bloody. Whatever was keeping them alive was beginning to fail. They were all looking the same way.

Even Alex and the Angels were looking older now, too.

"As powerful as this monster is, it's a tool. It always has been. The Syndicate had it trapped all this time. They planned on trapping it after it beat you, but we all showed up, and it sent you to God knows where. The time stasis is here, it's buried.

This all went wrong. If you want to save her, you have to find it."

"The longer the Chronovore is inside her, the less of her there is to save, obviously. You can kill her. It would be easier than looking through this mess. Without a body or a stasis unit, it will just die, needs a host and all. Cody, whatever choice you make, there isn't much time. Wait too long, and it'll be too late for either one."

Cody dropped him.

"Damn it, Emily, why did you have to do this?" He looked up at the raging battle above and had a choice to make.

"Guys, keep her busy for fifteen minutes. Bryan said there was a mcguffin in the wreckage that can end this. I can save her if I can find it. If there is no progress after the time runs out, kill her," Cody told them through the intercom.

"Yeah, I got that, but what if he's lying? You don't know anything about it," Wyatt replied.

He looked at Bryan. "Guess I have to trust him," Cody replied.

"Hey, old man, what's this damn thing look like?" Cody asked. Bryan coughed. "Silver box. The Chemical Dragons intended to use it once she killed you. It can't be far," he replied, then collapsed again.

"Thanks," Cody said and flew off into the disaster.

Cody was frantically looking for something he didn't know anything about. The place was a disaster filled with metal and human wreckage. The wounded were screaming for medics and their mothers alike the farther he got from the battle. Some people were time twisted, half aged, turning to dust as they screamed. Cody turned his head.

There was nothing he could do about them.

The dragons had to have kept it somewhere easy to get to. It couldn't look like anything else—at least he hoped not. Cody landed beside and picked up a random soldier on the ground who didn't look hurt, just lost.

"Where is it? The weapon you planned to use on her?"

This guy was mumbling about home. His eyes were solid white. This man was in no condition to talk to anyone. Then he coughed, and dust came out of his mouth.

Cody dropped the man and backed off. Emily's influence was getting worse. "Damn it," he said and looked around. All of the buildings looked as if they were ready to collapse with rust.

"Going to do what I should have done in the first place. Scan for unknown energy." Cody usually didn't talk to himself much, but it helped him think once in a while. His armor began the scan. Everyone in the sky registered as unknown.

Everyone he knew on the ground did the same. The Angels were knocked out cold.

"Come on, God. I know you're out there. I think I earned a bit of help," Cody said to someone he hoped was listening.

Then, an answer. If he would have found it on his own or not, he'd never know.

"Thanks," he said.

A signal was detected close by. He rushed to the building and tore the door off the hinges, walking inside and following it.

When he found what he was looking for, he was confused at what he saw.

It was a silver box. No buttons. No instructions or openings. Just a silver box that he picked up. It fit in the palm of his hands, a perfect metal cube.

"Well, now what do I do?"

Cody didn't have any time to waste and took to the air, flying through the decayed roof of the building and made a line to where he left Bryan. The man looked closer to death. His skin was starting to crumble at the edges.

"You, tell me how to work this box, start talking." Bryan looked at him, then at the box.

"This is the stasis unit. Must have been the only one they could get their hands on. I doubt this will work on the Chronovore, but you can try it. Fire opens and closes it. This won't suck the monster out. No, this will draw the host and the parasite in at the same time, trapping them both in here. If it works, it won't work for long. This is too small. Those idiots got the wrong one."

"Good luck," Bryan finished. Cody looked at the small box and wondered how it worked, no time for that. He flew towards the fight. It was time to end this.

## 90

"Guys. I got something that might work. Dustin, I'll need fire. Everyone else, when this thing does what it's supposed to, you might not want to be near it." There was no response because they were too busy to talk back. Cody was in the danger zone in no time.

Dustin stood up. His armor looked weathered and broken. "I hear you. You need fire, you got it," he said. He even sounded worse.

He took to the air and flew right at Emily. The only way to burn her was to get close. He let his flames loose. The monster was covered in the stuff.

"Now or never, Cody, do it!" Dustin screamed. Cody wasted no time and threw the box into the white fire.

The containment box did what it was supposed

to do. It opened up, and all the white-hot flames were sucked in. Then the green energy started to be drawn in too. For a brief second, hope began to rise.

Then after that, it fell to the ground. Emily stood there, stunned, but she hadn't changed.

"Was that it?" Josh asked.

"I don't think it did anything," Wyatt replied.

"Nope, she's still the same old time eating monster," Blake replied. They had one choice left.

"It's just not our day today. Well, we can't say we didn't try," Dustin said.

"Guys, wait. Don't kill me. I'm still in here. I can see sometimes. Sometimes I can talk. Why do you think you five are doing better against me than everyone else is? I don't want this thing killing you or winning. Open the trap again and put me in. Find a way to remove the parasite!" It was Emily. They couldn't mistake that voice for anyone else.

"What do you think, try again?" Wyatt asked.

"It's worth a shot," Cody said. "I say we kill her while we have a chance," Josh replied. Cody ignored it.

"Dustin, fire, we'll give this one more chance." Cody didn't need to think about it. Blake rushed ahead, picked the trap up, and tossed the box, and Emily caught it. It looked as if the thing inside was ready to lash out.

Dustin unleashed his flames again. She was covered in fire, and the trap opened. There was a hideous shriek that cut the air.

Then the fire and the green energy mixed together into a vortex. The five of them watched as the intense brightness forced them to look away.

The ordeal only lasted a few seconds. When the light was gone, so was she. The silver box was bright green now. As it fell, Wyatt caught it.

"I think, at least for now, we won," Josh said.

"Yeah, sure," Wyatt replied as he held the cube in his hand.

"I can't help but feel this is too easy, anticlimactic, something like that," Dustin said, looking around.

The world began to shift back. Time was slowing down again, and things would return to normal. The Zodiac began to recover as well.

Alex stumbled through the wreckage. "What did you do?" he asked, still trying to catch his breath.

"Saved the world, again," Wyatt said, looking at it.

Alex looked at the box.

"No, it's a portal. The box. It's not a trap. I've looked into the heart of a black star. I've seen what lives there. We are dead. We are all dead. The chaos is coming for us all, crawling through the black of space. I've seen it once before. How could you use this?" he asked.

"So, did we still win or what?" Dustin asked and looked at the box, confused at Alex's sudden rant.

"Basic containment box." Cody looked at Bryan. In return, he was staring at what he had seen, shaking his head as it was all he could do.

Cody flew back to Bryan and glared into his eyes. Bryan could feel it.

"What the hell is this thing? It's obviously not what you said it was. Tell me." Bryan was shaken out of what he just saw.

"I didn't think it was that. It looks like a containment box. It's a portal to the far realm. There were only three ever recorded in history. I didn't think—I didn't know it was possible. They were supposed to be gone." Bryan said this, half thinking, half terrified.

"Maybe, just maybe, it's a new one."

Cody turned to the others. "You do not let that box out of your sight." Wyatt looked at it, not sure what he was looking at, however. "Right," he replied.

"The Syndicate knows about this by now. Let's get to the Viper and find out just what in the hell is going on. Now that the Chronovore is gone, operations will continue as planned. We can assume that resistance will be worse from here on out. The Angels took way too much damage. We're leaving them here. They can catch up or do whatever they want. Zodiac, you're either with us or in our way. Decide now," Cody said.

"No question. We were Guardians once, and some of us twice. This is what we were made for. We're going with you," Bryan said with a new sense of conviction.

They agreed, all of them besides Gemini anyway. He was talking to a burning tire, oblivious to everything that just happened.

"Alright. Squad, we've been delayed too long. Follow me," Cody said, and they all took off. The Zodiac corps followed them.

Samantha had to grab Cole by the back of the neck and drag him along. He was waving goodbye to the flaming tire before he joined them in flight.

"I'll miss you," he yelled as she pulled him along. Sam just rolled her eyes.

## 91

The Leviathan was moving toward the Pacific Ocean. Tracking the Delta Squad was easy. They didn't make themselves hard to find. It was almost like they wanted everyone to know where they were, but they did disappear for a few seconds. Likely just a weird glitch.

"What are we going to do once we catch them? They aren't our biggest fans, and I don't think they'll be in a talking mood," Amanda said, sitting on the deck of the Leviathan, legs dangling over the edge.

"I don't care what they think of us. They don't stand a chance. If they're smart, they'll give up," Skye replied, cold-hearted as always, staring ahead into the dark.

"Maybe, maybe not. They seem to be always

getting better at this fighting thing. Maybe we can find a way to avoid killing one another this time," Amanda replied.

"Oh, they'll see us. They'll wonder what we are doing back, then they'll wonder what we are doing with all of you," Tyler replied, walking toward them.

"Personally, I'm with her. Fighting with them is a stupid idea. No matter how strong you think you are, they I don't know, it seems like they get lucky," Tyler said and sat down next to Skye.

"Lucky, call it skill, they've done things, experience counts for a lot," Amanda replied and laid back, looking at the stars.

"It would take all of us to do this. Have you seen their power lately? We just got done scanning it, and the Leviathan couldn't read it. We don't know what they got themselves into, but they have changed. I doubt we'll ever catch them in this rust bucket of a ship. I'm guessing this will be little to no help at all if we get into a fight. Maybe we can take out the Viper," Skye said, always thinking ahead.

"Yeah, we'll take them down. We still have Joey on our side. If the Squad dares lay a finger on Amanda here, he'll go ballistic," Tyler said and laughed about it.

Amanda just grumbled and looked away.

"Yeah, that's always good to know. Cosmic powered serial killer has a thing for you. Guess what happens when you say no." She was not looking forward to seeing him again. Nobody was. He was impossible to track due to his nature and could be anywhere.

"Don't worry about Joey. He's just a kid with a crush. He shouldn't be that tough to bend to your will. It's kind of your thing, after all, right?" Skye asked. "Yeah. I suppose it shouldn't be too hard, but no telling what it will really be like."

It was then that they heard running behind them.

"Guys, you're never going to believe this, but satellite images just sent the news! The Delta Squad just beat the Chronovore, the monster is gone!"

It was Stephanie running out to tell them the news. This news was both good and bad. Good that they won, bad that they won on their own. Just how powerful were they?

"God damn, they saved the world again," Tyler said with a laugh. "Well it was either that or die," Amanda replied.

"The interference was horrible, but the monster was there for a minute. Then, in the next broadcast, it was gone—just gone," she said. It sent a strange chill in the air.

"No matter. I bet the Chronovore had some weakness they could exploit. We have no weakness. The plan doesn't change. We keep going," Skye said and pushed herself off the edge of the ship and flew into the storm clouds. She needed to think about stuff and wanted to be alone.

"I got a bad feeling about sticking to this plan," Amanda said and crossed her arms to fight off the phantom cold.

"Bad feelings are the only feelings I've had for a long time," Tyler replied and laid next to the Olympian.

"So, what do you want to do now?" Tyler asked. Amanda just smiled. "Thanks for the news update, Steph, you can go now," she said. "Yeah, I didn't like it out here anyway," she replied.

"That was kind of mean," Tyler said.

"You should go away too. Joey might get it in his head to kill anyone he thinks might be moving in on me, I'm better off alone right now," she said. Tyler hated that logic, but he wasn't afraid. "Joey isn't Silence, he's got all that power, but he's still Joey. Don't be too afraid of him," Tyler replied.

Amanda smiled.

## 92

Adam could feel it in his bones that the time stream had shifted again.

"Something big just happened," Lindsey said, "I feel weird," she finished.

"Yes, time is healing. Everything is running as it should," Adam replied as they walked down the empty road.

"Why in the hell are we walking anywhere? Can't we just teleport? Lindsey could look for a car in any direction for miles in just a few seconds. This is stupid," Haley complained.

"Yes, I know, but it's good to get some fresh air in the middle of nowhere and a little sun once in a while. Are you really in a hurry to get back into the action? The Squad will kill us if they see us anyway, and we'd just get in the way. We're better off here," Adam replied.

"No, actually, I was just thinking of getting a hotel room somewhere and being warm. That was all. Even my sword is starting to get heavy," she replied.

"Haley has a point. We don't have to be walking," Lindsey replied. Then something caught her attention in the distance.

"Look, a Syndicate convoy is heading into a town over there," she said. The other two looked but couldn't see anything other than dust being kicked up in the direction of a town. "I guess you're just going to have to trust me on it," she replied.

"Hand," Adam said and held his out. Haley grabbed on to it, and Lindsey did the same. In an instant, they were standing among the tombstones.

"Thought we needed a better view," he said and let go.

"What the hell was that?" Lindsey asked.

"Grave Walking. Necromancers can teleport between graveyards anywhere they want. Kind of a useful spell," he replied and ducked down as the convoy started to drive past. The other two followed him.

"Congratulations, you were right, it was a convoy. Now that we're here, what are we going to do about it?" Haley asked.

"I'll just kill them all. No worries," Lindsey

replied, and Adam laughed. "I have a better idea—go stand on the other side of the fence and watch," he said.

The two of them weren't sure what he planned to do, but they moved to the back and hopped over the fence.

Adam put his hands together.

"Persephone, Queen of the Underworld. I request a spark of your power, return the bodies that lay here to life so ancestors may protect the descendants," he said.

Nothing happened.

"Magic is stupid, let me go in there and kick some Syndic—" Lindsey's voice was cut off.

"You called on me?" A woman was standing there beside him. She was dressed in black but had a bright red flower in her hair. Her eyes were solid blue, she was taller than all three of them, and her skin was the color of ashes.

She didn't look real.

"Yes," Adam replied, but he didn't move.

She held out the palm of her hand, a flower grew out of her skin, then she dropped it on the earth and at once it spread out with tendrils, one for each grave.

"I suppose I can grant you this favor. I've always liked you, Adam. You should prepare for the future—it's dark," she said. Then she turned to look at the women. Those solid, dark blue eyes were on them.

"I like your choice of company—a bit whiny but respectable," she said. Then it was as if she was never there.

"Thank you," Adam replied, then turned and walked to the others.

"Who the hell was that?" Lindsey asked, her voice returning as suddenly as it was taken.

"Persephone," Adam replied.

"No way, a real Olympian. What is reality right now? I thought all that trash was just made up," Haley replied.

"Oh, not quite made up," he replied. Then the ground began to shake as Adam phased through the metal fence.

Then coffins began to tear out of the ground in rows, pulled up by that alien plant. The lids were torn off, and skeletons began to march out. Each one had been supplied with a long black sword in their right hand.

The army of the dead started their silent march toward town.

"That'll buy the town some relief. Imagine that—a necromancer doing something nice," Adam said and laughed at the thought.

"I'm still stuck on the Gods are real thing," Haley said.

"Well, get unstuck," Adam replied. "We need to

get to the Viper. If the Delta Squad saved the world, the very least we could do is try and save them from what's coming," Adam said.

"I'll do my best, but where do we even start?" Lindsey asked.

"We need to teleport," he replied.

"I hate teleportation," Haley said and sighed, "but, I guess we don't have much choice," she relented. Adam held out his hands and they all joined in a circle.

"Don't break the circle," he said, "and do your best not to look into the void," he finished.

"Why, what's in the void?" Haley asked. "Void things, madness made flesh, horrible things. Don't you ever read Lovecraft? He looked in the void and went crazy," Adam replied.

"Oh, I see," she replied, "I'll just keep my eyes closed," she said.

"Won't make a difference, you'll still be able to see. Just look at one another. Ignore everything else —all the noises, all the voices, everything. Understand? We won't be there long, but it doesn't take much," he said.

"Got it," Haley said. Lindsey took a deep breath and nodded. "Ready."

The Syndicate's plan had to be stopped, and as far as he knew, there was one way to do it. "And here we go," he said.

## 93

Mark was nervous. The Delta Squad had just beaten the Chronovore and were now on their way here.

This was not part of any plan he ever made. If it were up to him, these thorns would have been burned alive the second they were captured.

"What the hell are we going to do?" a voice asked. Mark turned. It was a random soldier who wouldn't have dared talk to him like this hours ago, but now, doom was on the way.

Mark thought about hitting him but didn't.

"Get ready for a fight," Mark replied. It was the only thing he could say. "Go," he said, and the man ran off.

Mark made his way to the office of the Syndicate's leader, but the office was empty. "Of course it's empty." There was a note on the front of the door. Mark tore it off.

"Stay the course, get to where you're going. It will all make sense," Mark read it out loud, crumpled the paper, and tossed it in the office.

"If we even make it that far," he said, turned, and started making his way toward the bridge.

It was a short trip to the bridge. He walked in, and it was a bunch of people arguing about what to do. It was clear to everyone the Delta Squad was coming in their direction. Mark walked to the main console and pushed a button.

"Everyone listen up. I know you are aware of what is about to happen. We are not defenseless. Do not abandon ship. Anyone who does will just die anyway. The squad will hunt you down, or you'll hit the ocean and drown there," he said and took a breath.

"Man the battle stations. Prepare yourself for a fight. We still have the advantage here. We're on a goddamn mile long flying battleship. It's armed to the teeth, and we're going to use every weapon we have. They aren't invincible, just hard to kill, but those bastards won't get any older than today. So, take a minute, get your thoughts together, then get ready to fight or jump off the side. Either way is fine with me, but decide fast," he said and let the button go.

Everyone on the bridge was looking at him.

"Guys. Either get ready to fight or hit the water. I wasn't kidding. Decide," he said, and the crewmembers had a second of hesitation in their eyes, then it disappeared.

It was clear they believed in the mission.

"Solaris, what's the status of the project? I think we're out of time," Mark asked over the intercom.

"Chill out, it'll be ready, you can trust me," Solaris replied.

"Yeah, sure, just be ready," Mark replied and cut communications.

Mark smiled. At least this would be the last time they'd have to see one another. He had no intention of walking away until they were dead or he was. He also didn't believe the Chronovore was dead. Experience told him that. After all, he was still alive, too.

## 94

Quentin had passed into the black, and there was no way back.

This book had to go back home.

The next gate he made it to was blood red. It almost looked like it was liquid, but it wasn't. It was cold. Maybe it was frozen blood. These gates were always so morbid, but he assumed they would be.

"Just like last time," he said and pushed the book against the gate. "Do your thing, book," he said, and just like the last one, it started to melt away into nothing.

He pulled the book and himself back, not knowing what to expect. For all he knew, there might have been some horror behind it. Not much he could have done about it now but get eaten.

However, on opening this gate, he felt stronger.

As if whatever energy was inside had charged him up.

He had more energy. The farther he went into the dark, the better off he was going to be. He wasn't sure what was waiting for him at the end of this, but he couldn't wait to find out. The liquid black void waited for him, and with a deep breath and a tight grip, he walked past it.

"Quentin, what are you doing? None of this is okay, is it?" he asked.

"Bro, it's fine. Just keep going. You have a few more gates to go, and once you get through, you can get the reward."

A voice in his head. Not his own.

"What? I mean, if you say so," he replied.

"Of course I do. I have all the good ideas. Keep going."

Quentin had never heard voices before. He'd always heard that it was a bad sign, but in this world he lived in, sometimes it was good to listen to the voices.

"What's the worst that could happen?" he replied and kept moving.

## 95

The three of them had chosen their names.

Nate made a fist and stared at it. It was his first time in a suit that he could call his own. "I like this, but it feels like it's cheating," he said.

"Yeah, but when that helmet of yours blocks a bullet, you'll be happy you had it," Paxton replied.

"Illusions are fun, but I like this a whole lot more. That Mustafa knows how to make a suit—this is awesome," Lance said and floated into the air with a thought but was wobbly. "Flying is still a pain," he said as he landed.

"Yeah, it's a whole new world," Paxton replied. "It will take some practice, so what do you think? Should we get some?"

Lance and Nate looked at one another.

"Sure, where should we go first?" Lance asked, and Paxton's eyes lit up for a second.

"There's a prison camp a few miles from here. We could, I don't know, liberate it?" Paxton replied. "First, you need names that fit the armor."

Lance and Nate shrugged. "I'm not really that good at code names," Lance replied.

"Well, I named them. Lance, yours is called Bedlam. Nate, yours is Malevolence. I thought it was perfect."

"Yeah, sounds good to me," Lance replied and tried lifting off the ground again. Better this time but still not stable. "Not sure about this flying stuff," he said.

"Come on, let's go have some fun," Paxton said and lifted off the ground. Nate followed him.

"You lead the way," Lance said, and the three of them flew to the west.

The three of them were sailing through the air. Just as Paxton had said, there was a camp there. Piles of fires in the yard. "Burning the bodies," Paxton said. "That is a smell I miss," he finished.

"Bro, you're weird," Lance replied.

Before Nate could say anything, Paxton dropped out of the sky and landed behind a guard. Before the guard could turn around, he picked him up and tossed him in a pile of burning bodies as if he were a toy.

The man screamed but couldn't escape as the

bodies had fallen on him. Paxton watched it all happen, the flames reflecting off his armor.

"This is going to be fun," he said as the other two landed behind him.

The guards in the yard stopped, drew their weapons at the invaders, the alarms began to blare, and the prisoners started to run to anywhere they could find cover.

"Kill the guards, try not to kill the prisoners. We're turning over a new leaf and all, but if you do end up killing a few, I won't tell anyone," Paxton said as his chainsaws extended. He moved forward so fast the guard in his sights lost both his arms in a second.

Then he fell over, screaming. Paxton crushed his skull under his heavy foot. "Shut up."

Nate looked at the guards. There were twenty-four left that he could see.

"This is taking too long," he said and concentrated on their hearts. "And done," he said. With a thought, they all fell at the same time.

"Dude, what did you do?" Paxton asked, looking around.

"They all died of broken hearts," Nate replied. "What? I didn't want to waste time. We got stuff to do," he finished.

It was then that from the far building, men in uniforms came running out as if something was chasing them, screaming, "Get them out," over and over again in a frenzy, tearing at their skin with knives. The three of them watched as the warden and the officers dove headfirst into the pile of burning bodies to get relief.

"Bugs under the skin is a classic that never gets old," Lance said. "This armor told me there were people inside and let me focus on them. This works great. Can we go now?" he asked.

Paxton sighed. "Sure, I guess. You take all the fun out of things, you know that?" Paxton asked. Nate shrugged.

Then he looked at the gates. "Oh, right. Liberate," he said. Everyone watched as the heavy steel gates crumpled like tin cans, then were tossed to the sides.

"You can all go now," Nate said to the people who were still hiding. "I'd go before the Syndicate sends reinforcements," he added and took to the air.

"Come on, I'm sure we'll have more fun when we meet up with the squad," Paxton said and looked at the one guy he got to kill. "I sure hope so, anyway." Then he took off. Lance just behind him, still trying to get used to flight.

## 96

"Josh, I have to know. How did you manage to live that long and not go insane?" Wyatt asked him as they were flying. He was sure they all wanted to know the same thing.

Josh didn't say anything.

"Come on, man, real talk and all that," Wyatt said.

Josh took a breath.

"Well, it's simple. I invented Yuletide," Josh said as if it explained everything.

"You did what now?" Josh shook his head.

"You moron. I invented Christmas." Wyatt was stunned. "You did what? How, why? I have questions," Wyatt said.

"The Lemurians were terrified of the dark. When the sun got low and all the horrible things clawed their way out of the swamps, oceans, and other places. They had good reason to be afraid. The Atlantis attacks ramped up as it got colder. I mean, cold for a Lemurian, anyway. As their newest leader, when the dark times came, I brought them the holiday. I couldn't call it Christmas, so I called it something else. It's simple."

"You invented Christmas. Every Christmas I've ever had in my whole life is because of you?" Wyatt asked. "Yep."

"I need a history lesson, tell me everything," Wyatt said.

Josh grumbled. "I should knock you out," Josh replied.

"Come on, we have a long way to go and this stuff is interesting, tell us more," Dustin said.

"I'm with them. I'd like to know more," Cody said. "Fine, I'll give you your exposition to pass the time."

"Humans and Serpent kind were similar in many ways. The serpent people were created by older things, humanity too."

"The slave races toiled to build horrible cities for untold ages and were their entertainment, slaughtered on a whim. The older things didn't care about what they had made, much the same way you'd care about those ants you kill without a thought."

Josh wasn't sure how much of the story he

should tell. He saw things, things he'd never want to see again or talk about.

"Eventually, the Earth's climate changed, and the old masters grew weak in the cold over time. Weak enough for the slaves to rebel, and even if they could not kill their masters—I doubt anyone could—they gained the help of two saviors. It's said they aligned the stars themselves to somehow trap and banish what remained of the old masters and their vicious legacy."

"I don't know who the saviors were, no one knows for sure. I theorized it was Bob and Theron," Josh said. "Why?" Cody asked.

"Mostly because of the figures in the mural. One was black, the other was green," he replied.

"Those two have their secrets, I guess," Blake said.

"Yes, now can I finish?"

"Sure," Dustin answered.

"Anyway, the serpents and the humans lived together for many centuries, but as things usually go, people grew apart. Humanity was always aware that they were created with the divine sparks of some higher power and began to worship the new gods. They believed they deserved the whole world and eventually left the Serpents on Lemuria and sailed the oceans to find their new home, Atlantis, a nation of humans."

"The serpents cared nothing for power. Life and

living were good enough for them, so the separation wasn't that big of a deal. They would always fear the return of the old masters. By the time I got there, they believed that when the sun dipped low in the sky and the nights lasted so long, it was a sign of the end of the world. It was terrifying because all the old things from the past crawled out of their hiding places when it stayed dark longer."

"End of the world, really?" Blake asked.

"Yes, now shut up and let me finish," Josh replied.

"When I showed up, I caused a big panic. Everyone was sure the end of the world had come. I told them that the world wasn't ending. I don't know if Emily did it on purpose or what, but I arrived on the day their king was killed, and Quarl put me up for the throne. It was chaos for a while, but I calmed them down."

"They were a good people, I could tell. We had lots in common. We both had quite the temper, quick to anger and all."

"When the end of the year came and the panic was setting in as it had for centuries past, I was reminded of Christmas, but I knew the traditional story wouldn't work for obvious reasons."

"I told them the boundaries of the universe were restarting. The light would return, and we should celebrate the renewal. I called it Yule. The first few years weren't easy. No one was willing to participate, called it a waste of time," Josh said, and before anyone could ask him what he did, he got to the point.

"I began to tell them the stories of what we did. How we were actually heroes if you could consider us that. How we fought the dark, and if we could do it, anyone could do it. It created a general, happy feeling in the worst of times."

"It was still scary. Many still died, but now we had a reason to come together, celebrate the light at the darkest of times," he finished. They never realized just how much he had to go through.

"Holy hell, Josh is Santa Claus," Dustin said.

"Now the red suit makes sense," Blake added.

"I guess something had to make it through to the modern era," Josh replied. "Are you happy now? Is that enough filler for you?" he asked.

"I'm good," Wyatt replied.

Bryan had been listening to the whole thing and flew beside him.

"Josh, you recounted everything we know from the decayed records we've collected. When this is all over, I wonder if you could tell us more about it. You can't be a Guardian and not like history. Nobody likes it more than me," he said.

"I'll think about it," he replied.

"It's all I ask."

"I hate to break up the holiday love fest, but does anyone have any idea where we're going?"

Blake asked. "I am getting tired of flying over the ocean," he finished.

"I do. We're going to where you hid the Viper, near the sunken city," Bryan said.

"You mean—" Bryan cut him off.

"Bad luck to say it out loud, but yeah, we're going there, I think," he replied.

"I saw it before it sank. It was in the process, but, yeah, that's one weird place. There are things trapped down there," Josh replied.

"I know. I don't know if the Syndicate knows that or if they have something planned, but if they do and have a plan involving that, it's game over, again," Bryan said.

"Why in the world are there so many world ending things in the world? Who thought that was a good idea?" Cody asked.

No one had an answer.

## 97

Joey was sitting on some stairs, thinking about everything when gunfire erupted from behind the old building he was in front of.

"What the hell?" he asked and stood up, flying up to the roof. He landed on the other side, looked to the street below. A small Syndicate patrol was shooting at a group of someone taking cover behind rubble from a blasted out building.

He pulled his hood over his head with a smile and stepped off the building, landing in the gunfire. The bullets bounced off his cloak as he turned to look at the patrol.

For a second, he didn't move an inch.

"No." The word came out in his twisted voice, then he flew forward. The soldiers didn't have a chance. He grabbed the first one by the neck and ripped his head off. The other two started to run, but Joey wasn't going to let them leave. He used the headless body as a club and smashed the legs down on the back of the one closest.

The man fell, Joey stepped on his neck, crushing it flat to the ground. The last man was screaming. Joey caught up to him in a second.

"You should have been a dishwasher, less stressful." Then he smashed the soldier into the wall. The cracking bones almost made part of a song, then he tossed the dead one to the side.

The people they were shooting at were already running away.

"Hey, wait a minute," he said, but they weren't listening. He was ahead of them in a second and they stopped.

"Who are you?" he asked.

"We're the resistance, thanks for your help but we didn't need it, we had a plan," the man, if you could call him that, said, acting his best not to be afraid.

"Right. Where do you get your orders?"

The four of them pointed their weapons at him. "Guys, did you not just see what I did? Do you have better bullets?"

"Here," a woman in the back pulled her phone from a pocket and tossed it to him. Joey caught it. "Just push play, newest orders are on there," she said.

He did.

"Your orders, anyone who can hear this, is to take out the Red Mirror. It is the largest prison camp the Syndicate has running. Also, it's where they keep a majority of their War Walkers. This will need to be a united eff—" Joey shut Heath's voice off and tossed the phone back.

"Where is this place?"

"It's the Air Force Base. Ten miles east from here. Heath's been ordering us to take the place for a week now, it's suicide. The War Walkers, they—" Joey held up his hand.

"I get it." He was sure he sounded harsh, but they didn't need to bring up any memories of their friends getting slaughtered. "Thanks for the help, get to cover," he said and took off into the sky. The group watched the stranger fly off.

"That guy's weird," one of them said. "Yeah, let's call it in and get out of here," another replied.

---

Ten miles to the east.

"Heath, great general of the Syndicate reduced to a talking head barking out orders. I guess my life could be worse. We could be that guy," Joey said.

"Yes, we could. What is your plan here, play the hero?" Silence asked.

"I have to prove I'm worth a damn. I have all

this power. I might as well use it." Joey said. "Fine, I guess if you have to," Silence replied, "but I still don't think you're worth a damn," it finished.

"Yeah, well, shut up and let me think."

"Oh, some great battle plan. I can't wait to see what you come up with. I think I know what you're gonna do," Silence replied.

Joey ignored it.

As advertised, the base was sprawling. Guard towers, thousands of prisoners, high walls, and of course, the War Walkers stomping around the place, keeping everyone in line.

Joey was sure this place would even give the Delta Squad trouble, but they were busy doing something else. Now it was just him.

"My turn to shine," he said, held his hand out, and watched as black energy gathered in his palm. He aimed at a tower—he was sure his aim was good—then he let the energy go.

"Just like I thought," Silence said.

## 98

The routine of the day was destroyed as the guard tower was hit by a solid black beam and exploded. The base came to life.

Tony was here, waiting for his execution, tied to a flagpole. The War Walker watching him turned to see what happened. Tony looked too.

"What?" he asked with a cracked voice due to dehydration. Then, to his surprise, a figure in a black cloak landed in the yard.

"Silence?" Tony asked. Now he was sure he was going to die. This was how it ended. Unexpected but acceptable, he supposed.

Tony had front row seats to whatever was going to happen next. Silence didn't move, but the guards rushed to meet him. They didn't dare get close as they opened fire. The bullets smashed into that black fabric, turning to dust.

Then, faster than Tony could register, the maniac was mere feet from the guards. Silence pulled a rifle away from one of the guards and spun it around to stab the man through the heart. Tony winced as the blood and barrel shot out the back.

"Christ," he said. The guards started to retreat, but it was too late.

Silence began tearing them to pieces as they ran. Tony closed his eyes. There were some things he didn't want to see, but the squelching sounds of ripping flesh and the screams cut short—there was nothing he could do about that.

The smell of the blood was intense, too.

It was over seconds after it began. Then the footsteps were getting closer. Tony opened his eyes to see the monster coming.

"Silence, what are you doing?" Tony asked. He was going to die anyway, so he didn't care. To his surprise, the monster stepped behind him and broke his chains.

"You know my name? I don't know you. Why don't you run? Go, you're free."

Tony knew something was different. "Silence, we've met before. You're different. Finish this, and when you're done, we should talk." Tony was taking a huge risk by doing this, and he knew it.

Everything told him to run like hell while he could, but he needed to know more.

Joey looked at this guy and knew he had to be someone from his past, someone important. "Right. I'll be back," he said and walked away.

"You'll be fine. I need to find something to drink," he said, started to look around but didn't have time. Three of the walking tanks had shown up. It was best to just get away.

Tony had always wondered why walking tanks were a thing.

They were thirty feet tall and looked like the evil version of the walkers out of *Star Wars*. Silence didn't waste any time taking notice. How could anyone not notice these things?

Tony was too close as the cannons on the side of the thing started to fire at Silence. The sound was so great he had to cover his ears and get low to the ground.

The shells turned the ground Silence was standing on into dark brown dust and smoke. Tony knew that wasn't going to do anything. He wondered how the Syndicate thought it would. Then it occurred to him that maybe the chain of information wasn't as good as he hoped.

It felt like forever, but the thunder of the cannons came to an end.

Tony looked into the smoke, but when Silence didn't come flying out to meet them, he wondered if maybe whatever had changed in the monster made him weaker. Or, maybe less intelligent, and he didn't dodge.

Then, just as Tony expected, the man in black flew from the smoke and underneath the walking tank in the center, then through the top. It exploded, sending shrapnel in every direction. Tony winced in pain as a shard of steel landed in his left leg.

"Son of a bitch," he said, wincing in pain. He reached down and tore it out, then held the wound closed until the healing factor took over, closing the wound.

Silence punched the one on the left in the side so hard that it was taken off its feet and flew into the wall, smashing through it. There was no restraint here. Whoever was in control of this power was furious about something.

The last tank did its best to turn and fight, but it was no match. Silence tore off the left cannon and swung the thing as if it were a bat. The core of the tank was ripped off its legs and went flying into the distance. Tony couldn't see where it landed, but it sounded like it landed on a building.

Silence tossed what remained of his bat to the ground and landed next to Tony.

"Now, who are you?" Silence asked. Tony decided to tell him.

"Tony. I'm Delta Squad too. Older version. You don't remember me at all?"

"No. I got into a fight with the Commander—pretty epic stuff. When I woke up, I was in charge of the power instead of Silence. He, it, is still rattling around in my head, but that seems to be all. He thinks you're a loser," Joey said.

"My name is Joey. You don't know me?"

"The kid who—yeah, I know who you are, the fan fiction writer," Tony replied, doing his best to not be terrified. A kid with this much power was madness.

One bad day could do a lot of damage.

"More Delta? I'm your biggest fan in the whole world. Maybe I can help you, or you help me, or something?" Joey asked. He was enthusiastic about the whole thing.

Tony had to think fast. Right now, he was a fanboy with superpowers. He had to stick with that.

"If you could help find my armor, we could take the Syndicate forces down twice as fast. And maybe some water?"

Silence crossed his arms.

"Buddy, for you, I'll do anything. You're the man," he replied.

Then the two of them lifted into the air with no warning. Tony kept his cool, but inside he was praying that whatever God might be watching wouldn't let him get killed. His life was now in the hands of the worst thing he could think of—a fan with the powers of a cosmic serial killer.

"All right, Tony, we're going on a ride, hold on."

"Yeah, if there was anything to hold on to, I would."

He hoped that Joey would be attentive enough not to slam him into the sides of any buildings or trees on the way, wherever it was they were going.

Even with a healing factor, it wouldn't be a good time.

## 99

Necromancers knew of a few ways to teleport. The first was Grave walking, safe and effective. The second was worse.

The sky was black, and the sun was a deep red. The three of them stood on an ancient road. Adam took a look around.

"This is where the missing go—planes, ships, people. They slip between the worlds through a portal and end up here, sometimes at random. Sometimes a hungry thing takes them. There is no escape without help," Adam said.

"This place is horrible, it feels sick, like the air is filled with blood," Lindsey replied. Adam nodded.

"Ladies, I suggest you be as quiet as you can. If they hear you, they'll want to taste you. Don't deviate from the course. We are here for fifteen minutes in this time. In the real world, it'll be as if no time had passed at all."

Haley looked around. The red light from the sky didn't reveal too much. She looked to the edge of the path and started to look over the edge.

Adam stopped her. "Trust me, please. You don't want to see," he said, and she stepped away from the edge.

Lindsey could barely see anything and hoped that nothing here could fly because they would never see it coming. Haley looked to the left. The ground beyond the path looked like a shiny black ocean with no waves.

The sun here was so red that the light wasn't good enough to see anything far away. It looked like a city was in the distance.

Something was slithering and twisting around the spires. Something black and horrible, now thankful that she couldn't see it. "Let's go," Adam said and started walking on the one thing that felt normal in this place, the others followed.

Adam led the way, but he was afraid. This place had a way of pulling groups apart. "Hold hands," he said.

"Why?" Haley asked. "This place doesn't want to let you leave. This path is the only link to the world you have. They will read your mind, and they will do anything they can to get you to step off. Once you do, you're done," Adam replied, keeping his voice as low as he could.

Lindsey grabbed Haley's hand. "He's right. I just saw my mom out there in the black, she was waving at me, and it smelled like the pumpkin pie she used to make. For a minute, I just wanted to go say hello," she said.

Haley squeezed a little tighter. "I won't let you go," she said and kept her eyes ahead.

Adam heard that and smiled, just a little. These things would have to work for their meal today, and he kept moving down the path. He just hoped they wouldn't see anything horrible as they moved forward.

Hope in this place was a dead concept.

# 100

"What's the big plan? Walk up to the team that fought the Devil and all the other big things and just zap them out of the sky, declare victory, and take down the Syndicate all at the same time? Because if you ask me, that sounds like a stupid plan," Angel said.

"Yeah, that's what I had planned this whole time," Megan replied and rolled her eyes, "no, of course not. Obviously, they have something they want the Viper for—"

Something hit the Leviathan, and the whole ship rocked to the side.

"The hell was that?" Megan screamed over the alarms, dragging herself to her feet. "I don't know, but we should find out," Angel said and got up. He was holding on to the table.

The two of them waited until the Leviathan rolled back to where it was supposed to be and ran toward the deck to see what was going on.

In minutes, the Horsemen and the Olympians were on the deck, ready to fight something that was strong enough to rattle their whole ship.

What they saw was not what anyone expected to see.

It was the black and orange armor Paxton used to wear, Blood Wraith. "Paxton, is that you?" Amanda asked, but there was a shrill laugh that was the response. This was not Paxton.

"Blood Wraith has returned, but who wears the armor? Does anyone wear it?" Chris asked, and it was an unsettling thought. For whatever reason, it tracked them down and attacked them. It shouldn't have been able to do this to the Leviathan.

The figure tilted his head.

"Teleported into your ship. Sabotaged it. Planted explosives. Oh, not enough to kill the ship, no. I just wanted your attention."

The armor teleported to the deck of the ship.

"Now that I have it, I have it. I have you, I have everyone." He spread his arms out, and those chainsaws came to life.

"You're still insane. Congratulations. I don't care who you are. Don't care why you're here, either. You're messing with the wrong people," Hades said and didn't waste any time. He charged the intruder at full speed, but was too slow.

Hades got a chainsaw to the back of his neck for his trouble. It was hard to hit someone who could teleport offensively. Chris was slammed into the deck, face first.

"Yeah, didn't go so well for you, did it, deadhead?"

A beam came at his head, but he was already out of the way.

"Hello Hera, you think you can get the drop on me? Do you remember me? Does anyone remember me?"

He had appeared at the beam's source and put the chainsaw next to her armored throat as he was behind her. "Yeah, I don't know who you are."

The chainsaw revved, and sparks flew as it made contact. "Let me get to your soft insides," he said, but she fired a beam into the deck and forced him to teleport away. Skye was thrown forward and hit the deck.

Brianna helped her back up. "Thanks," she said.

"Thank me later," she replied.

"Olympians, Horsemen. Greetings, you don't know me. Obviously, but I know you. I've been watching you this whole time. Oh yes, and you know, I think you can be the ones to help me take down the Syndicate. They all deserve to die, trust me, you want to help me. You can say yes, or I can, one by one, teleport you all into various walls of this ship and watch you suffer and die. Your choice. Think fast."

This was an unexpected turn.

"Hey, what's the deal with the madness and attacking us? If you want to team up against the Syndicate, all you had to do was ask. There was no need for the show," Megan replied, and the man in Wraith armor stepped back.

"What? I thought I would have to prove my worth. Show my skills, rough you up a little," he said in one breath at a rapid pace.

The Horsemen and the Olympians looked at one another. "Nope, asking works too," Tyler said, and the chainsaws retracted.

"Who are you, friend?" Matt asked.

"Who am I? I don't remember. I used to be Mac, then I was a David. I was a Delta member, yeah. I was supposed to die. I think, you see. A shot in the dark saved me. Oh, that crazy bullet. I looked at it after the raid, and it was so strange. I needed to know who saved me, who let me live. The bullet was made out of unknown elements. Nobody knew what it was or why it existed. I used to be a Flesh Tearer," he said.

"I needed to know everything. Nobody knew. The obsession grew, I suppose, and eventually I was locked away in a dark place. I was released, maybe they forgot about me. I found this nifty armor thing. It was locked in a cage, like me," he said.

"We are friends, or maybe none of that is true. I don't know. I know one thing. I need you, and now you're mine, we are one," Blood Wraith said and laughed.

"Carry on, nobody tells anyone I am here or that one dies first, all the secrets must be kept," he said with a laugh. "You'd better believe I am always watching you." He gave them the thumbs up as he walked away and disappeared.

"Well, great. We just got partnered with a crazy person, but at least we got to see the ice queen get owned, that was funny," Brianna said and laughed about it.

Skye glared at her, then walked away.

"Guess maybe she took that kind of hard," Brianna said, and the others watched.

Athena smacked her in the back of the head. "She could wipe you off the ship with one attack. Maybe you should show some respect, horse girl, yeah?" Brianna didn't feel pain, but it was a good reminder of just who it was they were flying with.

She almost forgot.

"Yeah. Looks like we get to have a rematch with the Delta Squad anyway. I can't wait," Hades said.

"How are we supposed to get there before the battle's over?" Matt asked and looked over the edge and couldn't believe what he was seeing. They were over the ocean. Seconds ago, they were over land somewhere.

"Never mind, techno magic to the rescue, I guess," he said.

"Teleportation is so weird," Angel said and looked over the edge of the Leviathan, looking at the black void below.

## 101

"Does anyone else feel like the world has changed?" Nate looked around, and there was something different he couldn't put his finger on. "Yeah, can't you tell, man? Time, it feels normal. Look at everything. It seems brighter, fresh," Lance said, looking around. Paxton didn't like this one bit. His whole inspirational speech was wasted if this was true.

"Guys, pay attention to reality for a minute. If the monster was beaten, that's fine. One problem solved. It was replaced with another. The Syndicate and--"

Paxton was cut off as he looked up and saw Grandmaster Silence flying through the air with what appeared to be a victim.

"Guys, is that who I think it is?" he asked, and

they all looked over.

"What are the odds of this happening?" Paxton asked.

"Astronomical," Lance replied.

"I still think something is pulling all the strings. Why would we just happen to see him close to us? It doesn't make any sense," Paxton replied.

"It's Grandmaster Silence. The guy is a pure monster, let him go do whatever he's going to do. He didn't see us, and we don't see him. Everyone goes home happy," Nate said, and common sense guided his words.

Paxton didn't want to see it this way. "We'll save the prisoner. It should be fun." He took off after the monster.

"Oh my God, we're going to die out here," Lance said.

"I guess we might as well die together. Let's go," Nate replied and flew after Paxton.

"Sure, why not," Lance replied.

Joey noticed he was being followed and turned to look. "What the hell are you supposed to be?" Joey asked as he saw these three scary looking armors chasing him.

"Don't stop, Joey, you can outrun these guys. No problem. Just keep going as fast as you can," Tony said, but Joey was slowing down.

"No, this is the opposite of running away. You

don't need to do this. Really, it'd be smart just to ditch them," Tony said.

"I got this, hold on," Joey said and dropped him.

Tony fell for twenty five feet before hitting the roof of a skyscraper. Joey didn't think anything of it.

"Alright. I don't know you guys, but I think I can take all three of you down, so start talking."

"No, you're evil, and I know it. Now that you let your shield go, I'll take you down," Paxton said and charged Silence as fast as he could. "Evil, me. You're one to talk about evil," Joey replied.

Joey could see this coming. He lifted his right hand and fired a massive, deep red, spiraling beam. It not only took Paxton out of the air, but the two behind him were thrown into the side of a skyscraper, starting the building on fire.

"Oh yeah, this is working out great. You didn't expect him to do the beam spam attack, really?" Lance asked as he picked himself out of the rubble.

"That could have gone better. Yeah, see. Grandmaster Silence is one of those names you run away from. Not towards, but away. Paxton, I like you, but sometimes you're stupid. Maybe if we just lay here a while, he'll go away and forget about us," Nate said. He didn't move from the new hole his body made as his armor cooled off.

"Guys, we're not dead. We can win this if we are smart, you know. I have a plan."

Lance just groaned at Paxton's words. "Oh, I think I've had about enough of your plans as I can stand for one year, everything hurts," Lance said, but Paxton didn't listen to them and took off back into the sky.

"Or, whatever. Damn it, this time we'll try something else, I guess," Nate said and lifted into the air, following Paxton. "Have you both lost your mind?" Lance asked, "I guess I don't plan on living forever anyway. Today is a good day to die," he said under his breath and took off.

Joey looked at them as they came at him again. "I don't like the looks of these guys. They're kind of scary," Joey said, "and I only have two arms, and there are three of them. What am I supposed to do now?" he asked.

"Oh, come on, man. You can take these three clowns. You have all of my power, and you're scared of them? Sure, they look bad, but you just took them all down at the same time. What do you have to be scared of?" Silence screamed inside of Joey's head.

"Alright already, shut up. I'll do it," Joey said and flew towards the enemies. "You're all gonna get it now." Joey wasn't that good at threats. He was kind of hoping it'd be enough to turn them away, but it did nothing.

Joey fired another beam but watched as they twisted out of the way this time.

"Woah, you guys are good at this stuff," was all he had time to say when he felt a fist with spiked knuckles hit him in the stomach.

"Silence, you must be getting old or something. Either that, or I'm that good," Paxton replied and was excited about it. He hit the monster, him, he just couldn't believe it.

Joey was in shock, but not much pain.

"Oh, that was a good one, but, look at you now. You're way too close to do anything else," Joey said just before he was thrown by some invisible force away from Paxton and through a building that was nearby, sending glass and dust in every direction.

"Yeah, but I'm not," Nate said, and the three lowered themselves down to Tony once they got close enough to see who it was.

"Tony, is that you?" Nate asked, and Lance almost understood what was going on.

"Who the hell are you?" Tony asked, still in pain due to his broken legs still healing and other things he couldn't identify.

"Paxton, Lance, and Nate," Paxton pointed them out.

"Great, idiots attacking idiots," Tony replied.

"Listen, that's not Silence, it's Joey. Attacking him will just piss him off. Too much of anything might unleash the real monster on the whole world. What were you morons thinking?" Tony asked.

"We thought he was going to use you for some horrible purpose. We didn't know," Paxton replied, admitting it.

"Well, let's hope he sees that you're just morons and not real threats," Tony replied and looked over as the building Joey was thrown into exploded with red energy, pieces thrown in every direction.

"Well, looks like we'll get to tell him this was all a big misunderstanding," Lance said. He was nervous.

Silence was above them now. His hands were covered with deep red fire along with his burning eyes and the rest of his black night filled cloak.

"Joey, wait. Hold on, buddy. Listen, it was a mistake," Joey was mad. Nobody did this to him and got away with it, but Tony, a former Delta member, was telling him something—this was a mistake? Maybe it was. He powered down and floated to their level in the sky just past the edge of the building. "What mistake was made?"

"They thought you were trying to kill me. They didn't know who you were. Look at them, Joey. They can help us," Tony said.

"I see they are useful. They could attack us, they look evil," Joey said and stepped on the solid roof.

"We'd rather be with you than against you. A full-out battle between the four of us would be stupid. We just look bad. We're on your side. We have the same enemy, right, the Syndicate?" Nate spoke up then. Joey thought about it.

"Yes, we do. Very well. If you can keep up, you can fight with us. If not, you are on your own." Joey didn't trust these guys but decided that you had to take allies wherever you could find them. Silence took off, and the other three did too.

Tony looked around.

"Damn it, Joey, you forgot me," Tony yelled out just in time.

Joey spun around and flashed back to Tony. "Sorry, I nearly forgot you in all the excitement. Let's go!" Joey said, levitated him again, and the two continued their journey.

"I'm still pissed you dropped me," Tony said.

"Oh, yeah, I misjudged the distance. You'll be fine," Joey replied.

## 102

"Why do we have to save the world from the Syndicate? It seems the only time we get into trouble is when we go looking for it. Maybe if we just let the maniacs go, things will work themselves out. They don't have the greatest track record of having things work out in their favor. If it weren't for the Squad, you know, us, they'd be long gone by now. I say we let them burn themselves," Josh said. He was serious this time.

Cody stopped in the air, the others did too.

"You've been lying to us for a long time, Cody. You've had enough power to stop many threats in the past, and you never did. You'd rather let our teammates die than stand up for them. Commander, you're broken. You stopped me with no trouble at all back there in the forest," Josh worked it out in his mind.

Cody crossed his arms.

"You think I've been holding back?" he asked.

"Yes."

Cody shrugged. "Trust me, don't worry about that now. We have a job to do." Cody was trying to stop this while everyone was watching. It never occurred to Wyatt that this happened, but now that he thought more about it, it made sense.

"Yeah, how did you manage to do that?" Wyatt wanted to know. Cody looked at his team, and the Zodiac Corps, who had stopped, had no idea what was going on.

"You guys are doing this here and now?" Cody was becoming frustrated.

"All we are going there for is two team members, and hell, they might have been part of everything up until whoever is pulling the strings decided they weren't useful anymore. We don't know. Why do we have to go back there? Josh has a point. This is too much for two people," Wyatt said.

"The Syndicate will crumble on its own, they are idiots. We can stop them on a large scale. Let them have the Viper for now. If they ever show up with it, we can just take it out. Make it come to us. Millions are suffering because we are going out here. We could be doing so much more," Dustin said. He kept quiet about going way out here, but it didn't make much sense to him why they couldn't help more people.

"Diab has a point. Until you can give me a better reason than because you said so, I'm done with this. I spent one hundred years, you know, in hell. I'm tired of it and won't be played by the Syndicate or anyone else."

He turned to leave. The others were feeling the same way—they were tired, they had the armor and the power to make a difference in the whole world.

"If you want to stop me, you're going to have to actually stop me," Josh said and turned his back to the commander and began to fly away. Now Cody had a choice to make. He clenched his fists and knew there was one choice to make now.

"You want to quit?" Cody asked and didn't know what brought this on. Sure, he didn't tell them everything, but there were some things they didn't need to know or maybe didn't even want to.

"You got it. You've been screwing us over for who knows how long. I don't want to deal with it anymore. I don't think any of us do. We almost all quit once. God knows why we came back to this nightmare of a life, but you know, I hate it. All we do, it's violence and pain. That's all it is. Now I find out you could have stopped who knows how much of it? How many of these Zodiac people are still alive because of you? How many enemies could you have killed off when you had the chance? Why do you keep letting the bad guys live?" Josh was furious with the commander, and it was all justified, every single word.

"You don't understand. None of you do. Why are you going on about this now? We have a job to do, we can't stop."

Cody was trying to tell them more with fewer words.

They didn't get it.

"Right, it's always our job. Walk into hell, never questioning it. Dealing with things that should have driven us completely insane, who knows, maybe we are. I mean, think about it. What kind of sane person would keep doing this for so long? We've been Delta for so many years now, we don't know how to be anything else. You could have saved us years of trouble, but you didn't. I'm with Josh. I'd like to know why?" Dustin asked.

"All of that makes sense. Do you know how many people I've had to kill? I can see them through my scope. I watch them as they explode. I don't know them. It doesn't feel like war anymore. It feels like normal life. When did killing start to feel normal?" Blake asked.

Cody knew this was all true, but something was wrong. He could feel it.

"The great and mighty commander, look at you. Hiding things from people who've died for you, risked everything in strange lands, just for you. For all the times you've held victory and turned it into defeat, you've always failed just as many times. You've held secrets, you've played us sometimes. We can forgive you for that, but what is it, Commander? Are you scared of what happens next? What happens when the fighting is over?"

"What use will there be for any of us then? I think you've been prolonging this as much as possible because this is all you know. It's all you've ever wanted to know. You like it when the world is on the edge, you like it when the world is about to die. Admit it. You've been using us to keep this constant battle alive," Wyatt said all of this, and he was angry.

It was worse than anger. It was emptiness.

Cody felt these words, they hurt worse than any attack he ever felt. Maybe it was all true. He wasn't sure. He always planned ahead, but for him, there never was an end to the battle. He didn't know how it would end, always figured it would end bloody for everyone. He had no idea how to respond to this sudden shift, besides one of two ways: reveal everything he knew or start punching them in the face.

Both things were unpleasant.

"You know, we've known one another our whole lives. We've been through all kinds of hell together. I know that sometimes you don't like me.

I get that. As a leader of a team, it's my job to know more than you do about sensitive situations. Some things you don't need to know. God, I don't even want to know. Every situation we get into, I have to wonder if this is the one that ends the world. I have to make sure everyone does their job. I know you think it's easy leading you idiots into battle. The reality is, it's never easy."

"Each and every time we engage any of these superpowered monsters, I think to myself, is this the time we all get killed? That falls on me. Your life is my responsibility. I accepted that years ago."

"Every detail, every event, everything that goes wrong—you don't think I don't notice that? In the madness, somewhere, I forgot a few details, and it cost us pretty bad. There is a massive plan at work. We are a part of it, an important piece. Do you really want to know what the end game is? Could you handle it? I don't want you to handle it. This is my responsibility. Nobody else needs to deal with this stuff."

"The Syndicate has to be stopped. I know this. I know you can't understand why I wouldn't give my full effort the past few times we've done this. I don't expect anyone to understand. Just know that what I did, and why I did it, was for the bigger picture."

Cody had their full attention, but he wasn't done.

"It's true that I was broken for a while. Ten years on a cross will do that to you, it's been hell for all of us. I remember everything. Don't give up on me, not yet, just trust me a little longer. We are almost done. You'll all get to go home soon enough and talk about these days in a godforsaken bar some place, like these were the good old days and everyone will think you're insane."

"We've burned with one another in ways no one else will understand. They won't be able to take it. Someday you'll realize this."

"We need to go there. We need to do this. We are the only ones who can."

The commander laid it all out. He didn't know if they understood any of that. It was all true, but with all that, he didn't tell them much. He wondered if this speech would do the trick or not. He'd soon find out.

"Well, if you are responsible for our lives, you won't mind if we just leave. Take a load off your mind and all that. You're good enough to do it all yourself. I'm out of here. Guys, stay or go. I don't care anymore. Our part in this game is over. The 'commander' can take care of it," Josh said and had it with his brother. The others started to leave too.

"Yeah, we can save a lot more people just doing our thing on the land," Dustin said.

"Sorry, guys. I won't let you leave like this. You may have earned many things, but you haven't earned the right to quit. I am the commander of the Delta Squad for a damned good reason. If you want to leave, that's fine. You need my permission first. You have to earn it from me, and there is one way you can do that. What one of you is man enough to earn the right?"

The commander's armor exploded with violent electric power.

## 103

The other squad members couldn't believe what they were seeing.

"Oh, we've seen this before," Bryan said, and the Zodiac Corps backed off a good distance to escape the storm that was coming.

"So, you can turn on the fireworks. Good for you, Commander. I suppose that doubles as a nightlight too when you get scared of the dark. I know you. You don't have it in you anymore to go after your friends. I don't think you have what it takes to be a leader." Josh defied him with the usual anger he had in him.

"I don't think you ever did. I'm out of here. You can't stop me, you can't stop any of us." Josh turned around to leave. They all did, to find the Commander behind them. "I wouldn't say that. As my responsibility, I have to make sure that all requests to resign are accepted."

"Guys, let's take the commander down and move on with our lives. I know you're not that scared of some blue pyrotechnics, right?"

"Of course not, you don't know how to be afraid, but I'll teach you a lesson," Cody replied, not moving an inch.

Josh burst into black and red flames and attacked the Commander. The two of them spiraled towards the ocean like comets. "Well, I guess this is always how it had to end anyway. I'm not really interested in taking the commander but—"

Dustin was cut off by Wyatt.

"Oh, shut up already. You know you've always wanted to see what the guy was made of. This time it's Josh who has the plan. Pretty awesome if you ask me. This will be fun," Wyatt said and knew something Dustin didn't. Blake didn't know what was going on either, but he had the suspicion that all was not as it appeared.

"Right then. Let's go have some fun and try to not get killed in the process," Blake said. The remaining members of the squad turned on their inner power, and it burned around their armors.

Josh took notice of an island. It wasn't far, and he aimed for it.

Cody and Josh slammed into the ground and sent up a cloud of dust in all directions. The earth shook. They landed with so much force a crater was made. The dust could not hide them.

The two of them jumped to gain distance. Josh didn't have it in him to talk anymore. The deep red fire flared, and he charged, feet not even touching the ground. His left fist swung, and Cody blocked it, but even this caused him to sink into the earth on impact. The shockwave blasted the leaves off the trees, snapping some of them into pieces.

Cody pushed himself back up and kicked Josh in the chest, sliding him back, gaining some distance between them, but it didn't last long.

"Quit? You can't quit now," Cody said and was so fast in getting back to Josh that the earth started on fire in his wake. With a right hook to the face, Josh was knocked down. The sound was thunderous.

"If you die, you can quit. Get up. Come on, you wanted this, come and get it," Cody yelled, standing over his brother, those dark blue and electric flames rolling off his armor.

Josh sprang back up and threw his left fist at Cody's face, but Cody just caught it.

"I fought the Devil, Grandmaster Silence, and 188. Do you think you ever had a chance against me? No, this is a lesson you need to learn. This is why you need to understand why I'm in charge," Cody said and pushed that fist back down.

When Wyatt's blade came down and hit Cody in

the right shoulder, it brought him to one knee. This was enough time for that other angry fist to strike Cody in the face in the form of an uppercut and send him flying into the air.

"Perfect timing," Josh said as he stood up.

Cody was putting on a show at first, but now he was mad. Two at the same time? Were they all in on this, or what kind of deal was this? He didn't care.

He righted himself just in time to catch Wyatt's blade in his hands. It was going for his neck at full speed. He twisted it all the way around so fast that Wyatt had no choice but to let go. Cody raised the blade up and heard the sound of Blake's bullet bouncing off the blade.

Cody returned the favor, tore the sword from Wyatt's grip, and threw it at Blake. Blake was surprised at the sheer speed it was coming at him. He barely had time to blink, but just before the thing tore through his head, Wyatt caught the handle.

"Cutting it a bit close there, you think?" Blake asked.

"Nah, I had a good two inches yet before you died. We're still good."

Dustin dived at the commander and unleashed his fire. His flames covered Cody from above.

Cody had just enough time to look up as the flames engulfed him. Dustin wasn't enough of an idiot to think this would stop him at all. As soon as

Cody burst through the flames, he was greeted with dual wrist lasers.

The commander was hit by both of them, but his blue electric aura absorbed the energy.

"Dustin, stop with the light show already." Then Cody flew right at him. The commander wouldn't be taken down with any of the small stuff. He decided to give it everything he had two seconds too late. That blue fist struck across his face with so much power that he hit the ground and slid on his back twenty feet.

Before he could do anything, Josh grabbed the commander by the neck from the side. Cody put his feet firmly on the ground. Josh found it hard to hold on due to all the fire. Cody pulled to the right, escaped his grasp, and took a step back. His right fist went into Josh's stomach, the other into his face. Josh refused to fall.

"Rage, let me tell you about rage. It's really--" Josh put his left fist into Cody's chin. The uppercut sent the commander flying high into the air. "Effective," Josh finished. Wyatt used his blade like a bat and slammed Cody back into the ground as fast as he could.

Cody didn't even get to bounce before Blake shot him three times. The bullets exploded on impact with ice.

Cody got up, and Dustin blasted him with more white hot flame. Cody was walking through them.

Josh flew into the fire and met the commander halfway.

"I suppose you want me to do something impressive right about now," Cody said, standing there.

"Yeah, show me who you really are. I don't think you have much more than this to offer," Josh said.

"Alright, remember what happens next for the rest of your life," Cody said and rushed Josh, pushed him out of the way, and leapt into the air.

A flying kick right to Dustin's forehead sent him off his feet, sending those two jets of flames into the sky.

At the same time, Cody fired his plasma cannon at Wyatt. Wyatt moved out of the way to the right, but moved right into the other plasma beam Cody fired from his other hand and was blasted out of the sky. Blake was nowhere to be seen.

"Come on out, Blake. I know you're around here somewhere."

A second later, Cody got hit in the stomach with a fist. It was the only surprise attack Blake would get, and it took the commander off his feet.

Blake put the barrel of the rifle against the commander's shoulder and pulled the trigger, blowing a hole through his armor and him. Cody reeled back from this, his blood burning as it poured out.

Josh came from behind, put his leg into the back

of Cody's knees, and watched him collapse. He followed with a punch to the back of the commander's head. When it connected, the sound was like thunder coming from the ground. It put Cody flat on the ground. Wyatt came down, put his blade through Cody's midsection, and drove it all the way in so the handle was even with his back, the blade deep into the ground.

"Wyatt, what did you do?" Josh asked, staring at the impaled body.

"With any luck, earned our right to quit," Wyatt said.

"That wasn't the plan," Josh replied.

Wyatt didn't have time to reply when Cody started to stand up. Josh and Wyatt backed off as Cody grabbed the blade and started to push it out of his stomach, inches at a time.

"Nothing like a good impalement to get the blood moving," Cody said as he reached around to pull the sword the rest of the way out. "This thing is dangerous. I don't think either of you should have it," he said and threw the thing.

It was too fast for Wyatt to catch. He barely got out of the way.

Dustin took to the air just in time. The blade shot across his right shoulder, making deep red sparks as it made contact with his armor.

"You big jerk, what was that for?" Dustin asked.

Cody was flying right at him. Dustin didn't understand why, when there were other people closer, but it didn't matter. Dustin opened fire with his miniguns without even thinking about it.

Those bullets were fast, harder to see. Cody was trying to stay out of the way, but the bullets tore into his armor and threw him to the ground.

Wyatt threw two knives at Cody. Cody twisted. One missed, the other he was able to catch with his left hand, spin, and throw it at Blake.

Blake didn't stand a chance to catch it. The blade tore through the armor's left side and hit his skin. Blake tried to pull it out before the electric discharge. It was too late.

The power made Blake fall out of the sky like a ton of bricks, and he hit the ground about as hard.

Dustin was quick as he rushed to Blake's aid. He pulled that blade out and tossed it back to Wyatt, but at the same time picked up that sniper rifle, took aim at Cody, set it to its automatic setting, and pulled the trigger.

He wasn't as good a shot as Blake, but it was hard to miss a bright target like that. The rifle was loud and violent. Cody was hit in the back as he was trying to avoid two more knives. Chunks of armor were torn off by the bullets.

Cody spun around and fired his own plasma blast at Dustin. Dustin tossed the rifle just before he got hit. Blake would never forgive him if he broke his weapon. The plasma struck his armor, and the ground exploded around him, knocking him back into the sand.

The shockwave of the explosion shook his insides, and it hurt everywhere from the vibration of the blast. The distraction allowed Wyatt to put three more knives into Cody's chest, and they all fired their charge off at once. Cody was almost taken down by this massive electric charge, dropping to one knee.

He pulled those blades out and threw them back, but they were weak and Wyatt was able to catch them. Josh rushed the commander and made five large slashes in Cody's chest with his bare hands, drawing blood in a spray with each one.

Cody dropped to his knees.

Wyatt came in for the kill with his sword from behind, but Cody figured he'd do this and got out of the way at the last minute by dropping down. That blade tore through Josh's side, all the way through, and blood gushed from the wound, never touching the ground as it burned away.

"Damn it," Wyatt said, pulling the blade out as fast as he could and pushing himself away from Josh, narrowly avoiding a plasma blast meant for both of them. They both felt the heat of this attack.

Wyatt pushed himself out of the dirt, spun around with his sword, and brought it up and down as fast as he could, putting that blade into Cody's shoulder, deep into it, and pushed the blade out, cutting even deeper. He felt the blade grind against the bone as he pulled it out. Cody formed that plasma cannon in his other hand and fired.

Wyatt increased his speed and turned to his side to avoid being hit by either one with some quick thinking.

Blake materialized behind Cody and wrapped his left arm around the commander's neck. In his right hand, he held his blade and shoved it into Cody's side up to the hilt. He wasn't sure if he even felt it because just after he managed to score the hit with the blade, the commander broke free of the grip but didn't let go of that arm and twisted it around so fast that there was a terrible sound of breaking bones.

Blake's left arm was broken, and it was enough to send him to the ground. Josh and Wyatt wasted no time in attempting to take the commander down from opposite sides.

Cody flew up to avoid them, but Wyatt was too fast. His blade nearly tore through his heart, but Cody twisted around so the blade missed and put his elbow into Wyatt's face at the same time, which stopped him cold.

Wasting no time with the other hand, Cody fired a plasma beam into Wyatt's chest and threw him back to the ground.

Wyatt lifted his helmet to cough up blood.

Cody turned to see Josh's fist in his face. This

punch crushed him to the ground and forced him into it.

Wyatt got tired of this. His helmet slid back down, and he caught his breath. He grabbed his blade and sat up, pulling himself out of the burned ground. "Okay, this ends now."

His blade began to glow a dark electric red, and he looked at the commander who was going after Josh.

Wyatt's weapon once nearly cut the Viper in half when it was like this. He levitated in the air. He was still in massive amounts of pain, and his armor was damaged as well. He didn't let this or anything else slow him down. He made sure he had a firm grip on the hilt of his sword, took a breath, then rushed through the air, pulling his sword back, ready to strike.

Josh saw Wyatt coming—more to the point, he saw that Hell's Razor was activated and ready for the kill. Josh said nothing and could have blocked the next punch that was coming, but he took it and fell to the ground instead.

Cody didn't have a chance. He turned around, and the next thing he knew, Wyatt's blade was tearing through the middle of him. Everything went black.

It should have severed him in half, but the Nano armor sealed up as soon as the wound was made.

Cody collapsed as Wyatt's sword returned to normal.

Everyone held their breath as they watched this.

Josh narrowed his eyes and waited.

The Zodiac members were stunned to watch this. In this spot of isolation, the commander was killed by Wyatt in a fit of rage befitting Josh's own personality.

"Do you think we should tell them now?" Sam asked. "Nah, I think they worked it out," Bryan replied.

The twelve of them watched as smoke rose from the tiny dot of land in the ocean.

"How much longer is this going to last? We have things to do, don't we?" Derek asked.

"Yes, don't worry about it. It won't be much longer. I can tell," Ariana replied.

## 104

All eyes were on him. Cody could feel them. Oh, he hurt so bad there were few words for it. Wyatt was good at what he did, that was for sure. He expected it to be Josh. It didn't matter. Against all odds, he pushed himself up. It was agony to stand up, but he did it.

One hundred percent was a long way off, but pain was being replaced by something else. Rage— Wyatt would have killed him, should have.

Unacceptable.

Wyatt could feel it as Cody turned to look at him. In the time it took to blink, the commander cleared the distance between them. He reached down and grabbed Wyatt's blade by the sword end, lifted it up, and pulled the sword out of his hand.

"You know, that hurt. Maybe you'd like to know

how much. Using the magic weapons on me. Really, were you that desperate to win?"

He put the sword next to Wyatt's neck and said nothing more.

Wyatt was afraid that this was going to be his last day on Earth. He'd never been more thankful in his whole life to see the red and black blur slam into the commander, taking him away and that blade away from his neck.

He finally exhaled.

Josh put his foot on Cody's chest and held him there.

"Alright. I know you're just about to unleash a special kind of hell on all of us. I made most of that crap up, you know. I never intended to quit. None of us did. Wyatt overdid it a bit, sure. Make no mistake. If you hold back again and put us on the edge like you have before, I'll make what Wyatt did to you just now seem like a happy memory."

There was some silence between them before Josh offered his hand to help the commander up.

The rage disappeared. Cody relaxed. It felt good to relax.

"You're right. I've been holding back."

Josh held out his hand, and Cody took it and powered down at the same time. Josh pulled him up. The others figured it was safe to get closer.

"I won't hold back anymore. All of this stuff

ends today, but that doesn't mean you get to slack off," Cody said.

"Finally, the truth comes out," Wyatt said.

"Yeah, truth," Cody replied and looked at the group. Relieved that even after all this, they were still in fighting shape for whatever came next.

"Sorry for shooting you," Blake said, putting his weapon back.

"No problem, it was a good shot, well done," Cody replied.

"Can we take a few minutes to, I don't know, recover? That was a nightmare—you were going to kill us, man." Wyatt put his sword away as he said it.

"Yep, but you know the rules. Always be ready to die," Cody replied. "Yeah. I think I did a couple of times," Dustin said.

"Anyways, let's get to the Viper. We've wasted enough time," Cody said.

"It's about damn time," Josh replied.

"Everything hurts, I'm getting too old for this," Cody said as he lifted into the air. "We're all getting too old for this," Wyatt replied.

"I need a drink," Dustin replied.

"I guess we'll let them figure it out on their own. I'm too tired to fly over there right now," Blake said, and even if it was effortless to go to them, the thought of doing it was tiresome.

"Yeah, they'll figure it out," Wyatt replied.

The five of them started to fly.

---

"So, did anyone actually see any of that?" Ben asked, looking around.

"Those bastards were moving so fast, it was hard to see," Samantha replied.

"I saw it," Cole said. He had a huge smile on his face. "They were so mean to one another. I don't want them to be mean to us," he said, and his smile disappeared.

"I saw it too," Brad said, and the others looked at him. "Gemini's right. They were vicious," he finished. Bryan nodded.

"This is the area where we know one of the things lies beneath the waves. The madness tears at the unprotected brain. I thought that was what was happening here. Apparently not," he said, trying to figure it out as they started to follow the team.

"Rage guy must have had all this planned from the beginning. If this fight took place inside of a city or anywhere else, everyone would have been killed," Tiffany said, looking at the damage as they flew over it.

The entire island was scorched. Nothing on it remained alive that she could tell.

"No kidding. I guess they are all friends again.

Ten minutes of fighting, and they seem to be okay again. Strange bunch." Gemini said.

"Maybe this was a message for us, too," Sam replied.

"Yeah, don't screw with them once this is all over? I picked up on that," Bryan replied. He was sure they didn't need their armors anymore. They found their true powers—it was a new situation, or an old one. He couldn't be sure.

# 105

The two ships met over the sea under the light of the full moon.

Old enemies destined to destroy one another from the time they were built, at least that's what it felt like.

The Olympians, Horsemen, and the Wraith stood there on the deck, ready for battle, to destroy their common enemy.

The Syndicate had no allies left besides the Generals who remained on the ship.

Nobody knew what was on Blood Wraith's mind. He had no reason, an interjection of chaos in a well-laid plan. "So, now that we are here, what are we going to do about the Viper? Do we blow it up or take it?" Skye asked.

"Both, my little emo princess. We take it, then

we blow it up with everyone inside who didn't die," Blood Wraith said and extended his chainsaws.

"Seems like a waste of a good ship," Brianna replied.

"The ship is tainted with darkness, can't you see? It has to be erased. It's a scourge on the world," Wraith replied.

She didn't see anything weird about it, but maybe he was right.

Mark was not planning on getting any sleep tonight. He was sure the Squad was going to show up, but instead, it was his old ship.

"Sir, what should we do?" someone asked, and Mark wasn't sure why they hadn't just started shooting yet. Worse, for whatever reason, they were standing on the deck, out in the open like idiots.

"I'll talk to them, let's see what they want first," he said and pushed the button to the outside speakers. They were on the deck, they'd hear it. Also, they all had power armor.

"Attention, you on the Leviathan. Feel free to surrender at any time. Neither of us has anything to gain from fighting. You have ten minutes to decide what you want to do. If you don't or refuse to give up this course of action, we'll have to destroy you. Remember, I know every weak spot on those shields and the place to attack on that ship to make it worthless in just a few shots. It's your call," Mark said to them.

Blood Wraith laughed out loud, and everyone who heard this message was not affected by it in the least. "The old school club over there doesn't stand a chance against us. What are they thinking?" Chris asked.

"No sign of the Delta Squad or the Zodiac dwips anywhere. I wonder where they are?" Stephanie asked and secretly hoped they would be here by now but couldn't explain why.

"Olympians, Horsemen. New crazy guy. Let's just get this over with. It won't take long. Just don't be reckless," Megan said, and the Olympians floated in the air.

The three Horsemen prepared themselves. Once those shields were down, they'd join in the fight. The wait was not a long one, as Zeus unleashed a mighty thunderbolt from her hand and blasted through the Viper's shields with one devastating attack.

The energy it created set off a chain reaction that made the whole shield fluctuate and dissolve into sparks of energy that turned into nothing.

Mark narrowed his eyes. "They made their choice, poorly," Mark said and picked his blade up. He watched the Blood Wraith armor move. No, it wasn't Paxton. Someone else was wearing that, but he had no idea who.

The others were exactly as he remembered them, and he hit the button. "We have company. They decided to attack. I'm sure you felt it. They'll be too close for the main guns in a few seconds. Take them all down. The more superpowered freaks we can kill, the better our future is going to be," Mark said into the intercom.

Then he walked to the doors leading to the deck to meet them.

## 106

Mark made his way out to the deck, and the enemy was already waiting for him, moving in a line in his direction.

"At least they look cool when they move like that," he said but wouldn't let them see him smile. It was a few minutes before they were close.

"Just you?" Megan asked. Mark held his blade over his shoulder and shrugged.

"Welcome to the Viper. I know you have this idea in your head that this will be easy, but you haven't learned your lessons yet—there is no easy. There never has been, there never will be. I give you one last chance to turn around now."

Mark's smile never left.

The Olympians and the Horsemen took this as arrogance.

"The Squad may not be here, but that doesn't mean we need them. We can take you," Chris said.

"We also have you outnumbered if you didn't notice. There's one of you. We scared all your people away," Aphrodite replied.

"Yes. Them. I was expecting them to show up. Not you. If you refuse to run, well, you know how this goes by now," Mark said.

"Screw it, this will only take a second," Angel said, walking forward, towering over Mark until he blocked out the light of the moon.

"War, you were always my favorite," Mark said and looked up.

Angel swung that burning sword faster than any human should have been able to dodge, but the blade hit nothing as he moved back mere inches and watched it dig into the Nano steel. Mark swung his own blade and hit Angel's shoulder. The sword cut through the armor a few inches and sent sparks in every direction.

Angel was shocked. This shouldn't have been possible.

"I've taken on the whole Squad at the same time. Alone. You're just a brat with a big gun. You're in way over your head today."

"Well, you're half right, but I've been practicing," Angel said and reached for Mark with his free hand.

Mark stepped to the right, jumped on the arm of

the beast, and ran up the arm. Then he put his foot down on the Horseman's back, blade to the back of the neck.

"Well, I hope you thought this through a little better or had something else planned. It's not looking too good for you." He looked up at the rest of them. Mark didn't want to kill them yet. If he could get them on his side, all the better.

One more chance.

"Who else wants to try? Brianna, Tyler? Come on. I put you in this armor. Did you not think I might have a plan B?" The others didn't seem too interested in attacking the General, well, not one at a time anyway.

"Well, you better attack all at once. It's the most viable option. You're still just kids. You don't know how to form plans. Here, let me show you."

Mark jumped off the back of War and charged the group.

Tyler tried to shoot the General coming right at him but missed. Mark was too fast. His fist slammed into Tyler's face and knocked him off balance. On impact, some of the bones in Mark's hand broke, the skin ripped, and he bled for a few seconds. He ignored that, it healed in just the same amount of time.

Wasting no time, he spun around and put the wide side of the blade into Brianna's head. He was moving too fast to give her the edge, so the blade turned into a bat with so much force it knocked her off of her feet and into Angel, sending them both to the deck.

Tyler tried to attack again but was far too slow to pull the trigger. Mark jumped into the air and hit both of those rifles to the side with one swipe. The other free hand punched Tyler in the side of the head, knocking him down.

"Speed Blitz for the win," Mark said, was hit with a lightning bolt and sent flying down the deck.

"Idiot," Megan said, lowering her hand. "Also, I thought you three would be more impressive than this," she said.

"He's a former member of the Delta Squad, not entirely human," Angel said while standing up with the others. "Also, I didn't think he was that strong," Brianna replied, shaking her head.

"I've been training myself for a long time. Ever since I saw you, I knew I wanted to fight you. I just didn't think it would be like this, thought you'd be stronger," Mark said as he stood up.

He looked at the Olympians.

"You," Mark said in an angry voice and began walking towards them, smoke still rising from his body.

"Us? You want a piece of us too?" Megan asked.

"No. Not a piece. The whole thing." The steel floor of the Viper turned into liquid and shot upwards into a bunch of long spikes. The Olympians blasted into the sky to avoid them, only to be in line with Max and Jake, hidden by the night behind them.

They fired their beams into the six of them from behind in a surprise attack. Those energy attacks tore into their armors and knocked all of them forward.

"Nice reflexes there, Olympians, but you should have stayed home," Dan said and fired from his hidden place in the dark. His special ammo hit their marks and exploded upon impact, covering them all in flames. Making them fall out of the sky and hit the deck.

The combined power of Max and Jake's power knocked them out.

"Good work, team. Now that they are good and pissed off, they'll follow us anywhere. Proceed as scheduled," Mark said and looked at Blood Wraith, the only variable in this situation he didn't have a plan for.

"So, what's your story, saw boy? Revenge or looking to prove yourself? I don't have time for either," he said to him, and Wraith took a step back, shocked.

"How did you know? Are you psychic?"

Mark was annoyed with this reaction.

"Yes, I kind of am. Now, I know you might be looking to get even with the Syndicate, but you got to understand that everything has changed a great deal since your day," Mark said and took a few careful steps forward.

"Changed how? I must know. How did they change?" Mark knew this guy had to be insane.

"This ship, it belongs to them, and by them, I mean me. I own the place now. How do you think you were released? It was me. I hoped that you'd find a nice quiet place to live, but now that you're here. What are your plans?"

Blood Wraith shook his head, trying to understand. He wondered if Mark was lying or not. He couldn't tell. It didn't matter.

"My plans are to kill everyone involved with the Syndicate, and if you own it, I guess that makes you the top of my list. Not that I actually made a list. I'd be crazy if I made an actual list. Who does that?" Wraith said and took a familiar fighting stance.

"You're Delta," Mark said out loud and figured he might have a challenge. "Damn straight I am. Or I was, or something. I don't care. You and me, let's go."

Blood Wraith started running at him.

"Wait."

He stopped in his tracks. "What?"

"The reason all of this happened is coming here, to this ship. The most powerful version of the Delta Squad. If you help me kill them, we can have our fight when we're done with them. It'll be better that way, I promise."

"Fine. I'll kill you later." His chainsaws retracted, then he disappeared.

"Jake, Max, put those idiots in the containment chamber. It should keep them quiet, then get ready. They'll be here soon. Jake, fix the floor," Mark ordered.

Mark glanced at Max before he could start talking. "Don't start."

The Olympians lifted off the deck. Jake started walking.

"Can't we just kill these morons?" Jake asked.

"Yeah, as soon as we figure out how to take their armor without breaking it," Mark replied. "Same goes for the horse people. See, I'm always thinking ahead," Mark replied.

"I mean, we could just peel the armor off their dead bodies. I don't mind getting messy," Jake said. Mark considered it.

"It could be trapped or something. Syndicate suits are really fond of the critical existence failure trap," Mark replied and walked away.

"Yeah, I suppose he's right," Max said and shrugged. "This way, horse people," Max said.

"What makes you think we're just going to come with you?" Angel replied.

Max pointed at Jake. "188, powers of a god, or close enough. I'm sure you'd rather not get blasted. Besides, the containment chamber isn't so bad. It has a nice bench," Max replied.

"He does make a good point," Tyler said.

"You know I like a good bench," Brianna added.

"Fine," Angel replied. The three of them were led away by Max in his golden armor. "I knew you'd see it my way," Max said.

# 107

The Viper hung in the air, all the lights were off. It looked like some strange alien beast was sleeping over the ocean. The Leviathan was the same way.

The team stopped before they got there.

"This is obviously a trap," Cody said.

"Yeah, but what are we going to do about it?" Wyatt asked. "I have a suggestion. We'll check out the Leviathan, you check out the Viper," Bryan said, and Cody didn't like that plan.

"And what's to stop you from shooting us out of the sky?" Cody asked.

"Nothing, you're going to have to trust me," Bryan replied. Cody turned to look at him.

"Trust you? All of you? People who made a deal

with a monster to kill us all? That's a hard sell," Cody replied. "Yep," Bryan replied.

"Oh, to hell with it. If we die, then our problems are over. Let's go," Dustin said, and Cody looked at him.

"I guess you're right. Keep that green box closed, too," Cody replied. "Squad, on me. Zodiac, good luck," Cody said, and with that, they flew towards the Viper.

Bryan smiled. "Ladies, gentlemen, we have a ship to take," he said, and they flew towards the Leviathan.

Cody and the others landed on the Viper's deck, it was empty. "Not what I expected," Blake said, looking around for anyone or signs of battle. Nothing seemed out of place. Not even any weird Syndicate flags. Blake was disappointed, he expected at least one. There was a lot of deck, however. Maybe it was just somewhere else.

"We're here for our people. Maybe they abandoned the ship?" Dustin asked.

"If they abandoned the ship, they had a good reason. We shouldn't find out what it is," Wyatt replied.

"No, we move forward and use the bridge to find what we came for. If they did abandon the ship, we're not leaving it here. Come on," Cody said and started walking towards the doors.

"Ghost ships, got to love 'em," Dustin replied.

They got to the doors to the bridge, and they opened. The bridge was dark, empty but undamaged. "Creepy. No sign of any violence. What the hell?" Josh asked what they were all thinking.

"Just don't think about it too much. Stay focused," Cody said and started toward the main console.

"Power's still on, everything works, too. They shut everything off," Dustin said.

"Stop. Locate Dana and Erin on the monitors. That's all we need to do right now," Cody said, but the surroundings were getting to him a little. Too many things happened on this ship just to assume nothing was going on.

Dustin switched on the console, and everything came on just like it should. He typed in a few commands. "The only signs of life on the ship are in the medical bay. Just two, it's them," he said and flipped to the camera.

"Oh," Dustin said. The women were there with tubes coming out of their arms, blood being drained.

"We need to move, now," Cody said and started running.

"Cody, wait, damn it," Wyatt said and took off, catching up to him. "Trap, remember? That's bait. We need to think about this," Wyatt said.

Cody took a breath. "We can handle it."

"Fine, whatever. Let's go spring a trap," Wyatt replied, and Cody nodded.

It was a short journey to the medical bay. However, when they got inside, it was easy to see the place had been converted into something else.

"Well, the place sure has changed since we were last here," Dustin said.

Cody didn't waste any time. He rushed over to Erin and Dana and tore the blood-draining tubes out of their arms. "Josh, stop the bleeding on Erin. I got Dana," he said and pressed his hands on the wound.

Josh did the same thing.

They were on death's doorstep by the way they looked, long since passed out. "Dustin, we need some water," Josh said.

Dustin deployed his minigun and used the nano system to create water. He used an empty glass jar on a shelf and filled it up. He didn't know what the Syndicate did to the ship, trusting it wasn't an option. Any water obtained from the ship might have been infested with nanites of some kind.

"Got it. It won't taste the best, but it'll do," he said and brought it over.

Josh held Erin's head up and opened her mouth. "Sorry about this," he said, and Dustin poured some water in.

She drank it but didn't wake up. Dustin moved over to Dana and repeated the process.

It was dark in this place, the tubes they were connected to led off into the dark.

"Drained. Something was living off of them," Josh said and looked into the black.

"Oh, that's your professional opinion? Way to go. I could have told you that," Wyatt replied, but shut up when Cody glared at him. Then shuffling in the dark got their attention.

"If they are still alive, get them out of here. This place isn't safe." A voice came out of the dark. The source came out of the dark. It was Adam. Nobody wanted to see this one, especially Wyatt.

"We can't trust him," Wyatt said.

"I know we've had some issues in the past, but if you can get back to the other ship, you'll have a safe place to keep these two. They are going to die if you leave them here," Adam said. "You have to get out of here because--." He never got to finish the reason why when all the lights came on. "Damn it," Adam said under his breath.

"Welcome, Delta Squad and whoever you are. Adam, is it?" A voice said, and a man walked out. He had green eyes. "I've been waiting for you to show up for such a long time now. What took you so long?"

"Who are you, and what the hell is going on? Tell us everything," Cody demanded. The man smiled.

"Name is Dean. I own this whole Syndicate. I

have for a long time, and brothers, let me tell you I am so tired of, well, pretty much everything." The name didn't ring a bell with anyone. They still had no idea who this guy was.

"Tired of what—" This stranger cut the commander off.

"Shut up. I'm not done. Let me explain and have some patience. Believe me, I know you're not good with that, but if you try anything on me, I'll make sure you regret it."

The Squad resisted the urge to kill this new out of place man who wore a dark business suit. "Oh, come on, not another lore dump from someone we've never met, no one cares buddy. We're in the middle of something here," Wyatt said. Dean looked at him.

"Just a minute of your time," Dean said.

"Fine," Wyatt replied.

"A long, long time ago, a group of six people got the gift of a lifetime on pure accident, or maybe it was by design—who can tell? You should know all about that. Those six were the first Delta Squad members. They joined up with the Syndicate in an attempt to make life better for the world. For a while, it worked, but eventually, they got tired of saving the world from its own idiocy and took off, never to be seen again," he said, smiled, then continued.

"So, replacements were found, and the cycle

continued. The idea of the Squad and what it could have been was crushed by the red tape and confusion of the Syndicate's expanding rules and power."

"Mister exposition, do you have a point to this history lesson, or are you just in love with the sound of your own voice?" Wyatt asked.

Dean looked at him. "That's strike one. Yes, I have a point, just listen." Those green eyes stared at him, and Wyatt felt cold for some reason. He couldn't explain it, but he did his best not to show it, so he just crossed his arms.

"The Squad, well, it became a weapon, and the Syndicate was responsible for all the threats it had to kill. The bloodshed—well, it got too much. The world was sinking into a bloody hell. There was no escape from it, and the Delta Squad was making things worse. Even when they won, and they mostly did, they lost sight of the true enemy. The Syndicate was always the true enemy. So, the original five members of the Squad met to discuss the future of the world."

With no interruptions from the team, he continued.

"They came to the decision that the world couldn't last the way it was going for much longer. We took over the leadership of this twisted thing. Nobody seemed to notice. The goal of the Syndicate was world domination, of course, but then everything was going fine until something happened. You showed up. You were to be the last Delta Squad in history. I ended my exile and offered to help the council. I foresaw all of this, you see, that's a long story and not important."

"Congratulations, you're psychic. Why did you just..." Dustin was frustrated. "Let me finish," Dean said.

"I told them their plan wouldn't work. They didn't believe me, not until you defeated 188 in combat, the most powerful being anyone had ever seen up to that point in the modern world. You making the presidency was a nice little twist too, but every time you stood up, we had to knock you down. We had to break you. Almost did it once when we got desperate and let that idiot Blue back into the world."

"Still, even then you found a way to come back from the brink. You were supposed to lose. You were supposed to die, and you kept on winning against impossible odds, we always had a plan to swoop in after you lost to take the threat down, but you always won." The man smiled, looked down.

"I am not sure how you kept on winning, but at the same time, for whatever reason, you refused to kill most of your enemies, some of them even switched sides. I decided that you couldn't be beaten. Not with any new form of enemy or whatever. Even the cosmic insanity didn't do it. Everyone is thankful you put a nice lid on that little mess, by the way. So, I came up with a new plan. I decided the only way to beat you was to do it like this."

"Our release, everything. It was all a setup for this?" Wyatt asked, looking at the others.

"Why, if you are who you say you are, why would you want this? It makes no sense. Why would you let all the monsters out?" Cody said.

"Simple. You could never just sit back and let things happen. If even one of you got involved, the rest would follow, pretending to be dead or retired, it didn't matter. This was the only way to do it. You were all captured, and during that time, we were able to take your blood—a lot of it. Wyatt, I'm sure you remember," he said with a smile, and everyone cringed a little at their own memories.

Rage was building, too.

"I know you'd want nothing more than to attack us, but I'm not done. Let me introduce you to the Dragon. We created another member of the family with the DNA we collected from all five of you, plus those two ladies there."

"All your power, but none of that emotion or desire to do the right thing. Isn't that amazing? You're about to die and all the chaos you let exist in the world is going to die with you. Your own blood is responsible for it. Meet the sixth member of the

Delta Squad. The Dragon," Dean said and stepped to the side, looking at the still dark wall, which lit up, revealing a figure. It looked like it was encased in armor through the blood.

"Adam, get Erin and Dana out of here," Cody demanded, studying this new enemy. "Maybe it's not done cooking yet?"

"Yeah, good luck with whatever this mad science project is," Adam said, put his hands on the withered arms of Dana and Erin, himself all disappeared.

"Would you like us to come back later for a fight or what?" Blake said and almost laughed. The others thought it was funny too. When they looked around, Dean wasn't there anymore. He'd disappeared.

"Oh, he pulled a Batman," Dustin said.

"Yes, he did," Wyatt replied, looking around but not seeing any place he could have gone.

It was just them and this thing. The thing's eyes began to glow bright yellow.

"Oh look, it's awake," Josh said, not knowing what to expect. It put its hand against the glass, and it cracked and fell to pieces sending the blood in all directions. They watched as it stood there at the edge of the shattered glass, doing nothing.

"We really need to put a ban on making new armor when this is over, this is insane," Dustin said.

"Yep," Cody replied.

"Oh, screw it," Josh said and walked up to it. As he did, its armor changed from dark blue to black. It was strange.

The figure itself stood just mere inches taller than him but didn't look as strong as Josh's armor did. It was a mix of all the squad members, but those deep yellow eyes just gazed ahead. They didn't give any indication of being alive.

He walked up to this thing and flicked its shoulder, just to see if it would fall over. There was no sound. The strange armor absorbed all the energy, even the sound.

The person, if it could be called that, looked down at the insult, moving for the first time. Then back at Josh, it lifted its right arm and flicked with what appeared to be the exact same amount of force.

When the impact sent Josh flying across the room and through the far wall into the hallway, it was obvious it wasn't the same amount of force. They were all stunned.

"Well, I didn't see that coming," Dustin said and prepared his weapons, but it still didn't move.

"Do we attack it or what? If we attack, it might do the same. Maybe it's a mimic," Wyatt suggested, offering the best possible scenario they could have been given, but it was just then that the Dragon took a step forward.

"Dragon, is it? I have a question," Cody said,

taking a step forward. "Why do you fight? You don't know us. We've never done anything to you. You have free will, don't you?" he asked. It looked at him, said nothing.

"Great, just another mindless idiot," Cody answered himself.

"Alright, plan B. Let's kill it and get this over with," Blake said.

The Dragon was already next to Wyatt and grabbed the hilt of his blade and pulled it out in one quick motion. Wyatt could only watch as the Commander grabbed the sword just before it carved into Wyatt's face.

"Move!" Cody screamed, pushing the blade away. He let go of it, spun around, and struck the enemy in the side of the head.

The Dragon took the hit, and its head turned to the side as if it had been hit by a pool noodle. Wyatt was already out of the way, but Cody found the thing had a hold of his arm. Cody was picked up and slammed into the wall like a rag doll. The steel bent and groaned under the pressure but didn't break. When Cody opened his eyes, it was gone.

"Screw the rules. I have supernatural powers," a voice said. It was so electronically altered that it was chilling.

Dustin was picked up and thrown across the room by nothing. He landed on the blood covered floor and slid toward the wall. Dustin turned over while he was still moving and shot at where he was. The bullets stopped, crumpled flat in the air and fell to the floor. He was sure his bullets had nothing to do with it. The Dragon reappeared.

"Oh look, you shoot, that's impressive, but I can do it too. Dig on this," Dragon said and laughed, held up its left arm. It morphed into a plasma cannon, then fired a deep blue energy beam. Cody got in the way of this attack and blocked it with his hands.

"Move."

He was sliding in his direction due to the sheer force of the attack. Dustin flew to the side.

Josh rushed the enemy and grabbed the cannon, crushing it with both hands, sending arcs of electric power in every direction.

"It's about time you showed back up. Maybe we can play a little more," Dragon said as it tried to throw Josh off, but he let go and avoided being thrown.

Blake fired three shots, but the Dragon caught the bullets in the air and crushed them with its free hand. "Well, look at you, almost being useful," it said as the remains of the bullets were dropped to the floor.

"Well, I had to try something," Blake replied and aimed again.

"Yes, because it'll work the second time," Dragon said just as Wyatt's blade pierced its chest from behind where its heart should have been. The Dragon looked down and fell to its knees. It almost screamed before it went silent.

"Wyatt, you did it. Right? It looks dead to me," Josh said. "Well, it seems dead. A bit anticlimactic if you ask me. I guess I was expecting, I don't know, more?" Blake said, walking up and tapping it on the helmet. No reaction.

Then it started to laugh. "Alright, I'm sorry. I was just messing with you." Then it leapt into the air, flipped around, and stood on the ceiling, pushing the blade out and holding it in his hands.

"Oh look, my blood. I mean, your blood or something, I'm not sure." It put the blade between two fingers and slid it down the length, cleaning the blood off. "Wyatt, let's see if you recognize this little trick." The blade began to glow deep red.

"No, wait. You don't know what that does. Come on, man, you'd use that on us so soon?" Wyatt asked. "Why not?" Dragon asked.

"Why not? Well, the rest of us have weapons just like that. Theirs are much worse than mine, and if you want to go down this road, you'll get to see it firsthand." Wyatt's counterargument was good enough, and the blade powered down. "I guess I don't need all that to beat you," it said.

Dragon sprang forward so fast nobody could react to it, except Wyatt, who missed the swing of the blade by mere inches. The other four tasted the edge of the sword. The attack sent them into the air, back into the wall, and falling to the blood covered floor.

"Guys, if we stay here, we're dead. Everyone out now," Cody said as the gash in his chest was closing.

Cody fired his beam at the Dragon, hitting it with a full powered blast in the chest and making it drop Wyatt's blade in the process.

It tore through the Viper, through all the decks until it ripped through the surface, taking the Dragon with it. Wyatt grabbed his sword and was the first one to follow after the beam subsided.

## 108

Wyatt and the others made their way to the surface and backed off as they landed. Mark and the others were waiting for them, standing with the Dragon, too.

"Well, look who's here. Nice to see you, Commander. It seems everyone wants a rematch with you, new armor and all," Mark said with a smile.

"Dude, chill. I got this. That goes for the rest of you guys. The Squad belongs to me. Anyone who wants to get in the way, well, go ahead. See what happens, you had your chance to win and you failed," Dragon said, shutting Mark up.

"Are you as good as we made you out to be, or was the old guy all talk?" Mark asked, not appreciating being talked to like that. The Dragon reached over, grabbed Mark's arm, and broke it with ease—

a sickening crunch everyone heard. This would be the only answer he'd get.

"Holy hell, are you alright?" Max asked.

Mark clutched his broken arm and pushed the bone back into place. "I'll be fine," he said under his breath.

"I'll blast it to dust," Jake offered.

"No, then we'd have to fight those idiots. Let's hope we get what we paid for," Mark said as his arm recovered and the pain faded away. Dragon ignored all of them and stepped towards the squad.

"Unfinished business. I guess you wanted to die under the stars? Whatever, it's all good to me," the Dragon said as it looked to the sky. "I wonder how I know what the stars are. Weird," it added.

"I kind of hope the Squad wins this one," Max said, and Jake looked at him. "What, this thing shouldn't exist. The sequel to Frankenstein here is just the first of thousands. We all know how the Syndicate works. If they made one," Max trailed off.

"Yeah, I know," he replied, seeing how it turned on them just now. There was no telling what it would do next.

"Let's get out of here, this is above our pay grade," Dan said.

It was then that common sense prevailed. "Dan's right. Let's get out of here," Mark agreed, and they made a quick retreat.

Mark pressed a button on his wrist.

"Screw it."

"What did you do?" Dan asked. "Opened the containment, let the prisoners out," Mark replied as the sounds of explosions could be heard deep in the ship.

Seconds later he Horsemen and the Olympians tore out of the side of the Viper and made their way to the deck.

"What the hell is that thing?" Athena said as she landed onto the deck. "Looks like practice, let's kill it," Angel said.

The Squad turned to look at the sudden intrusion.

"What is going on?" Dustin asked.

"I don't know anymore," Wyatt said.

The three horsemen were ready to do anything useful. The squad had saved the world and become personal heroes to them. This was their chance to make a difference.

"We got this one, take a break," Angel said, and without missing a beat, they ran towards their new target. The Dragon looked at them and shook its head.

"Yes, because rushing the most powerful one on the playing field always ends well. I'm not sure if you're that stupid, or you had to work to get to this level."

It wasn't quite sure what to do with these new

ones. So, it decided to kill them all. It seemed the right thing to do.

Dustin and Josh intercepted their path before they could do anything.

"Stay out of this. Trust us. This is one fight you can't help with. Stay over there with the others or get to the Leviathan. The Zodiac are already on the ship, tell them we sent you, hopefully, they don't attack," Dustin said.

The horsemen stopped.

"We aren't useless," Brianna said. "Trust me, I know, but there is a time and a place. This isn't it, please go," Dustin replied. The three of them looked at one another. "Next time, then," Angel said, and they backed off.

"Thank you," Dustin said. "Be ready for anything, if we fall, you're up. Watch how the Dragon moves, fights and most of all, weaknesses. Strategy," Josh said. All the sudden the horsemen and the Olympians understood. "Got it," Brianna replied and they started making their way towards the Leviathan.

"Now's your chance to run," Dustin told the Olympians. "Thanks, but we'll be staying," Megan replied. "It kills us, you're next, but we may need you so be ready," he said.

"Understood," she said and the group cleared the area, but they weren't far away from whatever was going to happen next.

Josh and Dustin made their way back to the others.

"Trying to get your friends out of the fight, admirable," Dragon said. "I mean, I'll kill all of them too once I'm done here, so, pointless, but I'm here for you first."

"Just us now," Josh said. "Delta Squad, let's kill this bitch," Cody said.

"It's about time," Blake replied, "What's the plan—" Blake was cut off when Wyatt acted first.

Wyatt moved faster than the others. He swung his sword, the blade hit the chest of the thing, and sparks flew on impact. Dragon grabbed the blade, twisted it to the right, and threw him to the side without moving from its spot.

Dustin unleashed twin jets of flame into the thing. "Damn it," He was sure the enemy was going to avoid the fire.

It did not.

The Dragon flew through it and at Dustin, couldn't see it in the process, but the Dragon didn't need to see. It needed to follow the fire. Dustin refused to give up on the attack.

Josh's fist came through the white flames and sent the Dragon up into the air. Then Cody's plasma blast that took full control of the momentum of the Dragon for a second.

Then the thing stopped itself, started to push back against the beam.

Dustin didn't waste any time helping Cody, combining the plasma and the fire.

"Wyatt, use your sword. Use Hell's razor. Any one of our weapons will kill everyone here, us, it. Everyone. Use your weapon now and end this while we still can," Josh said.

"Yeah, I'll use it, and the thing will turn it against us somehow. It's not worth it. We have to do this another way," Wyatt replied. Josh was pissed and didn't waste any more time trying to convince him.

The monster fired his own bright yellow beams from his hands. With one shot it sent them both towards the ship.

"You're going to have to do more than beam spam to impress me, boys," it said.

Rage didn't work against this thing. It had all of that in it. All of that power. Then Josh got an idea. It was risky.

"Guys. I have a plan. Alright. Blake, distract it. We need to group up. Do this, and I'll do the rest," Josh said.

"That's the dumbest idea you've ever had. What are you thinking?" Blake said, shooting at the Dragon, only to have the bullets smash against the chest and fall to the deck.

"Guys. Wyatt's being a little bitch. We have one more option," Josh said as he rammed the Dragon to keep it busy. It didn't work, sliding the monster back a couple of feet.

"What are you made out of?" Josh asked.

"All of you. Can't you tell yet? I have every bit of your strength, sure it's cheap, but you know what, I don't care."

Dragon punched Josh in the stomach so hard that his armor threatened to crack under the pressure and slid back against the nanosteel. Sending sparks from his feet. He opened his helmet to let the blood flow from his mouth, coughing. Cody saw this and agreed.

"Alright, Josh, what's your plan?"

He closed his helmet when the blood stopped. "When I give the signal, regroup on me. Until then, make this thing think it's going to win."

"That isn't much of a plan, but making it think it's going to win shouldn't be hard," Dustin replied. "Yeah, I don't like this plan," Blake added.

"I can hear you, please stop talking about me like I'm not here," Dragon said.

Cody flew at Dragon and attempted a plasma blast, but the Dragon grabbed his wrist and crushed it in his hand through the armor as well, the bones could be heard snapping at a distance.

"Oh, did you need that? I hope not. It sounded painful," Dragon said and, with the free hand, he slammed the broken mess into the side of Cody's head before he could reply. Sending him back into the dark. Dustin covered the Dragon with acid while he was distracted.

The acid sizzled on the armor.

Dustin was sure the Syndicate wouldn't have given this thing self repairing armor. It had to have a weakness of some kind. All they had to do was find it.

However, he wasn't sure if they would last long enough to figure it out.

"Thanks, needed a shower. Acid is just the thing after trash like you touched me, gross."

Blake rushed ahead, put the rifle against the Dragon's chest, and pulled the trigger. This time, the bullet went through and out the other side, sending a trail of blood. This made it drop to its knees again.

Wyatt threw a knife towards the wound.

Dragon caught the throwing knife in his hand, the electrical discharge did nothing to him once it went off, then threw it to the side.

"Alright. This is my very first day on Earth. I want to see what it has to offer. Wasting all my time with you guys is pointless," Dragon said and stood up.

"The time is now," Josh said, and just as he had requested, they gathered.

"Why, what changed?" Cody asked.

"Face it, we can't win here. We have too much

humanity in this fight, Commander." Cody got the drift.

"Too much humanity?" Wyatt asked.

Josh stared at the Dragon. "That thing isn't human, or it's more than human I'm not sure," Josh said. "We're not going to win without an edge, and we're going to get one," Josh said.

Wyatt looked up. "You don't mean what I think you do?"

"It's our only shot," Josh replied. "Sometimes the cure is worse than the disease," Wyatt replied.

The Delta Squad prepared themselves.

# 109

Josh turned to Megan and gave her the signal, pointed at her. Hoped it

The Olympian took a step forward. Dragon didn't know what was going on, just stood there and watched.

"See you on the flipside," Josh said. "Sure, if there is a flipside," Wyatt replied.

Megan raised her hands to the black sky, and from it came terrible bolt of power that engulfed the squad. Their armors absorbed the energy, and everyone who had ever witnessed what happened when one single squad member got hit by this got chills.

"We need to get the hell out of here," Mark said.

"Yeah, God damn, get to the Leviathan as soon

as you can," Megan replied. Everyone watching abandoned ship, teleporting and flying away.

The light was blinding, the heat just as intense. When both faded, something was different.

"Guys. We're still here, are you still, I don't know, you?" Dustin asked. No one had a chance to answer. Dragon was already on the attack.

Josh caught the fist before anyone could be hit. The force of the impact created a shockwave.

"I hope you enjoyed this day, it's your last," Josh said and punched the monster in the face, knocking it off its feet, into the air.

The Dragon regained its balance, landed on the ground, and rushed them all again without missing a beat.

Wyatt countered, rushed ahead and swung the blade. Dragon ducked out of the way and caught Wyatt's chin with an uppercut. Dustin grabbed that arm and bent it backward a second later. Josh punched it in the chest so hard the Dragon's armor cracked. Dustin couldn't hold on, and the thing went flying back, sliding to a stop on its feet, smoke rising from the friction as it did.

Cody fired his plasma cannon but missed when the enemy stepped to the side and right into Josh's line of fire.

The rapid fire of the miniguns caused Dragon to flinch, put its hands in front to try and stop the bullets.

Wyatt charged past him and swung his blade down.

He caught the arm of the monster and cut through it, severing the limb at the elbow sending an explosion of blood every direction.

The limb didn't even hit the ground as the Dragon took a hold of it and reattached it. The armor resealed the wound and it was healed.

"God damn this thing straight to hell," Wyatt said, a part of him hoped someone was listening, but nothing happened.

Wyatt tried to go for the neck, but this time Dragon grabbed the blade as it came and twisted it around into the metal deck. With the other hand, it gripped Wyatt's throat and lifted him into the air, his feet left the ground.

Blake ran ahead, pulled out his blade, and stabbed Dragon in the neck. The knife went in.

On seeing this, Dustin wondered why bullets wouldn't go through the armor, but a knife would. It didn't make any sense. The Dragon reeled back in pain, dropped Wyatt. Blake pulled out his blade and attempted to stab again.

Dragon wouldn't have any of it and reached out, grabbed Blake's face and picked him up. With one swift movement, smashed Blake into the steel. The impact caused the metal to cave in and blood to leak from Blake's helmet.

Wyatt recovered and attacked again. The

Dragon grabbed the sword in its hand and pushed the blade into the metal. The free hand threw Wyatt to the edge of the ship, leaving that sword behind.

The Dragon pulled it out and swung it around bringing the tip of the blade right across Josh's face, it made sparks on impact as Josh had to get out of the way at the last second.

The commander took advantage and came at the monster, kicked it in the head so hard its feet left the ground, and the sword was dropped.

Cody caught and threw it at Wyatt who was already on the way back. He caught his sword.

Blake lifted himself from the crater and flew at the Dragon and was going to do something, it was never known what because the Dragon turned to face him and grabbed Blake's arm and squeezed so hard that his bones shattered, his armor cracked, and the blood leaked out of the cracks. He screamed in pain as the thing held him there.

"I'm going to eat you, take off my arm, I'll return the favor," it said.

Josh tackled the Dragon, causing it to let Blake go. Then, standing this close he fired his miniguns into the thing's chest. The bullets tore through this time, and there was nothing the Dragon could do about it.

Its body fell to the steel, face first, and soon a puddle of blood began to form around it.

"It's not over," Cody said when Josh backed off.

## 110

"So, why are we just not making this thing into a puddle of goo and call it a day?" Josh asked.

"I don't think we have what it takes to do that. I don't think we can kill this thing, even if we wanted to," Cody admitted.

"Sure we can, I'll just cut off its head, watch," Wyatt said and walked to, and held the sword against the neck of the Dragon, who still didn't move.

"Every horror movie ever says this is a bad choice," Dustin said.

The Dragon wasted no time in exploiting this and grabbed the blade, pushed it away from its own neck, and guided the blade into Wyatt's closest foot, then into it. "Son of a bitch," Wyatt said.

Dragon took to the air, flying away. Wyatt pulled the blade out and took off after it, they all did.

The Dragon stopped, turned around, and saw they all were chasing it. It raised its left hand and fired a thick beam of plasma at all of them. The Squad got out of the way at the last minute, but the Viper got a hole blown all the way through it with one attack.

They all looked at this gaping hole and knew that this monster had far more power than it was showing with that one attack and it made them nervous.

"Okay, that's new" Cody said.

"Guys. Do you not see how I could kill you at any time I wanted? Look at the five of you. Facing down an enemy you can't hope to even touch. You are all going to die here."

"Screw you, too," Dustin said, his armor flared with power, he put his hands together and channeled a bright orange beam of power into the monster's direction.

The Dragon only had time to turn its head before it was blasted out of the sky and sent down in an uncontrolled fall. That was everything I had, guys, I can barely fly after that," he said.

"Dustin, what the hell was that, you could have led with that," Blake said.

"Didn't think we'd need it. Going to go recharge

on the ship," he replied and made his way back down.

The Dragon felt it. It didn't get knocked out. It had something new grip its mind. Something that felt like fire and something else it couldn't describe, rage. Nobody did that. Nobody.

The Dragon stopped its fall in midair and didn't move. It saw Dustin going back to the ship and with an incredible burst of speed it charged him. Everyone saw this and moved to intercept, none was closer than Josh was and he got there first.

Josh got in the way of an attack and watched as that shining armored hand plunged into and through his chest armor as the two of them hit the deck of the Viper. Josh felt the hand tear through his flesh and grip his heart.

Everything was going black. Josh didn't know if he was dying or his vision was being covered with all the blood, he could feel filling his armor.

The last thing he saw was Wyatt blazing past his vision, taking the monster off of him with more pain than he had experienced in a long time.

The Dragon hated missing out on a meal of any kind and the wild attack Wyatt came up with was turned on him and there was almost a repeat of what just happened to Josh.

"I'm going to rip you all into pieces, tear your hearts out and eat them."

Wyatt was smart enough to let go and let the

monster slide on the metal, escaping just as those claws reached up and tried to get him. Wyatt wasn't done. The Dragon pulled itself up and into the air in one motion, flew at Wyatt, not fast enough.

The Dragon reached out for Wyatt as he spun around. His blade flashed red as it came down on the arms of the enemy, severing them at the elbows in one clean strike. The left arm was closest and the Dragon was able to reattach it by leaning forward.

The right one spiraled away leaving behind a trail of blood. It was this the enemy went after, its own limbs were turned into bait against it as Blake fired his weapon at the enemy, but not close enough to do damage, the bullets didn't go through that armor.

"Worthless rifle," Blake was frustrated.

It grabbed the severed arm and reattached it just before Cody could stop the process from taking place.

Rage still gripped the mind of the Dragon. It was injured, it saw Dustin there and went for him.

Cody blasted the monster with his own cannons and pushed the thing off course and caused it to roll into the steel, away from Dustin who was shooting at it the whole time with his own miniguns to no avail. The Dragon wanted to tear Dustin into pieces, nothing would stop it from this goal.

The Dragon was approaching its target when

all of a sudden, it was stopped in its tracks. Something was holding it back. It didn't take long to figure out what it was. The monster was flipped over and thrown to the ground on its back to see an enraged Flesh Tearer at the other end of its leg. Josh had healed somewhat, but the wound was still fresh enough to bleed, the armor still damaged.

The Dragon tried to get away but couldn't. With a roar more beast than human, Josh pulled so hard that with a sickening, tearing sound, the limb and the armor that connected it were torn off from the body.

Josh took his new weapon and began beating the monster, hoping to kill it. Over and over again, the attack continued, and everyone could do little more than stare at the savagery taking place.

The last impact happened, and the Dragon had enough strength to wrap its arms around the leg and pull it away from Josh as it launched itself into the air. Josh was not about to give anything up, and gave chase. The others broke out of their trance and followed the two of them in an attempt to help. They watched as the monster spun upside down and tossed the leg into the air, flew into it, and the armor and limb reattached in a second.

Blake couldn't stand it. The others dove in for the attack for close combat, but Blake melted into the dark.

"Why are you working for the Syndicate?" Cody had to ask.

"Enemy, you are the enemy. The only one. After you, there is nothing. Before you, nothing. There is only you and your deaths that I am concerned with."

Cody knew right then and there that this thing had no real personality. It was doing what it was meant to do. It was just a living weapon.

"Guys, I know you want to kill this thing, but it was made to die. Killing it, or it killing us, it wins. We can't win here. No matter what. I think that was the point all along," Cody said with a hint of despair in his voice.

"Well then let's lose by making this thing die. Sounds like a plan to me," Josh said in more of a growl than a human voice.

"I agree with Josh this time. Let's chop this thing into so many pieces that it can't get back up," Wyatt looked at Josh. Josh didn't look back.

"You two have a point, but it's this thing's first day on the planet and it's already in a death match. Never had the chance to make a single choice on its own. Always being someone else's attack dog. What do you say? If you could choose your own way, what would you pick?" Cody asked.

"Simple. After I kill all of you, I'm going to kill everyone else. It's my talent. It's all I'm good at doing, well, that and I like cheese. Know where I can get some? Alright, I'm just screwing with you on the cheese thing. Yes, I do want to kill everyone. I'm the best and I'll prove it. You'll see."

"We could hook you up with one of the Zodiac ladies, get you all settled into a nice place to live. Dinner and a movie. All on us. Come on, what do you say?" Wyatt asked, and Josh couldn't believe what they were saying. Dustin wanted no part in this either.

"No, I couldn't do that because I'm—" it was cut off.

The distraction worked well, and Blake reappeared right in front of the monster and began to fire his sniper rifle into the thing at point blank range. This time the bullets began blowing holes into the enemy. The Dragon took too many shots and fell to its knees and to the side. More blood poured from the wounds.

Blake put the rifle to the monster's forehead and pulled the trigger.

## 111

"Nice work, Blake," Cody said and looked down at the monster. "Thanks, what are we going to do with it now?" Blake asked, what they were all thinking.

"Delta Squad. Retreat to the Leviathan. I need to deal with this on my own," Dustin looked over to Cody. "I know what you're thinking, but you can't do it." The commander looked over.

"Why?" There was a pause there.

"Simple. We gave up the security of the world, passed over the lives of millions so we—you—could save two people, we all went with your plan. There are still people on this ship. Hiding. They need a chance to escape. We have to start saving everyone. We need to be better than the enemies. We only do this because we want to win, then we give up. We can do better," Dustin had a point here that Cody had to agree with. "Okay," Cody replied.

"You have ten minutes to get everyone off this ship. Announce it," he looked away, saving Syndicate soldiers seemed like a bad idea to him. Even they were afraid of the monster their former bosses unleashed. They were all still human enough. Dustin nodded and hacked into the communication system of the Viper.

"Attention everyone still left on this ship. If you don't want to be dead within the next ten minutes, you get yourself to the nearest teleportation rooms and you get your miserable selves to the Leviathan as fast as you can. This is your only warning."

"Ten minutes doesn't seem like a lot of time. You're lucky I'm not as evil as you are. If I were made more of you and less of the others, Commander, I would have killed so many people already just to make you feel even more helpless about your situation. But no, I don't care about cheap death. I'm a tiny bit better than you. So, I assume you want to do the group battle thing for the next few minutes then it'll just be you and me, one on one to the death?" Dragon asked, still lying there in its own blood.

"We don't have to do that. We're all tired of you, whatever you are it doesn't matter," Cody said, looking down.

"I can't seem to move right now. Nothing

works," it replied. Cody couldn't help but feel a little sorry for it now.

"So, you really want to go through with this, commander?" Wyatt had to be sure.

Cody looked at them. "I have to. No choice. No matter what happens, the Syndicate must be destroyed. This genetic thing can't be allowed to live, it won't ever stop.

"Go, get out of here, and be good, okay?" he gave them an order. They looked around the ship, maybe for the last time, and took off.

Then he took off towards the Leviathan, the others followed.

"Well, I suppose you have a secret weapon, some kind of power you have to unleash or whatever. You need to say what you're supposed to in times like these once your little moment in the sun is over. Prepare to die, this is the end, see you in hell. All the fun things," the Dragon said and the commander backed off.

He was going to use all of his power. Something that had never been done before.

As soon as he began the process, something unexpected happened.

The ocean beneath them erupted in a blinding white light that shot up and surrounded the whole ship. It caught the

"Is this you? Are you doing this because I have to say this is the first impressive thing I've seen done all night from any of you," it asked the commander.

"No, this isn't me. What in the hell is going on?" He didn't know. Nobody knew. The pillar of light could be seen for miles in the dark sky in all directions. He knew giant beams of light from the ocean were never a good sign.

## 112

Quentin was in the dark inner sanctum.

He placed the book upon the pedestal and the seven crystals around the room began to burn with power. None of this made sense to him.

"I see, you weren't here to replace me after all. The mist plays tricks with your mind and sometimes the insanity of it all becomes hard to see. Looks like after all this time I failed my mission."

The man came out of the black, looking tired but strong, like a fighter Quentin would know that look anywhere.

"Failed, what is going on? What is all of this?"

Quentin, for the first time, was asking questions. Now that the book didn't need him anymore, it freed his mind.

"My circle of friends and I. We used to write about horrible things. The Abominations of Yondo, Haunters in the Dark places. Ancient towers to strange elephant gods and terrible wizards that existed in dusty lands. We all told the secret history of the earth in our own way. The black and nameless things that existed on the outside. We were all Guardians, but our minds wouldn't allow us to rest easy with what we knew. We turned it into fiction, the price to guard the veil or try," he said.

The man reminded Quentin of what he thought a cowboy would look like, about thirty years old. Just so sad.

"You did a terrible job guarding it. Getting here was easy," Quentin said.

The man looked up, his eyes still hidden by his hat.

"Just because you can do something doesn't mean you should. You could have walked away at any time. Didn't it feel like this was wrong?"

Quentin didn't know what right was anymore.

"Kid, you just unleashed the worst possible thing."

"Thing, what are you talking about? What is this?" Quentin still didn't get it.

"Reality itself, gone. These things are old, older than us, older than God, older than everything. They existed in chaos, no, they are chaos. Madness. They will undo the omniverse. They will undo reality. Once they find physical bodies to take, powerful enough to hold them, all will be lost. Only oblivion awaits. They will consume souls along with everything else," the man began to fade away.

"One last gift. I will allow you to see what you have let loose. May they eat you first so you don't have to suffer," the man waved his hand at Quentin and everything went black, only for a second.

He woke up on the deck of the Leviathan, gazing out into a massive pillar of light. "Oh my God, what have I done?"

## 113

Cody and the Dragon stood on the Viper, surrounded by the mystical white light. The light was as cold as ice, blinding, and just felt wrong—not bad, just wrong. It didn't belong in this world, or any other.

"This is all your doing. I know it is," the Dragon said.

This didn't make any sense. "Rookie, it's not me. If it were, you'd be the first to know. This is something else."

On the Leviathan, everyone watching this had about as much information on the thing as Cody did.

Nobody knew what was going on.

Not even the leaders of the Syndicate. They were just as in awe of this as anyone else.

Bryan didn't want to believe what he was seeing was real or even possible. He kept telling himself that the Light was coming from the Viper, not the ocean.

He also knew they were too close to whatever this was.

"We need to get the hell out of here, whoever can drive this tub now's the time to make an exit," Bryan said, not sure if anyone was paying attention.

Mark looked to the sky. The stars were not right. Something had changed. This was an alien sky, something unsettling about it. Then he heard Bryan. "Best idea you've ever had," Mark said, but he wondered what this meant—was there anywhere left to run?

Nobody was paying attention to Adam as he ran and leaped off the edge of the Leviathan and disappeared.

The Delta Squad knew that something was wrong. The first sign was that there was no explosion. They all expected the blast seconds after they came to the other ship. It didn't happen.

"So, what's the deal? Maybe we should go back over there?" Blake suggested it, and Josh didn't need to wait for any motivation.

He took off into the air and flew at the pillar of light as fast as he could. It was only light, but everything in his armor was warning of a proximity alert. He stopped at the edge and slammed his fist into the light. Sure enough, it was acting as a force field. He could barely see Cody on the other side. It was blinding.

Dustin made his way to Josh's side. "Look, man, this thing is emitting weird energy. It's off the damn scale. We need to go back, please," Dustin said.

Josh slammed his fist against the shield again and again, nothing.

"Fine," he said, and the two of them flew back together.

Cody and the Dragon began to see things coming out of the light around them. Neither could tell the other what they were seeing. It was hard to tell. Sometimes they looked like spiders, sometimes humanoid. Their bodies were always shifting. It was obvious that they didn't have a physical form.

"We've arrived." A voice—it was many voices at once—all speaking together.

"We, who is 'we'? Who are you?" Cody asked, demanding an answer from the spirits.

"We are the first."

The word 'first' rang a bell in his head. Something Bob had said to him. It made him depressed to hear this word. "Right, the first. The first what? Cosmic flashlight?" The Dragon replied and laughed.

Cody looked at the Dragon.

"Will you please try not to piss off the ancient

ghost things, just this once keep your mouth shut?" He said, then looked back into the light.

"Oh, the mighty commander is scared of a voice and some light. Shouldn't be surprised, after all. I always knew you were kind of a wuss when it came down to it."

"Yeah, because we're such old enemies and know one another so well."

"Enough voices, we require constructs. This one will do, the others will be found soon," all the voices screamed at them, and it sounded like thunder.

"Constructs?" It didn't take long for Cody to put it all together.

"Bodies. They need bodies, I get it," Cody said.

"Sorry ghost lights, but you're all out of luck. We're all still alive, and I'll bet you're powerless without a form."

"Powerless? No. Limited, yes." They replied and began to walk forward. "This one is mine. With it, I will obtain the others." A form said and came out of the light. Its eyes were black and stood out in all this light. Cody looked at the Dragon, reached out, and pulled it back.

"You just had to be a stupid genetic creation, didn't you."

Cody was pissed, surrounded, and now had to save another enemy.

"I am, but I'm pretty smart," the Dragon said as it was pulled back.

"You moron. You don't understand. You have all of our personalities, but because you were built, you might as well be dead. You don't have a soul, you're nothing more than a machine that breathes."

Cody was frustrated, but this had to be the explanation. The things needed bodies they could take. Dead ones.

Empty ones.

"Now I understand the deal, Mercy. If all these people were dead, I get it. Bob, you're a genius," Cody had to admit it. Making a deal with the monster all those years ago paid off today, at least, it might have.

"Well, I don't quite understand what a soul is, but it sounds special. Maybe once we get out of here, you can tell me what it is before I kill you," the Dragon replied.

The commander needed to get out of here, but it became apparent there was nowhere to go. "Looks like we get to trash the windbag then, right Commander? Sounds like fun to me."

"Sure, just, how do you suppose we fight something like this? Have a proton pack ready?" Cody asked.

Cody blasted the black eyed thing, but nothing came of it as the beam passed through the form and slammed into the light shield.

"Well, you stole my one idea. I'm open to suggestions," the Dragon replied.

Everyone saw that the commander had fired, but nobody knew what he shot at. They couldn't see anything. Now the Squad was starting to feel nervous about what the outcome of this would be.

"I'd ask Nero, but she's still out of commission. This looks cosmic to me. Doesn't it to you guys?" Blake asked, and they all agreed with his point. This looked way bigger than anything the Syndicate could do.

"It's my fault, I did this." Quentin's voice came forward, the Squad turned to look at him, everyone else did too.

"What do you mean? Start talking." Wyatt was not amused. None of them were.

"I can't explain. There was this book that talked to me, and I listened. I thought I was doing the right thing. Someone let me out of where I was. Sparky and I never knew who it was. The book, you see, the book wanted to go home. It told me how. I brought it home."

Josh pointed his weapon at Quentin. "What kind of book was it, tell me." The rage was boiling, but he seemed to know more than he was telling.

"I don't know, it was old, really old. It felt like it was made of leather and stuff. You know? It talked to me. Inside my head."

Josh narrowed his eyes.

"It couldn't be." Then fired on Quentin, blowing his knees to pieces, dropping him to the deck.

"That's for being stupid. I should kill you. Right here and now!" Nobody knew what was going on. Wyatt tried to force Josh's arm down, the arm didn't budge.

"What the hell? Josh, start talking," Wyatt decided to try words instead.

"When I was the leader of Lemurians, about fifty years in, their magic nut jobs asked for my help to obtain a book. I thought they were insane, so I agreed to go with. The things I saw those three days will haunt me forever, but the book was real. It wrote itself and as long as it was connected to the pedestal these things had limited power over the Earth. I don't know what they were, but we managed to get the book off that rock and it trapped their souls into seven crystals. I don't know how it worked. The book called me the Tyrant. It tried to convince me that if I returned it, I'd get things. It was an annoying book. I had it locked away after we couldn't burn it," Josh said with anger in his voice.

"You know. I was pretty sure that the space rock would have been enough to at least bury it forever. Looks like it made it through. The past always catches up to us but this," he trailed off and pointed the minigun at Quentin's head.

"Josh, wait. He didn't know anything. Don't kill him for this."

Wyatt stepped in front of Josh.

"Wyatt, you don't understand what this means. You don't understand anything. He deserves to die for this. We're all screwed because we can't get back there to remove the book. Even if we could, we wouldn't stand a chance anyway. We got lucky that time. Do you understand, only three of us made it back, and that was due to dumb luck."

Josh didn't lower his weapon.

"They've had millions of years to consider their next move. I'm sure they are more than ready for anything we might have to offer," Josh said, and he was afraid of the future. There was more he wasn't telling. Nobody wanted to press the issue.

"Josh, listen. If you know this enemy, you know what they do, their moves. You know what they want and what they need," Wyatt said, and this made Josh lower his weapon.

"You're right. I do. That's the only reason Quentin gets to live today," Josh turned around then to the light.

"You know, they didn't belong in our reality. They wanted the bodies of the dead, the strongest things they could find, and use them, not sure for what. We never found out. Now it all makes sense. I wonder if the Dragon has a soul?" Josh said to himself, and then a horrifying possibility came to his mind.

"Josh. What were these things?" Blake asked.

"I don't know," he replied.

"We thought it was a myth, you know. Not everything was real. We barely knew Lemuria and Atlantean legends. Really, we knew that the disaster that destroyed them both was far older than anyone ever realized. We kept a lid on the real history because the world wouldn't be able to handle this or most of the things we dealt with on a daily basis, keeping it safe," Bryan said, joining the conversation.

"No, the legends were real. These could send ideas into the heads of some of my people. They wrote about it in stories, scaring the hell out of people sometimes. Never knowing that it had a basis in truth," Josh said, but he wasn't speaking of the present, but the distant past.

"Well, we need to find a way to help them. Any suggestions, anyone? Now, speak up. All hands on deck," Bryan said, and there was only silence for a short time.

Then Gemini, who got a hold of the glowing green box, walked up and held it up. He didn't have to say anything.

"No, but at least you're thinking," Mark said as he moved into the group.

The Squad had no respect for him and they were

on the verge of killing just about everyone on the ship. "Listen, you armored dimwits. This light changed everything. I assume that whatever this is, nobody saw coming. Like it or not, if we want to get through this, we have to work together," Mark said, showing no fear.

"What's it going to be? We can just kill one another here or come up with a plan. Don't tell me that Cody was the only one who knew how to think?"

Dustin's hand came up around Mark's neck.

"He's over there fighting for his life and ours too. Let's not try and do anything we'll regret later on. Working together is fine, but we can go on without you."

Mark glared at Dustin, and everyone had their hands on their weapons.

"Fine. You've made your point."

Dustin let him go, Mark backed off.

"Still, what are we going to do about this mess?" Mark asked, and everyone kind of had the same wall they were running into. Nobody knew what to do.

Then the ones behind the Dragon, and most of everything else decided to join in.

"We need to shut that light off first. If we are to do that, it has to be done from the inside. There is only one who might do it," Dean said, and none on the Delta Squad wanted to hear this, but they knew if this guy could come up with this plan, the Commander would have to realize this soon. They all turned to gaze into the light.

"Let's get this ship out of here," Dustin said as the others watched.

"You know. We could have always just tried shooting the light with the Leviathan's cannons. that might work," Blood Wraith said after he appeared beside Mark and walked away.

"Oh hell, let's give it a try. Prepare to fire everything," Mark said and began to rush towards the bridge.

"This is a terrible idea," Josh said, but he couldn't come up with a better plan.

## 114

Cody and the Dragon were playing a game of dodging the monster. It was difficult because, as the thing was slow, it was unstoppable.

"This is insane. Are you sure there is nothing more we can do then run? Eventually, we're going to mess up and--" the Dragon was cut off.

"And nothing, until we think of something better, we keep doing this. If that thing gets you, there is no telling how powerful it will be. Don't think for a second that I am helping you because I like you," Cody said.

"Like you. I don't like you either. We had a match to finish and you summoned the flashlight ghosts."

Cody didn't want to explain to the Dragon any more than he had to.

"Shut up and fly already."

The two of them had been flying from the spirit down the deck when Cody saw Adam appear on the deck below them. He was waving to get their attention, and he got it.

The two of them landed.

"There isn't much time, guys," Adam said, then stopped talking for a second.

"How in the hell did you get in here?" Cody asked.

"Magic. Is that important? Pay attention," Adam replied.

"Alright, we are waiting," The Dragon replied and picked Adam up with his left hand. "Put me down, I'm here to help,"

Cody didn't trust this guy either.

"What's the way out?" Cody decided to play along.

Adam smiled, then his hand started on fire, and he placed it on the Dragon's head. The whole armor caught fire, the body fell to the ground.

"Killing it was your plan. I like that plan. You have to teach me that trick someday, wizard," Cody said and managed to catch Adam.

"Necromancer, not wizard," Adam replied.

"Whatever," Cody replied.

"Anyway, no, the Dragon isn't dead. I just gave it a soul," he replied.

"What, whose soul? I just... How did you do

that? I have so many questions right now," Cody replied, and Adam shrugged.

"Now you want lessons on mystic arts and darker things. It's really not the time. I need you to hold them off as long as you can. I'll be able to get us all out of here then. Alright?" Adam said and closed his eyes.

"News flash, Mister wizard. I can't do jack to that thing. I can carry you both but--" Adam reached out and grabbed Cody's wrists, and they burned with purple flames.

"Necromancer. Also, this is a spirit bane ward. Won't kill these things but it'll make them think twice about getting close, shoot them, trust me."

"Not much choice, considering the situation, literal spiritual warfare,"

Cody formed a plasma cannon and fired at the strange, stalking spirit, but this time the attack slammed into it and sent it sliding back.

"Now that's more like it, taking care of ghosts the American way, shoot them," Cody said and charged the monster. It reminded him of something, but he couldn't figure out what it was. Tall, thin, and didn't have a face, hard to look at with those empty, black holes for eyes. If they were eyes at all.

He launched himself at the thing and fired as he did it. The thing seemed unhappy that somehow it could now cause it pain.

"You tiny thing, you challenge us?" many voices asked at once.

"I do," Cody replied and fired again. The blue plasma beam with a purple spiral of light around it hit the spirit, knocked it back.

"Good, don't hold back, human," the voices replied. Cody rushed it, the closer he got, the worse he felt. Something about the light was eating away at his mind.

Doubt, fear, and panic were infesting his thoughts, it was hard not to listen. Cody punched the being of light and sent it to the deck, each impact created purple sparks on impact.

Cody couldn't stand being this close to it for long and backed off. All he had to do was play keep away from the ghost as long as he could.

Time in here didn't feel like it was moving. This alien light was messing with his head.

## 115

Cody kept his distance and shot the thing one more time. He was sure each time he did this, the magic was getting less effective.

This time when he fired, the light surrounding them shattered like glass.

The blast slammed into the Viper and sent the commander careening to the side along with the Dragon and Adam, all flying to the left as the Viper buckled in the air. The spirit resumed its attack on the commander.

"You ruined my host. What is your name? What are you?" the thing demanded with its many voices.

"I'm the Commander of Delta Squad," Cody replied. The thing stared at him and swiped its misty, whip-like arms at him, but missed.

"Delta Squad. We will remember this name. Once my family and I are free from the infinite, we will be sure to devour you first, slowly."

"Freed from the infinite?" Cody asked.

"Yes, dust thing. This light was our guide to re-unification. We will all be here soon."

Cody heard them and the distant sound of Adam's voice. This thing didn't make any sense to him. They were here but not here. He tried not to think about it, it was time to go.

He rushed to them both.

"You two, get to the Leviathan." Cody tore off a chunk of his armor and placed it on the Dragon's own.

"This should be enough. Now go," Adam saw this and looked up at him.

"No. There has to be another way," Adam replied.

"This light is a portal. It has to be stopped. There is only one way to do it. We need a fighting chance. Go now. You have three minutes. Don't argue with me. They'll understand."

"I'm the one who knows magic. What are you going to do?"

"Don't know," Cody replied.

Cody watched as they both vanished, just before the light shield repaired itself around the ship. "Your family reunion is going to have to wait,"

Cody said, looking at the Leviathan beginning to move away.

"Finally, common sense prevails."

## 116

Adam and the Dragon were the last two things anyone expected to appear on the deck of the Leviathan. Blake rushed the two of them and picked Adam up, lifting him with one hand to eye level.

"Where's Cody?" It was the only thing any of them wanted to know.

"Stayed behind. He said there was no other way. Said you'd understand the reason. More monsters are coming through the light. We have to get this ship out of here," Adam said, and Blake dropped him.

"You heard the Commander. Let's get out of here," Blake said.

"We're never going to move fast enough.

Anyone who can help push this thing, let's go," Bryan said, and the Zodiac group took off.

Jake did as well. He didn't need to be told twice to help. The Olympians did the same.

With all of them working together, they managed to move the ship to what they thought was a safe distance.

Then they returned to the deck.

The Delta Squad stood on the edge of the ship. The others kept their distance but did the same.

The massive pillar of light in the distance flickered out all at once. The Viper hovered there for a few seconds, silent. For a brief second, everyone could believe that everything was back to normal somehow. That the commander found a way to kill the light and end the threat.

It was then that a blue flash erupted on the deck of the ship and spread out in all directions. The shockwave sped towards the Leviathan and hit with the force of hurricane winds. Everyone was pushed back.

The ocean below buckled and sent high, boiling waves out in every direction.

They watched the Viper explode.

The fire was as bright as the sunrise, the noise, the heat, and the wind came with it. Still, the squad held their ground. As soon as it began, the whole thing seemed to be over. The flames disappeared into the sky, the wind died out, and there was nothing.

The Viper was gone.

They all expected the commander to come flying out of the night, so they waited. No one dared say anything.

Then a hand rested on Josh's shoulder.

"He's gone."

Josh looked over to see Theron there. Standing behind the Squad were the ones they had sealed away.

"The seal was connected to Cody. His life force. When he died, it went with him," Cyranthis said.

Nobody was in a good mood. Not even Bob, who stared off into the distance where the Viper used to be.

"You."

Josh grabbed Bob by the collar of his shirt. "Bring him back to life. You can do it," Bob looked at Josh, there was no fear in Josh's eyes now. Right at this second, Josh didn't care who or what Bob was.

"I'm sorry. There's something you should know." Josh let him go. Before Bob had a chance to say anything, something was coming over the wind, a horrible screaming that every living thing on the planet would be able to hear.

"What is that noise?" Wyatt asked, looking around.

"It's rage. Your commander messed with an ancient and powerful plan. Screwed everything up in a way none of us ever saw coming. Gave his own life to cut off the path. The Omniverse is tiny, and to find their way here, they needed a guide. Cody put a stop to that by blowing up the Viper. That noise you're hearing is rage. You might call them our family. Many beings or just one large one. The far realm has a foothold on your reality," Bob said.

Bob and Theron seemed nervous.

"Let them come. Let them all come," Josh said. For there was nothing left for the Squad to do but fight.

"Why can't anything just be over, just once I'd like to win and not have something horrible happen," Dustin said. He was tired, hungry, just miserable.

Bob looked around.

"I see he kept the deal as best as he could. Kept almost all of them alive. It'll limit their choices. They'll need bodies used to holding power, Otherwise, they'll burn through them in minutes until they can access their original bodies. So, it might be a good idea to come up with a plan to stop them before they do that."

"Our world, our fight. You can help if you want. We owe it to Cody and all the others who've died to get here to win on our own," Wyatt said and stormed past everyone.

Blake replayed the explosion on his visor. This was all he had been doing since it was over. He didn't even notice that the others had reappeared. He saw what no one else did. Just before the explosion and after the blue flash, there was a spark of green.

This almost made him smile, but he wouldn't get anyone's hopes up yet. He didn't have the heart to be wrong at a time like this. The battle was over. The war was beginning, everyone had to be at the top of their game. The Leviathan was moving toward the west coast of America. The stakes were simple.

Life or annihilation.

## 117

Bob had never intended for the Commander to die like this. It was a bad day. "Why did the fool blow himself up?" Darius asked himself.

"Well, it seems to me that he did it to save us all. By my calculations, that light was spreading through the Omniverse. Without that link, they'll never find their way here and likely just go back to sleep. There are very few power sources in this world strong enough to channel the light," Cyranthis replied, lying on the deck.

The information didn't help make anyone feel better.

"Tell me, should I know something? What is it you needed to tell me?" Josh asked Bob then, showing no fear to anyone who stood there anymore. He didn't care.

Bob looked at him.

"None of us here can bring anyone back to life. Don't you see? The enemy you face is something worse than me. There is a long story behind it, but to the point. We've lost most of our power," Bob said and then nodded, smiling.

"You what, how?"

Josh took a step back, the scale of this new enemy becoming real to him. "Yep, sorry. Can't do anything about your commander. None of us can," Bob said and looked around.

"Tell me, Josh, is it? Is your planet worth saving? You do realize if we just find a way to blow it to pieces, the nexus will be broken forever and the whole light of the Omniverse will dim. Rendering the first ones blind to the fact we were ever here to begin with. This was kind of my plan the whole time," Bob said and sat down in a chair that was never there before.

Theron gave a burning gaze toward his brother then.

"How many times do I have to tell you? We are not destroying the Earth, or the Omniverse."

"It's never not going to be a plan, bro," Bob replied.

Blake was not paying attention to anyone. His complete focus was on their still passed out enemy. "Who is this monster?"

Adam stood there on the other side of the body on the deck.

"Unknown. It didn't have a soul, chances are the body was grown in that armor and has never taken it off. We don't know anything about it. I reached into the Soul Vault. No idea who I got. I was aiming for 'champion', but you never know. These things are random," Adam said, which did not move the barrel of Blake's rifle away from the sleeping dragon's head.

He had no reason to let his guard down. The Commander considered this thing worth saving so he wouldn't pull the trigger just yet, he didn't what the weird ghost thing to get another body. The groups here seemed to split off to their own sections of the deck, keeping to themselves for now.

With the death of the commander, enemies and allies alike seemed to be lost, everything had changed.

The wailing sounds of rage echoed through the sky, all over the world, all at the same time and they provided an eerie backdrop to the whole feeling everyone had.

The Delta Squad was hit the hardest. Anything anyone might have felt at the time, the remaining four members had it worse. It was more than just a member of the team. It was family who died for them. There didn't seem to be any way to make this right.

Wyatt was alone, sitting on the edge of the deck. He almost considered pushing himself off and letting gravity take over. So many thoughts went through his head that when the hand came from behind and pushed him off the deck, it caught him by surprise.

"What the hell?"

He fell a foot or so before he retook control and came back up. Mark was there with a big smile on his face, the only one among the group to have one.

"The one I hated the most gave up everything to save me. That's pretty handy if you ask me. Less work I have to do later."

Wyatt was at Mark's throat in a flash, blade against the skin. "Who says you'll get the chance to do anything past today?" Wyatt asked.

"Two things. One, you couldn't kill me even if you wanted to on account of the body snatchers, second. It's all hands on deck for this threat, well, besides you know, Cody," Mark said with a smile as Wyatt pressed the sword, drawing blood.

"I'm sure nobody will miss you. For some reason, he wanted you, and the rest of your kind alive for this. If those were to be his last wishes, then I'll keep you alive since I can't kill you anyway." Wyatt drew his blade across and slit Mark's throat, watching the blood pour out onto the deck of the airship and his body fall to the ground.

"Don't worry. I'm sure you'll recover," Wyatt said as he cleaned off his blade on Mark's clothes and put it back, then walked away without looking back.

# 118

The Syndicate resistance had to stop and gaze in all directions as the sound of an unearthly screaming came through the air.

"What the hell is that noise, was that us?" Tony asked, looking around. They had just smashed a Syndicate broadcasting tower to pieces.

"No, that wasn't us," Joey said, knowing what it was, and that Bob and all the others had returned as well. He could feel it.

"Something big happened. Can't you feel it? It's the end of the world, of everything," Joey said, trying to look in the direction of the screaming, but couldn't find it. These words didn't make anyone feel any better, they were supposed to be winning something, but now it just seemed like everything went from bad to worse and there was no way out.

"Well, if you're right. We better make ourselves useful somehow. Might as well die with our boots on," Lance said. "We go west. We should meet up with the others as fast as we can. I have a feeling that we don't have much longer to go before everything goes sideways," Joey said.

Nate shook his head. "How do you figure?" he asked.

"I can't feel the source of Silence's power anymore. That's never a good sign," he replied.

"Good thing we got this armor," Lance said.

"Yeah, good thing," Paxton said and looked to the West. The constant screaming, if it could be called that, was chilling.

"It's been one hell of a day," Nate said.

"Yeah, welcome to my world," Tony replied and with that, the group took off and started flying west to meet up with the others.

---

Heath, Roger, and Nick had made their way back to Blackfire Island, they stood on the shore of the island, the sky was grey with clouds, no sun would get through this wall. The rage-filled sounds in the sky gave them all chills as they heard it.

None of them knew what this meant.

The only thing there was to do was listen.

This was beyond anything they knew.

They first heard the sound ten minutes ago. It was reported on several news channels all over the world at nearly the same time.

When they left the command center, they knew that somebody had done something wrong. They couldn't put what they felt into words. That was impossible. Throughout all their experiences, they had never heard of anything like this, not even in past reports.

Heath crossed his arms and thought of something to say.

"Well. I guess this means Cody must have screwed something up. This stuff only happens when he screws up. He tends to do that. A lot," he said.

"Well, with a code name like Venom Sting, you can't expect too much. I mean. Just look how Mark turned out. Nut job there. He screwed up too. I sure am glad I never got that title. Seems doomed to fail, case in point, the endless screaming of rage in the sky," Nick replied, the others all agreed with this.

"Rage screaming. Sounds more to me like the wind from Nate's hurricane, remember that?" Roger asked.

"Yeah," Nick said.

"So, who wants to play cards? I have a deck. We got food. We can make it a regular picnic here on the shores of Blackfire," Roger said with a smile.

"Sounds like a plan. I'll find a grill and fire it up.

It's the end of the world. Might as well go out on a positive note," Nick said and laughed, they all did.

None of them had a clue that the Viper was destroyed, not that it would make much of a difference at this point anyway.

All they had was now.

---

Dana and Erin were awakened by the horrible screams in the air, out of one nightmare into another. They both had IVs in their arms, but nothing else.

"You alive?" Dana asked.

"I think so, where are we?" Erin replied.

"Leviathan medical bay," Dana said and sat up, everything hurt and she felt empty inside. "Great," Erin replied and sat up, pulled the needle out of her arm, then managed to stand up.

"Let's see what we can see."

Dana had been here before.

Dana led the way. The ship was dark and confusing, with a console at every corner. She wasn't sure why it was like this, but she didn't build the ship.

"Nothing has changed," she said. "Lots of life signs on the top deck," she added. "I Hope it's not whatever is making that terrible sound," Erin replied.

The two of them walked on, and after a few twists and turns, they made it to the deck.

"What the hell is going on?" Erin asked. Nobody was fighting.

At first, they figured they had died and this was some kind of punishment, everyone together in one place, tolerating one another. The wailing from the sky didn't help anything either.

This had to be some kind of hell.

It wasn't until Dustin walked up to them, out of his armor.

"Glad to see at least something went right today," Dustin said to both of them, and neither of them had a clue what was going on. "Let me start at the beginning."

Dustin explained everything he could to the best of his ability.

It was a sad story.

Erin looked around and saw no commander. However, she did see the new armor and despite everything, she smiled. It worked.

Then Dana saw the dragon lying there, and her eyes went wide.

"Blake, kill that monster. Kill it right now," Dana screamed at him. Blake turned his gaze for a second when he felt his rifle get pushed away.

"You might want to kill me. That's fine. First, let me figure out just who you are," it said, and leapt up. Blake didn't shoot. Something was different, and he watched as it landed some distance away.

"Who am I? What am I doing here?"

Everyone turned to watch this take place. Now the terrible and great dragon seemed terrified, surrounded by everyone.

"Wait, guys. Don't kill it. Don't even shoot at it," Adam said as he came running towards the scene. They barely listened to him. "Give me one good reason not to," Josh replied, both miniguns pointed at it.

"It has a soul now. It doesn't remember anything up to this point. It's brand new, or very old. These things are random," Adam said and carefully approached the dragon.

"Calm down. You've been through too much for us to explain just yet. Tell us who you are," Bob and Theron approached, wanting to know who the new one was just as much as anyone else did. It looked around at all the strange looking beings, then its left hand came up to its face.

"I am," the dragon paused, reached for the helmet and was able to remove it to reveal the face of the enemy for the first time when the horrible screaming in the sky stopped.

"What?" Josh asked and looked up. Nothing had changed.

Then out of the sky, Death's armor fell and

landed in the center, green and yellow sparks flew around the bone white body. It stood there, silent.

Bryan threw Theron's weapon to him, and he caught it without looking.

"Who are you?" Josh asked, still angry.

"Josh, back off," Bob said and pulled him back. Theron and Bob stood in front of him now. Josh was furious, but despite being 'powerless,' Bob pulled him back as if he were a mere toy.

"I found a body," it said.

"We see that," Theron replied.

The entity didn't move. "Your creation is an abomination. You must know you couldn't keep it hidden forever," it said.

"I kept trying to tell him that, but no one listens," Bob replied.

"One spark of light is that offensive, talk about a total snowflake," Theron said.

"Snowflake?" Death asked.

"Don't worry about it. What do I have to do to get you to leave?" Theron asked.

"Cease to exist," it replied. "Not going to happen," Death raised his right arm, "I need this one," he said.

A solid black beam fired and hit Famine in the chest, blowing a hole through him. He fell to the deck, dead.

Brianna and Angel rushed to his side in a second, but it was far too late.

"Get back," Megan yelled, and the two of them did just before something burning green shot into the wound. The body jerked back to life, then it stood up, without missing a beat, moved to Death's side.

"Who are you?" Wyatt asked, figuring he'd get something out of this.

Death looked at Wyatt, tilted his head a bit, studying him.

"I am Terazine," he replied. The voice was human, but there was something unsettling about it. It was too perfect.

"I am Zauron," Famine's armor said in almost the same voice.

It didn't mean anything to Wyatt.

"We remember you, human." They both said at the same time and pointed at Josh. "We will demonstrate how much more we are than you, we will explore this world. We will destroy this abomination, there will be peace," Terazine said.

Terazine snapped his fingers and at once all the armor on the ship, the ship itself, turned off. The Leviathan was falling, and everyone encased in mechanical armor was now trapped in it.

"It is impossible that anything in this reality even stood a chance to stop us. We have deemed them unworthy of existence," Zauron said and looked around at everyone there who were statues.

"Now we take the bodies we need," Terazine said, and his hands burned with blue light.

"Well, you know. We had to give them a chance," Theron said and leapt into the air, bringing the blade down on Zauron's arm as he came up to block it. Theron's blade tore through the armor and hit the now invincible flesh underneath.

"I remember you, child. You and your brother broke free of the chaos to do something. How'd that turn out for you?" Zauron asked, and it was then that Bob tore into both of the new enemies and knocked them both off the ship with black bolts of lightning. Theron landed on the deck.

"That was laughable. You are no threat. We will assist the others, then we will wipe you out all at once. Enjoy your time while you can, children."

Then the two were gone. Theron returned power to the ship and the armored ones. "What the hell was that?" Wyatt said, retracting his armor, everyone who could, did.

"A preview of things to come," Bob said and walked towards the edge of the ship.

"They like to fight. It's all they know. No, they wouldn't kill all of you here. They want to make you suffer first, punishment. So very human of them. War never changes," Theron said, and his sword disappeared.

The Delta Squad members looked at one another and for the very first time were lost as to what to do next. This threat was above their paygrade, and they knew it.

"Guys. We're going to need everyone on this," Wyatt said, and he hoped that he, being the second in command of the Squad, could handle his new promotion.

The last thing he wanted was to be responsible for the end of reality, but before giving in to despair he looked around and saw around him the most powerful fighting force this or any other world he knew of had to offer.

It didn't matter if this was enough or not. It would have to be. The last line of defense was going to be tested.

End of Book 6.

# ABOUT THE AUTHOR

I wrote my first "novel" when I was 16 years old in High school, it started out as something I just wanted to try, but the thing ended up saving me in English class when I told the teacher and she allowed me to turn the thing for extra credit. I still don't know how that ended up working, but it did. I managed to turn the thing into a trilogy before I graduated high school.

Now, in 2018 I hope to see my writing career go further than I ever thought possible, and with time I know this will just be the first steps into something truly amazing.

To learn more about Jesse Wilson and discover more Next Chapter authors, visit our website at www.nextchapter.pub.

Delta Squad - Black
ISBN: 978-4-82419-751-1
Large Print

Published by
Next Chapter
2-5-6 SANNO
SANNO BRIDGE
143-0023 Ota-Ku, Tokyo
+818035793528

3rd September 2024

Milton Keynes UK
Ingram Content Group UK Ltd.
UKHW031350011224
451755UK00003B/248